# TWO GUYS
*from* Verona

# TWO GUYS
## *from* Verona

a novel of suburbia

## JAMES KAPLAN

GROVE PRESS / *New York*

*Published simultaneously in Canada*
*Printed in the United States of America*

FIRST PAPERBACK EDITION

Library of Congress Cataloging-in-Publication Data
Kaplan, James.
    Two guys from Verona : a novel of suburbia / James Kaplan.
      p.   cm.
    ISBN 0-8021-3623-0 (pbk.)
    I. Title.
  PS3561.A559T87   1998
  813'.54—dc21     97-30168

Design by Laura Hammond Hough

Grove Press
841 Broadway
New York, NY 10003

99 00 01 02   10 9 8 7 6 5 4 3 2 1

To the memory of

WILLIAM SLOANE JELIN

(1951–1996)

Home-keeping youth have ever homely wits.

—Shakespeare, *The Two Gentlemen of Verona*

# TWO GUYS
*from* Verona

# 1

Poor Joel.

Will was staring at his best friend, who sat behind the wheel of his '69 Impala, low in the tattered, foam-hemorrhaging bench seat, arm thrown over the windowsill, still in his jeans and white, short-sleeved, V-necked Sub Shop shirt: he'd come straight from work. The moment before, Joel had turned to Will and asked, casually: "So—you going to the reunion?"

A simple-enough-seeming question. Yet Will couldn't help wondering—with scorn, with triumph, and even with a measure of sympathy—how had Joel *come* to this?

Sympathy was what Will ostensibly offered Joel on their drives, sympathy for the life that had gone so wrong, for all his friend could have been. Imagine—as Will sometimes liked to, imagining being one of his few legitimate hobbies anymore, though not one he'd have admitted to freely—what Joel could have been! If. If his father hadn't gone, then his brother; if whatever had happened the year after high school hadn't happened. The break. They called it. Such bad luck. Looks, brains, musical talent, athletic skill: Joel had had big possibilities. Broken. Will, on the other hand, had had all these things in moderation, just a little bit of each, had capitalized on them . . . *and went to work for your father*, the familiar voice in his head, the carping one, said. All right, so he'd gone to work for his father. He could've blown it. Some would've. He hadn't.

They were in Joel's car, the big boat, turning right, from Longview onto, of all things, a street strange to Will. On the passenger side of the big bench seat, he stared at the white-on-green street sign as it wheeled by, said the name to himself. Heatherdell. He must have passed this street a million times, over forty years; yet he seemed never to have seen it before. Was this possible?

And why turn here? he wondered. But with Joel, you usually went right on wondering. With Joel, it was always best to go with the flow. "The reunion? I don't know," he said. "You?"

"Oh yeah. Sure thing. Wouldn't miss it."

*Poor schmuck*, Will couldn't help thinking now, recalling the invitation he'd almost put out with the junk mail. Twenty-five years. Horrifying enough in itself, but silly too. All that remembering. All that *reminiscing*. Will, usually, went to a good deal of trouble to avoid thinking about the past, a place that, to his mind, was seductive but vastly overrated. The future was what interested him. That was where the money was.

And, anyway, who went to twenty-fifths? Twenty was the big one, the one everyone who could still bear themselves went to. And Will had missed it, standing in a delivery room, watching Danny cannonball out between Gail's raised and spread legs, her usually sleek thighs chubby-looking and painted with brownish gold disinfectant stuff, Danny glistening blue, puffy-lidded and annoyed-looking. Of course Joel had attended the twentieth—and reported later, in his own way. And now he was up for another? Why wasn't he embarrassed to go at all? He was funny about things like that, beyond embarrassment, in a way. Maybe it was one of the things that had broken in the break.

Will was not beyond embarrassment. Embarrassment was a big part of his life: remembering or avoiding it occupied much of his time.

Fortunately, he'd been pretty successful at avoiding it lately. (He thought of his portfolio—a major embarrassment-antidote—and smiled. It always gave him a warm feeling to think about his portfolio.) So maybe, then, he should go? Did unembarrassed equal proud? He thought of the invitation again, the tickle of titillation he'd felt picking it up, followed by the horror—twenty-five years! best not to think about it—and the piping child's voice that had interrupted. Always interrupting.

He looked at Heatherdell. A little leafy nothing street, a side street in the suburbs. Longview was something else. You drove down Longview for just that—the long view. That was the thing about the suburbs, Will thought. You could usually count on them to deliver just about precisely what they promised. Longview took you alongside the whateverth holes of Greenbrook's golf course for an unremarkable half-mile, a couple of big ranch houses on the other side, sold no doubt on that basis—GOLF VU!—and then, just like that, there you were, on the edge of the precipice, with everything spread out underneath: the valley, and then, twenty miles off, the shimmering, spangling City. It always took his breath away, a little bit, the long view.

And then, just at that point, Longview plunged down the side of the mountain—like those mad prospectors in *Treasure of the Sierra Madre*, like Wile E. Coyote in a Warner Brothers cartoon—plunged at a San Franciscan angle down to the blue-collar flatlands far below, past Tudors and Dutch Colonials and ugly postwar boxes and big sprawling brick ranches (filled with the ghosts of 1962 ease: finished rec rooms and intercoms with gold grilles and bedrooms that had once belonged to children now grown, rooms long ago filled with white sunlight and expensive toys), all clinging like mad to the side of the hill, holding on to that good life for dear life. But there, back up at

the crest, Longview earned its name. And the funny thing about
Joel—poor Joel—was, one of his oddities (and there were quite a
number) was, he hated that view.

"What do you want to look at *the city* for?" he'd sneer, whenever Will requested they come this way.

How many times had Joel even been to the city, over the past
five or ten years (or twenty, or twenty-five)? Here was a subject of
some interest. Will had tried to draw him out on it. And while Joel
was more than drawable-out on many subjects, this was not one of
them. He actually seemed to have lived in Manhattan once, a long
time ago, just after graduation. Joel in Manhattan: now there was a
thought. But that had been another Joel. Ancient history: he didn't
like to talk about it. How many times have *you* been to the city lately?
he'd say, if Will asked.

Joel, I go all the time. My work takes me there once a week,
minimum. Two or three times, more often.

Ah. And how do you like it? Going to the *city* all the time?

It's not really about going to the *city*, Joel. It's just my *job*.

I can live without it, Joel would shrug, staring off to that place
he stared off to. End of discussion.

Take a little street like Heatherdell, though, and Joel could
really get excited. The strangest things did it for him. His car, for
example. The Impala, green originally, had oxidized to a grayish color,
or, rather, collection of colors; this was one of the subjects you could
draw Joel out on, or, rather, that he'd draw himself out on, especially
with a little Scotch in him: color. Green in particular. There are at
least four thousand greens, he'd say; then he'd start listing his own
special spectrum: I'm in a Hurry Green; Sad on Sunday Green; Men
at Work Green; and (Will's favorite, because it was one of the few he

thought he began to understand) Long Beach Island Refreshment Stand in the Fog Green.

What is color as an abstraction? Joel would ask, rhetorically but heatedly. One of the things that drove him crazy was wordy definitions of colors, and those dictionary illustrations of prisms and color wheels and the like. Color is personal, he'd say. Color is a moment. *Jade* is a shell of a word, a crappy convention to get a stupid conversation started, a way to get people to feel less by assuming they agree. What matters is *my* jade.

This was Joel.

Joel might not like looking at the view on Longview, but he could rhapsodize about the two side-by-side green traffic lights, disk and left arrow, at the intersection of Northfield and Cedar, that were *two different greens*—Nothing But Trouble Green and So What Green, respectively, to the best of Will's recollection.

(And if there was anything Joel deplored, reviled, detested, it was burgundy-colored cars. Which, unfortunately, the suburbs were full of. They made his brain ache, he said. And Will's car was burgundy-colored. Thus they rode in the Impala.)

"So what's on Heatherdell?" Will asked, as casually as possible. Joel tended to react badly to direct interrogation.

"Ah," Joel answered. And no more.

So they drove along Heatherdell, a nothing little suburban side street lined with postwar ticky-tack boxes, albeit boxes enjoying a certain amount of separation from each other. This, plus the houses' tangential, down-the-block proximity to Greenbrook CC—even though there was no golf vu per se—would put their prices, Will guessed, in the mid to high threes. Amazing what ticky-tack cost these days. Real estate was much on his mind lately. Why? He could

only guess. Was he becoming the person he had always dreaded? The
carping voice again. Right now, he didn't much care. He was staring, half-potted—the Chivas, in its brown bag, sat midway between
them on the bench seat—out his open window, at Fisher-Price play-
houses, at Little Tikes swing-sets, at those ubiquitous, orange-
bodied, yellow-roofed Cozy Coupes, like Flintstone-mobiles, as
common as toothpaste. Will thought of his own Cozy Coupe, parked
by the back driveway; and, unavoidably, thought of Gail, and Danny
and Rachel, waiting for him, and felt duly, dully guilty.

   Joel was driving slowly, at his usual trolling speed, the Impala's
big engine thrumming like the engine in a fishing scow. Parents up
and down the block were probably darting worried looks out their
windows, thinking about dialing the cops, Will thought: big rusty
car, going slow, two middle-aged guys in it casing the kid stuff.
Perverts.

   Only Will was casing the kid stuff, however. Joel was casing the
*leaves*.

   "Now, what would you call those colors?" Will asked him.
Trying to get into the spirit of things.

   "Which?"

   "There." Will pointed to a big red-yellow-and-blue plastic
castle in the side yard of a gray box of a place with rust trim. He knew
the product well. Big slabs of crenellated, nonrecyclable polystyrene—the little arrowed triangle on the bottom might as well have
read FORGET ABOUT IT. Assemble it yourself, up-against-it dad, while
the kids yowled around you. Three forty-nine ninety-five at Toys
'R' Us. A shitload of unbiodegradable trouble, it would outlast the
Sphinx, the Great Wall, Machu Picchu. He looked at Joel. People
without children, he thought, knew nothing.

   "Red, yellow, and blue," Joel said.

"That's it?"

"That's it."

Suddenly Joel stamped on the brakes; Will slid forward. Bent his knees, extended his right forearm to the glove compartment. Sober or smashed, he was worthless, but when he was just a little drunk, it seemed to him, his grace was absolute. A tail-twitching squirrel, sex-addled, no doubt, paused and glanced up at the planet-sized Impala, its improbable savior. Scooted over the curb, ingrate. Home. Will replaced himself; Joel caressed the gas again.

"And the leaves?" Will asked.

"Which ones?"

"Any."

Joel sighed. "Where do I start?" He was patient with Will most of the time, when he wasn't being mildly, obscurely mocking. The mockery gave Will some trouble: he was never quite sure when he was being made fun of, for one thing. For another, part of him wondered whether Joel, as an object of sympathy, ought to be making fun of anybody in the first place.

But then, for an object of sympathy, he had a certain weird aplomb. Scraggly dark beard, noble goddamn nose, brown-black eyes. His eyes always reminded Will of the dark of the moon. Mooning at trees. A quick, clever glance over to Will. One black brow high. "Although this street, strictly speaking, is a cheat," Joel said.

On two shots of Chivas, Will was in Joel-mode. He could almost keep up. "Where's the Heather? Where's the Dell?"

"You impress me, white man."

The street dead-ended, the houses petered out among stands of birch, of aspen, of whatever-the-fuck. Quaking oval leaves, soon to die, in the tender orange light. The air hayey-sweet, with a cool menacing edge. September again. There was no stopping it. Purple in the shadows. White trunks and brown trunks. A developer's dream back here, Will thought. And yet, strangely, still undeveloped. The street dead-ended, but in front of them, to the right, lay a weedy gravel drive jogging off under the pines. And Joel turned onto it.

"Are we supposed to *be* in here?" Will asked. Stones were banging the Impala's undercarriage.

His only answer was the *boom boom boom* of the car's engine, the squeak of its springs. Joel had slowed to walk-speed. The drive curved around, under the dark trees, for fifty yards: there, ahead, was a rusty mesh gate. Open. On the other side loomed the back side of a big, low, modern house. Joel stopped. There wasn't much to the rear of this place, it was all façade. Expensive façade. Three-car garage, basketball hoop, brown cylindrical central-air vent. A little strip of lawn, some flagstones. Not even enough room for a pool. Will recognized the style. You could probably get it in the mid-sevens. And still have the address, the taxes—everything but a backyard. But wait—what *was* the address? Joel was smiling.

"My God," Will said, taking a moment to get it. "Woodwick."

Joel killed the engine. It died with a Donald-Duckish shudder; the wind blew. Will's mind turned over as he tried to figure it out. They seemed to have come around some sort of back way. Longview was in Cedar Grove. The ticky-tack boxes of Heatherdell were in Cedar Grove. Woodwick was in Verona. Where, how, had they crossed the line? The gate? The route between the two towns had been etched in his brain always—you descended Longview, curved and curved down to Wyoming: a five-mile avenue that ran along the mountain's side like a line on a topographical map, and named, no doubt, in some access of nineteenth-century town-planning grandiosity. "Streets named after places usually go there," Joel liked to say. "Except Wyoming." So—right on Wyoming, on into Verona, with the tender feeling crossing any sort of border always gave him. And then, too, Verona was home. Verona-alongside-the-Hill. Woodwick was another matter. Woodwick was Kike's Peak, the Golden Ghetto. The plateau of postwar, overpriced houses was accessible by two ascents only, each perpendicular to Wyoming: Juniper, and, a mile south, Overlook. These were the ways to Woodwick, Verona, New Jersey.

And yet, here, under the pines and through the gate, was another way. Here was the secret border, hidden in the pine needles.

The hayey breeze rose up again. "A wrinkle in time. A dimensional fold," Joel said.

"I never knew this was here."

Joel stared at him, spooky-eyed. *"Because they didn't want you to."*

"Shit. I'm suddenly having this massive déjà vu." The light, the oval leaves, polystyrene castle, rusty gate. It seemed, for the moment, more certain than anything Will believed or knew.

"Acid flashback, man."

"I never took acid."

"I took enough for both of us."

"I should probably be getting home, Joel."

"Hey—what if we drove through there and it was 1974?" Joel said.

"Oh God. Anything but that."

"Nixon resigning? The Captain and Tennille?"

"Please. Hey, Joel, really—I should get back. Gail and the kids'll be—"

Joel wasn't interested. "Now," he said. "Look through there. You recognize that place?" He was bending down over the wheel, squinting, pointing, like some N. C. Wyeth Chingachgook, through the rhododendron, down the driveway, and across the Woodwick street to another long, low house, white stone and purplish gray wood. A dense dark blue lawn, a lawn like a breathing creature. A stunningly self-sufficient-looking house. Also stunningly familiar-looking. But how? Will wondered. The perspective was all off.

"No. I—" he began. The wave of déjà vu had receded, leaving an empty swath of sand—empty except for a single silvery minnow, jumping, flickering.

"Cindy's?" Will said.

"Bingo," Joel all but whispered. He was staring reverently down the driveway.

Now Will knew what street that was. He'd had to think backward, in time and in place, turning the whole street map around in his head, driving in his mind up to Woodwick on Overlook, heading through the wide, quiet streets, up to Cindy Island's house. And past. That was the thing: he had always driven past Cindy's house. He sighed. "Hey, Joel," he said. "She doesn't live there anymore. She's gone."

"Maybe this way she's not." Joel turned the key and the car lurched forward, thrumming, down the driveway and onto the street, over the border and into Verona, in the magic evening light.

# 2

*Ooh, myy Sharona. Dit dit dit dit dit dit dit* myy *Sharona.* The song is on; Joel dances the dance on the dirty duckboards behind the counter: not much of a dance, just a little kick and shuffle. His own words: myy *Verona.* In honor of. Is he happy? Hard to say. Does he like the music? Sometimes you dance just to keep from dying. It isn't much of a dance, this dance—just move the feet. One, two, one two three. Long, long ago, in another life, he took cha-cha lessons, with Earl. Joel and three other boys (one of them Will), four girls. Someone else's house every Saturday. Cokes and Mallomars. You got to see the houses, smell the smells. Clean carpet, mysteries in the Tudor shadows. And feel the girls. Twelve; budding. All baby fat under those blouses. You touched with electric fingertips. Smiling Earl, in a sharkskin suit. Handsome Earl. Was Earl gay? *Was* Earl gay? Interesting question. They didn't have gay then—not, at least, that Joel knew about. Handsome, deep-voiced Earl had blond curls and a shiny gray suit. He was strange, that Joel could tell, even then; but he didn't seem to be strange that way. No looks, no touches; no, he wasn't in it for the boys. Maybe for the girls? He didn't seem to mind dancing with the girls—just, of course, to show how it was done. What did the girls think? Was Earl weird? Joel would have to canvass them—where were they now? . . . *to an ophthalmologist in Bethesda . . . the mother of three lovely . . .* No they weren't. Not if he didn't want them to be. Ronni, twelve, plump in a tight red blouse.

Budding. Electric under his quivering fingertips. *Bayyy-by*—do the cha-cha-cha.

Two fifty-three, Mountain Dew time. In a minute it'll be two fifty-four, but it isn't, yet. Sick sun outside the Sub Shop awning. None in here. Larry slicing provolone. Dancing, Joel shakes oil (Mountain Dew Yellow) and vinegar (Heartsick Burgundy) from bleary rectangular bottles with metal meatuses onto the shredded lettuce (Tent-Caterpillar Green) and sliced tomato (gray-red).

"You want onion?" he says to the guy. The guy—toothpick in his mouth, newspaper under his arm (odd object, filled with grave black assertions; Joel doesn't quite see what people see in them), belly poking out under his Montclair-at-Midnight-Blue PANTONE CONSTRUC-TION T-shirt—belches. His face is yellow: a dismal sort of yellow, the hopeless hapless yellow of a row house in Union. He looks like he's eaten about three lunches already today. What does he need another one for?

"Whut?"

"You want onion with that?"

"Onion?"

"Yeah."

"I don't know, you decide." Grin. "Surprise me."

OK, you get onion, buddy. You get lots of onion. Big surprise. Joel stacks onion on the lettuce. China-white onion, green at heart. Like me, Joel thinks; like Nabrubus.

Here they are.

Green at heart, like me. Bottle Green and Leaf Green and Day-Glo Green and Green Apple Green and verdigris. Gray-green and orange-green and brown-green. Moss and spruce and celery. And the green he remembers, but can't remember.

And M & M Green. Young and in Love Green.

Chia Pet's eating big peanut M & M's, popping them out of the bag right into her mouth with blood-brown fingernails, looking sideways at him, secret. Green M & M between orange-brown lips. A ring in her nostril. That secret sideways look. At him. At Romilar.

Romilar is seventeen, maybe. Long, baggy, olive-drab shorts, clamdigger length; surfer sandals. Some kind of Mexican shirt, multicolored: it hurts Joel's eyes to look at it. Earring on each ear, black hair long on top and shaved around the sides. Two piggy rattails in back. Thievish baby-face, all strut and menace: half-Spanish? Quarter? Smug. Slitted eyes. Faint pencil mustache. And even though Joel knows that it's all a hurt pose, rebuke to the absent father, et cetera; that one inch underneath he's no tougher than a puppy—Joel hates Romilar.

Chia Pet is something else. Joel knows who she is, for one thing, knows the big long brick house on Skyview, knows the vanity-plate numbers of all her parents' cars. Joel, you see, has toured Woodwick a little. To the point that the gray-green boat he drives, the '69 Impala, passes unnoticed: it's assumed he's someone's gardener or cleaning man. Joel has done research. Joel knows things.

He knows that Chia Pet's real name is Julie Berkowitz. That her father, Gary, graduated a year ahead of Joel, the youngest of four Berkowitzes who went through VHS. That three of the four still live in Woodwick. That Gary was the runt of the litter, a skinny wimp, a glad-hander and jock-sniffer. That he married Ellen Fleischman, from Joel's class, went into the family business, D. Burke Jewelers, and—bald—now wears a ponytail and a goatee and owns two Mercedeses, a sedan and a vintage Gull-Wing.

Chia Pet is, except for the extreme makeup and nose ring, something out of the Song of Songs: dark hair and big dark eyes, starey eyes. Like Cindy's. Small round breasts, silky hips and long legs.

Long, long legs. She's the same height as Romilar. A slightly strange gait, though—sidling, almost defective. Not as sexy as the rest of the package. The rest of the package makes up for it. Whatever she wears, summer or winter, must show three inches of belly. Today she's in ripped jeans hanging off her hips and an antique-blue halter, a George Washington blue, oddly staid color. Only the color is staid. Her shoulders are sharp. The white belly is slightly pudgy. The navel, too, has a tiny ring.

Chia Pet is, what? Sixteen?

Surely not as old as the song on the radio.

Cha-cha-cha.

*Dit dit dit dit dit dit dit* myy *Verona.*

"Hii, Joell." This is her game. She knows things, too: she knows how men act when she walks into the room, knows how far to push. She knows how Joel clams up when she comes in, looks down, drops things. An old guy, balding at the temples, weird around the eyes, old enough to be her father, really. Except kind of good-looking. For an old guy. A guy who should have gone places, done things: a guy who lives with his mother, a weird old broad, on Forest, just below Woodwick, under the crest of the hill. Chia Pet knows all this.

Romilar snickers.

Joel has summoned all his composure, dropped nothing, put his hands on the counter, looked them both in the eye. "Hi," he says. He even manages a smile.

Romilar is caught flat-footed, too chickenshit to cut Joel. His eyes look helpless for a second. "Tsup," he says, glumly.

"What can I get you?"

Romilar grabs her and sticks his tongue in her ear. She hunches the sharp shoulders, ticklishly, her eyes on Joel the whole time.

"Tell me when you're ready," Joel says. Friendly. Calm. Tolerant. A model citizen. He bags the fat guy's sandwich, rings him up. Romilar stares a hole in the cash as the drawer comes out. Chia Pet whispers in his ear; he laughs, still staring at the cash drawer. Joel closes it, smiles at them. Goes back and wipes off his knife.

Larry shoulders over, raises his chin at Romilar and Chia Pet. "Can I help yiz?" he says, in his rumbly voice, a voice like wind blowing out of a deep cave. All at once he glances down. "Hey, hey, sweetheart—no shoes, no service." Her feet are bare, the nails painted metallic gray-blue: a rainy-dusk-in-autumn car-color.

Joel stares at her toes, starts to dream. He could eat them. Slowly, one by one by one.

Romilar's smirk turns pained. "Aw, come *ahnn*, man," he whines.

"Hey," Larry says, shrugging. "Boarda Health's got me over a barrel. What do you want me to do, get shut down? You want them to close my doors?"

"Boolshit, man. I ain't comin' here no more."

"I'm terrifoid," rumbles Larry.

"What about no *pants?*" Chia Pet says, and yanks her jeans to her knees. There's nothing underneath.

Joel gapes. Larry gapes. Nothing. The long thighs are bluish white, the dark little bush sparse—trimmed? And Joel thinks—no, now he knows—he sees a glint of gold in there. Smiling, she does a bump and a dip, pulls the pants back up. Never having had to unbutton them.

Larry's mottled-red. "Nice. Very nice. What would your mother think?"

Romilar's smiling and shaking his head. His girl. "What would *your* mother think?" he says to Larry. His eyes are glittering, daring. He spits a tiny globule off to the right, right on Larry's floor, on the Board of Health.

"Get outta here, you pimp!" Larry picks up a carving knife. "And you, hoor!"

Romilar's smile fades. "Hey—fock you, man. I ain't no pimp."

Chia Pet slaps his shoulder.

Larry opens the counter-gate and advances, sandwich knife still in hand. "OUT!"

Romilar backs up slowly, eyes glittering. Giggling, shrugging her shoulders, shaking her can, Chia Pet dances out the door.

"Come on, fatty. You gonna stick me? Go to jail for stabbin' a unarmed jubenile? Come on, fatty."

Larry feints with the knife. The kid barely twitches. He shakes his head and backs out the door, smiling with pity. "Fat piece a shit."

Larry plops down in an orange plastic chair, almost buckling the legs. His rear end dwarfs the seat. He puts the knife on the table. Sweating, shaking, he wipes his forehead with his apron. "I'm gettin' out of here, I swear to Christ," he says. "I'm gonna sell and move to Florida."

# 3

"Jo-well," Irma called, hoarsely. "Jow-well."

She padded through the living room in her slippers and robe, Camel Light in one hand, fending off the daylight with the other. There was no light. The green-gold drapes were drawn against it. Around their edges it glowed anyway, the treacherous, inconceivable light of 1999. Into the kitchen. Too bright. Violet sat at the table, head in a tan turban—a pair of Caucasian-colored panty hose, actually—smoking a Marlboro, reading the *Daily News*.

"Mm-mm," Violet said, shaking her head at the paper. "Mm-mm."

"Violet," Irma said. "I'm looking for Joel."

"I ain't seen him."

"Is he in his room?"

"I ain't seen him."

"Do you know what time it is?"

"Clock's right over there."

The old white Sunbeam over the sink, with its black numerals, dirty dial, and sweep red second hand, said ten thirty-three. But ten thirty-three in what year? Irma didn't look at it. Nor at the turquoise G.E. table-model radio, with white grille and gold tuning knob, circa 1964, that sat on the counter below. "Have you done the towels yet?" she called, as she crossed the kitchen.

Violet shook her head with infinite weariness, exhaled a cloud of smoke, and turned the page. Irma opened a drawer next to the dishwasher. The drawer contained a decade's worth of rubber bands. Irma rummaged through the rubber bands as though, just possibly, she expected to find Joel in there.

"I said, have you done the towels yet?"

"And I *said* no."

"May I be so bold as to ask why?" Irma closed this drawer and opened another one, whose front compartment, for some reason, was full of ancient bottle caps—graying bottle caps from Cott's and Hoffman and Nehi and Veep and Yukon Club bottles of the sixties. She winced, and quickly closed the drawer.

"*I* ain't done no towels because *you* ain't got no detergent."

"Oh, and I told Joel to pick some up. Jo-well!"

Irma climbed the back staircase, holding the cigarette ash-up and shaking her head. The stair carpet—it had once been forest-green—was in bad, even dangerous, shape. Irma was shaking her head at Violet and Joel and the carpet all at once.

The carpet in the upstairs hall had fewer holes than the back-stair carpet, and this—along with leaving the painfully bright kitchen and the sight of Violet—stopped Irma's head-shaking.

She knocked on his door. "Joel?"

"What."

"Joel, are you sleeping? It's nearly afternoon."

"I'm not sleeping."

"I wanted to ask you something."

"Go ahead."

"May I come in?"

"I wish you wouldn't."

"Did you get us some laundry detergent, Joel?"

"That's what you wanted to ask me?"

"Violet can't wash the towels."

"This is what you wanted to ask me?"

"I'm asking you, Joel."

"Yes, I got laundry detergent."

"Violet said there wasn't any."

"It might help if she'd look in the basement."

"Joel."

Silence.

"I wanted to ask you—"

Silence.

"—if you've seen Steven's high-school book."

"*Which* high-school book?"

"His, you know—with the pictures of everybody."

"His *year*book?"

"That's it."

"It would probably be in his room, Mother."

"Do you think you could get it for me? When you have a chance."

"It's probably right in his room, Mother."

A long pause. "You know I don't like to go in there, Joel."

Silence.

"Joel."

"All right, all right, I'll get it. Later."

"Thank you, honey."

Silence.

"Just one more thing, Joel?"

"*What*, Mother?"

"I—I heard from Mrs. Dornberg again."

"Ah. And what did the lovely and charming Mrs. Dornberg have to relate? How is little Yvette these days? Still married to her handsome podiatrist? What *makes* a person become a podiatrist? What drives him to it? I'd love to know. Do ask Mrs. Dornberg that for me next time you talk to her, won't you?"

"Joel—she wishes you wouldn't."

"Wouldn't what?"

"You know."

"What?"

"The pachysandra."

"Mother, I'll urinate whenever and wherever I please on our property. If Harriet Dornberg is offended by it, so much the better. I can't think of a better use for my urine."

"She says the odor is—detectable."

"I should certainly hope so."

"Oh, Joel."

"What is it, Mother? You're not crying, are you?"

"Oh, Joel—how did we *get* here?"


On the other side of the bedroom door, Joel sits on his bed in boxer shorts, amid the cascading stuff of his room: shelves jammed with thirty years' worth of books, from the Hardy Boys to Catullus; school artifacts and pennants, disused sports equipment, loving cups, souvenirs. Football- and baseball-player dolls with bobbing heads. A hula-dancing coconut with lipstick, false eyelashes, a grass skirt, and a lei. A stack of Kennedy half-dollars in plastic cases. An old cork bulletin board covered with pennants, faded postcards, ticket stubs, school-play programs. Not a few empty Scotch and bourbon bottles.

Joel's boxer shorts are off-white—a tribute to Violet's laundering skills—with a repeating figure of a little tan man in brown plus fours swinging at a golf ball. Irma bought the shorts for Joel at Saks in Short Hills not long before. They are a size 40. Joel's waist and hairline aren't what they were five years ago—are especially not what they were twenty years ago, when he came back to live in his old room. Irma sees this—she isn't deluded—but at the same time she sees him as her *boy:* the jaunty, lively-eyed, black-eyebrowed boy who starred in Little League and won trophies at Camp Robin Hood. Thus, when she ventures forth, infrequently, in her big silver Cadillac (the car was Morris's until the time of his precipitous death, in his mistress's bed, the fall after Joel graduated high school), her small shoulders hunched by the years' gross indignities, a Camel Light stuck in a corner of her mouth, her head barely reaching over the steering wheel—and, not infrequently, a line of cursing drivers behind her: she adheres strictly to posted speed limits, and favors the left lane—when Irma goes out, it is often with the specific purpose of *getting something for Joel.* Her boy, the one remaining. Something: a tobacco-brown Lacoste, for example, which exudes a brownish, faintly burnt, corned-beef/haberdasher aroma when unboxed, an aroma that intensifies as the shirt is unfolded (if the shirt ever gets unfolded), the pearl-headed pins and tissue removed.

If the shirt gets unfolded. For more often than not the shirts— and the Bermuda shorts and golf slacks—end up stuffed in Joel's dresser drawers, still pinned, sales tags (the prices thoughtfully removed) still attached.

Joel's dresser and closet are packed with crisp, unworn sportswear. He could pass muster at any country club, if he cared to. Mostly he goes to work, then home, or drives around in the Impala, around and around and around the streets of Verona, trying to figure out why, as the houses and streets stay the same, nobody and nothing comes back. Why nobody *explains.* He always wears the same two pairs of jeans, the same two short-sleeved shirts (white; NASA engineer–style). His one accommodation to his mother being in the underwear department: he faithfully wears all the boxer shorts, socks, and sleeveless undershirts (identical to Morris's) she buys him. Underwear he can use. The rest he can leave alone.

Joel is writing. The tip of his tongue protrudes slightly between his lips, his nostrils are wide with concentration, his dark eyes stare at the faintly lined pages on his lap. He writes in an old Hebrew-school notebook, its cover a winter-afternoon indigo, with a slightly darker tape binding: a thing of beauty. On the cover, which is on the book's right side, is a picture of a bearded medieval sage and the mysterious legend (in Hebrew) RAMBAM. There are spaces for the student's name, address, and the teacher's name: all these are written in in Joel's faded fourth-grade script. The teacher's name was Mrs. Schreiber. At the top of the cover, Joel—the modern Joel—has inscribed, in bold black block letters, NABRUBUS.

Joel keeps to the book's scheme, proceeding from right to left over the yellowed, faint-blue-lined pages, although he writes, of course, in English. Hebrew was always a mystery to him, its dark, forbidding, vowel-less characters more successful, to his mind, as shapes than as letters. He writes in pencil, Eberhard Faber number 2. He keeps a box of them, freshly sharpened, on his night table, next to a shot glass and a bottle of Chivas. (The Scotch is from Morris's private stock, a case in the basement he received from a grateful client in 1972.) Joel writes:

> *Your thighs are longer than your pimp's attention span.*
> *I have no such problems, Melissa.*
> *If the burden of memory is burning, I am on fire forever*
> *with the thought of those thighs,*
> *and the thin thatch above,*
> *the gold ring*
> *calling my tongue-tip.*

He pauses, pencil hovering over the page, and reaches with his left hand for the Scotch. He breathes in the peat-smell, sticks his tongue in the amber liquid. It burns. He takes a sip, swishes it in his mouth, sighs, and lies back, notebook closed on his stomach, pencil resting at his side.

He's having a braingasm. This happens sometimes: he remembers and remembers, without limit, like falling through space. It was pale green . . . he sees the color . . .

. . . and then bumps the side of the shaft, and the floor. He can't remember what it was.

His room is painted blue—dragon's-egg blue is how he's always thought of it, a cool color, chalky and, by now, a little sad. It's been that color for a long time: since fourth grade, when Irma, encouraged by a raise Morris had received, decided to redecorate. Carpeting, paint. Furniture. The works. A mural of ancient Rome in the dining room: a potent stimulus for Steven's and Joel's play-fantasies. Morris bought a huge tank of tropical fish, with an ultraviolet lamp to accentuate the exotics' colors. The tank sat on a stand on the sunporch in another empire, the empire of childhood. Joel remembers standing with his mitt after Little League, staring at the colors. Burning.

He opens the notebook and draws a line through ~~calling~~. Above it he writes, instead, *tempting*.

*tempting my tongue-tip*

He smiles a little at the improvement and dips his tongue, once more, in the Scotch. Burning.

He closes the book again and looks nowhere, a dissolute emperor in the latter days of Rome.


A long time later. There's no clock in his room; Joel has gone to work, returned, eaten a peanut-butter sandwich and drunk a glass of water, and gone back to his bed, where he has sat and stared as evening turned to night. Now he screws the top back onto the bottle—good Scotch, he feels, is especially volatile—and replaces the pencil and notebook on his night table. The house is quiet, it has that tangible silence, abetted by the outdoors, of middle-of-the-night. He gets up, puts his bare feet in the thick tan carpet. The carpet smells like feet. He remembers the smell of this carpet when it first went in, a sweet acrylic stink, full of hope, that he has all mixed up in his mind with a Friday afternoon in fall and the smell of Irma's meat loaf. With bacon on top. He remembers being happy. Has the sharpest memories of being sharply happy. Was he, in fact, happy, or is it the remembering that makes it so? Now that happiness is no longer possible (is this really true? he thinks, for the barest flicker of a moment, of her, of her blue-white thighs, as though this impossibility were the one thing that could change his life), knowing the answer seems crucial. He was nine, the leaves were crispy on the ground, the October air bell-clear and Irma's meat loaf greeting him at the back door. And the carpet smell. New new. He was happy.

The hall is dark, darkness and the dark brown smell of something Violet cooked for dinner (he dimly remembers Irma calling him for dinner, calling and calling) flowing up from the stairwell. Through the kitchen door, around the corner, the refrigerator clears its throat and hums. He goes down the hall a few paces, toward Violet's room, turns the faceted glass doorknob on his left. It turns easily, but the gray-blue door sticks. The door has always stuck. He knows the trick: he leans down on the knob, and the door glides in. Whisking the fur of the carpet.

The ambient night-light—glow from a bulb over the Dornbergs' garage door, shining through hemlocks and rhododendron, blended with the more-distant gleam of the streetlight—swims, in tree shadows, on the wall, over book bindings and trophies. He thinks of Steve swimming, at El Dorado, the old swim club on Mountainside (where the hospital is now, acres of parking lot covering what was once the most poignant pleasure dome, under the sign of a seahorse), before Morris's real money came in, before they joined Westmont. The smells of Coppertone and hot asphalt and agitated chlorine and french fries; the heaven of sticky-cold ice-cream sandwiches; "The Loco-Motion" on the radio. Little Eva. Steve, broad-shouldered and slim-hipped, showing off his butterfly. Joel thinks, as he sometimes does, of Steve's body underground, the actual body, this moment, its precise state of rot. And Morris's, right next door. Morris seeming somehow better able to fend for himself down there. As if such a thing were possible. He switches on the light.

The yearbook, with its puffy-pebbly black cover and red embossed *Flagship '69*, is just where he knew it would be, is in fact where he left it last time Irma wanted to look at it, as she periodically does, to attempt to moor herself in time's crashing surf, its riptides and undertows. The black-and-white photographs, on the heavy, cool-smelling pages, smile out, confidently and wistfully, but in each case eternally, the seventeen-year-old skin firm and taut and beautiful, the eyes clear. He looks at the faces breathless, as though he were walking through a tomb of fallen soldiers, reading the inscription under each square image: *A certain gold GTO . . . Nights at the shore . . . Luv ya Janice . . . Be true to yourself . . . Linda & Bobby forever . . .* Steve's picture, the square jaw and strong nose, dark Assyrian curls and close-set eyes slightly averted, a warrior-god, gazing toward posterity. *A man's reach should always exceed his grasp.* Dot dot dot.

The room is as it was then, the Bancroft racquet in its press leaning in the corner, the Rawlings Hank Aaron mitt on the shelf, the bed made (and remade, by Violet, every week) under its green-plaid spread. The smiling bobbing-headed dolls with football helmets

and baseball pinstripes, the model Corvette, the forest-green Camp
Robin Hood pennants, the texts of a lost time: *Exodus. The Man,* by
Irving Wallace. *Guinness Book of World Records. Geronimo, Wolf of the
Warpath. Time Yearbook 1927.* All thirty white-and-green deluxe-
bound volumes of the *World Book,* with yearbooks from 1965 to
1973 . . .

Dot dot dot.

He opens the *Flagship* again, first to the *B*s. Gary Berkowitz,
with his big nose, badger jaw, small, resolutely unreflective eyes.
Funny her father should have small eyes. Were Ellen's big? Gary
Berkowitz. *Jewels are in his future.* Stunning foresight. Putz. Joel turns
to the *H*s and *I*s. To—as it happens—Gary's cousin and Cindy's sister, Wendy Island. *Adults are obsolete and the hell with them.* Good old
Wendy. With Cindy's big eyes but not her mouth; who could have
that one-in-a-billion mouth? Wendy's jaw was a little too firm. A
good, cheerleading jaw. And her dark eyes, even though they were
Cindy's eyes, knew that Cindy was the one. Wendy's eyes were kind;
they forgave the world for stopping in its tracks, mouth dropping
open, when her younger sister went by.

Kind Wendy told Joel where Cindy went, when no one else
would talk to him. And so Joel followed, to the place he thought of
as There. And found Cindy's eyes far, far away. Her room, though,
was very nice; you could see a pond, there was a deer. And her skin
so, so white. She was still so beautiful.

Joel closes the book and turns off the light.

He pads down the stairs in the dark, the book's cover cool and
pebbly under his fingertips, the darkness also a tangible thing,
caressing and enveloping him as he descends, like the warm waters
of a pool. The kitchen linoleum cool and smooth beneath his bare feet,
the refrigerator humming its monotone tune: Always. He lays the

yearbook on the counter, next to the radio, and opens the back door. There's a small vestibule, where wet boots (fragrant black rubber, with those slotted, finger-hurting, black-metal clips) and muddy shoes used to lie—especially once the carpet was installed, and all children went, by edict, shoeless in the house. Now the entryway contains only a disused galvanized milkbox, marked BECKER FARMS, with a faded, legless blue image of a cow. Becker Farms, now no longer in existence, had a miraculous train ride, the roofless silver cars (like milkboxes themselves, Joel thinks) pulled by an actual steam engine over fields, through woods, a layout that may have been three-quarters of a mile but seemed, at the time, like an entire continent. He remembers reclining in his seat, seven, as the train crossed a brook and passed, through lazy cloud-shadows, into a stand of trees with a pine-needle floor. Life was good. Where Becker Farms was is now an office park of identical bronze-mirror-glass buildings, distinguishable only by their numbers.

Out the back door, wearing only the golfer-patterned boxers. The night is cool and damp; it has a mulchy aroma, combined with some frown-brown odor Joel has never smelled before. Like the inside of a vitamin bottle. He sniffs: he doesn't like it. Some cloud of industrial pollutant, wafting over from Linden? How would anyone ever know? The sky—flowing from west to east like a great river of orange-gray slush—doesn't begin to offer an explanation. He crosses the lawn, the overgrown grass cold and wet between his toes, to the pachysandra-rhododendron border that leads to the Dornbergs'; he wades into the bushes and pees meditatively and for a long time, Dornberg-ward, making sure to project the stream as far into their yard as possible. He thinks again about Cindy's faraway eyes, her white white skin. Back across the yard, onto the driveway's hard uneven pebbly asphalt. He steps out of the shorts, and, tucking the waistband behind his ears like a chef's toque, gets into the Impala. The vinyl cool beneath his bare behind. The engine makes a big sound in the dead night.


Ten minutes later he's there, over the gravel, under the pines. It's dangerous this time of night, he knows: the Impala's throbbing boom penetrates walls and closed windows, communicating itself, the way low sounds do, as danger. Bathroom lights are on here and there; someone must be awake, sick or worried about making the mortgage. He's thought before of what it would be like if somebody called the cops; smiling, he's pictured himself being handcuffed, naked, against the squad car, his underpants perched on his head, while the roof lights flashed and the good householders of Heatherdell stood on their stoops, clucking in their bathrobes. Another one brought in.

But he also feels he won't be caught. He's invisible, he feels, especially once he's cut the engine. He shuts the car door, carefully. The shorts—whiter even than his flesh, they will glow in the dark— he has left on the seat. The wind is cool on his skin. When he was ten or eleven, he used to open his bedroom window in the middle of the night and go out on the roof. In his pajamas at first; later, without them. A narrow slate eave, giddily steep, led up to the top of the house. He tried it once, twice, three times, always turning back. Then, one night, he conquered his fear, foot by sweaty foot, and finally made it all the way up, where he perched on the roofline, nude in the moonlight, and surveyed the world that would be his.

Now the world belongs to others, and he's careful to stay in the bushes. And all he wants to look at, through the branches and across the street, is the dark window that once was her room.

# 4

$W$ill was dreaming. His dreams had been very satisfactory lately, not pleasant necessarily, but high in color and jeopardy, rich in incident. They nearly always involved driving—escape and travel in marginal machines, planes and cars with rudimentary engines, or no engines. His dreams were a good place to go when his wife—when his *life* was not. In the dream, he knew he was dreaming, but forgave himself. He forgave himself everything. In the dream. He and Joel were riding in Joel's car, in Woodwick. Joel's car was new. That was the thing Will couldn't get over. It even smelled new. Its boatishness had a crisp Chris-Craft-itude to it: they floated along, noiselessly. The car was also a convertible, which, in true life, it wasn't. In the dream it was: the dream was good. Joel and Will sat, smiling, in the new-smelling Impala, like Egyptian gods in a sun-barge. Osiris and Ra, cruising. In the bronze light of 1974. It was Indian summer, late afternoon. The hot air had an undertone of purple cool, of death. It was September. Cindy stood in her front yard, in a green-gold bikini, her dark hair in a Barbie flip. Her eyes made up Egyptianly, she stood in a 1974–ish pose, one thin arm akimbo, the other turning out and rising, palm up, as if holding an invisible tray of drinks. Cindy stood in her bikini, smiling slightly under the makeup. Her skinny body wasn't much—there was something uncomfortably anatomical, a whiff of the camps, about the protruding wings of her pelvis, the long stretched concavity of her belly, the flatness of her chest under the bikini's shiny top.

But at the same time, its defiant skinniness was sensual, over-powering. Will yearned to cover her, to feel her sharpness, to fill her up. She smiled, just a little. Her face was extravagantly beautiful. This was what no one could forgive her for. She looked like a dark Grace Kelly, and Jews weren't supposed to have such looks, especially with-out benefit of surgery. Her wide, thin mouth curved up very slightly, Deneuveally, at the corners. It gave her a look of contentment. Will knew the opposite was true. But in the dream it didn't matter. Her smile was an invitation. He was out of the car, floating across the fruity-smelling grass. That smell, Will realized, was death, dying. The cicadas were hissing, hissing. Cindy reached behind her back with an eerily flexible thin white arm and undid her bra. Her small breasts were goblet-shaped, their meltingly soft under-curves lambently greenish white—the color of a lake's surface before a thunderstorm—and the conical brown nipples excruciatingly, shudderingly tender, like the softest, youngest blossom. Will reached between her legs, felt her warm, damp firmness, the bone underneath, then spread the fingers of his right hand under her buttocks (the middle finger in the crack, its tip on the tiny, swollen bud), and lifted her, substantial but weightless, his left arm pressing into and arching her spine. Aloft, she smiled and leaned her head back, looking down at him through slitted, sable-lashed eyes. The cicadas hissed and hissed; the hot wind blew, with its hayey smell of dying grass, its purple undertow of fall.

And the strangest feeling came to him: that he was dreaming Joel's dream.

Will realized now—he was awake now, but didn't want to be—that he had seen Cindy's mouth, precisely, on a fat woman at the Livingston Mall the previous Saturday. The woman, in vermilion bicycle pants and a flowered top, had been wheeling a stroller with a screaming baby in it; a glum, frizzy-haired little girl walked alongside, holding on to the stroller's diagonal strut. And the fat woman, in the midst of all this, looked placid, drugged or tranced, her beautiful mouth weirdly content. She had a superb, peaches-and-cream complexion, and auburn hair. . . . Cindy? Will, holding his own children's hands, shook his head at the apparition. Cindy was nowhere. Cindy had disappeared. That was the way things went. Away. He hated the past: traitor.

The gerbil was skittering in its cage, frantically clawing at the colored plastic, trying to escape. It would never escape. And Rachel was standing by the bed. Will was in Danny's bed, Danny having gone into his and Gail's, as was his habit, somewhere around 5 A.M. Danny's bed, in Danny's room: whale poster on the wall, dresser-top packed with stuffed animals. Danny's bed was barely six feet long. As was Will, who had to curve himself like an S when he slept there, which, these days, was every morning. It was the combination of this mild contortion and lying on his left side, so as to face the shelter of the white wall (he slept on his right side in his own bed), Will was convinced, that made him dream so much in Danny's bed.

Or was it something else?

Rachel stood by the side of the bed, staring at him. A pretty little girl, three, brown-haired and solemn, with a small port-wine archipelago on her chin. Islets. He always wanted to reach out with a damp paper towel and wipe them off. There was a process for removing them, with lasers. It cost a lot, and insurance wouldn't cover it. Of course Will and Gail would do it for her, but not just yet. When she was older and could handle surgery better. And when there was more money.

"Hi, sweetie," Will said, hoarsely. "How ya doin'?" He reached out to pat her head. He was suffering from two more or less opposing problems: his bladder was full, and his penis was stiff. The former demanded leaving the bed, immediately; the latter prevented it while Rachel stood there. Or until Will could will himself into flaccidity. He tried to think of sad things—numbers, money, death. His bowsprit, however, had declared jaunty independence.

"You hungry?" Will asked Rachel, mussing her hair. "Want some breakfast?"

"Daddy?" Rachel said.

"Yes, sweetie?"

She screwed up her face as if she'd smelled something funny. "When I get old, will I get dead and buried?"

Will looked at her. The gerbil skittered and skittered. It wasn't the first time Rachel had read his mind. (Or had he read hers?) She was holding the funny-face, waiting.

They had been through this. What did you do? Tell the truth, and they wouldn't leave it alone. If you lied, you felt stupid.

Lie. "No. How 'bout some breakfast?"

"Danny said I would."

"Danny's a meanie. What's he doing?"

"Watching cartoons."

What else. Will thought of Da Vinci, of master drawings on heavy paper. *Cartone*. Cardboard. Boxes. Money. Death. What would Leonardo have made of Scooby-Doo? Badly drawn, at the very least.

"What's Mommy doing?"

"Sleeping."

"And what's Danny doing?"

Rachel laughed. She liked his dumb-guy act, and the face that went with it. "Silly Daddy."

That did it. He sat on the side of the bed. "Lemme just pee, then I'll rustle you guys up some grub."

"Mommy said I would get dead and buried. When I get *olden*."

"Huh." He patted her on the head. "Let me just think about that while I pee."

Down the hall. The dumb perpetual din of cartoons rising from the living room. The bedroom door cracked, she lying on her side among the rumpled sheets. Small. He had always liked that she was small. Now he tried to remember what else it was that he liked about her. He leaned in the doorway. "Traitor," he said. Eyes closed, Gail waved him away with the back of her hand. Danny was a kicker. Which maybe made Will the traitor, for having left the bed. But Danny didn't want him these days: so what could he do? Change to the dream-bed.

Rachel was waiting for him outside the bathroom door. "Is Fiona coming today?" she asked.

"No, honey. Today's Saturday."

"I don't want her to come anymore."

"You don't? How come?"

Pout. "I don't like her."

"But sweetie, you *love* Fiona."

"I don't. I hate Fiona."

"Who's gonna watch you when Mommy and Daddy go to work?"

"Susie."

"Rachel, Susie's *four*."

She grinned, with gapped teeth. "Silly Rachel."

"Come on, Silly Rachel. Let's go downstairs." He put out his hand. And—one of the most miraculous things about small children who happened to be your own—she took it.


"Who's Donna DiMichele?" Gail said, picking up the invitation. She gave it the correct Italian pronunciation: Mee-*kay*-lay. Gail

had briefly majored in art history, before coming to her senses and
switching to prelaw. It popped up at bad times. They were in the
kitchen; she'd just stepped off the StairMaster. Blue-and-white com-
pression shorts compressed her skinny behind. A fluffy white towel
(Ralph Lauren) hung around her neck as she drank Poland Spring
from a Dansk mug. Surely, Will thought, he, or she, had seen a commercial, or a TV show, or a movie, with a woman dressed exactly like
this, and drinking designer water from a Dansk mug: sometimes,
lately, Gail seemed to be standing inside quotation marks. Likewise
their kitchen—magnets on the Sub-Zero, drawings on the bulletin
board. Ceramic bottled-water dispenser, Viking restaurant stove,
Sendak calendar full of events and appointments. What of the disappointments? It helped, sometimes, to be surrounded by things.
Cozy clutter on the counters, a steak-y cutting-board smell over all.
Sometimes it didn't help. He stared at her. Wife. The second, and
surely the last. Surely? Here they were in the present moment, a
bubble advancing perilously through time. *It's now, it's now, it's now*,
he thought, looking at her sweating cheeks. Now again. What next?
Over the yard, the sky was blue. Three possibilities: Blue. Gray.
Black.

What color had the sky been in the dream?

"Dim-mi-shell," Will corrected her. "Dawna Dimmishell," he
intoned, an anthropology lecturer. "*Jersey* girl."

"So who is she? Prom queen? Former flame?"

"Yeah, right." He looked up from the *Times*, and saw that an
answer was required. "I remember her as big, and kind of terminally
perky. Sort of pathetic, you know? Always in everyone's business.
Living vicariously. The best-friend type. I guess she never married.
Poor Donna."

"So—you want to go?"

She stared at him with light blue eyes. He remembered, once, not being able to get enough of her eyes, which, together with her dark hair and wicked jaw, had stirred Klimt fantasies in him. He recalled, with distant excitement, her looking down at him from on top, a little cool, a little distant. It had fascinated him at first; it had not worn well. Now her eyes cross-examined him. He thought of the dream: he was guilty. "To my twenty-fifth high-school reunion?" Will said. He recoiled at the sound of the words. Then thought about it for a moment. "Yeah. I do want to go. Oddly enough."

She took a drink of water. "Huh."

"Why? You don't?"

"I *will*."

"But you don't want to."

"Do I have to want to? I said I'd go."

"I'm gonna owe you on this, huh? I'll go to yours."

"Big deal. Seven years from now. Anyway," she said, after another drink. "I don't want to go to mine."

"Why not? You're successful. You're not fat. You have two kids—you can bring pictures!"

She drank again, peering at him over the edge of the glass, a look he had to gird himself to return.

"What?" Will asked.

Danny was in the doorway. "I'm hungry," he whined, wincing, as though the unpleasant possibility that such a thing could happen to people had just occurred to him.

"I'll make you a sandwich," Gail said. Danny ate peanut-butter-and-mayonnaise sandwiches for breakfast.

Will pointed at his son. "Zing! You're a sandwich!" he said.

Danny shook his head, rolling his eyes. He had an advanced state of irony for a boy who still slept in his parents' bed.

"Oh," Gail said. "The car phone's broken."

"What?"

"I dial out and I get this fast beeping. Did you pay the bill?"

"Of course I paid the bill. I pay all the bills, in case you hadn't noticed. Did you happen to notice how much the car-phone bill *was* last month, by the way?"

"Please. Don't start this again."

"I just wish you wouldn't use it to *chat*. It costs about eight times as much as a regular phone."

"I don't use it to chat. Would you just call them, please?"

"It's really basically for emergencies. Remember why we bought it?"

Danny's eyes were moving back and forth between them, as though it were a Ping-Pong match, and he were the ball. "MommyI'm*hungry*," he groaned.

"Oh, I know what it is," Will said. He actually snapped his fingers.

She just looked at him, refusing to abet his moment of triumph.

"This stupid security code. So people can't steal your number out of the air. It's more to protect the dumb company than us, we were never liable anyway. I mean, if somebody calls—I don't know, Uzbekistan or something—on your number, they have to pay."

She squinched her eyes, unwilling to take it in. "So what do we have to do?"

"It's not that hard. I'll program the code onto the autodial. You'll just have to press one new button before you dial out." He smiled, her technological rescuer.

She wasn't buying. "Could you do it this morning?"

"*Mommy.*"

"Okayokayokay." She took the Skippy out of the grocery closet. To Will: "Could you. Please."

"I have to find the manual—I don't know. I have a lot of stuff to do today."

She put a hand on her hip. "Like what?"

"Cleaner, Chinese laundry, I have to stop by the office for an hour—"

"Ride around with Joel . . ."

"I was planning to, a little bit, later, yeah."

"Were you planning to work your children into your busy schedule at some point?"

"Come on. That's not fair."

"Why do I have the feeling you'd rather spend time with your schizophrenic friend than with us?"

*Because it's true.* "That's not true. Anyway, he's not schizophrenic anymore, he's on medication."

She was making Danny's sandwich, cutting the crusts off. "Oh yeah. Which one? Jack Daniel's?" She handed a yellow plastic plate to Danny, who took it to the counter. He got up on a stool, on his knees, picked up a half-sandwich, and opened a J. Crew catalogue.

An arresting thought suddenly paused in Will's mind: How was it that he happened to be living in this house, with these people? And what was worse, things staying the same or things blowing up? He shook his head. Just for the moment, he had no idea.

"I'll fix the phone," he said. Just to have an exit line.

# 5

Smooth Route 80, as it approached Paterson, turned potholed, as though in some sort of homage to the brown-brick city's dilapidation. Will was in his burgundy Volvo, a '95 with 96,482 miles, the shocks starting to go, dots of rust beginning to flower on the famous rust-resistant finish. It was unpleasant to be reminded of the car's mortality on rough road, unpleasant to think he'd have to drop fifty grand on a new one soon. What were they going to call the year-2000 models? Uh-ohs? He didn't like this; he didn't like any of it. (When he wasn't in love with the future, it terrified him.) He turned up the radio. The rock station he usually listened to had changed its format the other afternoon, *bang*, just like that, no warning. Suddenly it was "Music for the Millennium," songs he'd never heard before, flat-sounding young people keening about political breakdown, ecological disaster, virtual reality. And, of course, love. The impossibility thereof. All to the drone of native, acoustic instruments, Jew's harps and didgeridoos. Or something.

> *Losing my ability*
> *to forgive your mobility*
> *the worst is my timidity*
> *and the impossi, possi, possi-bility*

keened the singer, whose gender Will couldn't determine. Naturally love was impossible if you sounded that flat, Will thought. But then, it was impossible anyway.

He liked the music, in a depressed way. It went with the tan
fall sky, the opening vista of the dirty city, the old factories and, here
and there, pushing up through the William Carlos Williams brick-
face, an ugly glass tower. It was a Saturday morning; traffic was light.
He turned off onto Straight Street, stopped at the signal, pushed the
auto-lock button as a black kid in big bell-bottoms walked by.
*Whunk.* You couldn't be too careful these days, there were carjackings
all over the place. The kid turned back around and gave him a forgiving smile. Funny: Will had seen this kid before, no mistaking
him, a handsome kid with a big Afro, perfect, eggplant-colored skin,
close-set, tragicomic eyes—eyes from a back street in Alexandria, A.D.
40—and European features. Where? Crossing Verona Ave., downtown near the Sub Shop, a couple of weeks before. Strange: How
often did you see, for the second time in a day or a week or a month,
and in a completely different context, someone absurdly tangential
to your life—maybe the meter-reader doing his shopping, or just
somebody you'd happened to notice on the street?

Life at large, Will thought with sadness, was not like this, not
like the game of Concentration, the old TV memory game, where
Hugh Downs stood by, young and grinning, as you called for the
square to turn over and reveal itself as an exact match for the one
just turned. And you won a prize. Hugh Downs, wrinkled and
snaggle-toothed and ancient now, an apologetic anchorman with a
game-checkered past, didn't match up with his young, grinning self.
Nobody played Concentration anymore. People appeared once, then
vanished for good. Take Cindy.

*Take Cindy*, he thought. He thought of the dream. Joel's dream.
Of taking her. He squirmed stiffly in the leather seat.

Will pulled into the lot and parked, counted backward from
thirty, to soften up. It was a little easier these days—although the
presence of Layla's car, a repainted lime-green Festiva with flower

stickers, didn't help matters. He thought, defensively, of movie stars who were older than he was, who still looked good. Harrison Ford was almost sixty, for God's sake. There. He got out, locked up, walked across the lot and up the steps, pushed the security code on the keypad by the door. Glancing, just slightly, to the back and sides. He thought of the black kid again, the ancient forgiving tragicomic eyes. The door buzzed.

She sat at her desk with her stack of invoices, looking up as he came in. Her bronze hair pulled up into double top-knots; that was the style again. "Hi, Layla," he said, a little too heartily. Deflectively. "Hi," she said, feigning shyness, as she eyed him up and down: her messages, at the very least, severely mixed. She fluttered her lashes, half-smiled, and looked back at the invoices. Smiling as she sat there. He stood in the middle of the office, listening to the buzz of the fluorescents.

"Quiet on Saturday," Will said.

"Yeah."

"Give you a lot of time to catch up?"

"Yeah."

At time and a half. Still, this was the arrangement: weekdays the phone rang off the hook, she could barely get any paperwork done. So her coming Saturday mornings was the cheaper alternative to hiring someone else. Just thinking about it made him feel fiscally responsible—until he looked at her still sitting there smiling to her-self. Something had to be done about this.

But what?

"Layla?"

"Uh-huhh." Not looking up.

Sexual harassment is a terrible thing, Layla. Especially when you started it. "Did those McMillan people ever call back?"

She shuffled through the phone messages. "Thursday, yeah."

You horny old dog, her eyes said. What are *you* doing here on Saturday?

"Could you call them Monday and tell them we want a sample?"

Half-smile. "Uh-huhh."

Impertinent, Will thought. He depended on it.


"My God, I've turned into a caricature," Will groans. "I'm in love with my secretary." Joel looks over at his friend, at his salt-and-pepper hair and smooth, unlined face, and thinks: That's because you're an idiot. They're riding down Longview, away from the crest—by Joel's choice—in October sunset light. Away from the crest because, one, Joel hates the view, and two, going this direction, at this precise hour, at this exact time of year, the slanting sun, in clear air, gives the trees and bushes on the golf course shadows that seem to have actual volume, like dark transparent objects. They pass a shady corner where the orange light, having traveled ninety-three million miles and passed through the smudged lens of the atmosphere, has shot cleanly down a side street and struck a stop sign with such force as to turn it into a shield of fire. Openmouthed at the sight, Joel glances over at Will, whose mouth and forehead are twisted into an agony of ironic lust. Useless. Joel thinks of José Ferrer in *Lawrence of Arabia:* I am surrounded by cattle.

A big sapphire Mercedes comes along in the opposite direction. The face of the woman behind the wheel is childish but hard. Strange how often this is the case with expensive cars, Joel thinks.

He taps the brakes. Another pricey vehicle, a lake-black, spanking-new BMW, zooms out the country-club entrance and falls in ahead of them. At twenty-seven miles an hour. An old lady is hunched urgently at the leather-padded wheel.

"Have you ever noticed," Joel says, "that when people are in a hurry to get out from a side street in front of you, they invariably, *invariably*, slow down the second they actually *get* in front of you?" He's smiling. Behind his own aqua plastic wheel, in his Sub Shop whites, he feels, and looks, as relaxed as the Buddha himself. "I had this hypothesis once that it was some kind of optical illusion, or maybe something to do with angular momentum. Now I recognize it for what it is."

Will takes a deep quaff from the brown-bagged bottle of Wild Turkey. "It gets worse," he sighs. "Her name's Layla."

He glances over at Joel. Who has no reaction. Who, smiling slightly, is twiddling the wheel with the thumb and forefinger of his left hand.

And then looking to the left, where he notices a ranch house. But not just any ranch house. Two hundred feet long if it's an inch, a bad 1954 Bauhaus/cruise-ship mélange, in tapioca, with blood/rust accent panels trimmed in brushed aluminum. Joel shudders.

"This is what history has come to," he finally says. "Nostalgic parents naming their child after an Eric Clapton song."

"'Layla—you've got me on my knees,'" Will croons, off-key.

"Please," Joel says. "What about Gail?"

"Who?"

"Ha ha."

"What about her?"

"Love, honor, obey? What about all that stuff? What's that, window-dressing?"

"You've never been married, have you, Joel."

"I'd say that's a fairly cynical way of looking at things."

"It's not love, exactly," Will says. "I mean, I guess it's lust, but it's a—a particular *kind* of lust."

"Tender. Caring. Maniacal," Joel says. "Third-sector lust."

"What?"

Joel barks a quick laugh. "Someday you should pay a visit to the fourteenth sector," he says. "Now, there's a fine sector." He motions for the bottle. Will gives it to him. "My sector."

"What the fuck are you talking about?"

Joel drinks. "No, I'd say you're mired in, say, the third or fourth sector. A mere lust-primitive."

Will sighs again: sometimes you just have to let Joel go. "Layla Layla Layla," he says. "Why would anyone be *named* Layla, if not to be lusted over?" He stares out at the orange pines tilting past. "I mean, my God. You should see this woman."

They've come to a light at Longview's western end. To the right is an on-ramp for the Kennedy Parkway, north; across an overpass, another ramp for the parkway in the opposite direction. The old lady in the black BMW, stopped ahead of them, either wants to take the south ramp or has forgotten the right-on-red rule. Joel guesses the latter.

"Or here's another thing," he says. "Jever notice that when a whole bunch of cars are stopped at a light, and then the light turns green, they never ever all start going at once? I mean, they *could*. They could. Instead you have to build this stupid chain of reaction times. I mean—people don't *trust* each other." He drinks from the bottle and shakes his head.

Will stares at him.

"I remember when they built this road," Joel says. "People would sneak onto it at night, before it was finished, and drag-race. Remember? Remember when Don's was a log cabin?"

"You're not listening to me."

"Clown paintings on the walls? Simple, hearty fare at fair prices? Our fathers with big cigars, in Cadillacs? Who art in heaven? Where are the Morrises of yesteryear?"

"Joel."

"Listen, the third sector has simple needs. Two squirts and you'll be bored silly. Not to mention in deep shit."

"Oh, you're so fucking superior," Will says. "What is all this sector crap, anyway?"

Joel raises the bag to his lips again. "The fourteenth sector is the velleity I can't explain. The fall of light on a cheek, the tilt of a nose. The delicate interplay of exquisite memory and subtle perception that makes me me, and boxes you out irretrievably. Lust-peasant that you are."

"Yeah yeah yeah. So who's got you so hot and bothered?"

"I'm sorry—the fourteenth sector is beyond your abilities to comprehend."

"Oh, so there really is someone."

"Perhaps."

"Come on, who?"

"Gary Berkowitz's daughter. If you must know."

"No."

"Ah, yes."

"Come on. *The* Gary Berkowitz? Cindy's cousin? Skyview Drive?"

"The one."

"God, the fact that he could reproduce is truly scary." Will opens the glove compartment. Which is empty except for a neatly arranged pair of gloves. "How *old* is she?"

"Oh, I don't know. About sixteen, I think."

"Jesus, Joel!"

"Fourteenth-sector lust is profound."

"Profoundly fucked-up, you mean."

"I've seen her naked, Willy."

"You're gonna go to jail!"

"Tut tut, my son. You underestimate me."

Will thinks about it. "So what did she look like?" he asks.

"Ah, Layla, Layla. How soon he forgets."

"Six*teen*." Will shakes his head, shudders. "It's like—I don't know. Unripe fruit."

"Only to the jejune imagination."

The light turns green. Joel gazes at it for a moment before taking his foot off the brake. He was wrong about the lady in the black Beemer, who crosses the bridge: toward the mall, no doubt. Joel watches her head down the long lane of trees, into the October sunset, on that most serious of missions, shopping. At last he moves forward, heads down the north ramp, and merges, carefully, staying in the right lane once he does, at about thirty-five. "I've finally figured out why people go slow in the left lane," he says. "A master theory."

"But nothing's going on with her and you, right?" Will says.

"It has to do with right-brain dominance of spatial perception. That, and the fact that the heart is on the left side. Old people, scared people, seek that sheltering divider."

"Nothing is, right? Going on."

Joel points to his head. "Only in here," he says. "Where it counts."

# 6

Gail's car was a '98 Cassiopeia, Toyota's great answer to the previously missing link between station wagons and minivans. The Cassiopeia allowed hundreds of thousands of suburban parents, heretofore adamant about their distaste for fading into middle age at the wheel of sexless child-buses, to capitulate with honor. It had four-wheel drive, big chunky performance tires, and a sharp, snarling grille; it looked surprisingly trim on the outside, and it seated eight with comfort. It made everybody happy, and Toyota's only problem was turning out enough of them. Gail's car was plum and black, with a brand-new, long white horizontal scrape across the passenger's-side rear door where she had misgauged her distance from the cantilevered under-corner of a tall, silver-shiny truck delivering hot, fresh croissants, brioches, and baguettes to the Bloomingdale's bakery at the Short Hills Mall. It was Will's devout opinion that since women were in a constant state of chaotic uncertainty about the shape and outlines of their bodies, their cars, which after all represented an extension of the body, came in for far more dinking, scraping, scratching, and denting than men's cars did. He felt absolutely sure about this, but he held his tongue even when the latest scrape appeared, because he was in deep-enough shit as it was.

He had kissed Layla. She had given him one too many of her bold, inquiring stares when they were alone in the office on a Saturday morning, and he had finally responded, tentatively at first, then bending her backward over a gray steel desk, his tongue extended down her cigarette-smoky throat, his hands, electrified, on the hard horripilated nipples under her thin, ribbed tank top. Her midriff was bare. He had moved his right hand to her warm concave belly, and started to journey south, beneath the tight belt of her jeans, toward the steamy forests of Ecuador, when there had been a knock on the front door.

He deflated instantly, his heart banging in his ears. He was expecting no one; he never was on Saturday mornings, that was part of what charged the atmosphere, the thick dreamy aloneness. It was Gail. It was not. It was Federal Express. A stupid, needless Saturday delivery from an overeager potential supplier. ("Hi Bill!" read the note inside, which he eventually looked at on Monday morning. "It was great talking to you on the phone today, and I thought you'd really like to see this. . . .") Layla signed for the package as Will stood in the background, unconvincingly pretending to look for a letter on the desk. The driver, seeing Layla's mussed lipstick and smelling sex, smiled slightly before telling her to have a nice day. She closed the door and turned to face him.

She was playing with a tendril of her bronze hair and staring at him, quite frankly, with a half-smile. *I've got you now*, her look said. Resumption was clearly fine with her. Her nipples agreed. And it was equally clear to him that resumption was impossible. He signed her checks, for Christ's sake. He thought of this first, before he thought of Gail and the children. He signed her fucking checks. He knew exactly how much she took home, wherever home was. He had a sudden mental picture: a two-family, with brown vinyl siding and a steadily barking dog.

Will attempted a smile back. "I was stupid," he said. "I'm sorry."

She walked toward him, smiling. "Don't be sorry," she said. She put her palms under her belt and over her hipbones, never taking her eyes from his; pulling out the belt so he could see her narrow hips.

And he'd waked up. In Danny's bed, hard as a rock, staring blearily at the four-tiered pile of stuffed animals, like stacked bodies in some atrocity picture, on the bookshelf. Danny could no longer lay claim to the animals, couldn't quite give them up. So they lay, stacked, for day after day, their smiling faces upside-down and side-ways. Will had felt like crying: there were actually tears in his eyes. He wanted to go back to the dream.

He wanted to make it real.

It thrilled him; it terrified him. He couldn't go to the office Saturday; he must.

It was a Thursday night, the night of the reunion. He and Gail were riding in the Cassiopeia, she driving, in a fine rain, up the mountain. They'd stopped at a light by a giant spotlit radio-transmitting tower behind a Japanese steakhouse. The station they were listening to began to crackle like a Geiger counter. "That restaurant," he said, pointing, "used to be Hirsch's Mushroom Farm."

"A mushroom farm?" She sounded bewildered.

"No, a restaurant. That's what it was *called*," he explained. "Davey used to be terrified of mushrooms. He couldn't imagine anything worse than having to go to Hirsch's Mushroom Farm for dinner. We used to torture him with it, threaten to take him there." Worse than that. He remembered playing with his brothers in the neighbors' yard, golfing a giant toadstool at Davey with a sand wedge, laughing at the look of absolute horror on his face. The pure sadism of childhood.

"That was nice of you," Gail said, in a marking-time voice. Bored. He bored her. She was mouth-breathing the way she did, staring up through her glasses, which rested on the end of her pointy nose, out the wet windshield. "Do we turn right here?"

"Yeah. The biggest fight my parents ever had was over that. My mother said—"

"What is this person *doing*?" The car in front of them, a jade-green Effluent not much bigger than a couple of Portosans, was lingering in the intersection, turn-signal blinking right, but unmoving. Gail leaned on the horn, which blared, two-toned: a good expensive Toyota horn. Show that piece of tin a thing or two. The Effluent crept forward timidly, still blocking the way.

"They're lost," Will said.

"I *know* they're lost. They should pull over and get their goddamn act together." She leaned on the horn again, then swerved out to the left, over the double yellow line, and passed the Chevy. "Assholes."

"Hey. You want to go back home?"

"Yes."

"We can, you know."

"And you'll have wasted your hundred and fifty dollars."

"So? Do my bit for the alumni association."

"No, no. I need to get my tepid roast beef, need to smile at people I don't care about, need to dance to greatest hits of the seventies. What *were* the greatest hits of the seventies?"

"There weren't any."

"I thought so."

"We really don't have to go, you know."

"You do."

He thought about it a moment. "You're right," Will said. "I do."


They filled out their own name tags, in purple Magic Marker, at a bridge table in the crowded vestibule. The pleasant stink of the Magic Marker instantly taking him back, for a vertiginous second, to junior-high ad campaigns, epiphanies on oaktag. The world was there, then, to be designed: a clean sheet of paper. He returned to now, surrounded by middle-aged bodies, friends of his parents, perhaps. He slapped his tag on his tweed breast, pressed Gail's onto her pale gray linen jacket, a corny-looking thing on an expensive-looking thing. She rolled her eyes. But the tags got immediate results. "Hey! Willy!" An enormous hand was clapping him on the shoulder. A behemoth of a man, six-five and two-fifty at least, with a salt-and-pepper beard and silver-rimmed glasses. A small, plump, mousy-pretty woman stood next to him, smiling apologetically in her demure satin neck-bowed dress. The giant's name tag read DR. KEN KATZ.

Ken Katz? Ken Katz? It didn't even vaguely ring a bell.

"Ken! Kenny Katz!" Will said, reading the tag and frantically thinking back. Not *Kenny* Katz? From *gym* class? Fat and acned and not terribly bright? All at once Will remembered being forced to wrestle Kenny in one of those absurd gym matchups, being weighed down by his overwhelming flesh and body odor. Good God! What strange magic had made Kenny Katz a doctor and won him the love of a good woman?

"Hey! How ya doin'?" Kenny boomed. "You look great, kiddo."

"So do you." And in fact, it was true. Kenny wasn't handsome, but his small eyes had acquired an intelligence and a probity, an authority even, that Will would never have imagined in his wildest dream. "What branch of medicine are you in, Kenny? Ken?"

"I have a doctorate in social work. I'm a shrink."

"Really!"

Kenny shook his head. "It's a shrinkage industry these days. Meds is where it's at. How 'bout you, Willy?"

He was suddenly aware of the vaguely disapproving presence on his left. "Oh, this is my wife, Gail," he said. Gail reached out, forthrightly, and shook hands with both of them. Smiling tightly, but not unwarmly. Will liked this about her, liked her lawyerly assertiveness and confidence. He envied them. And she looked good. Straight and lean, shoulders back, dark hair glossy, proud. A million hours of aerobics, sweat equity. Not pudgy and graying around the edges, like Kenny's wife.

"Sorry, sorry. This is Belinda," Kenny said. The mouse-woman smiled and nodded, afraid. Of Kenny? Well, who wouldn't be? Will tried to imagine him on top of *her*. What women had to put up with. "You were saying, Willy?"

"Oh—me? I work for my dad. Cardboard boxes." He shrugged.

"Hey—people need boxes," Kenny said.

"They need a lot of them, fortunately."

Kenny laughed. "Whatever pays the bills, man. Wanna go in?"

"Sure." He took Gail's cool hand, a little ostentatiously. She allowed him, just. "How you doing?" he whispered in her ear.

She raised an eyebrow. "Fine." Meaning, You're the nervous one, not me. She *was* fine.

The room was wide and forgivingly dim, filled with round tables and milling strangers. A bandstand in the center, the two guitarists, the bassist, and the saxophonist all middle-aged themselves, lean and sly and knowing. Waiting to play. JAY JACOBS AND THE JETS was printed, in rakish script, on the bass drum. Jay sat behind his kit, sleek and tan, grinning in his big square glasses, talking with a pretty woman, looking more or less precisely the same as he'd looked twenty-five years ago. He had done well, had made a name as a rock sideman, had played for a while with some band that opened for the Stones. Will had seen him on TV. He remembered Jay at a ninth-grade touch-football game on a close gray October afternoon in Stoddard Field, with that same successful grin. Will vaguely remembered feeling oppressed by the humidity, dropping an important pass, the fat ball slick and grassy. Would his own life be different, he wondered, would he have caught more passes, if he'd cultivated a successful grin instead of worrying about the weather? He tried one now, just for a second, stretching his cheek muscles, jutting his jaw.

"Will Weiss." A tall black-haired woman in a purple dress grinned back, handsomely, and extended a jeweled hand. DONNA DIMICHELE, her name tag read, in perfectly matching purple. It crossed Will's mind for a second that she'd coordinated the colors. "And his lovely wife . . ." She read: "Gail." A compact, big-haired, small-eyed, satisfied-looking man in a shiny coal-colored suit stood by her side. "This is Mario," Donna said.

There were pleasant nods and handshakes. Mario was smiling wisely. What were people so wise about? Will wondered. What did they know that he didn't? "So—you planned all this, Donna?" he asked, waving at the room.

"I'm pawtly to blame, yes." It was very formal and serious, this Yes, like something a cop would say. It indicated the supreme importance of the occasion. Donna looked good. Will was quite sure he'd never said a word to her before in his life. She'd been just another figure in the high-school frieze. As he'd been to her.

"Mario, did you go to VHS?"

The smile grew even wiser, extending a beatific indulgence for Will's ignorance. Will noticed now that Mario wasn't wearing a name tag. "No, no, I'm from Rockland County," Mario said, in a lulling, grown-up, musical voice, as if this explained everything in the world: the particle-wave theory, Bosnia, death.

Will wanted a drink. Immediately. Why couldn't you just say this? Smile quickly: *I want a drink. Goodbye.* "So where'd you guys meet?" he asked, instead.

Mario and Donna glanced at each other. Donna twinkled. "We're not married," she said, kittenishly. Mario twinkled back. He was wearing a wedding ring. "We work in the same office. Suburban? The realtors?" She said reel-i-ters.

"You two live around here?" Mario asked.

Will glanced at Gail. Answer, please. She was smiling in what seemed to him a dangerous way. He was going to have to pay for tonight.

She nodded. "On Beechdale. In the Norwood section."

"Oh, I know Beechdale very well," Mario said. "That's a lovely street. Which house?"

"One twenty-one," Gail said.

Mario and Donna looked at each other for a second. Mario nodded gravely. "Beautiful house."

"Beautiful house," Donna said almost in unison, nodding along.

"We handled it for a while, before the previous owners— changed their mind," Mario said.

"They said they didn't want to sell through a realtor," Will remembered, aloud. The Gundersons. The old gougers.

"We would've recommended they not price it over three-fifty."

"You're kidding," Will said. They had bought for $429,500.

"But they were very obstinate," Mario said. "They had to sit with it for quite a while, as I recall."

"Until we came along," Gail said. Smiling. Will had wanted to tell the Gundersons to take a hike; she had insisted. She had a feeling about the place.

"Well. You got the house you wanted," Mario said.

"And you've done lovely things with it," said Donna. "You've really realized its potential." This gave him a creepy feeling: as though she'd walked around inside when he wasn't home. When had she done all her observing?

"Are you a large family?" Mario asked.

"Only two kids," Will said. "So far." He smiled at Gail, who widened her eyes at him.

"So you'll definitely be wanting to expand at some point," Donna said.

"Except you'd have to cut so drastically into that pretty back yard," Mario chimed in. "You know, we have some lovely places right now, at some surprisingly affordable prices. The market's a tiny bit soft—not that you'd ever have any trouble selling *your* place."

"The one on Hartshorn would be fantastic for them," Donna interjected.

Mario shook his head in grave agreement. "Fantastic."

"Hartshorn?" Gail said.

"Twenty-nine," Mario said. "You know, the big Tudor?"

"That place is for sale?" Gail said. "God, I *love* that house."

Will shot her a look.

"Another elderly couple," Mario said. "It needs a little work, but the space is fantastic. The possibilities in that place—" He shook his head again.

Will noticed that Donna was squinting over his left shoulder, fluttering her long coal-y lashes with the effort of seeing without her glasses. "Joel Gold," she read. She looked alarmed.

Will turned around. Joel was wearing a summer suit around two sizes too small for him, and a brown Lacoste shirt, untucked, with an inspector's sticker still stuck to the hem. His belly preceding him. He held a clear plastic cup of Scotch.

"This is some affair, no?" Joel said. He gestured around the room with his cup. Jay and the band began to play. The song was "Love Will Keep Us Together." Joel winced. "Although something terrible has happened to a lot of these people," he said, looking around. "Their *faces* have disappeared."

"I didn't know you were coming," Will said.

"Wouldn't miss it for the world. What if Cindy showed up?"

"Joel—"

"Hey, if Tommy, why not Cindy?"

"Tommy?"

"Tommy Dano's here," Joel said. Mario and Gail looked blank. Donna's mouth opened.

# 7

The main thing about Tommy Dano was that he was dead. He had been the first of their class's casualties, killed in a car crash the summer after senior year, on Route 206 in rural northwest Jersey, near a camp where he was working. Three other counselors had been in the car: they'd just been shaken up. The luck of the drunk. Tommy, in the front passenger's seat, had been thrown clear and broken his neck. Another form of luck.

Tommy was a sweet boy, friendly and lost, with a big bright irresistible smile. (In the yearbook, he and a girl with equally large teeth had been chosen Most Cheerful.) Joel had been fascinated with him for a time, because Tommy was black. Light brown, actually. How did you live in the suburbs if you were that color? Tommy and his family managed, somehow. They had a small house on a side street downtown: not a bad house, not a bad street, though too close to businesses and stores. Joel had never set foot in it, though he'd walked by a few times, just to look. He'd wondered what went on in there, a house full of black people. The surprise of seeing Tommy triggered two memories. One was of junior high, in the boy's locker room. Tommy had a long, smooth, whippy dick, uncircumcised. He liked to twirl it, flip it, show it off. And one afternoon, he pulled it back between his legs, tucked it back between his buttocks, bent over, and turned into a girl. With a big, white-toothed grin. It gave Joel a strange feeling: the effect was very convincing.

The other memory was of about a year later, in the Community House, where Joel had gone to shoot pool one afternoon. It was a dusty, old-fashioned place, with a brown air of the 1930s; Joel had spent a lot of time there during junior high, intoxicated with the smell of chalk dust, imagining that he was perfecting a special skill in pocket billiards. Then, in tenth grade, he'd grown bored and restless with the Community House—whose equipment, as though in agreement with him, was all falling apart—but wasn't sure what else to do with himself. One hot spring afternoon, he walked in to find Tommy shooting pool by himself. Tommy was grinning and stumbling, poking the balls off the cushions, even off the table. "Oh, I'm high, man," he said. "High high high." He walked around the table with his warped cue, playing his imaginary game, crooning, over and over, in a high, sweet voice, "What's your name? Who's your daddy? He rich—is he rich like me?"

And that had been it for Tommy. Until now. "What are you talking about?" Will hissed, once he'd taken Joel aside. Gail was enmeshed in further real-estate discussions with Donna and Mario: Will was surprised and gratified and worried all at once that she seemed genuinely interested.

"I swear to God," Joel said. "Standing by the men's room, in a green suit. He looks good."

"Are you OK?" Will asked. Joel was smiling a little too brightly.

"Never been better."

Will glanced at the bandstand. A few couples had begun to dance—insofar as you could dance to "Love Will Keep Us Together." "A *green* suit?" he said.

"Iridescent," Joel explained. "Kind of overcooked-asparagus. Canned, really. You know Green Giant canned asparagus?"

"You're insane."

"But very successfully medicated. And frequently well-behaved."

"How about tonight?"

"Assessments will be made at the end of the evening. By an international panel of judges."

"Joel? Joel *Gold*?"

"Hey! Patti!"

The woman, whose tag said PATTI CAMPESI MINTZ, was bleached-blond, tan, hard-looking but handsome-pretty. Pug-nosed. Extremely well tended. She wore a black pantsuit with a low-cut halter top under a vest made of dozens of tiny mirrors. Her chest was freckled but breathtakingly bulbous. Will gave it a good look, especially the dark central valley. He wouldn't mind spending some time there, he thought.

"Joel!" she cried. They embraced. Now Will remembered, blinking at the distant, dissonant image in his mind. Patti Campesi. Her hair had been black. There was a picture of her in the yearbook in absurdly long false eyelashes, a varsity jacket, and tight faded jeans, lying on the roof of a Pontiac GTO with her legs splayed.

She held out a tan hand to Will. On the other, drink-holding, hand, he noticed, was a diamond ring the size of a small doorknob. "Hi, I'm Patti," she said.

"Will."

"We traveled in different circles, I guess," Patti said.

"But you and Joel—?"

They looked at each other and laughed. "Oh, we—" Patti began, but then they started laughing again.

"We worked on a project together," Joel explained, after a minute. "In biology. 'Life Cycle of a Newt.'"

"It led to further experiments," Patti said, crinkling her pug nose. "In biology."

"Patti, Patti," Joel said. "I still think of you sometimes. At night. Very fondly."

"Ditto," Patti said. She turned to Will. "We had fun," she explained. "But we lost touch."

"I'm going to get a drink," Will said. "Could you excuse me?"

"So you got married, Patti," Joel said, ignoring him.

"Of course I got married," she said. She held out her left hand. "What does this look like?"

"It looks like sporting equipment," said Joel. "It looks like a crystal golf ball."

She put her fingers to the base of her throat and laughed a squeaky donkey-laugh.

"Excuse me," Will said, backing away. Neither of them looked at him.


"So Joel," Patti says. "You're married, too?" Her voice is the same: hoarse, sexy. He always loved her voice; it seemed up for anything.

"Me? No, no. I live at home."

"You're kidding me."

She scans his face. It's dead-serious.

"Still? On Forest?"

"Same place."

"I remember the basement," she says, smiling with wonder.

"I remember, too."

"With the fake palm trees on the poles?"

"Still there."

Her forehead wrinkles. "You're really still at home, Joel?"

He nods. "Just me and my mom. And Violet."

She puts her jeweled hand on her freckled chest. "No. The crazy cleaning woman?"

"Still crazy after all these years."

"My God!" Her eyes search his. "You were always kind of crazy, too, Joel."

"Yeah, well, I built on that a little bit." He sips his Scotch. Now the band is playing "Benny and the Jets." "If they ever made a movie of our high-school years, the sound track would be unsellable," he says.

She laughs her throaty-squeaky donkey-laugh, touches his forearm. "You always tickled me so," she says.

"Yeah, I remember the feathers."

An odd look crosses her face, sad and lustful and faraway. "Me, too."

"So what about this rich husband of yours? He's not funny?"

"Norman? Oh, Norman's a barrel of yuks."

Joel screws up his mouth. "'Norman'?"

"Most people call him Junior. He hates that, though."

His eyebrows rise. "Junior Mintz?"

She nods, dead-serious.

"Now, me, I would wear that name as a badge of honor. I mean, has the man no sense of humor at all?"

Patti stares at him for a moment.

"Ah," Joel says. "I see."

"No, you don't." Now she raises her eyebrows, and shrugs. "People get married, Joel."

"That's not exactly the most ringingly romantic thing I ever heard, Patsy."

"Well, you've never been married, have you, Joel."

"Why is it that all my married friends are so cynical?"

"Most people our age are married. Maybe they're cynical about something else."

"Like being our age."

She searches his eyes again. "So—why don't you call me sometime, Joel?"

"You sure that's a good idea, Pats?"

Patti smiles quickly and sips her drink, watching him the whole time. "No," she says. Smiling.


From the bar, Will could see Gail, across the room, still talking with Mario. Donna appeared to have slipped off into the party. Now Gail and Mario were laughing about something, and he touched her forearm. Just for a second. She kept laughing, as though it hadn't happened. But it had. Will had seen it.


"Tommy?" Joel whispers. "Is that you?" He came over having to take a wicked piss, but all at once here's a significant distraction: Tommy Dano, still leaning against the wall next to the men's room in his asparagus suit, smiling dreamily.

No answer. Joel leans up close, but can't quite catch Tommy's eye. He moves his head in an arc around Tommy's face, but it's like the opposite of one of those portraits where the eyes follow you: Tommy's eyes are always staring just off to the side. Despite the smile. For a second it makes Joel think of a hologram. Maybe that's what Tommy is? But who would go to this trouble and expense to play a ghoulish joke? And besides, the only holograms Joel has ever seen are citrine-green and rainbowy around the edges, spectral and technologically primitive, like an old Edison gramophone cylinder.

This Tommy, if artificial, is CD-clear. Joel's mind races through possibilities: some accidental incursion of future technology, another time-warp deal? Bad Scotch? But he feels OK.

"Tommy?" he repeats.

"Hey, man." Tommy still won't meet his eyes. And his light, Most Cheerful voice has an odd, tunnely overtone to it, like a backward recording.

"Joel Gold? We were in Hogenauer's social-studies class together?"

"Hey, man."

"Hey, Tommy. You look good." And he does: he hasn't aged a day, although the shiny suit is a strange touch. For reasons he can't fathom, the brownish green makes Joel overpoweringly sad. The suit has, he notices now, no lapels, like something from the future. And no name tag, either. Joel looks down. Tommy's brown feet are bare. The white toenails are beautiful.

"I feel good, man. Ow. Feel fiiine." No eye contact.

"Are you high, Tommy?"

"Never been higher."

"So—what are you up to these days?" Joel's bladder is killing him; he has to keep shifting from one foot to the other. Relief is just behind the door with its silver profile of a top-hatted gent, but for some reason it feels important to keep talking.

"Never been higher, man."

"What do you think of this party? Rotten music, huh?"

The big smile is fixed. "Yeahhh."

Joel's about to burst. "I— Could you excuse me one second? I'll be right out, I promise. Don't move, OK?"

Fixed smile, no answer.

"Just stay there, OK, Tommy?"

Naturally when Joel comes out of the men's room, Tommy is nowhere in sight.

As if in a dream, Will, carrying his beer and Gail's Chardonnay, couldn't get back to her: the room was too thick with people, and every third grinning face was someone tangential, yet not quickly dismissible, from his past. Donny Mars, once a fluffy-haired English-class show-off, now a bald professor at Antioch with the same buck-toothed baby-face. Carol Iosso, the object of a five-year unspoken crush from grades eight through twelve, now no longer blond and nubile but handsomely womanly, mysteriously single, and—again as if in a dream—pointedly flirtatious. She was a filmmaker in Hoboken. No time, no time. Will chatted for a moment, then held up the Chardonnay, apologetically. My wife. Carol's eyes, in fare-well, contained the invitation he had always longed for and now would never respond to.

Timmy Shaughnessy, dauntingly rugged and deep-voiced in tenth grade, a rebel, now an unrecognizably jowly, patently alcoholic, airport-limo driver in Worcester, Mass. Why had he come? Timmy, too, was bald. Baldness had attacked his classmates like some ravening plague that battened on hair. Here was Steve Marcus, the smoothest poker player and alpha male of Will's sophomore group, whose smoothly whiskered, handsome face, with its single dark eyebrow, had stared down many a shaky bluff. Bald. (And in tow to a clutching, dominant-looking Linda.) Steve Grossman, white basket-ball star, all-around cool guy (and Carol's high-school squeeze). Bald. Dick Overby, tennis captain. Bald! Bald! Will reached up with a cupbearing hand and stuck out a pinky, as though to scratch his scalp, but really just to make sure his hair was still there. (That morning, Danny, over his FiberPlus Cheerios, had helpfully noted, "You're not *really* bald, like Max's dad; you're just a *little* bald.")

And then, here and there, jutting out from the crowd, were faces weirdly preserved, like Mesozoic flies in amber, in virtually their precise ancient state. Unaged, more or less. (They were all men. All the girls had become women, attractive or un-, but some of the boys had, inexplicably, stayed boys.) Was this luck—heredity—or were these few simply doing the opposite of what Timmy Shaughnessy had done? Not everyone who had aged badly had been so vigorously self-destructive as Timmy. The answer, Will thought, must come from both the habits and the genes of fathers. Will thought of his own, still unlined face, and then of Jack's, well preserved except for the bags under the eyes. Neither he nor his father had smoked a cigarette in years; both were strictly one-drink-only men; both had a certain long-lashed vanity, integral to their souls, that neither would ever acknowledge to the other.

And here was Mario, with his bulletproof hairline and thick dark pelt, his long lashes and tan cheeks, gazing intently at Gail, who looked flushed and excited—and who already held a cup of wine. "Mario's been telling me about some houses that sound terrific," she said. "He feels it's definitely time for us to upgrade."

Mario smiled at Will as if he'd just beaten the crap out of him in tennis. "Definitely," he said.

# 8

Mornings in the Sub Shop are long, afternoons much longer. The breakfast rush lasts almost till ten; after an hour-long pit, the welcome distraction of lunch traffic starts to wander in. Then pile in. An interlude like war—flashing knives, barking voices—then, at one forty-five, silence. Certain clock-hand configurations make Joel's stomach ache. Ten thirty-three is one: the bottom of the pit. One forty-eight is another. The big hand beginning its agonizing uphill toward a peak on a desert's edge. The afternoon is a wasteland, with one oasis: at three, he can take a fifteen-minute break. Usually he stays in. Where would he go in his white shirt and apron? He sits with a cup of tea and stares at the changing shadows out on Main, as the schoolkids filter in with their alive eyes and bright loudness. With their smiling demands, their assurance the world will love them forever. Chia has stayed away since Larry's outburst, but Joel has caught her eye a couple of times as she lingered, just for a second, outside the window, giving him that look just to make sure he doesn't forget. He doesn't forget. The boy has been completely out of sight. Have they broken up? He chuckles, not humorously, at the old reflex, the brief resurfacing of high-school hope. He's been writing: it's best that she and the boy stay together, her betrayal is all the sharper. He likes to imagine them together, imagine all they do, every sweaty bit of it, every fleck of saliva: the pain makes him feel alive. In the pit of one forty-eight.

Jingling, and a faintingly lovely smell of roses. And leather. In the Sub Shop. He looks up, at Patti, in a black-brown bumpy jacket, big-shouldered, fancy, like rhino hide. Many gold bracelets. Big bright smile.

"Hi."

"Patti," he says, with mild surprise. He remembers his manners, stands, kisses her perfumed cheek for the second time in a week, the second time he's seen her in twenty-five years. Her skin is softer than it was back then, with the incipient faint down of middle age. Her eyes are a little wild; she can't stop smiling.

"So," she says. "Wanna take a little ride? Do some catching up?"

He spreads his hands, shrugs. "I'm working." Larry's leaning his vast bulk against the counter, his pale hard eyes, just slits over the pillows of his cheeks, fixed on two skinny junior-high boys in porkpie hats, dressed-down-rich-looking, standing with the glass cooler door open, whispering as they decide on sodas.

"Hey," Larry rumbles. "I'm not paying to cool the room with that."

The boys grin at each other, in delicious amusement at the deep-voiced, menacing fatty. "OK," the one on the left pipes, squeakily. The door stays open.

"Can't you take a break?" Patti asks. "Personal time?" Still smiling, but looking intent.

"I, uh— Larry?"

"Yes, Joel."

"Can you do without me for a little bit? I have to, uh, help a friend with something?"

Long-suffering, Larry's favorite tone: "Yes, Joel."

Patti squeezes his arm. "I'm parked right outside."

★ ★ ★

The inside of the big Benz is butterscotch leather, a slightly fruitier scent than her jacket. Joel also recognizes the unmistakable odor of car-wash air-freshener. The car's carpets exude a fluffy, just-vacuumed turbidity. So she has prepared for him. A pleasant confusion overtakes him, along with the confusion of perfumes. Patti puts her long-fingered, white-nailed, gold-jingly hands on top of the steering wheel—it's also wrapped in leather—and he notices, once again, the enormous wedding stone. She shrugs, grinning. "So," she says. The blush begins from her earlobes, which are pierced with tiny gold-set pearls.

"It's good to see you, Patti." His tone is genuinely pleased, also questioning.

"I'm picking you up," she explains. "Is this too aggressive of me?"

"No, not at all. I mean, I'm glad for the—diversion."

"I want to see your basement," Patti says. The blush rises through her cheeks.


They park on Forest. The driveway is empty, the garage door open. The garage doors, and their moldings, are painted a dark, ancient green, the color of autumn twilight, the color of the morning Joel saw Morris for the last time as he set out for work—and play—in the silver Cadillac. Which, Joel now notices, is out. He stares at the ancient green, the dried-blood brick of the house, the sooty empty cave of the garage. Old Jersey license plates hang on the cinder block: cream on blue, black on cream, white on black. For some reason, Joel suddenly remembers an elementary-school trip to Trenton, to the governor's mansion. Glancing into the back of the long black limo, he learned the single civic fact he retained from that day: the governor smoked Salems.

"Irma's out," he says. Puzzled. "Slowing up traffic somewhere."

"Why? Doesn't she leave the house?"

"Only when the migratory urge sets in," Joel says. "Sale at Saks or Bloomie's."

She squeaks her donkey-laugh. He looks at her, smiling in bemusement. What does she want?

Something. "What about Violet?" Patti asks, quickly, as if she were planning a crime. Grinning, all the while, as she savors the ancient name.

"Thursday. Maid's day off."

"Excellent."

"Excellent?"

She hugs herself and shivers. "Brrr. I hate winter," she replies.

"It's still fall," he corrects, the instant before he realizes he's simply being prompted to open the door. The smell, in the vestibule porch, is a primeval amalgam of stuffed cabbage and ammonia: Home. The chief charm of visiting other kids' houses, long ago, was always smelling the strange smells, sorting them into color-coded categories. He remembered the dark-gray-green carpet-and-roast-chicken scent of certain rich Jewish households; the tan, electric-train-coal-smoke bouquet of gentile basements (and the prim, off-white, cinnamon-grocery-closet fragrance of their kitchens). The sunset-orange-brown-cedar perfume of unfinished attics; the pot-roast-gray tang of steam heat rising among strange cooking on a winter Friday afternoon.

Patti's girlhood house—he'd been there only once or twice; for certain logistical reasons they'd soon switched to Joel's—smelled like a furniture store. It was a big, white-brick postwar pile on a half-acre of perfect flat lawn in the northern, newer section of Woodwick. The carpeting too was white; on the living-room wall was a painting of Patti's older brother, Pete Junior, as a Roman centurion. Joel was sorry, once they changed to his place, not to get to go there anymore.

"How are your parents?" he asks. They're standing in the kitchen; the silence is like a blanket. The red second hand on the Sunbeam clock sweeps its important way around the dirty dial. Three-fifty. Larry will have his head.

"My father passed away four years ago," Patti says, matter-of-factly. "My mother lives in Rembrandt Ridge—you know, the new high-rise where Borgenicht's used to be? She has a boyfriend."

She shrugs: this is the way time goes. A nice, sugar-cone-fragrant ice-cream store with knotty-pine paneling yields to a colossal glass condo monstrosity; men topple like oaks in a storm and are put underground to rot. "Your dad passed away a long time ago, didn't he?" she asks.

Joel nods. "The fall after we graduated," he says. "'Seventy-four.'"

"Ah," she says, looking around the kitchen and nodding as though she were assessing the fixtures.

"The basement's over here," Joel says, going to the door in the corner.

She smiles. "I remember," she says.

The kitchen odor modulates, on the warm basement steps, into a laundry-room-fresh-paint aroma that never fails to please and excite him. The basement is only partially finished—the furnace and Morris's old tool bench sit in blue furry darkness behind beaded curtains—but the finished section, though simple, is clean and dry and gay. Tropical fun is the theme. After Morris and Irma's second

trip to Honolulu, they hung coconut mats and Hawaiian travel post-
ers on the walls and wound the steel support columns with burlap
to make them resemble palm trees. The leaves, next to the ceiling,
were green oilcloth, with slices cut in them, for realism. Coconuts
with smiling painted faces and exotic-colored parrot feathers com-
pleted the décor. It's all still here. Everything is still the same as
it was in 1966. Violet cleans regularly down here, keeping it nice.
Strangely, though, she never touches the windows: only the bleary
gray-brown light filtering through their dusty panes indicates the
passage of thirty-three years. Or twenty-five.

"My God," Patti says, openmouthed. "It's exactly the same. It
even *smells* the same."

"Time warp," he says, with a serious smile.

She walks over to the corner, where an ancient portable record
player, covered in aqua vinyl, sits on a gold-aluminum TV-dinner
table. "It's still here," she almost whispers, as she reaches down and
opens a record box, also covered in vinyl—brown, with an ivory
plastic handle. The box is full of 45s, the meat of Joel's collection.
Every once in a while, he comes down to the basement to listen to
them, and dances, when the spirit takes him; you can stack a half-
dozen at a time on the turntable's central cylinder adapter. The
records are primarily from the sixties, when the music was still great:
Motown, Beatles, Stones, Kinks, Animals. Good party tracks,
with that extra heft in the sound, the big woof that 45s had. Before
music became a replica of itself. Patti picks up a handful. "'House of
the Rising Sun,'" she reads, reverently, shuffling through them.
"'Mickey's Monkey.' 'Mr. Postman.' 'Tell Me Why.'" She shakes her
head.

"Does it work?" she asks, pointing to the record player.

"Sure."

She opens the lid, turns the knurled white-plastic ON knob. The little orange indicator light glows, after a second's hesitation. There are tubes in there. She removes several records from their sleeves, aligns the big center holes with her long witchy thumbs, and sits them atop the cylinder. She turns the play switch—Joel can feel, with her, its bulky spring action—and the bottom disk plops onto the turntable. The fat white tone-arm jerks over and settles down over the record's rim. Suddenly scratchy sound booms through the single speaker. The song is "Rescue Me," by Fontella Bass.

Patti extends her arms, the bracelets jingling. "Dance?" she asks, with a half-smile.

He takes her hands. He can dance. So can she. She still has her leather jacket on; she's wearing black stretch pants and black suede heels. She has nice legs—he remembers them—and she likes to show them off. He holds her hands and watches her dance, his own movements slow and muted, a background for her performance. She never takes her eyes off him. He remembers she was a good dancer, but she's gotten better: age and knowledge have loosened her, made her more self-assured. She gestures expressively with her shoulders, even does that neck-juke that black women do, her chin staying parallel with the floor as her head shing-a-lings from side to side. He laughs with pleasure at the sight; the sound of his laugh surprises him. "You can dance," he tells her, raising his voice above the music.

"Thank you," she says. "So can you."

"Aw, come on—I haven't done anything yet." He lets go one of her hands, twirls, dips, and comes back to face her. He raises her fingers and jitterbugs her around, then releases her and goes into a medley: a modified Hitchhike, Swim, Mashed Potato, Hully-Gully.

She follows him move for move, watching him, improvising around the edges. Then the record ends. The arm swings back; another 45 drops.

They're both sweating. "When a Man Loves a Woman," by Percy Sledge, begins. They look at each other and laugh. Patti wrinkles her pug nose. "Whew," she says, taking off the rhino jacket and flinging it onto the Ping-Pong table. She's wearing a white silk blouse, cut low over her swelling freckled chest, that makes his fingertips tingle and the back of his tongue swell expectantly: Feed me. She beckons once more and he takes her in his arms, his right hand resting on the small of her back, which, he's surprised to feel, is taut and firm. He thinks, uneasily, of his own flaccid midsection. He was an athlete once.

"You work out," he says.

"Part of my busy day."

Her discontent is palpable, even in the midst of her pleasure. As if to get closer to its source, Joel puts his nose in her hair, down among the dark roots, and grows dizzy with the smell of roses. "I don't know anything about you anymore," he murmurs, as they slow-dance over the rattan mat.

"What can I tell you? Twenty questions."

"Do you have any kids?"

"Whoops—sore subject," she says.

"Because of the kids you have, or the ones you don't?"

"Maybe we should make this ten questions."

He leans back and looks at her. Her eyes are closed, her smile is sad. "I don't have to ask you any," he says.

"No, I want you to. I like it," she tells him. And adds, "Norman says I'm his kid."

"Do you love Norman?"

There's a pause; he's afraid he's done it this time. But then she opens her eyes and says, "What ever happened to what's-her-name, the one you were so in love with? With the angel face, and no boobs?"

"Cindy."

"Yeah."

"I don't know; she kind of disappeared," he says. Only half-lying. "You didn't answer about Norman."

"Norman. You'll have to meet Norman."

"I will?"

"Everybody should meet Norman. Everybody likes Norman. Everybody that isn't afraid of him."

"And you?"

"What do you think?"

"Some of both?"

"Joel." The record ends. The ratchety little mechanism goes through its rinky-tink routine, obediently dropping another disk. She's staring at him, daring-ashamed.

He stands back. "What?"

"I want to do what we used to do down here," she says.

"You're kidding, Patsy." He looks at her. She's not. This is the secret, the crime she's been planning.

The new song is "Mickey's Monkey."

"We were kids, Patsy," Joel says, as the horn section kicks in. "We were bored. It was a way of getting out of doing biology."

She grabs his chin. "I want you to. Will you do this for me, Joel?"

It had begun this way, when they were lab partners in junior year: he had told her about the Friday-night and school-holiday-afternoon poker game he occasionally sat in on, and she had begged him to teach her to play. And so, instead of studying the stages of amphibian embryos, he had instructed her on the subtleties of seven-

and five-card stud, High and Low Cotati, Anaconda, even Night
Baseball. They began playing for nickels; she quickly suggested they
switch to clothes. Once she lost everything, the question became
what further stake she could put up.

"In money poker, you can go light," he told her, as they sat, he
in his underpants, she wearing only a gold ankle bracelet, all fleshy-
white and grinning, with her arms over her knees and the fanned-
out hand of cards barely masking the round, wide-nippled breasts (as
erect as he was, he noticed) that peeped out at him along with her
shining eager eyes.

"What's that?"

"If you want to bet, but you're broke, you take your bet out of
the pot. If you win, you keep it; if you lose, you owe that much extra."

"I'll go light my panties," she quickly said, pulling them out of
the pot—a pile of both their clothing—and putting them between
her feet. The lacy gold anklet drove him crazy.

"You're pretty confident. OK, what do you have?"

She lowered her cards, smiling in triumph. "Three eights."

He placed his cards down, instructively, one at a time. "I have
a straight," he said. "Three through seven."

"Don't the three eights beat the seven high?"

He shook his head. "It doesn't matter what the straight is,
straight wins," he said. "Pair, two pair, three of a kind, straight, flush,
full boat, four of a kind, straight flush," he recited. "I've only seen a
straight flush once—Howie Kahn had one over Christmas vacation.
But I think he cheats."

"Oh," she said. And she dropped the panties back in the center
pile, her feet moving apart ever so slightly, letting him have a look
at all of her. She smiled, almost shyly, and he felt a disabling pressure behind his eyes. His reptile brain. It would be something like

this later, the time it broke. He broke. But that would come long after this. The light in the basement seemed distorted. He took hold of the waistband of his underwear.

Patti put her hand on his leg. "You didn't lose them. They have to stay on." She grinned. "But I owe extra. What can I pay?"

Joel shook his head in confusion, his imagination shut down. Nearly fainting—almost all the blood in his brain, after all, had traveled from his head elsewhere—he listened to her idea: she would be his native slave. He could tie her to the coconut trees. But—and it was a big but—his pants must stay on. There was no arguing the matter. She was terrified, it turned out, of getting pregnant. Her older sister Debbie had gotten knocked up senior year, and had ended up going, behind their parents' backs, to a butcher in Irvington who'd hurt her and made her bleed. And deeply shamed her. She still had the dreams. The abortion, in Patti's quick retelling, was more of a sin than the sex.

"If you break the bargain, we'll never play again," she warned.

But then she smiled once more. Anything else, anything at all, was fair game. As long as his underpants stayed on. It made his head hurt, calculating the possibilities, and impossibilities. Nevertheless he tied her, wrists and ankles, using the burlap strips on two support columns, about six feet apart, behind the Ping-Pong table, and they played the game. They played many times over the course of the year, and it was always the same. She was his, in every way but the obvious. Creative use was made of the basement's colored decorative feathers, of Ping-Pong balls and paddles, bars of laundry soap, even 45-rpm records. And Joel's underwear never came off. He learned much about female anatomy and sexual response, and lost many pairs of briefs that year, smuggled furtively out to the trash in plastic bags and buried beneath other garbage.

But, inevitably, the game grew tired and obligatory and me-thodical, all its surprise gone, as summer vacation approached. And so they parted as friends; senior year, they smiled, wistfully, as they passed in the hall. Nostalgia was pleasant. She was dating a football player; he had started seeing Cindy Island. Joel particularly remem-bered Patti's expression, as she and her slab of a tackle walked by Joel and wan Cindy one Friday afternoon in the school's Gothic-arched, brown-linoleumed front foyer: a complicated mix of triumph and envy, longing and satisfaction. His feelings, too, were complex—Cindy, at the time, wouldn't do anything more than make out. He scanned the football player's smug brick-face and wondered what *they* did together.

"What did you do?" he asks her now. They're still dancing, dreamily, to "Heart of Stone." "You and the football player?"

"Football player?"

"Senior year."

"Oh, Bobby." She half-grins at the sound of the old name, then shrugs. "Just fucked. It wasn't so special. You and Cindy?"

"Not much." A funny look comes over his face: what he means to say, but can't, quite, is that not only wouldn't Cindy sleep with him, then, but that later, when she did, it wasn't so great. It was terrible, as a matter of fact. His intense love for her made sex confus-ing, made kissing and wanting the most erotic things of all.

Patti leans down, as though to catch his eyes at a more reveal-ing angle. "My God. You're still stuck on her, aren't you."

"Come on. I haven't seen her in—in years."

"On someone, then?"

"Hey. Pats." He sweeps his hand around vaguely at the house, the environment. "This is my life. You've seen it all." He's matter-of-fact about this, even a little amused, beyond self-pity.

"I can't believe it," she says, reaching up to caress his cheeks with thumb and forefinger. "You know, you're still handsome as hell."

He joins his hands over the small of her back, in the dear dimple at the top of her butt, pushing her hips against his. He's thinking, in quick succession, almost simultaneously, about Patti's breasts—he wonders how, exactly, they've changed; they seem to have gotten bigger—and then about Cindy's white white skin, and Chia Pet's chalky, pouchy little belly, the long blue thighs and abbreviated bush. The extravaganza of flesh makes him semihard, his brain is turning like an asteroid in space. "Oh, Patti Ann," he breathes, into her sweet hair. Partly by way of apology: he doesn't love her. And yet . . . He pulls a few strands of her hair, accidentally inhaled, out of his mouth. "We never did technically make it, did we."

She shakes her head wryly. "Sure came a lot, though."

It's been a long time since he made it with anybody, is what he's thinking. He's thinking of the pond outside the window There, the place Cindy went, the deer's white underparts, its big black whiteless eye staring. Cindy in the half-darkness, half-smiling.

"So come on, Joel," Patti whispers, hoarsely, into his ear. "Fuck me *now*. Fuck my cunt, Joel. Ream my asshole. Come on, big boy, put it in me."

This produces the reaction she was looking for; smiling, bracelets jingling, she reaches for him. As the hoarse, tearing sound of Irma's voice spills down the stairwell: "Jo-well? Are you down there?"

# 9

When he closes his eyes, lying on his bed in the half-light, he can see her so perfectly, walking down the hall, can see her brown-black hair hanging around her slim jaw like raven's wings, her slightly smiling dream of a mouth, can even see the corny Popsicle-purple dress with the big-ringed silver zipper down the front, fashionable in this awful time. It's 1973. Joel catches her dark warm-distant eyes as she approaches; she pays him the compliment of raising a hand from the books she's cradling in front and pushing back one wing of her hair. He holds her look and they both stop, each cagily circling to the side for a second.

"What?" she says, her smile a little more pronounced. She has a small cleft in her chin. He could move in there, he thinks; he could move in and set up shop and stay for good. Behind her is a showcase full of swimming trophies (Steven's name is on four of them). The brown-linoleum hall smells like eraser dust and fall and now her, a pale-gray-violet going-away smell.

"What?" she repeats, almost laughing now.

They've never met. He knows too well who she is, and he's fairly sure she knows who he is; the protocol says they should act like strangers, but his eyes demand better.

"Why are you wearing that color?" he asks.

Now she does laugh. It's not a particularly lovely sound, a little too deep and not very happy. He likes seeing her pearly-perfect teeth, though: a triumphant tribute to good genes, orthodontia, and regular checkups. *"What?"* she says, her brow wrinkled.

"It doesn't do anything for you. It just sits there being purple. Like a show-off."

Strange talk to be coming from a good-looking guy in a varsity jacket (tennis). "What's your name?" she says, mock-suspicious, as if she knows the answer already.

"Why don't I take you shopping?" Joel answers.

She looks off to the side in caricatured disbelief, but when she turns back to him, she's smiling. "OK," Cindy says.

They take his car, to Lord & Taylor, in Millburn. It's a Friday afternoon in October; the light orangey, the air clear and cool, the kind of afternoon when you know you'll live forever. They play Jewish geography as they ride, and find out all they seem to need to know about each other for the preliminaries to be satisfied: Wendy, Steven, Westmont. But the preliminaries don't speak to what feels important now. Rich silences fall, silences full of promise rather than discomfort. She huddles cozily in the seat next to him. Walking across the parking lot full of big cars, he takes her hand. She looks at him, wondering how he knew he could do this, and smiles.

He tows her unerringly through the lavender-scented aisles, among the staring ladies, just as if he knew where he was going, to a slim black dress on an eyeless mannequin. "There," he says, pointing.

She goggles at him. "Do you have any idea how much this *costs*?"

"Trust me," Joel says. "You'll look amazing in it."

"May I help you?" a saleswoman scowls.

"She'll try this on," Joel says, pointing to the mannequin.

The woman looks the two of them over, shakes her head, and then has a thought: rich kids. Their money is as good as anyone else's. She smiles unattractively. "Certainly," she says.

When Cindy comes out in the dress, a salesman across the room gapes over the shoulder of the woman he's helping. Joel gapes, too. Cindy smiles at herself as she turns in front of the three-way mirror.

"It looks like it was made for you," the saleswoman says.

"*I can't buy this,*" Cindy stage-whispers to Joel.

"*I'll buy it for you,*" he whispers back.

The saleswoman smiles.

"You're crazy," Cindy says. "Joel, we just met."

The saleswoman blinks. Joel calculates as he stares at Cindy: he can cover it from his Bar Mitzvah account. The money's supposed to be for college, but it's his, he can do whatever he wants with it. This is what he wants to do.

Cindy shakes her head. "No. It's very sweet of you, but I won't let you."

The saleswoman drums her fingers on the glass counter.

"Cindy—" Joel begins.

"No, Joel," she says, looking as if she's about to cry, and runs back toward the dressing rooms.

The saleswoman stares daggers at Joel. He shrugs. Just then a lady full of clicking jewelry places herself in front of the saleswoman. "Can you help me," she says, and the saleswoman, with a last glance at Joel, nods.

"Certainly," she says.

Joel goes over to the dressing-room door, looks both ways, and slips in. There are four curtained enclosures; only one of the curtains is drawn. He walks up to it and says her name.

She pulls the top of the curtain over—her shoulders are bare, her black eyes wide and moist. "Joel, you are *nuts,*" she says.

"I'm sorry, Cindy, I really am," he says. "I—" He shakes his head, his vision unexpectedly going blurry. "You just looked so *beautiful.*"

"Oh, Joel," she says, shaking her head at him, "Oh, Joel." And they're kissing, the curtain held between them, his hand reaching around, his fingers alive on the warm bare base of her back.

# 10

On Fridays the cleaning woman came, a tiny, spherical, sour-faced Salvadoran named Esperanza. Will had seen her once or twice, when for one reason or another he'd left late for work: she stepped out of the taxi with her thick lips and squinty eyes twisted into a sneering scowl, as though the world had betrayed her in an especially poignant way. Her black hair hung in a long, unreasonably jaunty-looking braid; she wore a short leather jacket with a jungle scene embossed over the breast, and waffle-textured turquoise acrylic pants. Was she as angry as her face looked? There was no way to tell. She moved quickly, kept her gaze fixed downward, and spoke about six words of English. She was paid in cash, eighty dollars for five hours of work. Once Will tried to remember how Esperanza had first come to them, but the answer was lost in the mists of time. She was the latest in a series of Salvadorans, Yolanda and Alícia and Luz, each of them sad-faced and hardworking. Each of Esperanza's predecessors had left after a term for some uncommunicable family emergency. Will guessed terrible things had happened, were still happening, to all of them. The world whipped you when you were small and poor. One morning, Gail told him, Esperanza had shown up with a black eye and bruises on her cheek. She'd thought, guiltily, that she ought to ask her about it, but the language barrier, which prevented all but the most rudimentary communication, kept her from even fumbling toward a question. Moreover, she didn't like Esperanza.

Gail worked three days in the city, doing commercial real-estate closings for Bache, Halsey & Stewart. She had worked for the firm for ten years, and had made partner just before Danny was born. Between her full-time salary and Will's, they'd really had some money in those days. Occasionally he thought of the time nostalgically: they'd gone to Ocho Rios, to Vail; they'd been lovers. (Especially in Vail.) Being lovers, they had made babies. Having babies, they had ceased being lovers. Then Gail cut back her hours, and things got tight. With two children, they needed more money than ever, but these days she told him, again and again, that she wanted to quit work altogether. She hated real-estate law, she'd grown bored with it, even though she was good at it. And the firm, men mostly, nodded and smiled at her part-time mommy arrangement and loaded her up with more work than she'd had when she was putting in five days.

Tuesdays and Fridays she was off. Fridays Esperanza came. Gail hated it. She'd tried to get Esperanza to switch to a day when she was gone, but had learned, through calendar-pointing, that the cleaning woman was booked solid; some days, apparently, she even cleaned two houses. Where did she get the energy? "Seven hundred a week, say, all cash, free and clear," Will mused. "That's the equivalent of, what? A sixty-grand taxed salary? Shit, she's practically middle management."

"We're always bumping into each other," Gail complained. "I can't even take a shower after my workout without thinking about when she wants to get into the bathroom. Meanwhile I'm supposed to feel bad that I'm not off somewhere, slaving away like her. She just doesn't *see* me doing my slaving. To her, I'm just the rich white señorita."

"Señora," Will corrected.

"Whatever."

Every Friday morning he dutifully left four twenties, folded, on the kitchen counter, under a purple glazed-clay doggie Danny had made at nursery school, beneath the telephone. And every Friday evening when he returned, the twenties were gone, and the house was a mess, the kitchen floor spotted with cookie crumbs and twist-ties and cat food and sandy shoes, the living room strewn with cookie crumbs and sand and Legos and shoes and action figures.

"Wait a second," Will would say. "What, exactly, am I paying for here? You hate her, and the house is a pig-sty."

"It's messy," Gail said. "It's not dirty."

"Ah. I fail to grasp the subtle difference."

"Lynnie was over all afternoon, with Sarah and the twins."

"That would explain it."

"Meanwhile, you could do some picking up, too."

"I could pay myself the eighty and clear a profit."

"Meanwhile" was her latest verbal tic, and it drove him crazy. It had crept into her vocabulary, he calculated, sometime over the summer, probably from Lynn Zembowski, Gail's best friend. Short, perky, curly-haired, and relentlessly unintrospective, Lynnie seemed, to Will, exactly the kind of person who would say "mean-while" a lot.

Will thought about Lynnie sometimes, bent over and naked, smiling back at him. Perkily.

"Mario called this afternoon. He wants to show us some houses."

"Who?" Will said, though he remembered slick little Mario all too well. He watched his wife's face carefully for any suppressed smirk, any telltale trace of hidden lust. Two days a week would give her plenty of time for an affair. In some weird, perverted way, the idea turned him on. A little.

"You remember—the realtor, at the reunion."

"Oh yeah. Mr. Miami."

"I thought he was nice."

Aha. Or not? Would she defend him if she were really *shtupping* him? But what if she were just considering the possibility? Then she would defend him. To rationalize her good taste. "Yeah yeah. Six-percent nice."

She ignored it. Poutily: "We've been talking about looking."

"Looking is one thing, buying is another. We're cash-poor right now. And what about if you stop working? Any more mortgage'll murder us."

"Not if I stop. When I stop. You were going to ask your father for a raise, remember?"

They both suddenly became aware of the fact that they had conversed uninterrupted for a full three minutes. Conceivably this could mean the children were dead, or comatose. The thought passed between them when Gail's eyes flicked toward the living room, a microscopic gesture that would have been undetectable by anyone other than her husband.

"Could you take a look in there?" she asked. He did. Danny was not smothering Rachel, or vice versa; they were lying on the rug, a foot apart, staring at the TV, mouths ajar. Cute. Piercingly cute. All at once—even though they were right there in front of him—he missed them.

"Hi, guys!" Will called, loudly, waving broadly, as though he were flagging down a ride on the interstate. Their eyes stayed glued to the tube. The tinny music played; the adult actors' nasal baby-voices fluted; the candy-colored cartoon figures hopped and darted. "Bye, guys!" he called, and returned to the kitchen.

"*Rugrats*," he said, giving her a look that attempted to establish an ironic reconciliation, based on a commonplace between them: their shared helplessness at how much TV they seemed forced to let their children watch. She refused the gambit. Her eyes still held the hard stare of a half-minute before, pressing the question. *You were going to ask your father for a raise, remember?*

"What?" he asked, playing innocent.

"You know what."

"Look, we've already discussed this. We agreed I would wait till after the first of the year."

Now they were staring at each other, their mouths as ajar as the children's, at loggerheads. The first of the year, he thought, with amazement. The new millennium. The idea frightened him. He tried to picture the date printed at the top of the front page of the *Times:* he couldn't, quite. Maybe there would be no more world then—what would money matter?

"You were the one who said you wanted to wait; I didn't agree. Anyway, what if we need the money sooner?"

He slumped his shoulders and stared at the photographs on the side of the refrigerator, Danny and Rachel mugging in big sunglasses, in a mocking lost world of summer and surf. He remembered for a dizzying second what it had been like to be a child at the beach— the salt spray, the dancing sun on the water, the promised endlessness. But endlessness had fled, and there was no escaping its two opposites. The latter of which was money. He and Gail had been around and around on the raise question a hundred times. Will's father, nominally semiretired, still kept a close eye on cash flow, and Weiss Containers' corner of the Northeast's cardboard-box business had been tight lately, threatened by Leviathan, a coalition of New England competitors with a better distribution network.

Jack Weiss had started his company in the late forties, and had built it into a medium-size family business with old-fashioned book-keeping habits and limited sales penetration—the sales force being primarily Jack, who was basically the whole show, most of the business based on his contacts and bluff personality. Will, a good administrator, simply lacked the selling temperament. So now, in the company's latter days, contraction was the issue, not expansion: the hope was not to grow but to avoid shrinking, in order to maintain the company as an attractive takeover target for just such a group as Leviathan. There had been nibbles, but, as yet, no definitive offer. "Your job is to be a good steward," Jack had told Will, often, in his gruff business-voice. "I don't want any fire sales on your watch." The last time Will had mentioned needing more money, Jack had grumbled something about a bridge loan, essentially an advance on his inheritance: Will had pictured one of those long shaky rope-and-plank spans in the Andes. He didn't want a bridge loan.

In the meantime Jack, handsome and trim at seventy-four, tended his portfolio, did yoga, and played computer chess with a Seattle E-mail pal. Louise Weiss, who still had a hint of girlish prettiness at sixty-nine, did good works for Jewish charities, played tennis year-round, and entertained in the neat Cedar Grove condo they'd bought when they sold the house in '95. The sale of his childhood home had felt like a betrayal to Will. His older brother Brooks, a urologist in Mahwah, liked to make fun of his hurt feelings, but there they were. It still felt strangely wrong to go to his parents' apartment. It had a sweet, breakfasty but slightly sterile space-capsule smell, and a quiet ambient hum, the aggregate of all the place's state-of-the-art life-bettering devices, Sub-Zero and trash compactor and burglar alarm and humidifier and Sony Digital Home Theater and Jack's never-turned-off Compaq Presario, the gorgeous prismatic tropical fish of its screen-saver drifting by with blurping bubbly sounds.

The hermetic silence of the condo gave Will the creeps; it had a mortuary, end-of-the-line feeling to it, right down to the perfectly tended birch and rhododendron outside the Thermopane. And yet, on the edge of the millennium and their own lives, Jack and Louise were gay there, even conspiratorially giggly; they appeared to have rediscovered their sex life.

Which was more than Will could say. "If we have an emergency, we can borrow off our equity," he told Gail. Knowing she knew this better than he did.

She instantly pulled rank. "If we buy a bigger house, we'll have to hand in all our equity, unless we get more money first," she informed him.

"So let's stay," he shrugged, his eyes trying once more for humorous reconciliation.

Gail narrowed her own eyes, mock-exasperated at his mulishness. Was this a thaw? Or simply a ploy? "It's just a couple of hours tomorrow morning," she said. "Lynnie said she'd have the kids over."

"Aha! So you already made the appointment!" he said, grabbing for her rear.

She nodded, smiling. Neatly dodging his grab.


Mario drove (what else? Will thought) a big dove-gray BMW, one of the new ten-series, a car that cost—if you bought it outright, as Will felt sure Mario hadn't—as much as a house itself, or at least a house in certain parts of the world, maybe a little farther to the east in Essex County. Closer to Newark. Farther from Newark was most definitely the direction they were headed now, Mario at the wheel in yellow-tinted aviator glasses and a houndstooth Saturday sports jacket, like a tycoon on his day off. What did realtors make, anyway? Maybe Mario had some sort of side business. Maybe he was a wealthy investor who dabbled in real estate for his amusement. Sure. Gail was in the passenger seat, Will in the back, with plenty of room to stretch out on matte white-tan leather so soft, it felt like doeskin.

They were driving up Hemlock, a long, semicircular shunt that branched off Forest halfway up the hill, then rejoined it, refreshed by opulence, near the top. It was an earnestly sedate, wildly over-pricey street with a few modern glass boxes cantilevered out over the glen on the right and three or four massive, velvet-lawned stone or stucco Tudors on the left. The reason for this pointless detour through unaffordable territory? Mario, Will guessed, was mood-setting, softening them up somehow.

"So—where are we heading?" he perked up, from the back seat. He had decided on a tone of amused agreeability, both to make him-self feel better and to let Mario know he wasn't putting anything over on him. There was also a slight edge of irony to his voice, which Mario either didn't pick up or chose to ignore.

"I want to show you two houses this morning," Mario said. His voice had a singsong to it, businesslike, a bit didactic, not entirely unpleasant: it sounded as though he were telling a story to children. It certainly wasn't unpleasant riding in his plush car. Gail was smil-ing in anticipation of Mario's next conversational pearl. "One is the one I mentioned the other night," he said, doing Will the honor of turning partway around in the driver's seat to glance at him.

The other night. It had been almost three weeks since the re-union. Was Mario's time-compression an assertion of intimacy or a kind of resolute dumbness? Will couldn't decide (sales not being his own specialty) whether the realtor's blank cheeriness was disingenu-ous or merely blank.

Or were Gail and Mario having conversations she wasn't tell-ing him about?

"You mean the one on Hartshorn?" she asked, sounding disin-genuous, rehearsed, herself. Will got it now: she and Mario had discussed this house already, and he was being led by the nose. When had they had these discussions?

"Yes, that's the one," Mario singsonged, like the bad actor he was.

Now it was Gail's turn to swivel toward Will. She was smiling, he thought, like a girl who knew she was getting just what she wanted for her birthday. She rubbed her hands and put them between her knees, hunching her shoulders cozily. It was a crisp morning—the first frost had arrived the night before—but the car was warm enough. If only, Will thought, she wouldn't wear this, her partially satisfied house-lust, like a fur coat. At that moment he had a brief, unwilled, exceedingly unpleasant sexual fantasy, containing a guilty crumb of excitement, about his wife and the realtor. He tried to smile back at her.

Hartshorn was up the hill on the other side of Wyoming Avenue: a long block of brick and stucco Tudors, built just before the Depression, and a little too close together, though well-lawned and nicely maintained. The neighborhood was a definite step up from theirs, but not a step all the way up. The street ended in a cul-de-sac called Hartshorn Court, and a narrow border of spruces, on the other side of which was, all too visibly, the middle drive of Arrowood, a development of expensive but attached condos whose front (and least-desirable) units faced onto Wyoming. The development climbed the hill in three Babylonian tiers, the topmost of which had a magnificent view of the city to which most of the resident men no longer commuted. (One of Jack's requirements for his own posthouse residence was that it not have such a view: "I've seen all I want of that place," he grumbled.)

Mario parked along the court's curved border. Staring through the spruces at the condos, Will had a two-ply vision: he remembered clearly, from some Hebrew-school car pool or other, driving down

Hartshorn late on a winter afternoon, staring through the spruces at what had at the time been someone's big, snowy backyard, and trying to get it through his mind that it was the very same yard that lay hidden behind the huge, dark, rambling house that stood aloof (and doomed) above Wyoming Avenue. Such transformations of perspective, such axis-turnings, had once seemed magical to him, as had brooks of every sort—they spoke, with real voices—and borders of all kinds, especially borders of trees through which you could disappear and reemerge somewhere else: the next yard, the next block. But he censored the memory, brutally: magic was in short supply these days. The transformation that now stood in front of him—the utter disappearance of the huge house and its backyard, and their metamorphosis into Arrowood—seemed less magical than merely sad.

They got out of the car, and Mario raised his chin, and his eyebrows, at the house on the uphill side of the court. It was a white-stucco and gray-fieldstone just-postwar, boxy but solid-looking, with a built-in one-car garage and a small, sloping, neatly trimmed front yard. "Grandma and Grandpa's," Will muttered into Gail's ear. She gave him a look—he was playing on the wrong team.

"This house has a few surprises I think you're going to like," Mario said. "One is the backyard."

"Big?" Gail asked, obediently. Stooge, Will thought.

"*Huge*," Mario whispered, wrinkling his long tan nose gleefully: they had climbed to the neatly flagstoned front stoop, where discretion was clearly called for. "You'll see." The doorbell sounded, muffled: the classic descending major third, with a rich, chimey echo that hinted at plush grandparental expanses within. At least the storm door didn't have a circled initial, Will thought.

A white face appeared behind the middle of the front door's three rectangular windows, which rose left to right; the door opened.

A stooped, grizzled man stood before them, in black-and-white plaid pants, bedroom slippers, and an orange zippered sweater-shirt with huge pointed collars. His mouth was slightly open, his eyes drooped blearily. His entire expression seemed concentrated in thin-winged, sharply flared nostrils, which didn't look welcoming.

"Suburban Realty, Mr. Abel?" Mario said. "We called earlier?"

"Yeah yeah," Abel said. "You're always calling. Come in, come in."

Everything Will could see, hear, and smell confirmed the promise of the doorbell's echo, and suggested he was an invader in a foreign territory: the foyer and staircase were wallpapered in an off-white, pseudo-*chinoise*, fake rattan, and carpeted in a dense ancient gray-green pile; the air was suffused with a sweet, heavy, pot-roasty aroma. Somewhere within, with an echo that suggested the kitchen, an all-news radio station blared inanely.

"I'm going back to my soup," Abel told them. "Look around, as if I could stop you. And don't forget to close the closet doors this time."

"Yes, sir," Mario said, the soul of phony probity.

"Don't mind my wife, the nurse comes at one," Abel said. "She doesn't bite. My wife, I mean."

"We'll try to be quiet, Mr. Abel," Mario said.

"Not so goddamn able these days," the old man muttered, before shuffling back to the kitchen.

"Well," Mario whispered, becoming himself again once the old man was gone. "Now," he said, sizing up the premises, "I want you to use your imagination."

Gail gazed at him adoringly, ready to make her imagination his.

"The carpet is gone; the floor—all original oak—is bleached and pickled," Mario intoned. He pointed to the wall. "This god-

forsaken paper you replace with a French-farmhouse print from
Pierre Deux or, if that's not your style, Laura Ashley. Or just paint,
a funky antique color; young people are doing that more and more
these days—" A quick, sly, sweeping look made sure they'd received
the flattery: they were young. "A girl I know in Millburn even paints
faux wallpaper."

Gail was locked in, staring at him with an almost sexual inten-
sity. Almost? The faux wallpaper, Will could tell, had taken her over
the line, worked her into a lather. If only—the carping voice chimed
in—sex engaged her imagination to the same extent! He liked her
when she came, it made her less businesslike. But the terrible thing
was, Will was using his imagination, too. He couldn't help himself:
he *could* see the pickled floorboards, the French-farmhouse print, faux
or *vrai*—what was worse, it didn't look bad.

"An Oriental runner on the staircase? Eh?" Mario said, roping
in their approval before moving on to the stairs. Gail and Will nodded, like the sheep they'd become. "Now I want to show you something incredible," the realtor said. He nodded sideways and headed
up the steps.

The upstairs hallway, carpeted in the same thick stuff, was dark
and hushed; it smelled also sweetly, not of pot roast, but of something medicinal. A front bedroom, small and undecorated except for
an ancient-looking Hobart pennant pinned at a forlornly perky angle
on the wall, relic of some long-departed college-bound son, looked
out on the court, where nothing was happening, where nothing (Will
thought) had ever happened, and nothing, except for the arrival and
departure of cars and delivery trucks and the final ambulance, would
continue to happen, until the very crack of doom.

"Now," Mario said. "Little bedroom, not much to it, right? OK,
stick with me now. What if you knock out *that* wall—keep it in your

mind and follow me," he commanded, as he led the way down the hall, where another door was slightly ajar.

He gave a kind of grazing half-knock as he opened it. An ancient woman in a pink bathrobe fastened to the neck sat in one of the room's twin beds, tubes in her nose connected to a tall green oxygen tank by the bedside, a wire clipped to her withered fingertip attached to a flashing monitor on a table. Her gray, watery eyes somehow both registered them and stared past.

"Excuse us, Mrs. Abel," Mario said, loudly enough to be heard outdoors. "Suburban Realty?"

She gazed over their shoulders. "She's basically out of it," Mario stage-whispered. "OK—so that wall is the one that comes down," he said, pointing to the left, past a heavy antique dresser on whose glass top lay a silver-backed hand-mirror and hairbrush set that somehow haunted Will: he glanced superstitiously at the old woman's thick silver hair. "And then what you have is one gi*gantic* master, with a clear shot from the front of the house, where you have that terrific city view—" Mario drew his hand across the imaginary skyline; Will realized, guiltily, that he had somehow failed to notice it. "—to the rear, where you have a beautiful vista over the backyard to those trees." Mario now directed their eyes to those trees. You did indeed have a beautiful vista, and Will's imagination, fully if reluctantly enlisted, now saw the ravishing light and size of the altered, successfully brutalized master bedroom. All theirs.

He quickly calculated the mortgage, at seven and change. They would be up to their eyeballs. Beyond. Doing the dead-man's float in debt.

Mario walked toward the back of the room, with its vista— quite useless to the old woman, Will guessed—of ultraquiet backyard and dark trees. If you stared long enough at that border of woods (trimmed and maintained at a cost he could begin to guess, and had factored into his calculations), maybe something remarkable would appear, a magnificent stag or a unicorn. It was the kind of thought he had sometimes, unwilled, before falling asleep, a fugitive magic thought from childhood, when the earth was still alive. He thought of lying in this room, growing old here, less and less alive. It spooked him. He glanced at Mrs. Abel's eyes, which appeared to flick toward him, then revert to their stare. "Now, *this* is a bathroom," Mario said, expansively unfolding his palm into the doorway as though he, and he alone, had just discovered the concept of bathrooms.

Will and Gail took a look. It was a bathroom, all right, salmon-tiled and huge—roughly the size, he realized, of Danny's bedroom. The frosted-glass-enclosed stall shower was one of those old-fashioned car-wash-type affairs, with three nozzles in vertical array; the separate tub, anachronistically long and deep, had an aluminum hand-rail mounted on the tiles that looked more recently installed than the old chrome fixtures: a health-aid for Mrs. Abel, no doubt. Will's ears and hairline were prickling; the blood had risen to his face. There was an entire life in this bathroom, a life now ebbing, and they were intruders. Grave-robbers.

"Now," Mario said, forgetting to whisper. "Here's the most amazing thing of all. They're asking six-fifty, but with her and the stairs, you can bet they're in a hurry to unload fast. My guess, you can probably get them down to the high fives, maybe six-ten, tops."

Gail's eyes were wide.

"Pardon my French," Mario said. "The place is the fucking steal of the century."

# 11

Joel and Irma, in Morris's silver Cadillac, pull into the semi-circular driveway of Westmont CC, the great brick-Tudor pile of the clubhouse looming up, in the flat white November light, like something both oversubstantial and insubstantial, something in a dark dream, a dream Joel feels he may very well have had last night. Maybe. His eyes hurt. Irma's at the wheel: Joel has let his mother drive, partly out of a certain physical incapacity—he drank a lot before bed—and partly out of irony, for the perverse pleasure of seeing the angry traffic stack up behind her on the double-yellow-lined back roads winding into Cedar Grove. Not very trafficky roads to start with, especially on a Sunday afternoon, but there's a kind of magic to Irma: she stirs up honking jams out of nothing. She takes them in stride, shoulders hunched, Camel Light stuck in the corner of her vermilion mouth, harlequin glasses glinting. "Awright, awright awready," she mutters, without much urgency, as the drivers behind her lean on their horns and tear their hair. "Troublemakers." She has always taken twenty-five- and thirty-mile-per-hour speed limits precisely literally, feeling, as near as her son can figure out, that these were simply the speeds you ought to *go*—except when another sign tells you to STOP.

Morris's spirit hovers over Westmont. He loved the country club so much, for the cigar-smoky camaraderie of his golf and pinochle games, that he paid outright, when business was flush, for several of its rooms and facilities, feeling that the resultant plaques, around the clubhouse and grounds, would guarantee him a kind of eternal life. (Hence the Morris Gold Game Room; the Morris Gold Starter Shed, by the first tee; the Morris Gold Memorial Veranda, overlooking the pool.) On the slim chance that he himself might not live forever, he specifically set aside a generous sum in his will to assure lifetime memberships for his survivors. (A sum, ironically enough, that loomed large next to the rest of his estate, whose chief component was a small trust fund that paid the taxes on the house, bought groceries, and subsidized Violet's meager salary. Morris tended to spend it as he got it.) His survivors, at this unimaginably late date, of course number exactly two: Joel and Irma. So Joel is a member of Westmont. Here is another vast, pleasing irony. He owns several golf shirts, caps, and gloves (all unused: Joel has golfed twice in his life) emblazoned with the Westmont crest, crossed hot-pink golf clubs against a background of dark, densely threaded pines, under a transcendently artificial navy sky.

The pines, naturally, are the wrong green, a shiny bumptious textile medium green, but the dark sky in the logo haunts Joel: he frequently sits on his bed late into the night, a glass of Scotch in one hand, and a pristine golf cap in the other, gazing into this object of meditation, the Westmont-crest sky, sky of an unimaginably distant summer, a kingdom by the sea, whose mingled, powerfully erotic scents of hot freshly trimmed fairway grass and grilling hamburger combine with the memory of a certain song—"Wah-Watusi," by the Orlons—to distill the deepest primary colors of pleasurable memory, colors like jewels from Ali Baba's cave, colors now faded by over-experience into banality, except when caught at precisely the right microangle, late at night, on a bed, with Scotch.

This is Westmont in his memory. The club itself is another matter: Joel avoids it whenever possible. (Today, a silly brunch

Irma has bugged him about for weeks, not being one of those occasions. Having put her off a dozen times for other club events and nonevents, he knows that going just this once will let him put her off a dozen times more.) His dislike of the place has nothing to do with the clubhouse and golf course and grounds, all of which he loves; it's just the people. If it weren't for the people, he'd go to Westmont all the time.

"Joel Gold!" Shirley Feldbaum, tan in November and mildly osteoporotic in her fawn-brown pantsuit, with avid ravening eyes and an underbite, is holding his fingertips and shaking his hands like reins. The underbite is what's always worried Joel about Shirley—it gives her a look of leading with her chin, of being about to devour whoever or whatever is in front of her. Which, in the past, might not have seemed completely terrible: Joel remembers when once, projecting jaw and all, Shirley had a Body on her, in a black one-piece by the Westmont pool, shapely legs, trim middle, and real headlights, the last fervently admired by all the Donnys, Larrys, Steves, and Jeffs around the patio.

The headlights are still there, astonishingly high- and firm-looking, but dropped a little now by the beginning of a dowager's hump. And, like Irma, Shirley is a dowager, Arnold having succumbed a year or so ago to his particular variant of the disease that liberates wealthy Jewish women of-a-certain-age-beyond-a-certain-age from the gruff-voiced men who snapped them up as dewy girls, grunted on top of them to produce the sleek dark-eyed children who went off to summer camp and college, and grunted a few words over coffee in the morning for forty years. Shirley's eyes are as merry as if Arnold were simply on another of his business trips to Puerto Rico, on many of which he conducted business. "Tell me what you're up to these days, Joel," she rasps.

And this is it, this is why Joel can't stand coming to West-mont—not because the seventy-nine different greens of the grounds and golf course aren't, at any hour of the day, sublime; not because the clubhouse foyer, with its flagstone floor and high, noble-flirtatious scent and heraldic rosters of golf and tennis and swimming champions (in gold leaf, on morning-brown oak), isn't magnificent; not because the dining room, with its blood-purple carpet and big round beckoning tables and breakfast-of-the-gods aroma, doesn't stir his digestive juices like no other place. Joel can't stand coming to West-mont because he has to spend the whole time, every time, explaining to the bemused membership (who at least, at last, have stopped trying to fix him up with their daughters; who could he be fixed up with at this point?) what he's *up* to. And while precisely what he's up to seems reasonable enough to him, mostly, the driving-around and thinking and drinking and writing and being naked parts don't quite seem translatable to the above-middle-age membership of West-mont—almost all of whose children are themselves producing fortunes and broods of dark-eyed children who go to summer camp and college.

"Pretty much just piloting the Concorde," he tells Shirley. "I've had to scale way back on the hunting ever since the accident."

Irma's eyes are heading up toward the sunny-tan rafters. Motes are lazing around up there in the white light: motes, Joel feels sure, that contain Morris. Shirley's underslung smile has grown uncertain. "Accident?" she says.

Joel pats her on the shoulder. "I'm feeling *lots* better," he says—a perfect moving-off line if ever there was one.

The buffet tables groan epically this morning, with expensive smoked fish, chafing dishes of eggs, platters of huge bagels, crystal pitchers of freshly squeezed, non-bright-orange orange juice, recent juice from actual oranges. Friendly fellow food-service workers stand behind the tables, ready to correct the tiniest error, satisfy the slightest whim of the Westmont members. Joel is salivating wildly; he could easily take a fork and dig in right at the buffet table—but Irma has grabbed his arm, is wavering at his side, a feathery firm weight on his elbow, angling him off ineluctably from the food and toward a round table containing Howard and Iris Silverman.

"Aren't you hungry, Mother?" Joel stage-whispers, pulling back toward the food.

"I just want to get us situated first," Irma says, pulling, irresistibly, toward the Silvermans.

The Silvermans look like twin bull terriers. In fact, Iris Silverman looks so much like a dog that Joel wonders if there was ever a time when she didn't, whether she ever enjoyed a dewy girlhood whose smooth cheeks and pert bosom inspired the young Howard—who is, if anything, even homelier than his wife—to want to make more Silvermans. Like many older couples, they resemble each other; unfortunately this looks better on Howard, whose puffy, ravaged, flaming-cheeked face has a certain canine, stoical nobility, while Iris just looks mean.

But neither of them is mean, they're just the Silvermans. Howard, tucking into his scrambled eggs, barely looks up as they sit down. "Irma. Joel," he says, dutifully, and gets back to it. Iris, having taken a nibble of a bagel, is sipping her coffee, prepared to be sociable. "How are you, dear," she asks Irma, gravely, knowing the answer to expect.

"Ach. So-so," Irma says, tapping her Camel into a green-crested Westmont ashtray.

With gratitude and mild disappointment, Joel remembers that
the Silvermans are one of the few Westmont couples who don't seem
to *care*, particularly, what's up with him.

"Can I get you some food, Irma?" he says, brightly.

She gives him a little wave with the back of her hand. "Go. Get.
I'll wait till the mood strikes me," she says.

Howard dabs at his mouth with his napkin and croaks a little
tune: "'Wait till the sun shines, Nellie,'" he chants, in a George Burns
burr.

"He's happy when he eats," Iris notes, drily.

Something like a smile flickers around Howard's rheumy blue
eyes. "One of my few remaining pleasures," he says, winking at Joel.
Who winks right back.

Joel pushes out into the room, which is churning with various
currents: the Founders' generation, of the vintage of Irma and
Shirley and the Silvermans (Joel gives a folded-hands, conversation-
preempting, Indian *namaste* to Morty and Millie Dinnerstein; a crazed-
eyed fingers-to-stomach-to-breast-to-forehead Levantine salute to
the Shapiros); as well as—a recent development—a number of new
members, of Joel's generation . . . and even, incredibly, younger.
Dark-haired and prosperous-looking in crisp pressed Levis, spotless
Nikes, and gold Rolexes, they have assured, servant-ordering eyes
and sleek, confident children who look like photocopies of the children their parents used to be, the children Joel grew up with, only
with new accessories—tiny wrist-televisions and sneakers that light
in different colors as they skip along.

Joel recognizes some of the parents from around the pool thirty
years ago, and earlier: there's Sherry Moskowitz (currently, although
Joel doesn't know or care, Sherry Bohrer), who once fed him a spoonful of dirt in nursery school—a taste he's never been able to get out of

his mind—Sherry who, unaccountably, has ripened into a plump-cheeked matron in some kind of clingy black athletic shorts made of an insecty, iridescent fabric. Fly-colored. The view from behind is tragically bad. Why, Joel wonders, would she feel people want to *look* at that?

"Why, Sherry?" he says, getting in back of her in the buffet line.

"What?" she says, turning around. The tone of her voice and the look in her eyes, at first, are those she might use with an incompetent sales clerk at Bloomingdale's. A small girl and a smaller boy, in front of Sherry, goggle at Joel, who, admittedly, is oddly dressed, in one of Morris's brown polyester suits, circa 1974 (the pants are about three inches too short), and a burnt-orange Lacoste buttoned to the neck.

"Joel Gold!" Sherry says, starting to reach out a hand, then letting it drop at the sight of all that polyester. "Where have you been *keeping* yourself?"

"I will show you fear in a spoonful of dirt," Joel says, grinning.

"Huh?"

"You know what I wonder, Sherry?"

She blinks. "What?"

"I wonder what Dannon ever did with all those great old flavors it phased out. Remember Prune Whip? Orange-Pineapple? Piña Colada? Think there's a yogurt heaven out there somewhere?"

The little girl tugs Sherry's sleeve. "Who's he?"

Sherry, warily: "An old, old friend of Mommy's."

"Your mom used to like to show me her underwear," Joel tells the girl, who laughs out loud, then, with a look from Sherry, hides her mouth with her hand.

Sherry, not smiling, pats the child on the back. "The line's moving," she says. And now here's the husband, tall, with frizzle-hair over bald bays and big, clear-plastic-rimmed glasses over tiny eyes. He's also in athletic wear: a crinkly, idiot-blue warm-up suit with dramatic black racing stripes and chevrons and the odd oxymoron POLO TENNIS in big persimmon block letters on the back. He closes in protectively on Sherry's shoulder, with a sidelong glance at Joel.

"Which one?" Joel asks him.

"Pardon me?"

"I was wondering which one—polo or tennis?"

The guy does the same stutter-blink as Sherry—maybe it's what drew them together—and turns around.

"Your wife used to show me her underwear," Joel says.

The guy pretends not to hear.

"Once she wasn't wearing any."

The husband turns back around, loaded for bear. "Listen, pal—"

There's a tap on Joel's left shoulder, a hoarse whisper in his ear: "*I'd* show you my underwear. *Especially* if I wasn't wearing any." He can smell who it is before he looks: crushed roses. The scent causes a little dazed vacuum to form between his eyebrows.

"Patti! Jesus, what are you doing here?"

She's wearing a white tennis skirt and a cable-knit white sweater over, as far as Joel can tell, nothing. A delicate gold necklace jingles on her freckled chest. FORTY-LOVE, it reads, in diamond-chip script. "We're members," she says. "What's your excuse?"

"My excuse—" His eyelashes flutter in confusion a second, then he nods his chin toward Sherry and her husband. "My excuse is that these people are being rude assholes."

The husband starts to turn around again, but Sherry restrains him. "Barry," she hisses, under her breath, shaking her head, as Barry twitches with lemme-at-him.

Patti takes Joel's elbow, rubs his forearm. "Are you OK, sweetheart?" she asks.

He flutters his eyes again. "A little—you know. Elevated."

She keeps rubbing his arm. "You hungry, baby?"

"Ravenous. Not that fuckin' Irma seems to care."

"That's OK. That's OK. Here." She gives him a plate. "You take some eggs."

He does as he's told. The friendly food-service professional behind the buffet table is smiling a warm, secret smile, a smile of food-service solidarity. And more. A diamond glints from his eyetooth. Holding his eggs, Joel stares at the diamond, then at Patti. "Is that really you, Pats?" he asks her.

"In the flesh, sweetie. You all right now?"

"I'm glad to see you, Patti."

"I know you are. I'm glad to see you, too. Norman's here."

"Junior?"

"Norman," she says. She smiles simply but firmly, at once educating him on the name question and informing him that her husband is near.

Two enormous hands fall on her shoulders. "Who wants me?" The voice, leonine, seems to emanate from bass speakers slightly to either side of the man behind Patti. Wearing a maraschino blazer with wide lapels and a black shirt with a pink pattern of palm trees and native huts, Norman Mintz is only a little taller than his wife, but his hands are gigantic, as is his nose, whose tip, a story in itself, is divided into two distinct tan bulbs. Sparse sandy hair is combed over the projecting dome of the forehead, a hank on either side thrusting forward like the laurel wreath of a Roman senator. It's a tragic, overarticulate face, the face of a clown or second-string character actor, the slitty eyes challenging the world to find it amusing.

"Norman, darling, this is Joel Gold, an old high-school friend."

"I don't like old high-school friends. Are you *shtupping* my wife?" Junior's smiling a little—just a little.

Joel grins. A giddy idea floats up through his chest, the idea that he tell the absolute truth. Patti, seeming to read his mind, looks concerned—but then why, if the truth be told, should she be? "No," Joel says, with perfect honesty.

"Ah. And did you ever *shtup* my wife?"

Grinning even more broadly, Joel shakes his head. This is easy. "No."

"Mm-hmm. And would you *like* to *shtup* my wife?"

Joel is virtually incandescent. "I'll plead the Fifth on that one." All but undetectably, Patti lets out a little breath.

"Good. Good. The man gives the right answers." Junior's wary eyes search his for a second. "And oddly enough, I seem to believe him." He sticks out a huge paw, which fully encloses Joel's. "Norman Mintz," he says. "Don't call me Junior."

"Junior?"

"Some people do. Don't."

"Aha. Joel Gold."

"Nice to see you, Joe."

"That's Joel, actually, Norman."

"You golf, Joe?"

"It's Joel, Norman. Not really, no."

"Tennis?"

"Used to. Not anymore."

Junior throws up his hands. "So what good are you?" he roars. Patti is stifling a grin.

"I have a certain amount of imagination and a fair eye for color. Other than that," Joel says, "not much good at all."

"Listen to him. What do you do, Joe?"

"Joel. I work in the Sub Shop, downtown. I make sandwiches."

"You make sandwiches?"

"I write a little verse on the side. I remember things."

"You make *sandwiches*?"

"Yup."

Junior nods sideways at him. "This guy's a character!" he tells Patti.

She's giving Joel a Look. "That's what we always said at school."

Junior claps Joel on the shoulder, nearly sending him to the floor. "I like you, Joe! Maybe we'll golf sometime."

"I don't golf, Junior."

A thick silence. Junior looks almost apologetic. "Hey," he says. "What'd I tell you?"

"My name's Joel, Norman. With an l at the end. My eggs are getting cold," he says, turning to head back to Irma and the Silvermans, who, he's sorry to see, have been joined by another gray-haired couple.

"The guy's a character," Junior tells Patti, as he watches Joel cross the room.

# 12

"Yikh," Gary says, shuddering. "How can you eat that crap for breakfast?"

Chia, Julie, Gary's daughter, is sitting at the long table in the sunroom off the Berkowitz kitchen, surrounded by hanging plants, stirring a bowl of Froot Loops with a Snickers bar. Her method is unique: First she fellates the Snickers to soften the chocolate, then she uses it to stir the cereal, staining the milk a faint brown, a tint that goes oddly with the fluorescent-green and -red and -yellow Loops. Kohl-eyed, Chia watches Gary—he shifts uncomfortably in his seat—while she sucks the Snickers. Black is her color today. She recently redyed her hair shoe-polish ebony; she's wearing black lipstick—the black puffy lips against the brown chocolate—and plenty of raccoon gunk around her eyes. Along with all this: a thin black-leather dog collar sprinkled with rhinestones; a tiny black tank top (in November) that reads LIGHT-YEAR '99: EARTH IN PERIL, over a picture of the earth with a big red arrow stuck through it; black hot pants with suspenders; black calf-length parochial-school socks; and shiny black Minnie Mouses with four-inch heels.

"I like it," she says, stirring the cereal again.

"How you stay so skinny I'll never know," Gary, a quick-talker, says, glancing at her belly. "Coffee, Althea?"

The maid, moving slowly around the kitchen, shakes her head. "It's coming," she says.

"But not *fast* enough, not *fast* enough," Gary says, snapping his fingers on the beat and grinning as though he'd made the wittiest remark of the morning. "You're giving me andante, I need molto vivace." He waggles his eyebrows at Chia—who, even if she had eyebrows to waggle back with, wouldn't be inclined to.

"Hey, what's the deal with the dog collar?" he asks her. "It looks kinky."

She smirks with the side of her mouth he can't see. Gary shrugs, shut out.

"How does she stay so skinny?" he asks his wife, Ellen, who's just come into the sunroom. A tall, wide-hipped, glum-looking woman with paradoxically lovely dark eyes and long thick lashes, Ellen is dressed for her morning doubles game, in a crinkly white Brindisi warm-up suit and white Nikes. Gary's in his work clothes: pressed black jeans, custom-made pinstriped Paul Stuart shirt, string tie. His salt-and-pepper ponytail shakes from side to side as he glances animatedly from daughter to wife.

"Her day will come," Ellen says, taking her grapefruit juice from the sideboard. "She'll put on the weight like the rest of us."

Chia, sipping her Coke, nonchalantly gives her the finger.

"Ah, you're a cruel lady, Ellen Fleischman," Gary says, hugging her shoulders. Ellen barely takes notice. "But then that's why I married you." He snaps his fingers once more for the coffee the maid is pouring, turns to Chia. "How you getting to school?" he asks her.

"I dunno. Hitchhike, I guess."

Gary points at her. "Now, don't even joke about that. I'm driving you."

"So why'd you ask?" Chia says.

He squints cleverly as he slurps his coffee. "Just testing."

★ ★ ★

"You should be nicer to your mother," Gary tells her as they glide down Eagle Rock in the white Gull-Wing, whose black-on-cream Jersey vanity plates read GARY B. Now and then other drivers, always male, eye the beautiful car; Gary catches every glance, but, pretending not to notice, sucks his cheeks in slightly in a way that, he believes, makes him look more dramatic in profile. Chia notices this.

"Why? She's not my mother," she says. Gary's oldies station—the radio's playing "Sweet Caroline"—is making her head hurt.

He sighs at the one irrefutable argument, and says, for the millionth time: "Listen, we're your father and mother now, and we have been ever since you were a tiny baby."

She cocks a hairless brow at him. "Oh, I know you're my father. She's just not my mother."

Gary ignores the probe, the only way he can think of to deflect it. "We're both your parents."

"Uh-huh."

"And you should respect Ellen the same as you respect me."

"That's easy."

"I'm serious, Julie."

Chia cradles her patent-leather knapsack and singsongs, in a piercing baby voice that saws across Neil Diamond's rasp: *"I know who my mommy is . . ."*

It irritates Gary; he likes this song. "You're not seeing that punk anymore, are you?" he cuts in.

*"And my daddy tooo . . ."*

Gary clicks off the radio, a serious move. "Julie."

"What . . . punk?" She gives the word, a relic of some ancient era, an ironic emphasis. Meanwhile her heart's skip-tripping at the mere mention, the idea, of him. Of Romilar.

"I know all about him, Jules. And what he comes from. Believe me, I know more than you give me credit for. That kind of people start out scum, and end up the same way. Garbage in, garbage out."

*Romilar Romilar Romilar.*

"They lie, they steal, they use drugs. And they never ever stop."

*I lo-oh-oave you, babyyy* . . . he said. She thrills herself by remembering, by thinking how she would do any, anything for him. *Any*-thing. Would do, has done. How she, who has the whole universe inside her brain—this is her secret; she's told nobody, not even Rome; she feels quite sure about it—would make herself into an animal, or even a thing, for him.

"You said you were stopping drugs. You said it, and I thought you really meant it."

Which is the funny thing, the secret thing, the great thing, about Romilar. *We don't need that shit, baby. I seen what that shit do.* "I did mean it," she says. "I don't hang with those people anymore. I don't need that . . . stuff."

Gary looks over at her, beaming. She plays him like one of those instruments the angels play, like the one she saw that funny guy with a wig plucking in the super-old-fashioned movie on TV late one night. A harp. "Hey. That's really, really great, Jules," Gary says. "I'm gonna give you a big present for that—a big one. You think about what you want."

*Romilar Romilar Romilar.*

Romilar is shuffling down the sidewalk to VHS, wearing a checkered lumberjack shirt with torn-off sleeves, along with his clamdiggers and surfer sandals. On a hard bright morning in early November. It's a new thing these days, to wear spring and summer clothes all year round, no coats, ever, coats are wuss, are fraud. You always end up someplace warm, anyway.

"Hey, Johnny, aren't you co-old?" It's that lame Alicia, fuckin' little blond cheerleader from up the hill, she'd do him in a second, no challenge, wouldn't mean nothing.

"Look who thinks he's too good to talk to other pee-pull." She's in a holding pattern next to his face, moving alongside him, in his air. She does smell good, he'll give the bitch that. Without breaking profile, he takes a couple of sniffs.

"You like that?" Alicia says.

He raises his eyebrows a fraction, cocks his head, still not granting her a look: no big deal. *?* his balls ask. *Maybe*, his head answers.

"You wanna sniff me all over?"

Suddenly there's a thud; with a little whinny, Alicia staggers forward, kicked in the butt by Chia's Minnie Mouse. "Beat it, bitch," Chia tells her.

Alicia wheels around. "Fuck you, you whore, what right do you have to kick me?" she spits, in her whiny uphill accent. Alicia Korngold, her father runs some record company. Her parents have a pool shaped like a guitar.

As an answer, Chia fixes her with a kohl glare and starts to twirl her backpack, sling-style. *Whiz*, *whiz*, it sounds, higher and higher.

"I'll report you, whore," Alicia sneers.

Shrugging with profound indifference, Chia twirls the pack still faster, advancing, clearly meaning business. Half-tripping, Alicia turns and runs down the sidewalk. "Whore!" she shouts over her shoulder. "Herpes-bait!"

Romilar sniffs in amusement. His girl.

Bright eyes, down by his side. "Hey."

He struts along for a second, then, on an impulse, leans over, clamps a hand on her little round butt, and sticks his tongue as far down her throat as possible. With his other hand he hooks a finger under the tank top, gets her nipple hard, then, quick, takes his finger out, reaches around the back of her neck and tugs ever so slightly on the dog collar. Fainting, she opens her mouth wide, wider, to let him in, sticks her hand through his loose shirt and spreads her fingers on his stomach muscles. Like cobblestones. Her head sees a picture of some old street in Europe somewhere, the place they'll go together when they get out. Funny words pop into her brain, the way they always do: *Antwerp. Estaminet.* Dreamy, wanting to make the words stop, she starts to move her hand lower. He's pulling the collar harder; she can feel the pressure on her throat. Her breath stopping. A gaggle of tenth-graders, nerds, their voices not even changed yet, snicker as they pass by.

*I love you*, she whispers in his ear. And she means it, she's never felt this way before, about anyone or anything, not even Donny the puppy when she was nine.

Even though he's woozy himself, Romilar releases the collar, takes her hand off his stomach, and slaps her on the rear. "Later," he orders.

She shrugs, smiles. She's the pet; he's the master. "'Kay."

"You taste like chocolate," he grins at her.

"I'm your candy girl."

"Hey." He glances around. "Check it out," he says, pulling up one side of his shirt, where a black plastic handle, diamond-scored, nestles along his narrow hipbone.

Her eyes widen. "What the fuck—?"

He takes out the pistol, sights it at a passing car, whose driver, an old lady, goggling in disbelief, almost swerves off the road. "Boom!" Romilar yells, laughing, as she floors it up Boyden Avenue.

"Is it real?" Chia asks.

He looks insulted. "Real? Fuck, yeah. Real, and loaded." He squints down the barrel at a tail-twitching squirrel by the foot of a shaggy-bark tree. "Blam!" he shouts. The squirrel darts off. Romilar puffs imaginary smoke from the muzzle, giggles. "Squirrel meat," he says.

"Jesus, Rome. Where'd you get it?"

"Never mind that shit." Serious again, glancing around, he sticks the pistol back in his waistband, covers it with his shirt, and gives her his best seducer's smile, squinty, down along his cheek. The secret smile. "How'd you like to pull some shit, huh? Take some motherfuckers off? Like, um—you know—Clyde and Bonnie."

Her legs go all gummy at the thought of it. "You mean rob?"

"No—walk in the fuckin' park. Yeah, rob."

She smiles appreciatively. "You're crazy."

"Yeah, I was thinkin', like maybe that fat fuck at the Sub Shop. That other gonzo. Be fun to watch them shit their pants, right?"

She shakes her head, smiling. Crazy.

Suddenly Rome looks vastly pleased with himself. "Hey, that gives me a idea," he says. His eyes move up and down over her body for a moment, and her nipples get stiff all by themselves: she is his.

"What?" she says, breathless.

"He got, like, a major hard-on for you, right?"

"Who?"

"Gonzo."

She thinks of Joel, the way his weird dark eyes stare at her, the same as other guys, only different: the way his eyes also seem to know the same things she knows. She looks at Rome's shining, close-set eyes, thinking how strange it is that he doesn't know any of these things, but that he's the one she'd die for. It's the first time the idea has come to her—she would die for him. She imagines her dark blood everywhere, pumping onto the sidewalk, while her eyes stare no-where, like in a movie. It makes her all warm inside. And still smil-ing, she tells him again: "You're crazy."

Grinning back, Romilar says, "Yeah, I'm crazy."

# 13

Will and Barry Bohrer were tennis friends, which didn't mean they were friends, exactly—Will could hardly imagine himself and Gail socializing with bland Barry and his wife, Sherry (a bovine Bloomie's shopper, period, as far as Will could tell)—but that each man was vain about his tennis game, and each beat the other often enough to maintain, in one or the other, a steady level of irritation about getting revenge. The relationship lacked warmth, generosity, perceptivity—it even largely lacked humor. What it had instead were forehands, backhands, volleys, and serves. It was a friendship conducted, primarily, seventy-eight feet apart, from which perspective each saw the other as a small, sweatbanded, running, flailing, occasionally swearing, blur, causing pleasure (by making mistakes) or problems (by persisting in not making mistakes), as the case might be. True to his last name, Barry, who was tall, balding, and wore round clear-rimmed glasses, was almost aggressively uninteresting. His job—which, as far as Will could understand it, had something to do with betting which way the stock market would go, and getting people to buy into the bet—sounded even more boring than Will's, which at least had the virtue of an old-fashioned, glue-and-brown-paper tangibility to it . . . though Barry clearly made much more money: he lived in Woodwick and drove a big blue Benz.

Like Will and Gail, Barry and Sherry had a boy and a girl, roughly the same ages as Danny and Rachel. This provided the basis

for a certain root level of perfunctory conversation, in the locker room
or as racket cases were being removed at the net; the few times there
had been extended contact—once or twice, due to car-inconvenience,
one man had had to pick the other up and drive him to the courts—
had been agonizing. For Will, at least. Barry, behind his big glasses,
was thoroughly opaque. You sat next to another human being in an
enclosed space; wasn't there something you had in common? Your
town, your country, your very humanity? It seemed not. Mum was
the word. It seemed to be some kind of basic code that men shouldn't
say anything of emotional substance to each other; there might, somehow, be sexual implications.

But Barry's tennis game had a certain pungency, a wit even, that
his personality entirely lacked. He could often place his serve, for one
thing, and his favorite placement—skidding down the middle, in the
right or left court—occasionally caught Will flat-footed or lunging
impotently. His weakness was not, as with most players, his backhand (it was sliced and nothing special, but he could hit it back till
the cows came home) but his forehand, which was powerful yet fluky:
if Will kept on it, Barry's macho crosscourt responses were likely to
start sailing wide after a while.

In the spring and summer, Barry played at Westmont, where
he belonged, and Will played at the Little Club, on a leafy side street
in Verona: its four red-clay courts were brushed and swept by the
members. Will and Barry traded guest visits, though Westmont,
where you had to wear whites and schmooze with new money, had
an inhibiting effect on Will's game: Barry had the edge at home, and
indeed, if the truth be told, after the past summer, due to some lessons he'd taken from some New Age sports guru who ran a ranch in
New Mexico, Barry had an edge altogether. Suddenly he was showing up at the net, all six-three of him, and, with that implacable

adenoidal expression, plucking off Will's best passing shots and lobs. As the summer wound down and Barry took more and more games and sets off him, Will half-wondered if his tennis friend would snub him the next spring.

But instead, Barry phoned toward the end of October and asked Will if he wanted to play indoors over the winter. "It's at Playdium," he said, referring to the giant green-and-white prefab barn that sat next to a desolate stretch of Route 10 in Roseland. Why, Will wondered as Barry droned on about fees and schedules, wasn't this land developed? How could there be undeveloped land in Essex County at the end of the twentieth century? ". . . other guys aren't bad," Barry was saying now. "This Mintz guy, got kind of a funny serve but he's steady, and you know Gary."

"Gary?"

"Berkowitz?"

"Gary Berkowitz?"

"Gary Berkowitz, yeah."

"Gary Berkowitz plays tennis?"

"Oh, yeah. Gary beats *me*."

Will got Barry's point—if Gary beat Barry, Gary would certainly beat *him*—and pulled the arrow out of his side, one of the dozen wounds of any given day. It was, at least, one way to tell he was alive: when life was through wounding him, he thought, it would dump him by the side of the road.

"You're shitting me," Will said.

Barry, in his phlegmatic voice, assured Will that he wasn't. And so it began, Will's weekly humiliation at the hands of Barry, Gary, and Junior Mintz. Actually it all started with Playdium itself, which smelled funny. That was the first thing Will noticed, when he walked in, on the first Saturday morning, with his big pro-style tennis bag over his shoulder: Playdium smelled, vaguely, like lion shit. He half-remembered going to the old lion house at the Bronx Zoo when he was a kid, and being terrified not just by the thought of the lions escaping—a highly likely prospect, it seemed to him at the time, which no one ever talked about—but by the feral smell of the lion dung, which no one mentioned, either.

And Playdium smelled like that—not strongly enough so that any of the mostly wealthy men who played there, generally not soft-spoken types to begin with, would say, "Jesus Christ, it smells like shit in here! Can't they clean the fucking bathroom for the prices we pay?"—not that strongly, but just flickering around the edges, a warning whiff of lion shit that made Will's muscles tighten (and he felt scared and lonely to start with: his new tennis plan, in Gail's eyes, was yet another erosion of his family-Saturday time, and he'd left the house that morning to her silence) as he walked down the dark corridor between the heavy green-vinyl backdrop and Playdium's prefab outer wall to Court 3.

He was the first to arrive. It was warm and humid out there, and lion-shitty, and brightly lit, the big fluorescents buzzing up near the peaked ceiling, where wide-bladed fans turned slowly. The courts were separated by hanging gladiatorial nets, which stopped errant balls, but somehow made the adjacent play more intimate than if there had been no nets at all: on Court 4, to the right, two whippet-like young guys, they must have been pros, were hitting the living crap out of the ball, playing terrifying points that went on forever, using strokes that Will knew he couldn't come close to replicating on his best day. Their shots, in the building's echoey confines, sounded like small-arms fire. Once, when the taller, wirier, blonder pro aced the other one, the report of his ball hitting the backdrop—a fleshy, flagellatory *thwock*—made everyone nearby stop and stare.

The group on the other side, on Court 2, were four oldsters, wearing every conceivable manner of joint appliance, hinged knee braces and surgical elbow braces and inflatable ankle aids, as well as a rainbow of striped and checked and fluorescent wristlets and sweatbands. They were game old guys, moving a few fast steps then stopping, trickily massaging every stroke with their giant rackets, hitting stiff-armed but wristy trick shots that skidded dead or sailed straight up, toward the turning fans, over their openmouthed opponents' heads, to drop neatly inside the baseline. The old men made up vocally for whatever their shots lacked in pace—every tricky play generated groans or shouts of approval and dismay.

Barry and Gary emerged from the backdrop flap together, in close conference. This pierced Will immediately, just as Barry's comment about Gary being able to beat *him* had: Will now realized that the level of nonintimacy he failed to enjoy with Barry would never allow the kind of heads-close-together talking that Barry and Gary were now doing— about what? What conversational vein had Will failed to tap? The terrible thing was, he felt fairly certain (fairly certain) that whatever they were discussing wasn't even particularly interesting; what was most interesting was that he was left out. The schoolyard never died.

"Hey hey," Gary said, pointing at Will. "I know you, right?" He had a short but beaky nose, a tall mustache, and close-set blue-gray eyes. A long, salt-and-pepper ponytail seemed, by counterweight, to be pulling back the rest of his hair, recessively, from his high, sun-speckled forehead. A little gold *chai*, with a tiny diamond in the center, dangled from his long right lobe. What was the code again, Will wondered, which ear meant what, right or left? Lean Gary had a natural hunch that looked less like a slouch than a predatory crouch: his walk was an aggressive bowlegged strut, and Will noticed that his right forearm was thick and ropy.

They'd met before, on an occasion Will remembered but Gary either didn't or pretended not to. Junior year, a quarter-century ago. With fresh driver's licenses, Will and some friends had gone to the Claremont Diner at 1 A.M. one Sunday to eat the magnificent cheesecake and make fun of the other patrons, old nighthawks and middle-aged couples in rumpled formal wear and other late-evening flotsam. It was good sport then, mocking older people, they were ugly and wrinkled and you weren't, they were going to wither up and die and you weren't, not even remotely. The tired waitresses were fair game, too—anything for a laugh. Gary, with a big Jew-fro then and tremendous sideburns, had come in with Diane Ackerman, a petite blonde with a big chest but little else to recommend her: her nose was long and bony, her chin nearly nonexistent. Clearly Gary halfway recognized the boisterous kids from VHS in the end booth, and clearly he was embarrassed, both at the homeliness of his date and the obviousness of his modus operandi: to ply Diane with some cheesecake and chat, then drive up to the caddies' parking lot at Westmont and go for extra bases.

Mel, the gimlet-eyed night host, seated the couple two booths away from Will and his group, the kingpin of which was Richie Schneier, red-haired and flaming-faced and, so it seemed at the time, chokingly, heart-stoppingly funny. (He later became a government economist.) Richie's family were all comedians—especially his foghorn-voiced mother, Bubbles—but Richie was the champ. He could make material out of anything. Wallpaper paste; anything. Diane Ackerman was almost too easy.

Richie, seated in the back corner of the booth, by the window (Will was on the outside seat, with big, dumb Donny Friedman between himself and Richie), warmed up with some fake sneezing. Each sneeze ended with the clearly enunciated syllable "chin"—a pointed anatomical reference to Diane. Gary, facing them, clearly got the message, even though he pretended not to notice; poor Diane, in the dark, turned once or twice to see what the hubbub was. Richie then proceeded to throat-clearing. This was an older ploy, one Will had seen Richie use often, and to good effect, in study hall, where the monitor, an irritable spinster named Miss Ehlers, was ancient enough that Will had once found a carved graffito in a tabletop linking her romantically with Goebbels. The trick was to move around a lot of phlegm as loudly as possible and end up on a subtly altered but clearly pronounced voicing of the word "bullshit." It was a sure attention-getter and Ehlers-irritator—all the more so since there was little she could do about it. Richie's variation for this occasion was to substitute for "bullshit," in quick succession, any one of several colloquial synonyms for breasts—maracas, casabas, hooters, boobs. Gary stood up.

Will, on the outside, and Donny, next to him, were the ones who got leaned over. Wiry Gary grabbed Richie by the collar of his sweatshirt, pulled hard, and stuck a long finger almost onto his nose. "Listen, pizza-face, do you wanna go outside now and get embarrassed in front of all your milk-puke friends?" he hissed. Richie shrugged, a Harpo-like mask of comic indifference. "I guess my choice would be no?" he said. Richie always had a line.

Gary held his sweatshirt for a dramatic few beats, then let it go. "Try me again, puppy-shit," he told Richie, very quietly. "Try me, and see what happens." And, straightening his lapels, he went back to his Diane—no doubt having significantly improved his chances for later. That there were five of them and only one of Gary barely occurred to Will and his friends, any more than the fact that Gary was small and two of them, Donny and Eddie Gross, were big. Gary, no one doubted, could have taken them all.

Which heightened the engine-gunning, tire-squealing fun after

Richie—the five of them having left shortly after the incident, and while Gary and Diane were still at their table—pressed his face against the couple's plate-glass window and did his best Charles Laughton Quasimodo.

But if Gary had even a partial memory of the evening, or any bad association with Will, all seemed forgotten as he shook hands now, the picture of sportsy amiability. "I think we may have met, a long time ago," Will said.

"Yeah," Gary said—thick or sharp? He smiled impenetrably. "I think we may have."

Gary held on to his hand for an extra second. "So," Will said, after a second. "Where's our fourth?"

"Norman's running late," Gary said. "Why don't we warm up a little?"

This they did—in a way—with Will and Barry on one side and Gary alone on the other. Will stood on the left, and Gary simply hit all the balls, or seven out of every eight, anyway, to Barry. No one seemed to notice this but Will, who lowered his racket in annoyance—just in time for Gary to crank a backhand unreturnably wide, into the gladiator net. "Caught ya lookin'!" Gary called, merrily. He was warming up, getting into fine form, and Will could see that he really knew what he was doing on a tennis court: his shots were fast, heavy, and deep, underspun and overspun, and angled trickily. It was quite a polished performance. Barry just stood there and slapped forehands, as well as the odd backhand down the middle before Will could get to it. After around twenty minutes of this—Will hadn't even broken a sweat, and Gary was dripping and smiling—the vinyl curtain parted, and Norman Mintz appeared.

As late as he was, he wasn't moving especially fast. He wore an electric-blue warm-up, with aircraft-like stripes and chevrons in persimmon, yellow, and black, and a brand-new model of Nikes that Will had seen advertised somewhere for three hundred dollars. The shoes, Barracudas, had viewing windows in the soles, through which tiny toy fish were visible, floating in the patented TransGel system. They moved when you ran. Norman was carrying a pale tan leather racket bag and smoking a cigar. One of the old men on the next court wrinkled his nose at the smoke and made fanning motions. Norman ignored it.

"So who missed me?" he croaked, as he laid down the racket bag on the courtside bench. He carefully removed a chartreuse-and-black racket—also brand-new-looking, with the initials N. M. spray-painted, in black, on the strings—and dropped the cigar onto the court, where he stubbed it out with his Nike. The old man shook his head. Barry, Gary, and Will had dutifully reported to the net-post, where Norman was now slapping on cologne from a little bottle, with the biggest hands Will had ever seen. "If I smell nice, I play better," Norman explained.

"Norman, this is Willy Weiss, the guy I told you about," Barry said.

Mintz encased Will's hand. "He looks like a kid, except for the gray hair," he noted, drily, to Barry. The little brown eyes looked too deeply into Will's for a second, before drifting off, bored, to a point somewhere over his shoulder. "The other guy crapped out?" Norman said.

To his credit, Barry seemed mildly embarrassed. "Yeah."

"We had this one fella lined up, a ringer, he played semipro in Argentina or something," Norman explained, to Will.

"Ah."

"But Barry said you could play a little ball."

"A, uh, little. Yeah."

This proved to be exactly right. Will and Barry proved to be a singularly ineffective team against Norman and Gary, for several reasons: There was Gary's highly polished game, gaining confidence with each passing minute and built around a smooth, deceptive, fast-paced serve; there was Norman's quite strange left-handed game, not much of which came into play—Gary covered three-quarters of the court—except when he was serving. Norman hit what could be described only as a drop-serve: struck with a grunt and fiercely underspun, it just cleared the tape and virtually bored into the court just a few inches from the net. To return it, you had to charge in and try to dig the ball off the floor, by which time Gary and Norman were stationed at the net, giant rackets ready.

And then there was communication, the basis of good doubles: Will and Barry had none. Gary and Norman had "Nice shot, pardner!" and "Mine!" and "Yours!" and intense little baseline huddles, backs turned to their opponents. Gary even gave hand signals to Norman, ostentatiously indicated by the disappearance of his left arm behind his back (as a raffish little smile stole across his features) when he stood at net and Norman was serving, to indicate whether or not he was going to poach the return. Providing there was a return. Norman moved his screwy serve around the box well enough so that Will usually found himself diving and flailing at what felt, if he managed to connect with the whirling ball, like a plummeting elevator.

Will and Barry had no calls, no conferences, no congratulations, not even any commiseration, only silence. It got quieter and quieter on their side of the net, especially when Will was serving, for he soon began to double-fault. His ordinary serve—whatever that had been —had fled, and with it any looseness, rhythm, or sense of how to spin the ball into the box. What he had instead—as he stood at the line, his heart in his throat and his breathing constricted, staring at Gary (crouched, fiercely intense), Norman (infuriatingly relaxed, as though he were waiting for a bus), and Barry (his back, up at the net, somehow looked increasingly pessimistic)—what Will had instead was an arm made of concrete, the arm of a cadaver in a medical-school theater, each of the seventy-eight muscles clearly indicated, still giving the occasional spasm—a pity they couldn't function smoothly together, as they had done in life. (The same was true of his left hand, which on the toss had turned into a crab's claw: he literally couldn't get the ball to come out of it.) This was beyond choking: at first, when Will tried to counteract whatever was happening and just let go, his serves sailed beyond Gary and Norman's baseline ("Just out!" Norman croaked, gleefully). Soon, trying to ease off, he couldn't even manage to get the ball over the net—once he whiffed completely. Finally Barry raised a hand and came back to him.

"I'm sorry," Will said, miserably—furiously, really: for somehow this was really all Barry's fault. "I've just—lost it, somehow."

Barry's adenoidal stare was not unkind. "You just gotta throw the ball up and say, 'I—don't—*care*,'" he said, miming a service motion. One of his little lessons from New Mexico.

*I just have to be as big an asshole as you*, Will thought.

"Try that," Barry said. "OK?" Try *something*, his look said.

"OK."

Barry went back up to net. The score stood at 5–40 (one of Will's weak pops had just cleared the net the point before, and Gary, with nothing to lose, had gleefully creamed a crosscourt return that Will had, authoritatively but with no certainty at all, called out). Now Norman was receiving on his right side, his lefty forehand up the middle. Will dimly remembered some instructional piece in a magazine, about serving wide to the deuce court in doubles: it forced the receiver to hit to the net man. He had a vengeful vision of Norman getting all tangled in the gladiator net, going down in a heavy heap, as he lunged for Will's wide-breaking delivery. Also in his mind was that you were supposed to play it safe at 5–40, hit a second serve. He had no second serve. He had no first serve, either. He would show them: it would all change here. He tossed the ball up—he'd actually managed to get it out of his fingers this time, though not very far— and swung as hard as he could, turning his head toward the court just in time to see his serve hit Barry square in the right love-handle, with a smart, fleshy *thwack*.

# 14

The Abel house had sold, fast and preemptively, to a buyer with cash. Gail heard about it, heart sinking, in the nursery-school parking lot, after dropping Rachel off, from Marlene Cruickshank, the rich, skinny, pretty blonde who always wore workout clothes but never looked sweaty. Gail hated Marlene, not only because she was rich, not only because—after cranking out four (count 'em!) perfect blond girls, *pop pop pop pop*—there wasn't an ounce of cellulite anywhere on her body (in summertime, at the public pool, she wore skimpy, ostentatiously colored two-pieces that drew attention to her improbably toned midsection and perfect upper thighs, thighs that had, in that sensitive area below the elastic of the seat, not a hint of wrinkle or droop)—not only all this, but because, when it came to divorce, infidelity, illness, and real estate, Marlene prided herself on knowing Everything. Besides shopping, driving around, and going to exercise class, that was what she did: gather intelligence. Gail called her the Weather Girl.

Marlene always delivered her reports, unless the gravest matters were involved, with a sunny smile. She had plenty of reasons to smile, as far as Gail could see. Her husband, Craig, was outrageously handsome—Gail was convinced that he was either secretly gay or cheated on Marlene incessantly—and was a vice president at Smith Barney or Paine Webber or Peat Marwick, one of those two-name places. Craig traveled all the time (more fuel for Gail's imaginings), but, whenever

he deigned to reappear, always seemed to wear a calm, amused, masculine smirk, as if satisfied that his house and his harem and the world
around them had been properly kept up in his absence.

The Cruickshanks had more money than God—or so, at least,
it seemed to Gail. Belonging to the public pool and driving unremarkable, slightly run-down cars was their form of reverse snobbery, a
policy that didn't extend to their house, a huge, white, perfectly kept-
up Victorian, in one of the best old sections of Glen Ridge, that
resembled some sort of heartbreaking Platonic ideal (if a bit hyper-
trophied) of the American Dream House, a house from a paint ad—
or an ad for a brokerage firm. Gail had been inside it once, for a
nursery-school dinner, and had had to spend the entire evening literally chewing the inside of her cheek in envy. The ceilings downstairs must have been fifteen feet: they just went up and up. All the
1898 wainscotting had been perfectly restored to a waxy, rosy glow.
The gleaming, wide-planked floors were the house's special ornament.
Gail overheard Craig telling someone at the party, in his cool, braggy
way, that the original oak had been so hard, dense, and well-laid that
even now, 101 years later, they were still dead-level: a billiard ball
placed anywhere on the floor would simply sit there.

A billiard ball placed on *their* floor, Gail thought, would simply
get lost in the jumble of toys, or, given a little leeway, gather speed
and roll off to some other corner of the room. Their floors, so nice
when they'd bought the house, were not only warped but cosmeti-
cally a mess, spotty and waterstained from the front door on into the
dining room, distressed from years of ground-in mud and snow and
playground sand. What was more, whenever Danny and Rachel
bounded around the house, or jumped up and down—which was frequently—the wood gave off a hollow, booming sound; objects rattled
on tables and shelves. Sometimes Gail was scared (she knew it was

stupid, but she worried about it anyway) that the floor would just give way someday, that Danny or Rachel, or she or Will, or Esperanza (that would be OK) would just crash through into the basement. What if they had termites? Couldn't you have them for years and not know it? Once, on one of her infrequent trips to the cellar, she had seen a gigantic winged ant on the laundry table. She smushed it with a ten-pound bottle of Tide; brown bug-juice squirted onto the ceramic surface. Later she dreamed about the ant, with its big, eyeless, penile head: it was singing plaintively in Romanian. She wrote down her dreams sometimes—she'd be turning forty in the spring, the first spring of the new century, and she was trying to get things to fit together somehow. Lately they seemed to fit together less and less.

The floors were much on her mind, but she was scared to talk about them with Will. They barely talked at all these days, anyway: they passed each other coming and going—like ants, she thought, picturing the tiny black ones that always invaded the house in the summer, going after the plentiful supply of cookie crumbs. Two ants met going to and from the cookie crumbs; what did they have to say to each other? They were just in each other's way, that was all; they sidestepped and went about their business, in opposite directions, doing their jobs. She and Will.

Everything could be different, she felt, if they could get into a new house.

That was her plan: to get some money from Jack (there would be money if he sold the business, which he seemed almost certain to do; it might be a lot of money), spiff up this place a little bit, then sell and get out. She dreamed about, she hungered for, a walk-in closet. It was stupid, she knew, but why not? She was going to be forty, and she wouldn't live forever. She yearned, instead of opening the closet door and having boxes fall in her face, instead of having her dresses and sweaters smooshed together and wrinkled all the time, to walk among her well-spaced clothes in a big, light, airy closet, to smell their perfume, feel their swish on her cheek. And she had seen, as Mario took them through those old people's bedroom, the possibility of knocking down the dividing wall and putting in the closet of her dreams. She could see and smell and taste that closet, with its neat shoe-racks and sweet cedary scent, and now people with bags of cash had barged in and ruined everything. That was the way it always was with real estate, she thought. You had to be lucky, you had to stay right on top of everything, you had to be there fast with a lot of money, to be willing to bid higher than everybody, to not care about paying two mortgages until you could fob off your crappy old place on someone. You had to be fast, and rich, and crazy, and there was always somebody faster and richer and crazier than you were.

And that was the way it could never, ever be, not the way they were living now. Things were OK nice, but just. They were just going from paycheck to paycheck, on autopilot, putting a little aside for the kids' college, never enough cash in the bank (she had some stocks from her grandmother, but they were inviolable, for the deepest emergency; she thought of them as *hers*), always too much on the Visa, never enough to do what she really wanted, which was just to be able to *breathe*. To take a good, long, deep breath. Like that stupid Marlene, who looked like she'd never had any trouble breathing in her life. If *she* had that kind of money, Gail thought, she'd be happy to put up with that smug Craig and whatever he did on the side. (The idea suddenly made her feel funny: it occurred to her, as she thought of his superior thin-lipped smile and muscly hands, that part of her wouldn't half-mind putting up with Craig.) If *he* had that kind of money, she thought, meaning Will, she'd put up with whatever he did, even though she was fairly sure he'd never done anything besides come home tired and grumpy, and, every once in a while, late at night in bed, when he needed it and she was too tired to live, rub the small of her back, his signal. (What had happened to his libido? she wondered, remembering how ardent, how *ready* he'd once been. Lately he didn't seem especially interested in touching her; it was all by the numbers. When it happened.)

Shit, Gail thought. If I had that kind of money, I'd smile all the time, too.

"I was just wondering if I could seduce you," Mario said.

"Pardon me?" Gail said, putting her hand to her collarbone. It was Tuesday afternoon; she was on the kitchen cordless, blushing madly (it got worse and worse the more she tried to stop), wearing a paper crown. She and Danny and Rachel had just made the crowns, which the children, sitting at the dining-room table, were also wearing. Rachel was singing to herself and playing with some pieces of paper—or, possibly, singing to the pieces of paper. Danny, more tuned-in to things, was watching his mother with some interest. Seeing his knowing dark eyes, she blushed even more deeply.

"I have an amazing house to show you, maybe just a wee bit out of your price range," Mario said, silkily. "I was wondering whether you might like to have a look at it tomorrow morning."

Was that "you" singular or plural? "I have to go to work to-morrow morning," Gail said.

"Go a little later," he commanded. "This place is gonna fly."

"So how was your day?" Will asked. They were all at the din-ner table; he was smiling a little, fizzing with something, which wasn't at all like him at dinner, not lately; nor was it like him to open up the conversation: normally she had to keep after him, the tired, sad one. As if she were never tired or sad.

"All right," Gail said, her eyes questioning.

"Anything new?"

She had agreed to meet Mario the next morning, not saying anything about whether Will would come with her, presuming that Mario thought he would not. So she said nothing about it now, not quite knowing why. "Seduce you" popped back into her head, undismissible: *seduceyou seduceyou seduceyou.* She started to blush, but somehow succeeded in holding it back. Danny glanced at her. "Not much, no," she said.

"We made *crowns,*" Rachel insisted.

"Why? What's new with you?" Gail asked Will, over Rachel, in her cross-examiner's voice.

Will answered Rachel instead. "Is that *right?*" he asked her, in that big, excited voice you used with four-year-olds.

Rachel nodded, up and down and up and down. "Mommy was the queen, and I was the princess," she said.

"Great! And who were you?" he asked Danny. "Prince Matchabelli?"

Danny rolled his eyes and shook his head. Silly Daddy.

"Why? What's new with you?" Gail had to repeat.

"Oh, not much. It looks like we might have a buyer." He gave her a poker half-smile, raising his eyebrows.

The blood rushed to her lungs; she took a deep breath. *Then we can afford the house,* she instantly thought. Sometimes, sometimes, sometimes, things actually went the way they were supposed to go. "Who?" she asked, wide-eyed.

"Leviathan."

She slapped the table. "No."

"Danny was Prince Ertrop," Rachel said.

"Prince *Who*?" Danny said.

"Ertrop," Rachel said, with a small smug smile.

"She's *crazy*!" Danny said, pointing at her.

"I'm *not*!" Rachel cried, genuinely outraged.

"She totally made that up!" Danny said.

"I did not!" Rachel said, and burst into tears.

"Honey, honey," Gail said, rubbing her hair.

"So what's wrong with making things up?" Will asked the table at large, his good spirits inextinguishable. Rachel was calming down gradually.

Danny shook his head. His whole family was stupid.

"I thought they were balking at the asking price," Gail said, still rubbing Rachel's hair.

"They're still balking," Will said, happily. "They're just balking a little less."

"That is *so great*." If there was a buyout, Jack had promised to split the proceeds three ways among his boys, with Will, as the one son who had deigned to go into the business, to receive the largest share: 40 percent. Will had told her Weiss Container might fetch five million. It was a figure that had captured her imagination. But even if it were four and a half, she thought. Or say four. Times 40 percent, minus capital gains. Even so. She was, she realized, suddenly breathing deeply and freely.

"It's not bad at all, yeah," Will said.

"That is so *great*!"

"Well, let's not write checks on it yet," Will said. "Well"—he laughed, the fizz finally popping out—"maybe just one or two."

"Could I be excused?" Danny asked, scornfully.

Gail was smiling, giving Will a look she hadn't given him in—how long? Will smiled back.

"What?" Danny said, glancing back and forth at his parents.

"You can be excused," Will said, still smiling at Gail.


It was, for him, magnificent. He felt like a stallion, a charger; he remembered, as though waking up after a long time, how they had been at first, when everything had been new, when they had been lovers.

It was, for her . . . muted. Her excitement about the money—the money-to-be—infiltrated her passion at the start, distracting her from love, from their bodies, with fantasies about what the house might be like, about whether the walk-in closet would actually be possible. Right in the middle, she grew ashamed that she was thinking about that damn closet again, but she couldn't help herself . . . she put it out of her mind. By an act of will, she stopped thinking about the closet. Still, it put her out of things, somehow, she lost the rhythm; and then the oddest thing happened: above her, Will, just momentarily, turned into Craig Cruickshank, with his hard, smug face and hands, and she realized how very much this excited her, and she felt ashamed again. This second time was the killer. Too much shame. And so she pretended, which she hadn't done forever—lately she hadn't cared to try; either it was working for her or it wasn't—but she felt so bad for him, he was so happy and excited, and so she tried to be, too. But trying didn't make it work, so she pretended, and then it was over, and she was all worked up, over everything, and she knew she would sleep miserably that night.

"Mmm," Will said. "That was incredible."

She was silent. He turned to her in the dark. "How you doin'?"

"Fine."

He got up on one elbow. "Really?"

"Mm-hmm."

"Because I can—if you—"

She shook her head. "I'm fine, I promise."

He lay back with his hands behind his head. She could see him smiling in the gray half-light. "You know what I think I may do?" he said.

"What?"

"It's crazy—no, I may do it. I know I said we shouldn't write any checks yet—"

"What?"

"I might get a new car."

"You *should*," she said instantly, enthusiastically. She felt so guilty, over everything; she was getting the house, he should get something, too. A car wasn't much.

"Really?"

"Absolutely you should. I worry about you in that old thing."

"You really think so?"

"You should."

"Maybe I will, then," he said, smiling. He pecked her on the cheek and turned on his side; in four seconds he was snoring softly. She took a magazine from her night table and turned on the light.

# 15

Patti has been calling and calling, leaving messages, under pet names (Pats, Patsy, Patsilla), assumed names (Ms. Goodbody), and her maiden name (from Violet: "Miz Zambezi call"), at his house and at work; Joel hasn't returned any of the calls. He knows what she wants, and though part of him (ha!) wants it, too, the part that thinks doesn't want that, all of it, not now, now that he's seen the face and shaken the hand of her loud-voiced gangster. I may be crazy but I'm not insane, Joel thinks. Who knows what Junior could do to him, or have done? If she were married to a regular person, some lawyer or accountant, or some schmuck who just moved money around and turned it into more money—that would be one thing; but to risk winding up in the trunk of a car, for what? Then he thinks of the dusty-rose smell of her lank smooth hair, her slim firm waist and bulbous chest in the white silk blouse, her pug nose and dirty mouth and alive eyes, and, leaning against the counter, chopping lettuce, the butcher block pressing his apron right over his cock, feels a little faint. He leans back, shakes his head to shake the thoughts out. Just for something else to do, he glances at the Mountain Dew clock, sorry the moment he does, but unable to help himself. The time goes so much faster if you don't look. There have been days he's been able to hold out almost to noon. It's ten fifty-two, which is better than ten thirty-three, the time he usually can't help looking up, but not much: till they get past eleven, the clock hands have a whipped, hopeless look, like clock hands in one of the old Popeye cartoons. His stomach hurts.

Will is coming for lunch today, there's something he wants to tell Joel about, he sounded excited over the phone. Poor Will—what could he possibly be excited about? More money, in some form, is the only conceivable answer. Imagine, Joel thinks, being that unimaginative; imagine time only going in one direction, forward, forward, on railroad tracks, until it stopped going, which is what money makes it do. Money, he has tried to explain to Will, will only bring death faster. Money, he has tried to explain, is shit. There are so many better, nonshit, things to think about. Think of Cindy: out there someplace, then and maybe even now, in her room in the woods, smiling at him in the woods-light. Think of Steven, also smiling, his confident white smile, as he stands on the high dive, brown arms spread, in a holy halo of chlorine and Coppertone, as "The Loco-Motion" plays.

If time only moves forward, Joel thinks, where does that leave us? There's now, always a dicey proposition, and then all that future you know nothing about, that you can only *plan* for. Joel has no plans. There's a poem or two he thinks he might nudge forward; other-wise—when he thinks about it at all—he anticipates doing pretty much the same thing he always did, floating along, until the great adventure, the white-water rapids, of decline and death. Interesting stuff! Patti is an impediment to this scheme. She wants things to happen, to change; she wants Events. The wrong events. She offers fun in exchange for death or dismemberment. Is it love she wants? He has love. She can have his love, he thinks, surprised; she can split it three ways with Cindy and Chia. What she can't have is his time. Patti wants to yank Joel's time in the wrong direction, and he's not going.

★ ★ ★

One thirty-five. "You ever think about your future, Joel?" Larry rumbles, from farther down the counter. He's slitting open white restaurant-sized sleeves of Boar's Head lunch meats with his big knife, bologna and ham and olive loaf and head cheese, stacking the slices in the aluminum cooling trays, replenishing for tomorrow as the lunch rush slows.

"What future?" Joel asks, mildly. Coming from anyone else, the response might sound bitter or petulant; Joel is merely matter-of-fact.

"Don't you ever want to have a wife and kids? Settle down?"

"I'm pretty settled right now, Lar."

"Yeah, that's your whole problem. What are you gonna do if I drop dead? Or move to Florida? Hopefully not in that order?"

"Shit, I don't know. Maybe I'll become a transmission specialist."

"See, you're not serious. Maybe at your age you should be starting to get a little serious. What about that nice lady who keeps calling?"

"This is not a fruitful line of discussion, Lar."

"How'd you like to own this place?"

"What?"

Larry gives him a quick profile smile, his fat rosy cheek flapping, then goes back to his meats. "Easy terms. We got a little put by ever since Rose hit her number. And the market's up, so I don't need to make a killing."

Here's the yellow-faced guy in the PANTONE CONSTRUCTION shirt, a borscht-magenta one today, chewing on his toothpick, looking ravenous, an hour ahead of when he usually shows up.

"Breakfast?" Joel asks him.

"Huh?"

"The usual?"

The guy looks Joel over, eyes hurt and suspicious. "Yeah," he says. And then, after a moment: "Easy on the onion, huh?" He thumps his solar plexus with his fist. "Shit repeats on me."

"Ask me if I care," Joel says, scattering shredded lettuce on a sub roll.

"Huh?" says the guy.

"So—whaddya think?" Larry asks.

"I don't know, Lar. I'm afraid I lack the entrepreneurial spirit."

"Place generates a nice little cash flow. Plus, if they ever do that downtown makeover thing they've been threa—— Whoa whoa whoa."

Larry's broken off; he's pointing with his knife. At Chia, who's just sidled in, in big black circular sunglasses, which, if they're an attempt at disguise, are somewhat compromised by the blue-black beehive hair, shiny white lipstick, dog collar, chartreuse tank top over the expanse of white belly, with its navel ring, and low-riding striped bell-bottoms.

"I don't want your business, dear," Larry announces. The yellow-faced guy is staring at her as if God had just invented woman.

Two guys with identical short-sleeved shirts, ties, and beepers have also just walked in. One has a mustache, one doesn't. They give Chia a good look, too.

She puts a hand on her skinny hip. "This is *not* legal, you know," she says, clicking her gum. Green gum, pink tongue, white lips. "You're violating my civil rights."

"You tell me all about legal, sweetheart. You're the authority. She strips in public places," he tells the beeper guys.

The one with the mustache smiles. "Oh yeah?" he says.

"And her boyfriend, Mister Public Health, spits on the floor. Expecting him, sweetheart? Go on, out."

Chia raises her palms. "Listen. I'm by myself, I'm orderly, I want to buy a sandwich. Is that really such a big deal?"

Dead silence all around.

She gives a little twinkle, at Joel, of all things. "Plus you *do* make excellent sandwiches," she says.

"Sounds like you're being a little tough on the girl, buddy," the mustache guy pipes up to Larry, smiling at Chia. Who pulls down her sunglasses and smiles back at him, clacking her gum. Larry looks at the guy, looks at Chia, then shakes his head and goes back to his meats. The rims of his ears are bright red.

She comes up to the counter, with her slightly funny walk, and pulls the sunglasses all the way down her nose. "Hi," she says. Big white smile.

"Hello, Julie," Joel says, very smooth, though his heart is clunking. She smells like the flower show in fifth grade, he thinks, like lilacs on a country lane in the rain, like forever. Out of the side of his eye he can see Larry press his lips tight, shake his wattle. It's news to him, bad news, that Joel knows her name.

Chia's glancing around behind the counter as she smiles at him. "Cool," she says, apropos of what? The deli equipment?

With infinitely practiced ease, Joel slices Yellow-Face's sandwich diagonally in the middle, wraps it in waxed white paper, tapes the package up, and drops it in a bag. The guy is standing next to Chia, holding a huge Mountain Dew, trying to get a look down her Mountain Dew–colored top. "Six ninety-three," Joel tells him; still peeking sideways, still hoping, the guy pulls a ten from his pocket and gives it over the counter. Chia watches carefully as Joel rings it up. He's aware of the attention.

"You've got great hands," she tells him.

Stricken, out of his league, the yellow-faced guy takes his change and stares at Chia and Joel as he backs away.

"What can I do for you?" Joel asks her. He loves her, but he doesn't trust her.

"Do you play piano or anything? Guitar?"

"I've got other customers," he says, calmly, a little apologetically. The front door flashes its brief reflection of Main Street: Will has just walked in, all aglow, waving.

She shrugs her thin shoulders. "Provolone wedge, lettuce, tomato, easy on the oil?" she says, with what almost sounds like an apology back.

"*They're buying,*" Will whispers. He and Joel are sitting at one of the Sub Shop's five small circular tables, over next to the soda cooler, in the corner by the window. Two tables away, Chia is munching her sandwich, sipping Jolt Cola from a straw, and peering over her sunglasses at a white-and-rosy-buff paperback: *Steppenwolf.*

"Who's buying? What?" Joel says.

"Us. We're getting bought by Leviathan. After the due diligence, of course." Will, who's barely touched his tuna sandwich, is rocking in his chair, hugging himself—except for his big grin, the picture of someone in deep grief, Joel thinks.

"Of course," Joel says. "What's due diligence?"

Will shakes his head delightedly at his wry friend.

"So you're going to be rich?" Joel asks.

"Well, not *rich*, exactly. But a nice chunk of change—almost two million. Before taxes."

"Ah-ha." Bored, Joel's tapping his fingers on the table, darting glances at Chia. She catches him and smiles. He gives her a tight fake smile back and turns to Will. "Great," he says.

Will gets that pitying look. "You really don't care, do you."

"Not particularly, no."

"I got a new car."

"Ah-ha."

"It's beautiful—it's silver."

"Silver. Huh." Joel drums his fingers and purses his lips. "Well. Better than burgundy."

"And it smells amazing."

For the first time, Joel sounds vaguely interested. "Oh yeah? What does it smell like?"

"Like, um. Well—a new car."

Joel's face falls.

"Hel-*lo*." It's Patti, in a silvery fur coat, black leather pants, and a black-on-white polka-dotted blouse open halfway down, sunglasses propped up on her hair. "I was in the neighborhood."

Will rises, shocked by this apparition to a standing position, inhaling her scent, looking at her chest—tan in December—and re-membering her at the reunion. Joel remains seated. "Hey, Pats," he says, his eyes uncertain.

Brisk, bouncy: "Well, if I'm interrupting—"

"No, no, no," Will says, gallantly pulling over a chair from an empty table. "Please. Sit with us."

She sits, exuding a fresh furry draft of roses and leather, and turns to Will. "We met, didn't we."

He extends his hand. "At the reunion, yeah. Will Weiss."

Her hand is slim and slightly hard. "Patti Mintz," she says, wrinkling the brown pug nose. "Patti Campesi, back at VHS." All at once Will puts two and two together: Junior's wife. What a waste.

Yet something, it seems to him, is passing between them; she's smiling brilliantly at him. He wants her, now—in a mad moment, it seems he has never wanted a woman this badly. He wants to do it with her here, on the floor, on her fur coat.

"Will is about to be rich," Joel says sardonically, probing his canines with a mint toothpick.

"Well, not *rich*, exactly." Will's happy face belies his words.

"That's wonderful!" Patti touches his knee. "Congratulations!"

"It is kind of exciting, actually. We have this little cardboard-box company, and we're about to get bought by this big outfit up in New England."

She's gazing at him as raptly as if he'd told her he'd happened on the Fountain of Youth. Joel, having a rough idea of what's going on, isn't biting. Does he want Patti? He wants her. Does it make him sick with jealousy that Junior has her and he doesn't, that she's flirting with his friend? He isn't immune, though he also knows that her attention to Will is a tribute to her desire for Joel. (Isn't it?) But then, the strange part, her desire for him doesn't diminish his for her. It's interesting—and annoying. He stares out into the space between their two profiles, where Chia, perfectly framed—and also perfectly desirable (and perfectly taken)—looks up from her book (as though feeling his eyes), takes in Patti, whose fingers are still resting lightly on Will's knee, and raises a tweezed eyebrow over her dark sunglasses.

# 16

In each of her messages she leaves her car-phone number, and so finally—since though he's a crazy man, he is a man—he calls her back. Or tries. The first few times he gets that infinitely annoying car-phone recording, the voice of a failed DJ, full of hollow, slightly nasal, worked-up electronic cheer: "The TeleMax customer you are trying to dial is either out of range or has reached their destination. *Blease*—try your call again later . . ." Joel tries to imagine the home life of the cheerful-voice-man, his days filled with cheery announcements to his wife, children, pets. "The bathroom you are attempting to enter is currently in use. *Blease*—try again later." "The subject you are trying to raise is *not* one I wish to discuss. Blease . . ."

This takes him only so far. Reawakened erotic need (tempered by grave misgivings) is the reason he's calling, and so he persists, spermlike, salmon-like, willy-semi-nilly, until he gets her, rumbly sounding, out on the road somewhere.

"You're going shopping," he says.

"Joel?"

"Wait—no. Exercise class?"

"No, I'm actually going to renew my driver's license. It's the biggest pain in the *tuchis*." The signal breaks up momentarily "—glad you called," Patti says.

Joel says nothing. He's sitting in the kitchen, phone cradled under his chin, staring at a cigar catalogue. No one stopped them coming after Morris died, and so they keep coming, addressed to him: a form of immortality. It's four-thirty on a Thursday afternoon, gray and dead out. Work is over for the day, it's Violet's day off, Irma's on one of her rare excursions, visiting her cousin Hedda in the nursing home. He's lonely. He gazes at the Macanudos, the Joyas de Nicaragua, the wildly expensive climate-controlled humidor closets.

"Joel?"

"I'm lonely," he tells her.

"Where are you?"

"I didn't use to be lonely. This is all your fault, Pats."

"—not hearing you so well. Are you at home?"

"No one's in the house but the goddamn ghosts. The light is— the light is kind of gray-cat gray. Purple at the edges. Kind of sad but sexy at the same time?"

"So you're at home?"

"And this fluorescent light is killing me, but if I turn it off, *I can't see the fucking catalogue.*" There's a tremor in his voice.

"Wait. I'll come right over."

He turns the page. His hand too is shaking.

"Joel? Are you there?"

"Hey—Pats?"

"What is it, sweetheart?"

"I'm scared, Pats."

He can hear a screech of brakes, a horn honked in anger. "I'll be right over," she says, just before the line goes dead.

"That's what I'm scared of," Joel says, to himself.


She arrives, twenty minutes later, to find the lights off, his car gone, the house looking as if nobody had ever lived in it.

★  ★  ★

In the dream they both have, she comes over. And, after she holds him for a while, they gently go down the basement steps and play the game again at last, uninterrupted, updated, with an important variation at the end. A good time is had by all.


Patti begins to call again, leaving many messages.

# 17

W ill and Gail—Gail mainly—had decided to have their floors done. The Leviathan deal wasn't final yet, but they'd allowed themselves just two indulgences: a new car for him, new floors for her. And the floors, Gail rationalized to herself, were an even smarter investment than a car lease; they were a kind of insurance, improving the value of their present house even if Leviathan shouldn't go through (but of course it would), even if everything fell apart and they couldn't get the new house (the one Mario had shown her, a Victorian, with porches and high ceilings and wide-planked floors, on a twisty, rhododendron-dark street near the Glen Ridge border; it needed a little work—all right, it needed a hundred thousand worth of work over the asking price, eight ninety-five, which was more than a hundred more than what their budget had been before Leviathan). True, the place needed work, but it could be, Gail felt in her teeth and gums, the house, the house of her dreams, with the walk-in closet (Mario, who *understood*, showed her exactly where her closet could go, touching her shoulder as he pointed and giving her a questioning smile she returned in the glow of the moment, knowing what it all meant, feeling strange, bad but good, about it later) and everything, easy breathing at last, and the chance, at last, to grin back at that fucking Marlene Cruickshank. And—Gail thought now and then, with a sense of sober responsibility—even if everything went totally south, they'd still have nice floors.

She'd done the research on floor guys, more energized than Will
had seen her for years. Pete at the hardware store had confirmed what
she'd thought: there was really only one choice, Marvin Flanders, a
Verona legend. Gail knew the name well, but never dreamed she'd
actually be calling him. "An artist," Pete said. "He does a beautiful
job. But very, very expensive."

That sounded just right to Gail. An artist was what she wanted.
Besides, how expensive could an expensive floor job be? They
had Flanders over on a Saturday morning, while the kids watched
cartoons. He was a grave potbellied little man with bottle-bottom
glasses, a fringe of kinky copper-colored hair, and an undefinable,
slightly English accent, as though he'd been to the best schools and
majored in wood. He was very well spoken—just the way an artist
should be, Gail thought excitedly. He circled the downstairs, pac-
ing off the rooms, bending to peer at the boards as he moved from
room to room, squatting down a couple of times to tap (and shaking
his head and clicking his tongue), ending his tour in the living room,
where he sidestepped Danny and Rachel, prone on the rug, as if they
were furniture. "Your floors are in desperate shape," Flanders announced, with a kind of dying fall to his voice that nearly stopped
Gail's heart. But then he said, "If I'd come any later, they'd've been
too far gone for me to save." She almost jumped in the air. When could
he start?

He could start right away, he told them abstractedly, sandwich-
ing them in between a couple of other larger jobs. Larger presumably meant more important. Gail didn't care—Marvin Flanders was
doing her floors! Almost as an afterthought, with a nudge from Will,
she asked him what he would charge for the privilege. He took out a
pad of personalized stationery (MARVIN FLANDERS—FLOORS WITHOUT
PEER, it read, next to a picture of a crown and scepter), stared at it

for an artistic moment, quickly scribbled some figures, and handed it to her. Sixteen hundred, for the downstairs. Sixteen hundred! Gail almost hugged him. Maybe sixteen hundred was what Pete at the hardware store considered very expensive; to the imminent beneficiaries of the Leviathan buyout, it was pocket change.

"This is such a *great price*," Gail told Flanders.

He stared at her, bemused, through the thick glasses. "I could tack on an extra five hundred if you'd like," he suggested.

Flanders mentioned, as he walked out, that all the furniture needed to be removed from the downstairs before he arrived on Monday morning.

"Oh," Will said, as the floor man skipped down the front walk and drove off in his logoed Range Rover.

"Why?" Gail said. "We can do that."

Will cocked an eyebrow at her. "We."

"I'll help."

"Uh-huh."

"I will!"

Later that morning, as a cold hopeless rain spattered on Playdium's corrugated roof, Will's double-faulting continued unabated. His nerves mystified him—good things were, after all, in the works. But somehow, if he looked at himself carefully, the very goodness of the good things felt oppressive. And the tension had become a living, breathing thing, with a life of its own, too big to simply banish. He tried to plumb it. Something about Norman and Gary definitely psyched him out: they were so sure of themselves, so seamless. Without saying anything, meanwhile, Barry seemed to have become ever more reproachful—in his looks, his gestures, even his walk. Will could hardly blame him—who liked to lose all the time?—still, he thought, couldn't Barry console him, or at least talk to him?

Why couldn't they have hand-on-shoulder conferences like Gary and Norman? Yet somehow it didn't seem right for Will to initiate talk with Barry: there'd be no way around framing any overture as an outright apology, and this seemed too pathetic.

As though double-faulting two out of three times wasn't pathetic enough.

And so Will was stuck, and as he pulled out of the parking lot he had to try to banish the taste of incompetence and defeat from his mouth, to concentrate instead on the happy side. The good things.

Saturday afternoon he moved furniture. Gail, as he'd anticipated, bailed out after the dining-room table, a Brittany farm piece that felt like two tons, and which they negotiated, with no small effort, sideways through the doorway and into a corner of the kitchen. "I have to be careful about my back," she explained. "Dr. Keever says my psoas makes me very vulnerable."

Will glared at her, stalemated by her psoas. (He pictured the muscle, long and glistening, as a living organism, part of the forces she'd arrayed against him.) Keever was a Main Street chiropractor with a lucrative practice among local women of childbearing age who ran, worked out, and played tennis. This covered virtually every mother with a car phone in Verona. Will assumed that chiropractic in general was a fraud, and that the tanned, Mephisto-bearded, turbo-Volvo-driving Keever in particular was ethically and sexually suspect. He had looked up the psoas muscle in the dictionary, and had immediately had to confront a mental picture of Keever manipulating Gail's loins and taking a hundred and twenty-five a week for the job. He wondered how far these manipulations went. There was nothing erotic about the fantasy: Keever was just a sleaze. Still, Gail and all her friends swore by him, and there was nothing you could say.

"Why don't you call Joel?" Gail suggested, with a look that contained at least three edges.

"Move *furniture?*" Joel said. "What's in it for me?"

"Joel, it's what friends do for each other."

"Are you sure? Where does it say that?"

So Will moved everything—everything but the couch, for which he'd have to throw himself on Flanders' mercy. Shelves and shelves of books had to be boxed and taken to the basement, and then the shelves themselves—big heavy old oak shelves they'd bought when they were happy—moved to the porch. But first boxes had to be found.

This proved surprisingly difficult. Will had assumed that his basement was full of old empty boxes, but in fact there were only three in the garage, one broken beyond repair and one waterlogged. The shoemaker's-children irony of this did not escape him. He could drive to the plant, but it would mean an hour on the road, round trip, not to mention calling Cookie, the factory foreman, and finally admitting, for the record, that he didn't fully understand the building's alarm system. And Cookie worshipped Jack and thought Will was a twerp, and this would only make matters worse.

Meanwhile the rain was still falling, and Danny and Rachel were bouncing off the walls, running around and around and around the downstairs, then booming up the steps, then booming back down and running around and around again, with high-pitched squeals that seemed to directly attack a part of Will's brain stem already rendered swollen and irritable by the wet weather, his tennis failures, all the good things, and the gigantic job at hand.

"Can't you take them *out* somewhere?" he called up the steps.

Silence. Gail, exhausted herself, was taking a nap. With the bedroom door closed. Every once in a while, when for one reason or other he had to feed the children, or bathe them, or just take them out for a meal, the true meaning of the full range of his wife's activities occurred to him, and he realized that he had, by far, the easy side of the bargain. It was not an idea that took hold and flowered at this moment, though: Danny and Rachel were whining for chocolate milk. Filthy from the basement and the garage, dripping sweat, he stared at them. "How about regular milk," he said.

They stared back.

He gave them chocolate milk in cups with tops and led them into the denuded living room and turned on the television. Thank God for it. The TV, of course, would be the last thing he'd move. There was some sort of survival game on Nickelodeon, with muddy-faced big kids in helmets: Danny and Rachel shook their heads at it. The Cartoon Channel had an idiotic animated-robot show, all the characters with those exaggeratedly round eyes drawn by Asian artists. "Yeah!" Danny said; Rachel looked as if she were about to cry.

"Listen, guys. Watch this for a while, then Raitch gets to decide next, OK? I have to go get boxes. Mommy's in her room."

He put on a baseball cap and raincoat. Rachel glanced over from the couch, still looking stricken. "Where's Mommy?" she asked, quavery-voiced.

"She's in her room, stupid," Danny said.

"Danny," Will warned.

"Well, she *is*," he said. "You *told* her."

Will shook his head at this irrefutable argument and walked out the front door. His new car, his consolation and refuge, sat in the driveway, rainwater beading perfectly, in tiny droplets, off its silver finish. He sighed at its perfection. It was one of the first generation of mildly off-road four-wheel-drive Saabs, superbly sculpted but as idiosyncratic as ever, the interior still pared-down and aircrafty, the ignition still on the shift console. Crazy Swedes. The advertising showed the car negotiating boggy fens and rocky hillsides, as mud spattered its shapely body, then emerging through a shower of rain to haul ass down the highway: A BRUTE OFF THE ROAD, A CAD ON, the headline read. Will's sigh of pleasure turned into a hiccup as he thought of the slightly breathtaking lease payment. *Leviathan, Leviathan*, he cooed to himself, like a lullaby.

With his seat heater on and the wiper clicking cozily—nothing like brand-new blades!—he drove to town. On the way down the hill, he looked at his neighbors' houses and wondered how much money they had. It was the great mystery. Whatever they did or didn't do in bed was far less interesting. Who was living on Visa advances? Who had a pile socked away? There, by a driveway, sat an old dishwasher and refrigerator, waiting for the garbage men, and a Dumpster full of plaster and wall lath. The sight was both reassuring and envy-inducing: Someone was remodeling; someone was doing OK. Thus the suburbs regenerated themselves.

The only boxes the wine store had were elegant little compartmented Beaujolais cartons with chanticleers and fleurs de lis. Will took three, anyway, wondering if he'd have to give in and call Cookie; but then he had a sudden, lightbulb-like memory of a store way the hell down Bloomfield Avenue, Mailboxes Etc., that sold all kinds of packing material. Pleased with himself, he turned on the radio—the Saab had a superb sound system, mounted on some kind of viscous-liquid gimbals that could dampen the most violent off-road shaking—to the classical station, which was in the throes of *L'Arlésienne*, whose famous theme Will was able, in the temporary glow of self-approbation, to identify in three notes.

Bloomfield Avenue was very long and very straight, with very many traffic lights, and the neighborhood steadily worsened as he drove toward Newark. With a little twinge of guilt, he pushed the little key-logoed auto-lock button on his door, a movement that, with this car, you could at least perform surreptitiously, causing the locks to sink silkily—a definite improvement on the Volvo, in which you had to reach up to the windowsill and push the lock plunger in full view of whoever was walking by, producing that loud, embarrassing *thwunk*. Will would, he knew, probably never do any off-road driving; Bloomfield Avenue was probably as dangerous as it would get for him, sitting at a red light while three black boys, aged thirteen or fourteen, stopped in the crosswalk to gaze, with wide, overmature, insinuating smiles, at the shiny curvy silver car. One of them, tall and skinny and wearing a quilted, Communist Chinese–looking parka and yurt-hat, with absurdly long, curving earflaps, motioned for Will to roll down the window. Will attempted a smile, raised his hand in a that's-all-right gesture. Grinning, the boy ducked his head, insisting: Come *on*, man. We OK.

An eternity passed in a second as Will saw the headline: MAN DRAGGED FROM CAR. He waved to the boy again, the boy insisted again—and then Will saw the green-white-and-orange Bloomfield PD patrol car coming up the block. Emboldened, he hit the auto-down window button.

"Hi." He smiled.

"What kinda *car* is this?" the boy asked.

Will swallowed. "Saab Tundra," he said.

The boy shook his head, smiling. "Tole you," he said to his friend. And then, to Will: "Stick or automatic?"

"Stick."

"Aw *rat*." The boy extended a long palm; Will, understanding he was supposed to slap it, did the best he could over the windowsill. The boy's hand was leather-tough. The light turned green, and he drove off, waving to the boys, goosebumpy, his faith in humanity and his good taste affirmed.

The car phone burbled. He jumped. It was the first time he'd ever had a car phone, and he'd used it only twice, both times to call home: he'd never heard it ring. He relaxed. It was Gail, he knew; and, still smiling at his escape from violent crime, he decided to forgive her for not helping him with the furniture, for all her distance lately, for everything. He decided, in the instant before he pushed the green SEND button, to proposition his wife, over the car phone, from Bloomfield Avenue!

"Hi," he said, in hands-free mode.

"Willy," said the male voice, gravelly on the speaker.

Could it be? "Barry?"

"You got a moment?"

"Barry, is that you?"

"Yeah—look. You got a moment?"

"Barry, I'm *driving*."

"We should talk, Willy."

"Listen, Barry, I've had some tension, I know. I'm working through it."

"What the fuck are you talking about?"

What else did they *have* to talk about? "Tennis?"

"This isn't tennis."

"It's not?"

"No, look. I'm not sure how to say this, so I'll just say it. Junior Mintz is not a good guy to cross."

"Cross?" A slow blush began to creep upward from the base of his neck: somehow, Will knew, before he knew, what this was about. Still, he shook his head in bewilderment, acting, as though Barry were in the car with him. "Junior?"

"Norman. He's, uh, very—volatile."

Will realized he'd failed to upshift from second gear; he was going along at thirty-five, the car revving at the red line. He put it into neutral and glided to a stop at the next light. "Barry, I have absolutely zero idea what you're talking about."

"He's a jealous guy, a sensitive guy."

Sensitive? Uh-huh. "Jealous of what?"

There was a silence. The light changed; Barry sighed, loudly, over the speaker. "Not of, Willy. About," he said. "His wife."

Now, as Will thought of Patti's freckled chest and fur coat, his face grew hot. "His wife? Who's his wife? Shit." Will had just spotted Mailboxes Etc.—which he'd just passed, shifting and direction-finding and talking on the car phone all at once simply too much for him. He'd have to turn at the next intersection and double back. All the side streets were one-way.

"Willy—listen. What you do with your dick is your own business. She's an attractive woman. Just be careful. Be very careful."

Will was wondering, wildly, if this was somehow a message from her—if she was sending him a signal, somehow. He wondered how their strong mutual attraction at the Sub Shop, clear but unspoken, had been communicated to Junior. He was also thinking that this was the longest conversation he'd ever had with Barry, about anything. "I have to admit—I'm just not following you, Bar."

"Sure, OK. And Willy?"

"Yeah?"

"Get your fucking serve in, all right?"

And so the cardboard-box heir, the corrugated-cardboard prince, bought twenty number 16 boxes, retail! Five ninety-nine apiece—an insane mark-up, Will knew (wholesale, by the gross, number 16s went for eighty-nine cents a unit), but what could he do? At least they were decent boxes. They were stamped on the bottom with Leviathan's logo, the company name in bold capitals superimposed on an aggressive-looking whale, with a knowing smile and purposeful downturned eyebrows, in green ink. Arguably Will was contributing to his own welfare—though he knew the welfare he was really contributing to was that of Mailboxes Etc., whose grumpy owner, edgily secure that he had installed the strongest crime gate money could buy, and that the latest manager was probably not dipping into the till, yet, was at that moment improving his lie in a sand trap in Cozumel.

Will had pulled into the store's sliver of a parking lot after hanging up with Barry, turning around on a one-way street, getting momentarily lost, then going out of his way for about a mile. A single space, in front of the door, had beckoned; but as Will slowly approached it, carefully sizing up the clearances lest he park in door-dinging range, a big burgundy Buick, as in a dream or a cartoon, shot in out of nowhere. As the driver, a short goateed *gavon* (male-pattern baldness, silk Nets team jacket), got out and strutted toward the door, Will opened his window.

"Hey," he said. "I was about to park there."

The guy sized up Will, and the Saab, and raised his bristly chin, smiling easily. "What are you gonna do about it?" he asked.

Will thought about this as the guy went into the store. It was a good question: What was he going to do about it? He parked on a side street, activated the alarm, crossed his fingers, and bought his boxes. Miraculously, when he returned, the heavy unfolded cardboard flats under each arm, no one had stolen, broken into, or vandalized the Saab: there it sat in all its silver magnificence on a lousy street in a rotten neighborhood, rainwater horripilating its voluptuous skin. He glanced around nervously as he opened the car's big hatchback and stowed the boxes-to-be in the carpet-fragrant, capacious rear compartment: for a moment, as he bent over, his back was dangerously vulnerable to muggers or carjackers. Nothing happened. That, he thought with nervous relief after he'd locked up and headed off, safe once more, was the story of his life: nothing happened.

When he got back home, the kids were still bouncing off the walls, and Gail, unbelievably, seemed to be mad at him for staying out so long. That he'd been risking his neck in a dangerous neighborhood to buy overpriced cardboard so he could pack and carry, alone, twenty killingly heavy boxes of books down to the basement, so she could get her fucking floors done, did nothing to mollify her. She had a headache, she couldn't think about making dinner, she wouldn't look him in the eye. She was lying on the bed, *Vogue* tented over her face. Rachel and Danny, enjoying the new furniture-less acoustics of the living room, were skidding and pounding, playing the hollow-sounding floor like timpani. Will's head was starting to hurt, too.

"Guys, *please*," he said. "What's on TV?"

Danny, always alert to familial dynamics, looked puzzled and concerned. "Mom said we should turn it off."

"How 'bout a game up in your room? Baby Animal Bingo? With the door closed?"

"I'm hungryy," Rachel whined.

Will stared at them for a second, trying to summon up what it was that, so recently, had seemed so precious about his children. Or his wife. Couldn't she have given them something? He disliked cooking, and disliked even more making menu offerings to the children, each of whom hated what the other liked. And he especially didn't feel like cooking now: he felt depleted, exhausted, but not really hungry.

He went in the kitchen and opened the Sub-Zero, facing its contents but not quite seeing them. "How 'bout chicken fingers, guys," he said.

"Yeah!" Rachel called, from the living room.

"Eww," Danny said.

"Eggs?"

"Yay!"

"Eww."

"Oh, God—*I* don't know, guys. What about grilled cheese and soup."

Dead silence greeted this, over the plinking of cartoon sound effects. The TV had gone on at last. He became vaguely aware of a presence on his left, turned and saw Rachel. He closed the refrigerator.

"Daddy," she said, "what's owl money?"

"Owl money?"

"Skye says her mommy gets a lot of owl money. From her daddy."

"Owl—oh, *al*imony."

Rachel looked blank.

"Are Skye's mommy and daddy div—— Does Skye's daddy live there?"

She shrugged elaborately.

"See, some mommies and daddies don't live together—"

"Like Burford and Alice."

"Burford and Alice?"

Rachel shook her head indulgently at the depths of his ignorance. "On *TV*."

"Right. Like Burford and Alice," Will said. "So sometimes, then, the daddy helps the mommy out with some money—"

"Like owl money?"

"Exactly. Owl money."

"Do you give Mommy owl money?"

"No no no, sweetie, Mommy and I *live* together. We *all* live together."

Another look as blank as the stars. He stared into the child's black eyes, suddenly chilled to the bone. "Why, Raitch?" he asked, his voice cracking slightly. "Did Mommy say anything about al——about owl money?"

Another shrug.

He knelt and put his hands on her shoulders. "Did she, Raitch? Say anything?"

But the little girl just stared back at him.


He packed all the boxes, and carried the first one, important with its dense bookish weight, down the narrow cellar steps, trying to think calm thoughts so his back wouldn't go out. (Something in it was quivering, pondering the option.) Once at the bottom of the steps, he had to weave with infinite slowness and care through a head-bumping, ankle-scraping maze of overhead pipes and household debris to the basement's last conceivable available space, a windowless cinder-blocked cul-de-sac behind the furnace, where some defunct bamboo porch furniture could theoretically be shifted around, chesswise, to make room for sixteen boxes of books.

Theory and practice were two different matters. He cursed as he bent over in rank, dark, dusty confines, trying to make furniture that they didn't need anyway, that they should've thrown out years ago, fit around pipes and pieces of also useless old lath protruding from a disused tool shelf, the pride of the house's previous owner, or the one before that. Or the one before that. He wondered, gloomily, who would be in the house two owners from now, and where he would be, as he tried to play furniture chess without his back going out. But the oversized chess pieces didn't want to move; he kept banging up against the same infuriating, invisible ghost-obstacle, a piece of the foundation or a gas-valve cap or something, in an unseeable black space in the corner. And then, suddenly, finally, by turning the defunct bamboo couch upside down and upending it (and feeling something below his right shoulder blade give), he was able to free up a sector that, he thought, might accept his boxes.

He brought the rest of them down one by one, each a little three-act drama of possible injury, intricate maneuvering, and correct placement. Wire hangers dangling from the cellar's overhead pipes jangled merrily against his head, like triangles in some demonic orchestra, as he inched backward and sideways through the debris. From far away, two floors above, Danny's room probably, came the trebles and basses of unmediated screaming and banging—whether unhappy or playful he couldn't tell. No sound from Gail. Then, a while later, through the basement ceiling, he heard her unmistakable tread on the upstairs stairs, followed by the cozy clash of pots in the kitchen. The children's voices followed, and some temperate consultation, the sound of peace and order restored. He paused for a moment, trying to make out just what was being said, but all he could hear was the rise and fall of the three voices, in the middle range of tone and volume, a good sign.

But when he went up to the kitchen, Gail was another person, her face a ghastly yellow, puffy rings under her eyes; the children seemed worried and pouty. He tried taking a jolly tone—"Had enough?" he asked her, as she stirred some split-pea-with-ham soup at the stove—but it fell flat and dead in the white light of the kitchen. Danny stared from his mother to his father as Will's smile congealed. "There's soup if you want some," Gail told him, in a monotone. She turned off the burner.

"What's wrong?" Will asked, putting his hand on her shoulder. He had to ask again.

"My head's killing me," she said, barely audibly, slipping away from his touch. She sat at the table with the children and began to eat her soup, leaving him stranded and speechless at the stove.

He shook his head and went back to the boxes. He had taken down just eight. Eight more. After three his back and arms were aching; he was sweating freely, and ravenous. He paused and listened through the ceiling. The TV was booming. He went upstairs and found Danny and Rachel back on the living room floor, with *The Addams Family* on. In the flickering black-and-white light of the old show, Danny had a strange half-smile, more puzzled than amused; Rachel's eyelids were drooping.

"Where's Mom, guys?" he asked.

No answer.

He turned on a low flame under what was left of the soup, cut a few slices of cheddar cheese onto an English muffin, and laid both halves on the grill in the toaster oven. After a while he glanced back into the living room: both of them were asleep now. He went upstairs. Gail was back on the bed, with a Gardener's Eden catalogue.

"Hi," he said.

She turned a page, glanced at him with exhausted reproach, then looked back at the catalogue. "Hi."

"They're asleep."

She said nothing.

"Shouldn't we put them to bed?"

She turned another page. "It would be nice if you would."

He took a sharp breath, mentally counted to three. "I've got to eat something," he said.

She shrugged.

A piercing beep, throbbing and urgent, began to shrill up the stairs. "Shit," Will said. He boomed down the steps, ran through the living room—Danny and Rachel were still out cold—and into the kitchen, where black smoke was pouring from the toaster oven. The alarm was screeching away ear-killingly. He quickly unplugged the toaster oven, in which, he saw, a cheesy fragment of English muffin had broken off, dropped onto the heating coil, and burst into flame. The flame began to flicker out as the coil cooled. Then Will stood on a chair, a finger stuck in one ear, and pulled the battery out of the smoke detector. The silence throbbed. From this vantage point, he could now see that his inch of soup was boiling. He got down and turned off the stove; the soup had turned into gum. The smoke from the toaster-oven had died down, and the rest of the English muffin was edible, if black. He took it out, burning his finger in the process, and began to eat it standing at the counter.

The phone rang. He looked at it for a couple of rings, then picked it up. "Mr. Weiss?" said a young man's voice, quavery and cheerful.

"Yes?"

"My name is Leonard, and I'm being compensated by the National Patrolmen's Organization to call you. How are you this evening?"

Will hung up, hard. He scraped and ate the gummy residue from the soup pot—it wasn't at all bad—and put the pot in the sink. He ate the black remainder of the cheese muffin, then took an Oreo out of the Oreo-shaped cookie jar, chasing it with a glass of ice water from the water dispenser. There was a funny, metallic taste in his mouth that wouldn't go away—maybe more Oreos would do it. He gobbled cookie after cookie, staring out the kitchen window at the rainy blackness.

He ran some water into the soup pot and over his dishes, and went into the living room. Rachel first. He wedged his fingers under her inert torso, rolled her to her side, and heaved her over his shoulder fireman-style. Up the stairs and into her room, where every surface was covered with books, toys, and dolls, strewn as if in fury, as though by a madwoman. He slung his daughter onto her bed, turned the overhead off and the night-light on, and removed her jeans, marveling at her perfect little legs, feeling, under three or four layers of mental guards, a little frisson of sex, and quickly censoring it. There were fathers, many more than were known, he was sure, who acted on this. In some dim part of his soul, in the dim glow of Rachel's night-light, he understood them, and wondered what happenstance had made him one of the ones who did not.

Rachel was a camel. Danny's bladder, however, was pea-sized, and lately he'd been soaking the bed. As Will struggled up the stairs under the sandbag-like weight of his sleeping son, he wondered if the tension between Gail and him was somehow responsible for Danny's bed-wetting. At the top of the steps he put Danny on his feet and guided the sleepwalking boy into the dark bathroom, standing him in front of the toilet and pulling down his pants. He turned on the water in the sink and rubbed the nape of the boy's neck. "Come on, honey, pee for me," he pleaded. Groggily, Danny kept reaching down and trying to pull his pants back up. "Not yet, honey, not yet," Will said. "Come on."

Finally, after what felt like forever, a stream emerged. Misdirected for a second, it hissed on the tiles; then, as Will turned Danny's shoulders, came the sweet homey tinkle of water music.

He would wipe the floor later. He stepped Danny out of his dampened pants and steered him, trippingly, into his room, quickly yanking down the ball-and-bat bedspread and pushing him onto the sheet, then pulling the spread up over his son's shoulders and, suddenly sentimental, kissing his sweet plump cheek, slack with sleep. In the glow of the night-light, the toys on the table cast long shadows up on the wall. Will sat on the side of the bed and rested for a moment, staring at the shadows and thinking about the time, the day before yesterday, when he had gazed at similar shadows in his own room, and the time, the day after tomorrow, when Danny would be his age and Will would be gone, or getting ready to go.

The idea, all at once, made him miss his wife, made him want her, now. There would be no sex in the grave. Still, the hurdle of their argument—whatever it was—stood before him, unavoidable. Should he apologize? For what? He could think of something.

Yet as he approached the turning of the upstairs hall, he saw an unmistakable darkness, more than even a closed bedroom door would account for. Gail lay asleep under the covers, composed-looking, her mouth closed, complete, serene without him.

He would finish his boxes. But as he passed the dining room, he saw Gail and the children's dinner mess still on the table, and, through the far doorway, the kitchen and its brightly lit chaos beckoning unavoidably. He hated leaving a mess. And, he reasoned, cleaning up might, in the morning, pave the way toward reconciliation. If reconciliation were still necessary. Mainly he hated leaving a mess.

He cleaned the table, ran the disposal, and loaded the dishwasher. As he scrubbed at the gunked-on split-pea residue in the soup pot, the incurve of the pot's bottom somehow triggered an associative flicker too fast to trace, making him think of Gail's sleek profile, her lean jaw resting on the pillow. And all at once he wondered if she had ever been unfaithful to him. When she'd still worked full-time, there had been one partner at the firm he'd worried about; he could no longer remember the guy's name. He was tall, handsome in a ferrety way, penetrating in a way that Will could never be, and sardonic. The couple of times Will had met him, at Christmas parties, he had seemed completely impressive, and cynical about his own marriage to boot. And Gail had worked long hours then, late nights sometimes and occasional weekends.

If it had happened, though, it was over. It must be over.

And what about Mario?

Will held the soup pot up to the light, feeling its surfaces with his fingertips. There were still traces of crust, invisible.

It came to him: the partner's name had been Ted.

Will went at the soup crust ruthlessly with the Brillo, scouring at tall trim Ted, and then the pudgy little realtor, so much less sleek than the law partner, but with a certain slick charm of his own. He recalled, uncomfortably, that Gail used to have a thing about short men: they were commanding, she said. Will was five-eleven, lacking the command of either shortness or height.

At least he could clean a pot, he thought. He looked at it with satisfaction, all traces of Ted and Mario effaced. He put the pot in the drying rack and surveyed the kitchen. Sparkling. Done. Then he saw the forest-green Williams-Sonoma garbage can, brimming under its lid.

Would it kill her to take out the trash once? Shaking his head, he raised the lid and saw that a substantial overflow had been incompletely compressed, the grocery bag's paper handles smushed and grease-soaked, the underside of the lid smeared with what looked like congealed duck sauce. He dripped some green dish detergent on a wet Bounty and, on his knees, went to work on the lid. But the duck sauce was gummy and resistant; finally he had to use a Brillo, which scraped off much forest-green enamel. Disgusted, he dropped the soap pad and overflow garbage into a second paper grocery bag and took both bags through the mud room to the back door.

The house's three enormous plastic garbage pails were in a raccoon-proof shed at the bottom of the back steps; Will never made it. As he descended the rain-slick brick stairs, one handle of the first bag broke; as he reached, with the hand holding the other bag, to try and arrest the first bag's fall, he somehow unbalanced himself, catching the toe of his shoe and going down, in a heap, in the driveway.

His right hip and wrist ached. His fall had triggered the motion-detector in the driveway floodlight, the light revealing an impressive scatter of garbage on the asphalt. The fuller bag, grease-soaked, had disintegrated on impact; the fresh bag had simply spilled. He stood in the spotlight, looking at the damage. An icy rain was falling through the light onto the trash.

He did the best he could to clear the mess, leaving a heap of coffee grounds and a little pond of strawberry yogurt for the raccoons. Once, the floodlight clicked off as he knelt out of the detector's range; panting with fury, he had to wave an arm to turn it back on again. He was soaked and out of breath by the time he finished picking up. Odd, the range of thoughts that passed through his mind as he gathered garbage in the rain: first anger at Gail, then intricate plans for revenge, leading, inevitably, to sex. He imagined taking his wife from behind, but the image of her meager white buttocks suddenly reminded him of the thrilling double bulge of Junior's wife's freckled décolletage.

He wondered exactly what Patti looked like naked. (He thought he had a pretty good idea.) He thought again of his idea of fucking

her on her silver fur coat. The idea excited him intolerably. He imagined her smile, her brown arms, workout-sinewy, reaching up for him.
Brown arms and white breasts, spilled and flattened—but not too
flattened—in repose. Gail was, always had been, as flat-chested as a
boy. Lately Will found himself having guilty adolescent fantasies
about boobs. And Patti's boobs seemed just right.

He let himself into the mud room, turned off the kitchen lights,
and unbuttoned himself. His fingers still smelled of coffee grounds
and melon rinds, but it didn't matter, nothing mattered. Should he
try to visualize or simply drift, dreamily? It was always a question.
He chose seeing. He needed to focus in a little bit, to the precise
contours of Patti's dream-pelvis, and then he'd be there. She lay on
the silver coat, reaching up, and . . . just then, Layla walked in on
them, all mischief, reaching behind to unhook her bra. This was good.
Layla's nipples spoke volumes. He smiled: his harem. This was good.
And then, as he arched onto his tiptoes in the mud room, among the
swishy presences of winter coats, heaving like Hercules, all his labors
done for the day but one, the kitchen phone rang.

He was too close to stop. He came cramped, and staggered toward the warbling monster with his pants and underwear still shack-
ling his feet, snatching a Bounty off the roller to wipe himself as he
passed the sink. He managed to grab the receiver midway through
the third ring. "Hello?" he said, voice rising in disbelief and fear.

But he heard nothing but a deep, assessing silence on the other
end, and then a click.

# 18

Joel is driving up the hill after work, butt-tired, his hands reeking of vinegar and sweet peppers, the oldies radio on loud, playing Tommy Dano's song (*What's your name? Who's your daddy? He rich—is he rich like me?*), when he sees her by the side of Verona Ave., with her thumb out. It takes him a second to register it's her, but who else could it be? Neon-green pants, neon-pink halter top, black dog collar, slick black hair, dark purple lipstick. A little ratty black poodle-fur jacket, open, even though it's about twenty degrees out; belly and belly ring showing, as usual. He pulls over and stops, watching the rearview lest some joker hit him from behind. It's four o'clock, dim gray light, slate sky the color of pure sadness, idiot traffic roaring by.

Chia opens the door, clacking gum, sees it's him, and smiles. "Hi!" she says, as brightly as if they'd planned a rendezvous. Hops in. She's carrying a ripped-up blue notebook with seventies-style flower stickers on it and a paperback: *Psycho-Cybernetics*, by Maxwell Maltz.

"I can't believe you hitchhike," he says.

She closes the big door and grins. "I know," she says. "Me either."

He glances at the mirror, shifts into drive—the Impala complies, grudgingly—and pulls out into the traffic. "Hey. Aren't you cold?"

She shrugs. "You always end up someplace warm." She runs her fingers lovingly over the dashboard's flaking padding, checks out the back seat. "Great car," she says.

"Thanks. You going home?"

"Whatever."

Joel gives her a look. "Please define," he says.

She shrugs again, grins. "I don't know. I thought maybe you were going to abduct me or something."

This sends a little spurt of blood into his spearhead: he glances over to see what she means by it. But she's simply wearing her usual satisfied half-smile. She can't sit still; she keeps running her hands over the Impala's retro surfaces. "*Really* great car," she says. She fingers the chrome radio buttons. "You listen to the same station as Gary."

"Do I."

"Yeah, it sucks. Mind?" she says, the second after she's started turning the tuning dial.

"I guess not," Joel says. He's driven past Wyoming, where he would've turned off; they're at the crest of the hill, where the avenue enters the South Mountain Reservation. Chia tunes in some new music: it sounds like a Jew's harp twanging.

*Up shit creek again-nnn*

chants a soft, sexually indefinite voice, flat yet urgent. (Later the song, as much as he hates it, will come back to him, will come to seem, strangely, their song.) She bobs her head in time to the music, juking her shoulders, peering out the window, nodding at wherever they're driving. Where are they driving? He doesn't have a clue—just driving. They're in the esses, the avenue is winding through the forest. "Hey," she says, suddenly. He almost hits the brakes.

"What?"

"I got an idea."

"Yes?"

"Let's go see the deer."

He instantly knows what she's talking about: years ago, he can't even remember how long, it feels like the fifties, there was a rusty wire pen in the middle of the reservation, with a few scraggly deer inside. A bored park employee in a little wooden stand sold pellets to feed them.

"You're kidding. You think they're still there?"

"Why? Where would they have gone?" She actually looks serious.

But they're on the wrong side of the concrete divider—a divider that was installed on the twisty road, Joel recalls, after kids kept getting killed drag-racing. He has to drive two miles out of the way, all the way down and up through the reservation, and make an illegal U-turn at a traffic light, then double back into the woods going east. Chia dances in her seat to the music the whole time; he keeps glancing over, and she smiles, catching him. He smiles back, finally—he can't help himself, she's so beautiful and strange.

Here, back at the top of the hill, on the first ridge of the Orange Mountains, is the entrance to the reservation, marked by a heavily defaced pseudorustic carved-wood sign, yellow intaglio letters saying the park is open dawn to dusk year-round. It's almost dusk now. An orange-and-white-striped bar blocks the road. Joel pulls over into a gravel lot, next to the only other vehicle, a big black-and-chrome BMW motorcycle.

"I guess we have to walk in," he says.

"Cool," says Chia.

The darkening air, cold and clingy, smells like car exhaust and wet leaves, but, thanks to the gate, more and more like just wet leaves as they walk up the road into the woods. The trees seem to close in as they leave the parking lot behind; the sound of the avenue dies away, too, and it gets very quiet. Joel inhales the sad Thanksgiving-y woods-smell, remembering the time he dove into a pile of leaves in fourth grade and his fingers grabbed a loamy layer of wet stuff at the bottom, pebbles and worms and incipient earth, like the bottom of a grave. Chia's tottering along by his side on her clacking platform heels, looking around wide-eyed, hugging herself against the chill.

"What is it with you and the cold?" Joel says. He takes off his loden-green duffle coat—from Saks, of course; a gift from Irma—and drapes it over her shoulders. She's shivering. "You sure you don't want to go back?" he asks.

She blinks at him. "Why?"

"It'll be dark in twenty minutes."

She smiles and shrugs. "Hey," she suddenly says. There in the gloom, sure enough, is a rustic wooden arrow that reads DEER PASTURE.

They turn right, onto a narrow path full of dry leaves. Their feet swish as they walk along. The slate sky may be full of jets descending toward Newark, the path may be scattered with crumbled Styrofoam and Hostess wrappers, but the sound of swishing leaves is so beautiful, it makes his stomach turn over. "So how come you're not scared of me?" he asks her.

"Scared?"

"Strange old guy, works in a sandwich store—probably has all kinds of objectionable habits."

She stares him in the eye. "I bet my habits are twice as objectionable as yours."

"Huh," he says. And then, "You're not worried I have designs on you?"

She looks down at herself, plucking out the edge of the halter top, the waist of her pants. He can see she's wearing no underwear. "Where?" she says.

"Ha ha."

"I know you have designs on me," she says. "I also know you're not going to do anything gross."

"How?"

"Your eyes," Chia says. "And your hands."

"My hands?"

But she doesn't answer. "So how come you never left home?" she asks.

"I don't know. . . . What's out there that's so great?"

"Wife? Family?"

"My friends don't make it look especially attractive."

"You mean your friend?"

"Friend?"

"The one with the wedding ring. And the hots for that bimbo."

He stops short, his lust shifting like liquid sloshing in a tank. "Hey—Patsy's not a bimbo."

"Oh yeah? What would you call her? A library lady?"

"Come on. That's not fair."

Somewhere in the gloom a branch cracks. They look at each other silently for a second, breathing, listening. Farther along the path there's a light swishing of leaves.

"Maybe we should go back," Joel whispers.

She shakes her head. "I bet it's the deer," she whispers back, and strides on through the leaves.

"Hey," he says, catching up. "Try to make a little more noise." She stops.

"Pick your feet up and put them down flat instead of kicking through the leaves," Joel suggests. He demonstrates.

Chia grins, her teeth white in the gloom. "Cool," she says. "Where'd you learn that?"

"I was an Eagle Scout."

"Uh-oh," she says. "*Now* I'm scared of you."

After a minute they come to the edge of a clearing, a long gravel parking lot giving on to a road at its other end. And there, in the semidarkness, stands the rusty deer fence, precisely as he remembered it, as though time had melted. It startles him for a moment: How many years can it have been? How many things out there in the darkness are exactly as he remembers? Two? Three? There's even the old wooden feed stand. They stop and hear the swishing again, and a different sound, an animal voice, a high, guttural "Uh? Uh? Uh?"

"I don't think that's deer," Joel whispers.

Chia shushes him. She tiptoes a few paces across the gravel, then stops short. "Whoa," she says.

He sees what she's talking about: behind the wire fence twenty yards away they can just make out two figures in black, gender indeterminate, one on all fours, head down, the other crouched close behind. The guttural voice starts again, then breaks into a keening whine. Joel and Chia look at each other.

"History?" she asks.

"Roger."

Fifty yards down the path, he finally exhales. "*Not* deer," he says.

She shrugs. "Things change."

"Oh, my." He shakes his head, tries to catch his breath. "It's my least favorite thing about things, actually."

"So," she says, after they walk on a ways. "The bimbo's not a bimbo."

"Patsy? Nah. An old friend."

"Girlfriend?"

"Sort of, about a thousand years ago, yeah."

"But not anymore?"

"Not anymore."

"High school?"

"'Fraid so."

"You went to VHS, right?"

He nods. "Class of '74."

"Ooh. You *are* old."

"Thanks."

"Maybe you knew my mom?"

"Your mom?"

"Cindy Island?"

# 19

Marvin Flanders had done his magic and departed. The Weisses' downstairs floors were transformed into a paradise of waxy blondness, unblemished and magnificent. And Gail was happy—temporarily.

For one thing, she realized that the pleasure she now took in gazing at all that perfect wood was about to be considerably diminished by the replacement of their rugs and furniture—rugs and furniture that would look significantly worse than before simply by comparison to the gleaming new floors. There was an easy solution to this, but Will wouldn't hear of it. "The money's not in yet," he said, his lips getting that thin look she hated. "We've spent enough for now."

In truth, he was jittery. Leviathan's due diligence was taking longer than expected—were they getting cold feet? And the market was all over the place. The Dow kept flirting with ten thousand, then backing off: every week, robust employment figures, or some other happy economic malarkey, kept raising the specter of inflation and higher interest rates, causing nervous Nellies to sell.

Will had sold stock only twice in his life, and neither occasion had had anything to do with the economy at large, or making or losing money in the market—both times he had simply needed cash. He hated people who dicked around with stocks, doing little get-rich tricks, messing things up for the solid, unbrave, small investors like him, who religiously fed money into the market every month, waiting for that big righteous cash-in at the end. The Dow's fluctuations should have been of strictly theoretical interest to Will, whose close-to-half-million-dollar portfolio was strictly earmarked for college costs and retirement.

But he couldn't help it; he took it all very personally. He let the market affect his morale (sometimes he fantasized that his mood affected the market). He called his broker's automated line far too often, like an anxious first-time parent checking the crib at night. (Or, he sometimes thought, like a lover—for he kept the calls secret from Gail, afraid of her ever more pronounced disdain. And his broker, ironically enough, was Fidelity.) But, he reasoned, he had a right to be vigilant: losing ten thousand dollars—as he had, in a recent bad week—seemed like losing real money, even if something in him knew he was likely to make it back, plus two or three more, over the next few months.

And then there were all those skunks muttering in the background, in newspapers and magazines, about the Millennium Effect, the Big One: the crash that would make '29 and '87 look like kid stuff. The Medicare trust fund was about to go bust; Social Security would follow soon thereafter; corporate valuations were more overblown than ever, blah blah blah. The 2000s, the skunks were saying, were going to be Wild West City for investors: a lot of baby boomers would lose their shirts, and the only people who would make any money would be fearless young financial ninjas willing to gamble on offshore alternative medical technologies and other such malarkey, willing to ride the financial seismic waves, willing to fall and bleed and get up again.

It was all Greek to Will, or at least it was language he was reluctant to understand. He was a man of the nineties: keep investing and hope for the best. He knew he was skating on thin ice, but so was everyone. And at least he was still skating.

On the other hand, he was still convinced, deep down, that something was profoundly wrong with their floors. They still sounded too hollow. Something in Will's soul felt sure, despite Marvin Flanders' expert cosmetic manipulations, of the ever-present chance that somebody would simply crash through to the basement sometime. It was crazy, he knew: he had checked, and checked again, for the telltale sawdust of termite damage. Nothing. There was no rational basis for his fear. He had come within an inch of asking Flanders if, perhaps, their floors sounded hollower than other floors he'd worked on, but the little man's thick glasses and cold, slightly academic humor had intimidated Will; what if he made fun of him? (Why was he so scared of being made fun of?) In between sanding and buffing, Flanders liked to take off his airport-style ear-protectors, drop his mouth-and-nose filter, and boast, in a cool, understated, vaguely British way, of the big shots whose houses he'd worked on. That was all Will needed, to be the small shot who made it into Flanders' oral history through baseless fears about hollow floors. He held his tongue.

It was even hard to take complete pleasure in the silver Saab. In some part of his mind, he began to see it as a financial millstone, a monthly lease payment that could begin to look steep if things didn't go perfectly smoothly. (What if Leviathan fell through?) The car drove wonderfully—the smooth assured click of the gearshift was a particular joy—but Will also suspected he wasn't getting nearly the gas mileage the sticker had promised, eighteen city and twenty-seven on the highway. One morning he woke up—in Danny's bed, as usual; with the gerbil skittering, as usual—realizing he had dreamed about the Saab's gas mileage, had consulted some faceless Delphic oracle on the question, the oracle hissing, in scathing response, *Sixteen.*

What was worse, getting cheated on your new car's gas mileage, or dreaming about it?

And he knew precisely what would happen if he complained to the dealer: the car would be dutifully held for a day and examined (while he had to drive around in some cigarette-reeking lunch-pail loaner of a Dodge), and, after no problem was found, Bruno, the menacingly obsequious service manager, would call into question Will's shifting and tire-inflation habits. He held his tongue.

Then (he saved it for last in his thoughts because it was too hard to think about), there was the lunch with Jack. Once every three weeks or so, Jack and Will had lunch at Pal's on Eagle Rock Avenue, in the heavy, masculine, dark-wood-and-leather confines of the Wagon Wheel room, amid paintings of Custer and Buffalo Bill. The drill was always the same: after a little edgy patter about Gail and the kids (Will had always suspected Jack had a lech for Gail; nor did he especially like the appreciative way she looked at him), and some more chat about Jack's continuing E-mail chess rivalry with a Pakistani anesthesiologist in Redmond, Washington—after the pro forma preliminaries, business was discussed. And the gist, the undertone, the theme of the discussion was always this: Will might be in charge of Weiss Containers now, but only one person was really in charge while Jack Weiss was still around.

No matter how much of an intellectual handle Will got on the box business, he wasn't Jack Weiss. He never would be Jack Weiss. Will tended to feel hurt when accounts receivable weren't received, when suppliers two-timed him with bigger companies, when truckers cheated on mileage tickets. Jack, a master of distrust, expected all of it. He blew up at people, had tantrums; it got results. In his time, he'd developed exploding into a fine art—so much so that old-time employees, vendors, suppliers, and truckers were sometimes perplexed by Will's (seemingly) cooler, quieter style. "You ain't gonna yell at me?" a tooth-pick-chewing, bill-padding truck-driver had asked him a few weeks before—with disappointment, Will thought.

It wasn't that problems had rolled off Jack's back—the industrial-size Mylanta bottle he'd always kept in plain sight in his office was proof. But problems didn't seem to worm into him the way they did with Will. Jack, a former Marine, was a tough character. Small-hipped, steel-haired, brush-cut, he still did his sit-ups and push-ups. He barked at parking attendants and recalcitrant sales clerks. He would live forever.

But during their last lunch, the week before, Jack had told Will he'd found lumps in his armpit and groin.

Will's reaction had surprised both of them. He broke into a cold sweat and felt a seasick pressure between his eyes. His head grew light and he suddenly, urgently, wanted to lie down. His father was going to die. He stared at Jack, who looked puzzled and concerned—"You OK, Willy? You look terrible"—and felt puzzled himself, even as he felt sick. Jack looked so *good*. How could he be going to die?

"No, I don't feel so hot," he told his father.

"You're white as a sheet."

"I don't feel so great."

Jack summoned the headwaiter, with a curt, two-fingered ges-ture whose brisk economy Will had to admire, even in his condition: Would he ever be capable of such a gesture? Then he capitulated and lay down sideways on the burgundy banquette as the other business diners looked on with interest. He didn't care if they stared; he had no choice in the matter.

"I need some extra napkins and ice for my son," Jack told Nando, the maitre d', who was staring at Will—sideways, from Will's perspective—with what appeared to be real concern.

"Of course, right away, Mr. Weiss," Nando said.

Will sat back up.

"What are you doing?" Jack asked.

"I'm OK," Will said. He wasn't—although he was a fraction better.

"You're still pale as a ghost, kiddo. Why don't you lay back down?"

*Lie*, Will thought: his father never got it right. An extremely quick debate about lying down occurred in Will's woozy head, then gravity won out over reason. He tilted back to his side. It felt odd to be lying there in the middle of Pal's: he felt calm and panicked, sick and well, all at once. And there was this: what had just happened to him would never have happened to Jack. Never ever. But then, turning forty had finally taught Will what he was and wasn't, and a tough guy was one of the things he wasn't. There was even sort of a toughness in knowing he wasn't tough.

Nevertheless, now he sat up again.

"It's OK, Willy," Jack said, with unusual softness. "Stay down till you're ready to get up."

"I'm OK now," Will said. "Really." He felt a little better.

Jack, it turned out, was going in for tests. But in the aftermath of the lunch, it all seemed so unreal—both Jack's lumps and Will's near-faint—that Will almost forgot about it. Almost. *My father's going to die*, he tried saying to himself a few times, but the words felt hollow. How could Jack die? People got lumps all the time. Will didn't even mention the incident to Gail—partly because they weren't saying much of anything to each other these days, beyond the perfunctory necessities; partly because it didn't make him look particularly good. Mixed in there, too, in small measure, was the wish not to worry her—or himself, further.

One night soon afterward he awoke in the deep watches of the night, three or four o'clock, to pee. Standing sleepily at the toilet in the dark, he glanced out the window at the quarter moon, setting in the bare trees: it looked incorrectly sideways somehow, and full of a meaning he couldn't decipher, like a joke in a foreign language, Moonish. And Will thought, quite matter-of-factly: My father's going to die.

Gail ran into Lynnie at the school-bus stop on a bright cold Tuesday afternoon and asked her if she wanted to have lunch. On Friday. Lynnie's mascaraed brown eyes widened theatrically. "Have *lunch*," she said. "How *cool*. How grown-*up*."

This was Lynnie's version of "yes." Actually, she had a conflict—Lynnie always had a conflict; her schedule and the schedules of her children were planned out months in advance, to the nanosecond—but she could move a few things around, have her hair cut the Thursday after next at three-twenty, and lunch would be fine. They decided, since the satirical idea of Lunch had taken hold, to try Le Poivrier, a tiny, pricey French place that had recently opened in Cedar Grove. Le Poivrier had immediately been homed in on by restless suburban good-tasteniks (most of them hard-pressed to pronounce its name correctly), and given what Jack Weiss liked to call the Verona Gold Card Seal of Approval. Or, as Lynnie put it: "Small portions, big checks. *Perfectamundo*."

As Friday approached, Gail found herself unaccountably nervous. Or not so unaccountably. She had invited Lynnie to lunch mainly to tell her about a lunch invitation *she*'d received, from Mario. She'd been standing at the kitchen sink one morning, bleaching some chocolate out of one of Danny's T-shirts, when the realtor had called, ostensibly to discuss yet another amazing house that wouldn't last, and then, after a little banter, slipped in the question, smoothly, the way he did everything else: "Hey, why don't we have lunch?"

Her heart had jumped. "Lunch?" she repeated.

"You know, the one that comes between breakfast and dinner?"

She stared at Danny's T-shirt for a moment, noticing, with a mix of emotions, that her nipples had stiffened slightly and the saliva on the back of her tongue turned gluey.

"Gail? You there?"

"Yeah."

"I can retract the invitation if it makes you uncomfortable." Smooth.

She didn't say she was uncomfortable. She said she'd think about it. Now she was thinking about it. Everything felt upside down all of a sudden, with the floors so beautiful, the furniture rearranged and looking worse than ever, all that money about to come, the vast silence between her and Will. The other night she had turned to him in bed, nostalgically, and he'd turned away, patting her on the hip. "I've got a lot on my mind," he'd said, and she fumed for an hour, unable to get to sleep. Who didn't have a lot on their mind?

What she had on her mind now was what to wear to lunch with Lynnie. What was right for a French lunch in the suburbs? A work suit would be ridiculous; were pants too casual? She decided, finally, to buy a cute blue-black skirt and print top she'd seen in the window at Arleen Miller in Montclair. Deep-voiced Arleen herself was in the store that day, and persuaded Gail to spring for a grass-green kid vest, a wonderfully funky touch (at three hundred bucks), to complete the ensemble. Gail glowed as the young girl at the regis-

ter—dressed all in Arleen, of course—put her card through: the
purchase was faith in the near future, revenge on Will, and an acknow-
ledgment of Mario's tribute, all at once. It was also perfect for lunch
at Le Poivrier.


"You're *kidding*," Lynnie breathed, in her nasal voice, putting her right hand not quite where it ought to be, over her heart,
but slightly to the northeast, just below her left shoulder. It was
Friday; the two women were seated in a quiet back corner of the
restaurant's single, pseudo–Norman farmhouse room. Lynnie, Gail
had been happy to see, was in a rust-and-denim cowgirl thing, not
as good-looking as her own new outfit, but not so dowdy that Gail
would be embarrassed to be seen with her. Lynnie's taste could be a
little iffy. "*He* asked you to *lunch?*"

Her hand over her mouth, stifling a nervous laugh, Gail nodded.
"Oh my *Gawd?*"

"Why?" Gail asked. "You think it's more than lunch?"

"Lunch is *never* lunch—didn't you know that?"

At that moment, the solicitous, white-aproned, too-handsome
waiter—gay, Gail and Lynnie had instantly agreed—put their plates
on the table. As promised, the actual quantity of food, adrift in a pond
of tri-color pastel sauces and trimmed with what looked like wood
shavings, was minuscule. The two women ah-ed appreciatively, both
at the prettiness of the plates and the fulfillment of their expecta-
tions. "*Bon appetit,*" the waiter said, fake-flirtily. And as he left, to
their surprise, Gail and Lynnie looked at each other and suddenly
burst into laughter—at the waiter, at the restaurant, at themselves,
at lunches that were lunch and those that weren't; at everything.

★ ★ ★

On Monday afternoon, Gail called Will at the office and told him she had to work late. With a throb of guilt and inadequacy and titillation all at once, he thought of Ted, the tall, handsome partner. She'd been so bitchy with Will lately; maybe she'd broken off with Ted but was thinking of starting up again? Will shook his head. It was crazy; he was making all this up to begin with. The funny thing was, the second before Gail had called he'd been stealing glances across the office at Layla—or rather, at Layla's flat white belly, the three exposed inches of it, under brown-and-gold-striped acrylic, that he'd been unable to take his eyes off all morning. Shouldn't he say something to her about dressing this way? Then again, what could he say? With his wife in his ear, he looked over at Layla again.

"So," Gail said. She sounded flat—for a change—and rushed. "Can you bathe them?"

"Sure."

"OK."

"OK."

"So—all right," she said, clearly eager to get off the phone. "I'll be home on the ten or the eleven."

"All right."

"I have to go."

"Gail?" He almost never called her by name; this, and the almost pleading tone of his voice, stopped them both.

"What?"

He thought for a second. "Nothing," he said.


After finishing the dinner dishes he customarily allowed himself, as a kind of end-of-the-day treat, one call to the automated line at Fidelity, to see how the Dow had done, what his balances were.

In truth it was more compulsion than treat, and only pleasurable half the time, but it was something to do, and, tonight, a way of delaying bathing the children. They were pounding around upstairs, screeching.

"Will you stop that!" he shouted; there was a brief pause, then they started up again. He shook his head and picked up the kitchen phone. The funny thing, though, was that there was no dial tone in the earpiece—but it wasn't as if the line were dead, either. The sound had an open quality, a hollowness, and Will had the strong impression that someone was on the line, that it was one of those strange times when you picked up the phone to make a call and found someone already there, waiting.

"Hello?" he said.

There was a silence, then a prevocal intake of breath—somebody was clearly about to speak—and then a click.

If it were the movies, Will thought, he would say hello a couple more times, just to convey he'd been hung up on; but he didn't need to say anything. The line was dead.

At least he knew it wasn't Ted, he thought, with a grim smile. Then he stopped. Maybe that Mario? But it wouldn't have been Mario the other night at one in the morning. Maybe it was just the world, being weird. He dried his hands on the dishtowel and turned off the kitchen lights.

The phone rang.

"Hello," he said sharply—angrily.

"Willy?" It was Barry, sounding almost meek at Will's tone.

"Oh, hey, Barry. Did you just call a second ago?"

"What?"

"My line went dead just now. I thought maybe it was you."

"No?"

"Sorry. I've been getting funny phone calls."

Barry ignored it, reverting, in a flash, to his customary bossy drone. "You think you can get a sub this Saturday, Willy? I got a wedding in Boston."

"A sub? God." He blinked in confusion. Who did he know?

"Dad-*dyyy*," Rachel screeched, from the foot of the stairs.

"One second," Will told Barry, cupping his hand over the mouthpiece. "What is it, Rachel? I'm on the phone," he called, testily.

The child walked around the corner, tiny-hipped and red-faced, in just her flowered underpants. "Danny's *deezing* me," she said, and started to sob.

"OK, OK, here I come." Will uncupped the mouthpiece. "Listen, lemme call you back," he told Barry. "I'll try to think of someone."

# 20

Joel, for some reason Will couldn't fathom, was adamant about driving them to Playdium Saturday morning, even though there was an inch of fresh snow on the ground, and more flurries in the air, and Will was itching to see how the Tundra would handle it.

"Come on, Joel," he said. "I've got four-wheel drive."

"Two won't get us there?"

But it wasn't just Joel's bald tires Will was worried about. Now, instead of suiting up and getting neatly out of the house, he would have to stand around the kitchen in his tennis clothes, on call, until Joel showed up. Gail was sleeping late (or "in," as she said, an expression Will could never understand—in what?); Danny and Rachel lay on the ratty Oriental, in the newly blond–floored living room, staring, openmouthed, at cartoons. They (especially Danny) watched too many cartoons, he knew; he should read to them, he knew. Especially Danny, who, just lately, seemed on the verge of some sort of strange dyslexia: anything more than catalogue copy—or cartoon end-credits, for which he seemed to have a nearly photographic memory—was simply too much for him. Will made a mental note to do more reading with Danny. Soon.

He tried to read the paper at the counter for a while, dutifully paging through the first section and noting new trouble in Afghanistan, corporate start-ups in China, but he couldn't stop thinking about tennis. Now and then, in the past couple of weeks, he had been doing a little better: last Saturday he and Barry had come achingly close to taking a set off Junior and Gary. Will had been serving, and, though his heart was in his throat, he somehow managed to shoot out to a 40–15 lead, startling himself and everyone else on the court with four decent first serves in a row. The fourth was to Gary, who wound up for the kill and skyed the ball off the frame, up toward the ceiling fan, then gave him a sour look, a look that said, "You're not supposed to do this." Then, as Will began his toss for the next serve, Gary muttered something. It sounded like, "All right, motherfucker." Will's left hand seized, the ball just managed to escape his cramped fingers, but, furious, he swung at it anyway, sending it over the box, past the baseline (Gary ducked theatrically), and smack into the backdrop.

"Deep," Gary said.

Will gave him a long stare—and obediently hit the second serve into the net. Gary's thin lips curved ever so slightly up at the corners: the desired result had been produced. Form had been reverted to. Will double-faulted away the next two points, then, at ad out, hit a pathetic pitty-pat to Gary that came back, unreturnable, at two hundred miles an hour. Junior and Gary took the next two games, then six in a row.

Now Will was dreading going into battle with Joel on his side. True, he used to be on the tennis team. A quarter-century ago. And how many times had he played since? He was potbellied and out of shape. And as for competitive spirit—this was a forty-three-year-old guy who worked in a sandwich shop.

They were going to get slaughtered.

Plus, Joel was late. It took twenty minutes to drive to Playdium, in good weather, and it was a quarter of. Will walked into the living room and squinted out the window. No Joel. He looked down at his

children, then at the TV screen, where two villainous-looking crea-
tures were strapped, writhing, to laboratory tables.

"What *is* this?" Will asked.

Silence.

He asked again.

"*Space Ghost,*" Danny said, nasally. He was on what seemed like
his fifth cold since school had started—with the usual concomitant
ear infection, which meant another plastic bottle of pink Ceclor in
the refrigerator, at another forty-four dollars a pop. Will thought
about Leviathan, ominously silent for a week. He thought about his
father's lumps. He looked back at Danny and Rachel, the two of
them oblivious to all this, to death and money, conscious only of
the (barely) animated drama on the screen, where, Will noticed, the
characters' mouths moved when they talked, but their lips didn't
match the words.

"You *like* this?" he asked.

Danny nodded, tranced. But Rachel took the opportunity to
demur. She sat up and brushed one wing of her hair to the side, a
gesture that exactly matched one of Gail's. "*I* don't like it," she
whined. "I want to watch *Pretty Pony.*"

"*Pretty Pony*'s bullshit," Danny said, over his shoulder.

"What?" Will said. "Excuse me?"

"Whoops," Danny said.

Looking on with interest, Rachel brushed her hair to the side
again.

"You bet your bippy, whoops," Will said. "I don't want to hear
that kind of language from you, Daniel J. Weiss."

"Bet my *what?*" Danny said, smiling satirically at his ancient
dad.

"Did you hear me?"

Danny lost the smile, squinching up one side of his mouth. "Yes."

"You hear me?" Will repeated, pointing at his son, surprised at the heat in his voice.

"I'm *sorry*," Danny said, cross himself.

"Daddy, kwee have pancakes?" Rachel asked, a little too brightly.

At this moment, Joel's car horn blew—or rather, bleated weakly, one of its two tones having shorted out or frozen up, or simply died of old age. Will glanced at the VCR clock: ten of.

"Listen, Raitch, could you ask Mommy about that? I gotta go now."

"Mommy's *sleeping*."

"She should be up in a couple of minutes, OK?"

Rachel looked as if she were about to cry.

"Or wake her," Will said. He picked up his tennis bag. "I don't care. Listen, I'm sorry. I'm sorry. I'll be back in a little while." Now they were staring at him instead of the TV. He shrugged apologetically. "See ya, guys."

Neither of them answered as he went out.

Cindy had had a child out of wedlock, Julie told Joel. In 1983. And so Cindy's first cousin Gary and his wife, Ellen, childless, had adopted the baby—her. But the thing is, the thing is, the thing is, Julie told Joel, tripping over the words, the thing is I think Gary's really my father.

Gary?

Gary's dirty, she said, giving him a funny look.

Is that right, Joel said, searching her eyes.

Gary likes family, Julie said.

Is that right.

He always had a thing about Cindy, Julie said.

Who didn't, Joel thought, as he drove through the snow. The thing about bald tires was, you could get some fairly interesting skids going.

When Will opened the rear door of the Impala to put in his tennis bag, he saw the extent of Joel's equipment lying on the plaid-covered seat: a wooden Dunlop Maxply in an old-fashioned wooden press.

He picked up and examined the artifact. "You're kidding, right?" he said, as he opened the front door and got in, the Dunlop in his hand. Broken horn or no, the Impala's heat blower, turned up high, seemed to be working just fine: the car was filled with a cozy greasy old-fashioned car-heat smell.

"About what?" Joel said. He was wearing a white Lacoste shirt, fresh out of the bag, its price tag, still attached to its plastic twig, sticking straight-up from the back of his collar. The tremendous, wrinkled ivory shorts—they had to have been Morris's—looked as though they'd been in a drawer, under a lot of other things, for at least twenty years. Joel was also wearing black socks and blue high-top Keds basketball sneakers. Next to him on the bench seat sat a familiar-looking brown paper bag.

"This racket." Will held up the Dunlop.

Joel took it with his right hand, even though he was driving up the hill. "Isn't it a beautiful thing?" he said, turning it, examining its laminations. Will wished he would watch the road. "They really knew how to make 'em. Strings are a little dried-out, though."

"Joel, it's not 1974 anymore. The game has changed. These guys are packing graphite—they hit the ball a thousand miles an hour."

Joel put the racket down on the seat, picked up the brown paper bag, which contained a bottle of Wild Turkey, and unscrewed the top with one hand. "Hard hitters, are they?" He took a long swig as he turned right, onto Verona Avenue. "I always liked hard hitters," he said.

"We've met," Junior said, delightedly, as he reached over the net and encased Joel's hand. "This is an interesting fella," he told Gary. Will noticed that, for some reason, Junior wouldn't meet his eyes.

"Interesting *suit*," Gary said, noting the big shorts.

"I know your daughter," Joel told him, shaking hands.

Gary's smirk congealed. "You do?"

"Hey, my wife, your daughter—the guy definitely gets around," Junior said.

Gary looked uncomprehendingly at Junior, then at Joel and Will. "Why don't we play some tennis," he said.

The warm-up was strange. Two balls were in play: one between Will and Junior—who, even seventy-eight feet away, still wouldn't meet his glance—and one between Joel and Gary, who, in his purple bandanna headband and crinkly-silky black-and-persimmon jacket and pants, was giving his best imitation of a Tough Pro, turning his shoulders, squinting his eyes, banging hard, sharply spun shots to Joel's forehand and backhand, testing, testing.

It was impossible for Will to tell whether Joel was passing or failing the test, though it didn't look good. He returned a few of Gary's shots with dazzlingly beautiful form—but it was the form of twenty-five years ago, the form of Smith and Lutz and Rosewall and Ashe, elegant and measured and smooth instead of bombing it in. Not that he would've been able to bomb it in with that frame, those strings: all Joel's strokes, Will noticed with a sinking feeling, produced a soft, dull sound, as if they might not quite make it over the net. (He also suddenly remembered the discouraging tendency of Maxplys to explode in midrally—all that lamination was beautiful but not so hardy.)

And then there were Joel's mistakes, which were legion—mishits and just plain misses. He simply whiffed two overheads and three or four volleys. The problem, it seemed, was not just being out of practice—way out of practice—but being overweight. Any shot that called for sudden or extreme movement, stretch or jump or dive, appeared to be more than Joel could handle. After ten minutes, he was red-faced, sweating profusely and panting.

"Are you OK?" Will asked, with some concern, when they convened at netside. Men their age, he was thinking, could have heart attacks. Gary, loose and happy, was standing a few yards away, with his back to them, apparently telling a joke to Junior, who was nodding along and laughing in the right places.

Joel sat down in one of the molded-plastic chairs, huffing and puffing, unable to speak. "Relax," he said, catching his breath after a long moment. "I'm hustling them."

"You're *what?*"

He reached into the old-fashioned red-and-white-vinyl Dunlop racket-head cover, pulled out the brown-bagged pint of Wild Turkey, opened it, and took a long pull. "Here," Joel said, offering it to Will.

"You're crazy," Will said.

"What else is new. Have a drink."

Will pushed the bottle aside. "Listen," he said. "Joel. I don't think we should do this. I mean—I'm sorry to have to say it, but frankly I'm worried you're gonna keel over out there."

"*Look* at those guys," Joel said. His bleary gaze had traveled to the oldsters on Court 2, hacking out an endless point.

"Joel, I'm serious."

Lob, chop, volley; lob, chop, volley—the ball wouldn't stop going. "They look like an orthopedics-supply demonstration," Joel said.

"Joel."

Taking a tremendous swing, one of the old men mishit an overhead smash, causing the ball to land weakly and hop back over the net. The men erupted into laughter. "Atta boy, Sy!" one of them crowed. "Quiet!" someone yelled, deep-voiced, from a couple of courts down.

"Wow," Joel said. "Cool spin."

"Joel, will you listen to me," Will said.

Joel took a moment to return from a distance, then held the bottle directly under Will's chin. "I really think you ought to have a shot."

"Up or down, you guys," Gary called, blithely, over his shoulder.

"Up," Joel said. And then, to Will: "Take some."

Will made a screwy face. "I can't drink in the morning." He shook his head. "I can't drink and play tennis."

"Why not?"

"Up it is," Gary called.

"You can serve," Joel told him. And then, to Will: "Why not?"

"I—"

"Look at you. You're fuckin' gagging, you're so uptight. I'm sure you'll play at the *very* top of your form."

Will gave his friend a dirty look. It wasn't always the best thing, having known someone for thirty-five years.

"Look," Joel said. "These guys are total putzes. One's some kind of criminal, the other would love to be if he only had a brain. Maybe they'll slaughter us—" He paused.

Will waited a second. "And?" he said.

"And—so have a drink," Joel said.

And so Will did.


Gary served first. Four winners, just like that—*boom boom boom boom*. On the last one, a clean ace, Joel dived to his left to try and dig the ball out, got tangled in the side net, tripped as he tried to stand up, then tripped again. Will stared at his own sneakers and shook his head. Gary and Junior slapped hands. Joel went to retrieve the ball, which had shot off behind the backdrop.

"I've been taking some lessons," Gary explained to Will, with a little smile, as they changed ends. Will feigned a smile in return, then looked over to the green backdrop for his partner. No Joel. He noticed that the old men had stopped playing, and that three of them were staring at their own backdrop, where their fourth had apparently also gone to retrieve a ball. "Hey Harry!" one of them called, smirking. "What are you, lost back there?"

After what felt like a very long time, Will walked to the rear of the court—and Joel emerged from the fold in the hanging vinyl, looking delighted.

"Hey, it's really different back there," he said.

"Joel, we're getting killed here."

Harry came out of the curtain on his court, holding his lost ball aloft triumphantly. "Congratulations," one of his partners said dryly. Harry winked at Joel; Joel winked back.

"That's the most amazing guy," Joel said. "Take a guess how old he is."

Will put up his hands. "Joel, I—"

"A hundred thirty-five," Joel said. "Can you believe it?"

"No," said Will. "I can't."

"It's really different back there," Joel repeated. "Hey, nice serving," he said to Gary.

"I took some lessons," Gary repeated.

"Hey, they're really working," Joel told him. Gary beamed, accepting the compliment in full, as Joel and Will walked by. Junior took it all in, raising his big eyebrows. "You mook," he said to Gary. "He's hustling you."

Gary shrugged. "What do I care? He can't play for shit."

Will and Joel stood at their baseline. "You're loaded," Will said.

"Lemme serve first," Joel said.

"You're *drunk*, Joel."

"Come on. Gimme them balls."

Will gave him a look—then gave him the tennis balls. Joel put two of them in the pocket of the giant shorts, stationed himself at the baseline, and, with a brief, inward stare, tossed a ball up and hit it. The dead strings of the old wooden racket didn't make much of a sound, but Will, standing at net, saw the ball land almost noiselessly in Junior's service box and skim off toward the side net at what looked like two inches above the court.

"Hey," Gary said.

"Looks like it hit something on the court," said Junior.

"Play a let," Gary said.

Will looked back toward his partner. "What did it hit?" Joel asked, calmly.

Junior shrugged. "Must've been something."

"See anything?" Joel asked.

Junior walked up, hands on hips, and peered down at the court. "Huh," he said.

"All right, all right," Gary said. "Play it. Fifteen-love."

"Yeah?" Junior asked him.

Gary was standing in receiving position, squinting and wielding his racket like a samurai. He nodded. "Play it," he said. "Come on, big boy."

Will glanced back and saw Joel go into his service motion again, his eyes rolling up trancelike for a second as the toss rose. The racket was moving very fast just before contact, but then the strings seemed to just barely brush the side of the ball, which instantly went into a severe spin, landed in Gary's box, and jackknifed off to the left at shoe level. Gary made a disgusted face. "Come on," he whined. "Gimme something to *hit*."

But Joel wouldn't give them anything to hit. His serves sliced, dived, skidded—they did everything but land in such a place, and such a way, as to allow a solid answer. It was as if the ball had suddenly turned into a badminton birdie.

The score stood at 1–1. "Harry gave me a couple of pointers," Joel told Will.

After Junior's first serve to Will—the usual back-spinning corkscrew, which Will ran up and shoveled onto the waiting racket of Gary, who killed it—Joel took his partner aside for a moment.

"He always serves that same serve?"

"Yeah."

"Well, what are you standing back there for?"

"He moves it around sometimes."

"On purpose?"

"I don't know."

"Let's see," Joel said.

He walked in and stood a foot back from the service line to await Junior's next delivery. Taking note of it, Junior shook his head, smiling. "This guy," he said.

He served. Joel caught the ball barely off the court surface and redirected it into the air above and then behind the quickly inrushing Junior. It landed softly in the backcourt and hopped off into the corner. Junior and Gary looked at each other.

Fortified by Wild Turkey, Will managed to approximate some of what he saw Joel doing. Except for the serving, of course. His serve was the same old serve he always served, yet all at once, instead of mostly going out, it was mostly going in. The knots in his shoulders seemed to have melted; he was moving like liquid. He and Joel were covering the court like a dance team—a feat that was made all the easier by Gary, who had begun to unravel.

"Cunt!" he shrieked, after netting a backhand sitter. The oldsters kept playing unperturbed; the Japanese women two courts down glanced over nervously. Junior came over to Gary, wrapped his arm around his shoulder, and, with the gentlest solicitousness, guided him to the backcourt, where he patted him on the cheek as Gary stood shaking his head over and over.

"We got 'em on the run," Joel said. The score was 4–3, theirs, with Joel about to serve again.

"I'll drink to that," Will said, and giggled.

"Maybe you better slow down on the medicine, pardner."

"What about you?"

"Me? I got practice."

Junior was walking up to the net, waving his racket. "Gentle-men," he called. "Gentlemen." Gary was tossing his racket and ban-danna into his bag.

"I'm afraid we're going to have to call it a day," Junior said. "My partner is slightly injured."

"Gee, what happened, Gar?" Joel called. His tone was all sin-cere concern.

"I had this shoulder pull," Gary grumbled. He wouldn't look up from his bag. "Shouldn't have played today, anyway."

"Aw, I'm sorry, Gar. Hey—maybe I'll catch you another time."

Gary pointed at Joel. "Not if I see you first, asshole."

"Hey," Joel said, throwing his palms out and shrugging blamelessly.

Junior grabbed Gary around the shoulders and pinched his cheek. "Gary, Gary," he croaked. "Gary, Gary." He wrinkled his big nose explanatorily at Joel, his slightly walled eyes still avoiding Will. "He's in a little bit of pain," he said. "Makes him grumpy."

Joel held up the brown bag. "Drink?" he asked Gary.

Gary started to lunge at Joel, but Junior's giant hands held him back effortlessly.

"Easy, Gar," Joel said. "The shoulder."

"Fuck you," Gary said.

Junior slapped his partner lightly on the cheek as if it were all a joke, still holding Gary back as he pointed to Joel. "This is a very interesting fella," he told him.

# 21

"What does a girl have to do to get noticed?"

Joel looks up from the counter at Patti, who's standing in front of him in her silver fur coat, black leather pants, high heels, and big round sunglasses. She quickly pulls the lapel of the coat to one side—Joel sees that she's naked above the waist, and that what he sees is all he imagined—then closes it.

He swallows. "Um," he says. "Uhh—hum. That would do it, I guess."

"I need to talk to you," she says.

He looks over at Larry, who's moving his bulk, fast, around the back of the shop, getting out the lunch stuff. It's ten of eleven. "Hey Lar?" he calls.

Larry glances up, sees Patti, and smiles. "Yes, Joel?" he says, in a sweetness-and-light rumble.

"Could I take a little break? I'll make it up to you."

Still gazing at Patti, the big man sighs. "You're killin' me, Joel," he says. "I get stuck alone on lunch, I'm dead."

"I won't be long," Joel says. He looks at Patti, who's smiling strangely. "Ten minutes," he says.

"—twenty minutes," she says, at the same time.

Larry rolls his eyes to the ceiling. "Go," he says.

★ ★ ★

"What's up?" Joel asks, as they drive up Overlook. Patti's going fast, the rear end of the Mercedes thudding dully in the dips on the steep hill. With an old reflex, he glances back for the roller-coaster view out the car's rear window, and sees the white-tan street dropping away into the whole sad vista: bare trees, smug big houses, and, down and beyond them, the gray-bristled plain—relieved here and there, in the middle distance, by mud-brown apartment blocks—extending toward the sad blue-gray city.

"Norman's freaking out," she tells him. "He thinks his partners are cheating him, he thinks people are coming to get him, he thinks . . . Jesus—" She shakes her head. "He thinks I'm doing your friend."

"Will?"

She nods. Her coat has fallen slightly open over her chest; as much as he wants to look, he reaches over and pulls it closed. Barely aware of his hand, she glances at him: her sunglasses have slid halfway down her pug nose, and he can see tears rimming her eyes.

"But you're not, right?" He's half-kidding. Which also means half-serious.

It brings an explosion. "Jesus Christ, Joel! Don't be like Norman! I don't fucking *need* two Normans on my hands!"

He feels obscurely flattered, but manages to look contrite. "I'm sorry," he says.

She shakes her head. "Jesus Christ."

"I'm sorry, Pats."

"He's getting paranoid, and it's scaring me," she cries, hoarsely, sliding right past the stop sign at the crest of the hill as if it weren't there. "Goddamn it!" She pounds the steering wheel, half-sounding the horn. "I fucking *hate* it when he's this way."

"OK, OK, slow down, Pats."

"I *hate* it!"

"Slow down. You hear me?"

She takes him literally, slowing the car to a crawl. They're in the middle of Woodwick on a weekday morning; the only living thing in sight, among the large white houses, is the odd squirrel, foraging in the frozen grass. There's something about the particular brown-gray-green of frozen lawns, and the jittery hopefulness of squirrels, that Joel finds nearly unbearable; he shakes his head and looks back at her.

"I mean, is there any basis for any of this?" he asks her. "Are his partners cheating him? Could anybody be coming to get him? Who *are* Norman's partners, anyhow?"

"Momo and Salvi."

"Ah."

"Fuckin' Momo and Salvi. I *hate* their slimeball asses."

"And so, could Momo and Salvi, maybe, *be* mad at Norman about anything?"

She turns right, at the bottom of a shallow hill, onto Glenview—Cindy's old street. She drives for a minute, not saying anything.

"Pats?"

"I don't know," she says. "I don't want to talk about it."

"OK. We don't have to talk about it, Pats."

"I mean, I don't even want to talk about it."

"It's fine, it's fine."

Her tears are flowing. "We have a child, you know. Did you know that?"

His stomach bucks. "You and Ju—— Norman?"

She nods, once, almost imperceptibly.

"I wasn't aware," Joel says. "No."

"Could you hand me a cigarette?" she asks. He reaches into the little black bag sitting between them and fishes a cigarette out of a gold-foil-wrapped pack. He hands it to her, and looks back in the bag. Prescription bottles, Tic-Tacs, a white-wrapped Tampax, Visine, makeup cases . . .

"There aren't any matches," he says.

She points to the dashboard. "The lighter," she says. The cigarette is just barely hanging onto her open lower lip.

"Silly me," Joel says, pushing in the round plunger. "I haven't used one of these for years."

"In Overbrook," she says. "For all his goddamn little life. Spina bifida."

"I'm sorry."

The plunger pops out with its small click. He touches the orange-glowing coil—the faint electric warmth smells delicious—to the tip of the cigarette, producing an even more delicious blue cloud. Sucking in the smoke as if her life depended on it, she keeps glancing over to her left. "Ah," she says, and turns left onto a little houseless dead end, Pierce Court.

He's always wondered about this street. It runs up a small rise for only a hundred feet or so before stopping, on the edge of the reservation, at the base of a water tower, a great, looming, lollipop-shaped thing he's always been aware of but never entirely noticed before. There's a barbed-wire-topped chain-link fence around the base of the tower, whose cold, pale, sad white-green surface is dotted with rust and scarred with some elderly carved graffiti. Patti stops the car.

"What's here?" Joel asks.

But she's already gotten out. "Come on," she says, jerking her head sideways.

He closes his door and follows her. She's clumping purposefully through the dry leaves, into the woods, puffing on the cigarette, the fur coat swishing busily as she moves. Joel hugs himself as he walks: it's *cold* out—below freezing—and he left the Sub Shop without his jacket. "Where we going, Pats?" he asks, as gently as possible.

But she swishes on without answering. After a couple of hundred yards, up a ridge and down the side of a steepish hill, she stops. He stops, too.

They listen. The winter woods are utterly silent—a strange sound. Then, from the white sky, comes comfort, something: the tiny roar of a jet, miles above, headed west.

She tosses the cigarette to the side—it lands on a rock and dies slowly—then takes off the fur coat and lays it on the leaves. "I want you to fuck me, Joel," she says, matter-of-factly.

He stares at her.

"It's time," she says.

"It's cold," Joel says.

She kneels in front of him. "Here, I'll warm you up."

"Pats."

She opens his zipper; he says no more. All the while, he listens. The jet's roar fades off; the silence returns, absolute. The only sounds are her mouth and his shoes, skittering, as he tries to keep his balance in the dry leaves.

"Come on, Joel," she says, finally, unzipping the leather pants and lying back onto her coat.

He nods down between her raised thighs, their flesh hot by his ears, and—after looking for a second at what really seems to him like another face, one expressing desire as clearly as the one he's more used to—eats, greedily, tasting the harmonica taste he's dreamed of and missed for . . . how long now? Seventeen years, he calculates. He stops thinking. His prick is jammed into the icy leaves; it doesn't matter. After a while he rises up along her belly and, like a hungry infant, takes one breast, then the other, in his mouth, then her nicotine-sharp tongue, then her breasts again. Her body is wonderfully warm, but the air is so cold. Patti pulls the coat over both of them, as best she can, like a blanket; it keeps falling off, exposing his bare butt. The hill they're lying on—it smells like iron—rises up and up and up, then, after a long while, drops away, as steeply as a dream. They're tumbling, like Jack and Jill. The strangest thing—he keeps feeling, even as they fall through the deepest silence, that someone is watching them.

"Oh, Pats," he groans. "Oh, Patti Ann." He falls onto her. She's smiling, her still-wet, long-lashed eyes closed.

It's then that he looks up and sees the deer, not twenty feet away, staring. And thinks: Cindy.

# 22

He *listened*. And made her laugh: that was the thing. It felt, to Gail, as though she hadn't laughed in a long time.

"Oh—my—God," Lynnie whispered, putting her hand on her chest. "You're *joking*."

Gail stared at her, barely suppressing a smile.

"OhmyGod ohmyGod ohmyGod," Lynnie said. "You're *not* joking."

They were sitting, once more, in Le Poivrier, each with a mostly drunk glass of Chardonnay in front of her. Gail's glass was her second, actually: it had been halfway through the first that she'd decided to tell Lynnie about Mario; she'd briefly reconsidered, then ordered more wine to help her get through it. Now she looked baffled, happy, and ashamed all at once, and Lynnie couldn't get her mouth closed.

"What was it like—I mean, I don't even know what I should be asking you—where to *begin*."

"It was, it was—" Gail fluttered her hand.

"May I just interrupt a second?" Lynnie said, holding up an index finger. She was a little drunk: it turned her normal perkiness sententious. "I just want to say that I have slept with only *one* other person besides Howard in my *entire life*, that it was before I was married, and that this is *not* a boast."

Gail was staring off toward a corner of the room. "It was . . . you know," she told her friend, who didn't even begin to know. "Fun and sexy and dirty and scary and sweet—and *insane*. I mean, I'll *never* do it again. Never. I mean—Lynnie, you have to *swear* you won't breathe a word of this to *any*one."

Lynnie made an X on her chest. "As God is my witness." She sipped her wine, and looked kittenish. "So. Where'd you go?"

Gail put her hand over her mouth, then spread the fingers slightly and whispered through them: "Sheraton." She blushed hotly.

"Oh my G——you mean the one out on Route Eighty? With all the mirror glass on it?"

Gail nodded.

"Now, how do you do that?" Lynnie had suddenly turned practical: she might have been asking for decorating tips. "I mean, do you use cash or plastic, whose name do you register un—"

"You have to promise you won't tell anyone, OK, Lynnie?"

Lynnie stared at Gail, who looked, for a moment, as if she might be about to cry. "Gailie, sweetie—" she began, softly.

"*Not* even Howard. Please?"

Lynnie snorted, and drained her wine. "Please. Howard and I never talk about anything anyway."

# 23

The phone ringing and ringing, off in the muffled depths of the house, wakes him. Joel blinks at the clock—it says eight-twenty—and fights panic for a moment before realizing: it's Sunday. Poorly named in this instance. The weak December sun struggling with shadows like stone. He picks up the empty bottle lying by the pillow, looks at it, then tilts it up to drain the last few drops onto his tongue, where they burn sweetly, the sunlight that's missing. He has, he now realizes, been dreaming about Pats—the first time ever—and, more's the pity, Junior. A house by the sea, enormous waves, gunfire. He puts the empty on the night table, sits stiffly on the side of the bed, slips his feet into the new brown slippers Irma bought him, as a surprise, on Steven's birthday. The phone will stop ringing, he thinks. It doesn't stop. The slippers feel cool and smell good—like Hubert's, the Main Street shoe store long since closed and turned into a Blockbuster. The succotash-yellow carpet, tilted floor mirrors, big Keds display, March of Dimes jar on the counter, that black-and-silver foot-measurer with the width-slider that felt good against your arch. Always wondering if shoe salesmen made any money. They seemed so *jaunty*. And, suffusing everything, the intoxicating perfume of leather, promising that this pair of shoes would be the ones that lasted forever. Who knew? Maybe, despite space and time, Irma had simply stridden into Blockbuster and demanded, and received, a box of slippers, size 9E. If anyone could bring it off, Joel thought, she could.

There are three phones in the house: one in Irma's room (she keeps the ringer off, the heavy drapes drawn, her eyeshades on; early on a Sunday morning, lying next to the empty space left by the man she slept next to for twenty-five years, she might as well be a stiff herself), one in the kitchen, and one in the maid's room at the end of the upstairs hall, where Violet stayed five nights a week until she began having to take care of her own mother, now in her nineties. Joel pads down the hall to Violet's room, running his fingers, as always, along the dingy patterned wallpaper. Halfway down the hall, there's a seam, the paperhanger having misjudged and left a vertical line of partial and broken fleur-de-lis. It hurts Joel to see the broken pattern. When he comes to the seam, when his fingertips find it, what frequently happens is what happens now: padding toward him, from the old bathroom where coats in garment bags now hang, comes Steven, wet from the shower, with a white towel knotted around his waist. One dog tag around his neck, one clinking on his blue left big toe.

"Hey," Joel says.

Clink. Clink. Steven smiles a little, but says nothing. His eyes say everything. *You know*, they say. Steven's eyes stay on Joel as Steven walks by. Joel looks down at his brother's blue feet. He can smell wet hair and Dial soap—and something else. And something else. He blinks, and the hall is empty.

This is just the way it always happens.

The phone rings and rings.


The telephone in the maid's room is an old-fashioned black dial unit, with an actual bell built in instead of the electronic tootler they use nowadays: its ringing has a crisp, glassy-metallic tingle that cuts into his head like an axe. Who who who? he thinks, as it rings for the thirtieth time; and why why why? Nobody has died, at least: every-one has died already. Moving as fast as he can—not very fast—he grabs the heavy receiver. "This better be good," he says, into it.

"Joel?" the hoarse female voice says.

"Pats?"

"Joel, it's Julie. Julie Berkowitz."

He sits on the side of the old single bed. The light in the room, through the dried-out drawn shade, is rotten peach–pink. "Julie," he says, groggily, trying to make sense of it. "Is everything OK?"

"Not especially, no."

"What is it?"

"Listen—Joel. Could I borrow some money?"

"Sure. You pregnant?"

Silence on the other end.

"I mean, that's what it would be in the movies," he says. "Right?"

"I don't know if I'm pregnant. That's a good question, actually."

"This is the first time it's occurred to you?"

"It's not for that," she says. "I have a friend in—in trouble."

"But this friend isn't you."

"Me?"

"Right. Like the movies again. You *say* it's a friend, but it's really—"

"It's not me. It's my boyfriend—Rome. He's in goddamn jail."

Joel lies down on Violet's bed. A faint dusty smell of lavender rises up like a little song: *Jesus loves me, this I knoww* . . . "Ooh, Julie. I have to say, this doesn't come as a huge surprise."

"No, Joel. Listen, it's a bullshit bust. There's this asshole Verona cop—"

"Which one?"

"Stuie? Like, big muscles and a little dick? He's always strut-
ting ar——"

"Oh yeah, yeah. I know the one."

"Anyway. He's, like, totally dirty. I mean, Gary gave him a
hundred to fix a speeding ticket—Gary's *got* this hundred, folded
next to his license, and Stuie's the pathetic dickhead who took it.
Now he treats Gary like the other mayor or something."

"Uh-huh." Joel stifles a contented yawn. It's not completely
unpleasant coming back to the land of the living, lying and staring
at the spotty ceiling on a Sunday morning, listening to the plight of
a young damsel in distress.

"So Stuie's got it completely in for Rome, not to mention Gary,
so Rome's standing around with some friends on the street last
night—I mean, it was late, I know, he shouldn't have been—" Her
voice breaks.

"Julie?"

"I'm sorry," she says. "I was up all night. I mean, I was the one
he called."

"You weren't with him?"

She blows her nose, ignores it. "So this fucking *Stuie*," she says,
"tells them to move along, then drops a dime bag through his pants
leg or something and says it's Rome's. Which—I mean, he *knows*
Rome's been busted before, he used to deal but he *doesn't* anymore.
He doesn't even *use*."

"But you weren't there? With him?"

"No, I was home. Fuckin' grounded. Fuckin' Gary."

"But you believe him?"

"Believe — who? Rome?"

Joel can see it's hopeless. "How much do you need?" he asks.

He can hear her suck in her breath. "A lot."

"How much?"

"It's a thousand. But I *swear*—look, I have some stocks and shit, I just have to—"

He sighs, audibly.

Her voice softens. "Joel, I *know* it's a lot. I know. I could . . . you know."

He feels an involuntary thrum. Down there. "What?"

"I mean, besides paying you back."

Something in his stomach feels sickly sweet. He rolls over onto his side and looks at the phone as if it were she herself. "Julie, what are we talking about here?"

Her voice is small. "*You* know, Joel."

"No. No. I mean, you can have the money, period. Pay me when you pay me."

There's a silence. "Oh, Joel. I love you."

He blinks. "You love *him*, right?"

"Rome?"

"Yeah. Rome."

"Oh, yeahh," she sighs, her voice like melted caramel.

# 24

The Dow broke ten thousand on a Friday afternoon, on the announcement of yet another dip in employment, and in giddy anticipation of the turn of the millennium in two weeks. The news coincided with, or perhaps precipitated, an end-of-business-day call to Jack, at last, from Barney Jessel—Leviathan's owner, an old friend and adversary of Jack's—making an official offer of $4.5 million for Weiss Containers. That evening Jack relayed the news to Will, who, standing at the kitchen phone, started smiling, then couldn't stop. His lungs seemed filled with a light and expanding substance, maybe with light itself. *Rich rich rich*, he thought, his breath feeling cool and sweet. *Money money money.*

"That's amazing," he told Jack. "Incredible."

"What?" Gail said, from the dining room, where she and the children were sitting at dinner. Danny, who had turned his two index fingers into bull horns, was feinting menacingly at Rachel, who whined, "Stop it. *Stop* it."

Will held up a hand, both to the children and Gail.

"Incredible inshmedible," Jack growled, happily, on the phone. "You think I took it?"

"You didn't?"

"That *gonef*. I told him not a penny under five, or no deal."

God, Jack had balls. "So what'd he say?"

"He said no deal."

Something in Will's stomach did a little roller-coaster dive. Gail was watching him closely, her eyes widening. "Jack—" Will began, then said: "He did?"

"Correct."

"And then?"

"And then he hung up. Bang." But Jack was clearly relishing all this, clearly had a story to tell.

"But?" Will said, pleading.

"But I knew I had him by the short hairs. Don't you get it, Willy? You have to appreciate our value to Barney. West of the Hudson, to him, is terra incognita. The wilderness. We're his warm-water port out here."

"So?"

"So I looked at my telephone and counted to twenty."

"And?"

"And I didn't get to twelve before it rang again. Barney. Of course. Four point seven-five, he says, not a dime higher."

"And you said?"

"I said, 'Barney, I don't want to be a *chozzer*, but I don't want to be a schmuck. You know as well as I do that anything under four-nine is giving away the keys to the store.'"

"And Barney said?"

"'Four-eight, Jack. Take it or leave it. That's the very best I can do.'"

"And you said?"

Gail's hand was over her mouth. Even the children had picked it up, were watching him now.

"I give a big sigh, like he's really busting my chops. 'OK, Barney,' I say. 'OK. If that's the best you can do.'"

"Four point eight?" Will's voice had risen an octave. Gail was mouthing *Oh my God*.

"See, I would've taken the four and three-quarters, but I wanted to give Barney a little workout," Jack said.

"Jack, you're a fu——" he began, then looked at the children. "You're a genius," his son told him, quietly.

"Our lawyers meet with his lawyers next Thursday afternoon. So that's where our extra fifty goes."

"Four point eight," Will repeated to Gail, shaking his head, after he'd hung up.

"Incredible," she said.

"Four point eight what?" Danny said.

"Times forty percent, minus capital gains, plus the portfolio and house equity—God, even minus debt, we're officially millionaires," Will told Gail.

"Jee-zuz," Gail said. Her eyes were shining.

"Four point eight what?" Danny said.


"Oh," Gail said, holding up an expensive-looking cream-colored envelope. "Did you see this?"

They were standing in the kitchen later, the children finally asleep, straightening up and talking, in a pleasant daze, about the money. Usually, by this point in the evening, they were both exhausted; tonight they both felt as though they were going a mile a minute. It felt like a long time since they'd talked, since they'd had something to talk about. Everything seemed new, bathed in a golden glow. Anything was possible. Will looked at the envelope. An ambassadorial appointment? A bequest from a forgotten uncle?

"It's an invitation," she said. "New Year's Eve. Your tennis partner's house."

"Really? Barry?"

"It says Gary Berkowitz, Skyview Drive."

"Gary? You're kidding."

She handed him the card. *Welcome the Millennium with Gary and Ellen*, it said. *Dinner. Dancing. Black tie.*

"Fancy neighborhood," Gail said, raising a mischievous eyebrow.

He took her meaning. Fancy neighborhoods were now theirs to explore and assess, without fear of envy. Woodwick was now disdainable on a higher level, perhaps it was even slightly sympathetic. Their money, after all, would be new money, too. Will shrugged. "So maybe we'll go," he offered, in a tone that—he now remembered— he used to use, long ago, when they'd done things that were silly and fun.

Patti, it occurred to him, would probably also be there.

Gail shrugged back—he couldn't believe it—flirtatiously. "So maybe we'll go."


They made love that night, of course, and it was strange: he began as her charger, the rampaging millionaire, but then he started thinking about the money, and wondering precisely what it would mean, and how they would spend it, and the numbers proliferated in his head, distracting him, which prolonged her pleasure, and, finally, diminished his. Gail, though, was thrilled, transported, and thoroughly dirty-guilty, the guilt and the gold alchemizing into an excitement she'd never felt before, Will and Mario blending into an amalgam-man, funny and attentive and rich and perfect. Perfect. She lay smiling afterward—it was all so strange and funny—as he curled onto his side, thinking, thinking, into the night.

And this too stopped him: she hadn't been so passionate in a long, long time. But what, he wondered, had it had to do with *him*?

Tennis the next morning was not as wonderful as Will would have expected. For one thing, he'd told himself his news so many times that he was beginning to have to remind himself to be excited. For another, the lessons he had learned with Joel weren't quite applicable to playing with Barry, who was back in all his monosyllabic splendor. The court chemistry had returned to normal—Gary smirked as he ate up Barry's steady but eminently returnable serve, seeming to take a special pleasure in drilling killers at Will when he stood at net. Junior was his old, bluff self, though Will noticed that he still wouldn't quite meet his eyes. Worst of all, his double faulting had returned, not quite in full force, but in ragged adamant patches, which Barry now accepted with a grim, philosophical air. Will's little skill-uptick had come and gone, with Barry none the wiser. After each double fault, he felt like grabbing Barry around the neck and saying, "I was good, I was good, I was good—when I had a *partner*."

By the afternoon, though, Will had forgotten about his loss and started to think, with fresh little bursts of surprise once more, about his coming gains. He insisted on picking up Joel in the Tundra: the roads were still covered with the salted residue of Thursday's snowstorm, and, too, Will wanted to take enjoyment in the car he now knew he'd be able to solidly afford. Joel, though, seemed glum as he trudged down his driveway, his hands thrust into the pockets of his green duffle coat.

"Hey, I could've used you there this morning," Will said expansively, as Joel got in. Joel grunted. The inside of the car was lit with the rusty sunlight of a winter three-thirty; in this light, in profile, his friend's face, Will noticed, looked exceptionally puffy. His hair was sticking up in unkempt tufts. He looked as if he'd just woken up.

"You OK?" Will asked.

Joel tilted his head grudgingly. "OK, OK, I'm OK," he grumbled. His left hand came out of the coat pocket with a brown paper bag. "Drink?"

Will smiled happily and simply. "No, thanks."

Joel looked at him for the first time. "Oh no, it's money," he said.

Now Will was grinning.

"So it's finally come?" Joel said. "Your ship? You're a zillionaire?"

"Only a millionaire. Just."

Joel clicked his tongue. "Ah well," he said, unscrewing the bottle top. "Zillions can't be far away." He upended the whisky, shakily.

"You sure you're OK?" The Tundra, he was cozily delighted to notice, was handling lower Longview's ultrasteep uphill—just before the summit, the angle was so extreme that you looked through your windshield straight up into sky—with perfect aplomb, even on salty snow.

"It's funny," Joel began, as they bumped over the lip of the hilltop, and vistas of the white-shrouded golf course opened out on either side of them. "My God," he suddenly breathed. "*Look* at that."

"What?" Will said.

Joel pointed at the course with his bottle-holding hand. The sun had just vanished in the bare trees, but the snow still held a greenish reflection of sky. "Pretty," Will smiled.

Joel stared at him. "Pretty," he repeated. "You said 'pretty'?"

"What?"

"Christ," Joel said, shaking his head. He took another hit from the bottle and stared out his window. People with children, he was thinking, were idiots.

"Joel, listen—" Will began, irritatedly.

Joel put up a hand. "Wait a second," he said. "Do you smell chop suey?"

"Chop *suey*?"

"Irma used to make chop suey a long time ago. I thought I smelled it somewhere. I thought—God, maybe I have a brain tumor."

Will glanced over at his friend, who was hunched down against the door, cradling the bottle. "Look, Joel," he said. "You don't have to make me feel like an asshole just because I happened to make some money."

"*Au contraire, mon frère,*" Joel said.

"Meaning?"

"Meaning, if anyone's the asshole around here, it's gotta be me, *n'est-ce pas?*"

Will, who secretly felt this to be true, tried not to smile. "Joel, you're not an asshole."

Joel sat up a little and pointed to the left. "Let's cruise down Heatherdell," he said. "Go through the gate, see if Cindy's at home."

"Joel, for God's sake, she's—"

"Shh," Joel said, putting up a hand, shooting his friend a sardonic look. "Indulge me."

★ ★ ★

Heatherdell in the winter dusk was an enchanted lane of hokey Christmas decorations, the little box-houses festooned with giant Santas and candy canes and reindeer, and colored lights—lights that, for Will, triggered a confusing inchoate glop of happy-sad memories, memories he was just as happy to dismiss. He stared straight ahead as he drove. Joel, though, commanded him to go slow, and gazed right and left with shining eyes, taking gulp after gulp from the bottle. "Wowee," he kept saying. "Whoa."

Then they passed through the gate into Woodwick, whose big houses had no decorations and few lights. Lapsing into silence, Joel drained what was left of the bottle and sat glumly as Will obediently stopped in front of Cindy's old house, which was completely dark, its walk and driveway unshoveled. They sat there a long time, saying nothing.

"OK?" Will finally said.

"She's not fuckin' home," Joel said, thickly. "Not fuckin' home."

"Joel—"

"What? What fucking words of wisdom do you have for me? Huh?"

"I have to get back to my family."

Joel rolled down his window, admitting a draft of shockingly cold air, and hooked the empty over the car's roof and toward Cindy's snow-shrouded lawn. It fell short, shattering on the street. A porch light came on next door.

"Great," Will said, shifting into first.

"Get back to your family," Joel said.

"That's where I'm going."

"Get back to your fucking family."

"Joel."

"Take me home. I gotta get back to my fucking family, too."

Joel huddled into the car door, staring bright-eyed out the window as they moved through Woodwick. Then they turned a corner, and Will saw an apparition. Ahead on the left, among the dark white lawns, sat one big house entirely covered in colored lights. Flashing Santas, reindeer, giant candy canes. The display illuminated the entire block. "Jesus," he said. "Who lives there?"

"You're kidding me," Joel said, wiping his nose.

"What?"

"You're fucking kidding me. You've been living in Verona—how long?—and you don't know whose fucking house that is?"

"Joel, give me a break. I don't know."

Joel shook his head sadly at Will's overwhelming ignorance.

"Please. Joel. Tell me?"

"Sally C.," Joel said, in the tone of someone explaining something to a particularly ignorant child.

"Who?" Will asked.

"Sally Calamari, the big-deal mobster. Don't you know *anything* about your fucking town?"

"Jesus, look at that car," Will said, gazing at a long, cherry-red Cadillac with two men sitting inside. The driver, who turned his big sad face to them as they went past, was Junior.

# 25

Will walked out of the house two mornings later to find his tires cut to ribbons, all four of them, right in his own driveway. It looked as if someone had taken a long, loving time doing it. The Tundra sat down on its rims in the gravel, as if stuck in quicksand. The Cassiopeia perched triumphantly alongside, untouched.

He stood staring at this incredible sight, tears in his eyes. The thing of it was—how could anyone have known this?—Will loved his tires. There were certainly times he didn't even like, let alone love, his children; and he wasn't at all sure if he loved Gail anymore; but he always knew he loved his tires. (There had even been a night, not long after Jack had told him about the lumps, when he'd managed to lull himself back to sleep at three-thirty by thinking about them.) They were Nakamuras, wider than wide, with a tread you could sink the tip of your thumb into and—this was the best part— no bulgy sidewall, no raised white lettering. Will hated that corny look: it was like driving around on decorated balloons, it was for housewives in tricked-up Subarus. (Or Cassiopeias.) The Nakamuras were black and mean and subtle, guaranteed not to hydroplane, and they looked good dirty.

Now they didn't look very good at all.

"Jesus Christ! Who would do such a thing! Jesus Christ!" Will screamed, stomping back into the kitchen and flinging his briefcase onto the floor. Danny and Rachel, sitting at the counter with their bowls of cereal, were staring at him instead of the TV for a change. Gail looked outraged, but not about the tires.

"Will you *stop* it?" she hissed, fiercely protective of the children's ears. "What's the *trouble?*" Her tone was less than solicitous.

He told her what the goddamn trouble was, his pitch only slightly muted, and she shook her head at the vagaries of suburban life. "Someone ripped out half of the Richmans' pachysandras a couple of weeks ago and left them in the middle of the street," she said. "Kids are doing stuff like this these days."

"Kids?" Danny said, looking interested.

"Big kids," Gail explained. "Teenagers."

"Whoa," Danny said, impressed.

"Well, if I find out which teenager it was, I'm gonna serve him his nuts on a platter."

Gail gave him a faint, pitying smile. "That's nice," she said. "Teach your son how to talk."

Danny and Rachel turned their heads to watch for Will's response. He had none.

"Come on, guys," Gail told the children. "School time." They hopped off their stools like obedient ducklings; she zippered their fat bright parkas and helped them into their big backpacks as Will stood in the middle of the kitchen, his mouth still open. Gail put on her long lavender down coat, jingled her keys purposefully, and, without looking back once, led them out the back door. Rachel didn't look back, either. Danny did. "'Bye, Dad," he said. "Sorry about your car."

Will was three hours late for work that day. He could have taken a cab straight in or rented a car, but something primal made him want to stay with the Tundra until things were set right. Things weren't set right. A dozen phone calls later (insurance agent, Saab dealership, various tire stores within a thirty-mile radius; he spent a lot of time listening to cheery hold music and clenching his teeth), Will had found out just how special the Nakamuras were: there wasn't a full set of them to be found in the entire metropolitan area. They were on back order from Yokohama. So he had two choices—let the Tundra languish on its rims for seven to ten days ("optimistically," admitted the single even vaguely sympathetic tire-store guy, whose name was Attila) or buy other tires. He bought other tires. By a little after twelve noon, courtesy of a candy apple–red tow truck sent by Attila from Vulcan Goodyear on Route 22, the Tundra had risen onto a set of new Falcons—with bulging sidewalls and raised white letters—and Will's American Express account had a brand-new, fourteen-hundred-dollar hole in it. An insurance check for six hundred and change—the bullshit depreciated value of the Nakamuras—would arrive in its own sweet time.

After the tow-truck driver, an unreasonably cheerful and vigorous young–Kirk Douglas lookalike (greasy square jaw, gleaming teeth), had driven off, Will stood and stared miserably at his car. If he squinted, it wasn't so bad—but it was still bad. The whole aesthetic had been sabotaged, even from head-on, where you didn't have to look at the goddamn sidewalls: the new tires' tread was inferior, their chunkiness less chunky. They looked pencil-necked.

At least Layla, who had adroitly fielded his morning's worth of messages, was sympathetic to his plight: this sort of thing, she told him, prettily shaking her head, went on in her neighborhood all the time. "Maybe someone don't like you," she said, in her hoarse, delicious voice, with a regretful look. "Maybe, pardon my language, you pissed somebody off."

Will thought about it as he sifted through the messages. Who wouldn't like *him*? (Gail didn't seem to, especially, but he didn't think she'd slash his tires.) He was a nice guy, he paid his bills, he was always kind to pets and children. He may have coveted his neighbor's wife (and his assistant, as well as any number of incorrect objects of desire), but he had the good taste, or the cowardice, to keep it to himself. Of course he'd immediately thought of Junior, but then, just as quickly, had put the thought out of his mind: the idea of Junior slashing tires—or paying someone to slash tires—was just too absurd. As was the idea that Junior had any notion of Will's intricate fantasies about Patti.

Will tried to think of the last time he'd had an altercation of any kind, let alone said an unpleasant word to anyone outside of his immediate family. A schoolyard fight in fifth grade was the last thing he could remember. He was nice, too nice. He thought of the guy in the parking lot at the box store, asking him what he was going to do about it. What was he going to do about anything? Just move on through, sidestepping when necessary.

How, he wondered, would Jack have handled the whole thing? Today was Wednesday, Jack day: Will would have to report. He always anticipated their lunches with severely mixed emotions, never more so than now, when he'd literally be in and out of the office, pausing to return a few calls before jumping in his aesthetically compromised car to drive over to West Orange. Would Jack approve of his working a fifteen-minute morning? What would Jack have done about the slashed tires? Will knew the answer instantly, and it made his stomach hurt: Jack would've gotten to the office by any means necessary, as quickly as possible, and had his assistant—Rosemary, a ferociously loyal, and just plain ferocious, barrel-chested Italian widow who'd retired when Jack had—take care of having the car fixed. And, by the way, if Jack had wanted Nakamuras, Rosemary would have made sure he had nothing less, even if it meant bullying tire suppliers up and down the eastern seaboard.

It was a white December noontime, glarey with diffused sun-shine, and Will felt sad as he drove west on Route 80. The new tires hummed strangely. The light traffic was moving along nicely at seventy or seventy-five, the cars all a good distance apart, few of them containing more than a single driver, yet even this somehow made him sad. As did the music on the radio, some young person wailing, in a beautiful, quavery voice, to the accompaniment of a solo sitar—Will hadn't heard a sitar since *Sgt. Pepper*—about love lost on the Internet. Will remembered his own lost love, in the days long before the Internet, and felt a fresh pang at the thought of the name *Emily*, which he quickly suppressed by thinking of his portfolio. Remembering wasn't so good.

He would never be young again. Going ahead in time a number of years equal to the years since he'd last seen—her—where would he be? Driving on this same road, probably, in some kind of slightly more modern car, maybe with that new auto-drive system they were testing now, only there would be something vaguely dissatisfying and dehumanizing and even frightening about the auto-drive, and the car would have some slight unfixable mechanical problem, a jiggle or rattle somewhere, maybe, as well as unremovable crumbs wedged in the window-switch cracks, and the music on the radio would be even more incomprehensible, and he, Will, would be an incredible sixty-five years old, an incipient oldster with hair in his ears, on deck to be shuffled off to oblivion as the future went forward like a white, sunny highway, full of heedlessly beautiful young people who loved the new music and knew they'd never die.

And Jack would be gone. Of this Will felt certain, for even though the test results hadn't come in yet, how could lumps bode anything but ill? Lumps were like a revolver brought on stage in the first act: of this Will was certain.

★ ★ ★

"Non-Hodgkin's lymphoma," Jack said, matter-of-factly, taking a sip of his Beck's. He and Will were sitting in their regular red vinyl banquette at Pal's.

"Shit," Will said.

Jack shrugged. "Orkin says I don't even need chemo or radiation," he said. "Just a handful of pills every morning. He says I could go ten, twenty years."

"Shit," Will said, in a slightly different tone.

"You OK?" Jack peered, with a certain softness, at his sensitive son.

"I'm not going to faint again, if that's what you mean," Will said, irritatedly.

The older man looked amused. "You should've seen me when they came after me with that big needle at Parris Island," he said. "Out cold. I hit the deck so fast, they almost shipped me home then and there." Jack shrugged again. "Frankly, it's not the worst news I could've had," he said, clamming up quickly and glancing at the waiter, a very big-nosed man with close-set eyes, who put down their salads, smiling obsequiously at the tablecloth, and quickly withdrew. "But here's the thing," Jack continued. "The important thing." He hunched his thick neck down like a football coach, raised his gray eyebrows, and lowered his voice. "It's news that has to stay with us. Barney would love to renegotiate on a fire-sale basis."

"I—" Will looked confused. His mind was still fixed on the dire-sounding syllables "non-Hodgkin's lymphoma." It was a mean, chunky mouthful.

"Word gets out I'm under the weather, you know how people talk," Jack explained. "First thing you know, they'll be drawing me out of the picture in three months, six months, whatever sounds dramatic. And, no offense to you, Willy, but even semiretired, I still add value."

"I know." The clear implication being that Will alone was insufficient: only a caretaker, not a leader. But then this was old news. "I know," he repeated.

Jack took a big forkful of salad. "No word this morning?" he asked. The Monday after his offer Jessel had called back to put off the closing—"just a couple of days," citing, as an excuse, a new computer inventory system he was having trouble getting up and running.

"Not a peep, no."

"It's the war of nerves," he said, chewing. "Maybe Barney's got computer trouble, maybe not. The thought of buying retail drives him crazy."

"Hey," Will said, rubbing the small of his wife's back. "You asleep?"

"I was, almost."

"Oh."

There was a silence. So he was hurt, she thought. Great. She *really* wanted to go to sleep. "What?" she said, after a minute, wondering how impatient she sounded.

"I'm worried."

"About what?" she asked, even though she knew.

"My father. Leviathan."

She turned her head to him. "Everything's going to be all right. Go to sleep."

"My father has *cancer*." Even to himself, he sounded like a scared boy.

"He told you what his diagnosis was. He'll probably live a long time."

"You think so?"

"Jack's a tough guy."

This came, Will felt as always, at his expense. Still, it was true. And consoling. "I know."

"The deal'll happen."

"You think so?" he said. He sounded excited—childlike, she thought.

"Go to sleep."

"Wanna mess around?"

A pause. "My back hurts," Gail said. The door that had opened had shut again.

He rubbed her hip. "Poor psoas," he said. "Poor thing."

She lay unmoving for a couple of moments, then twitched him off. "Go to sleep," she said.


She lay in the darkness for a long time, worrying about the strangest thing: that it was all, somehow, her fault.

# 26

"Hey Pats?" He's on the phone in the back, after the lunch rush, as always trying vainly to wipe the smell of peppers and vinegar from his hands. The connection to her car is exceptionally bad: it sounds as if she's in the cockpit of a small propeller airplane.

"Joel?"

"Is everything OK, Pats?"

A momentary break in the connection. "—OK?"

"I hadn't heard from you, I wanted to see how you were doing."

"—isn't a good time, Joel."

"What isn't? This isn't?"

In a burst of static, a man's voice, clipped and rushed and ambulancey, overrides hers. All Joel can make out are the words "check check," at the end.

"Pats? You there?"

All at once he can hear her quite clearly. "Joel?"

"I hadn't heard, I was worrying a little."

"We shouldn't talk right now, Joel," she says.

"Do you have a cold or something? You sound f——"

"Lemme call you back in a few days, OK?"

"Is everything O——"

"Gotta go," she says quickly, hanging up.

★ ★ ★

She's been staring so long at this brick-red metal door in the back of the station house that she's surprised she hasn't stared a hole in it. Meanwhile the cops are all staring at her as they go by, especially fucking Stuie with his short sleeves and stupid-looking muscles, big man. She laughs to herself at the image of him she conjured, naked, infantile down there, and his smile goes funny for a second, almost as if she might be right.

She had to take the money to the court clerk, up a long staircase in a bright little room, two women busy talking to each other and laughing, making her wait till they were good and ready. Then the woman, with no smile for Chia, had to count the bills like eight times, *flip flip flip flip flip*, ten hundreds, straight from Joel's pocket, he'd been so sweet, barely even letting her thank him. What was in it for him? She would've done him, and he wasn't interested. Or he was interested—he'd as much as told her—but couldn't, somehow. Because he was old? The word *scruple*, as a verb, popped into her head. Could it be a verb? Funny, it had *screw* in it. She wouldn't have half-minded, he was sweet and she loved his hands. The hands had pushed the bills into hers and pushed her away. Go. Pay me when you pay me. She'd managed to kiss his cheek anyway. All bristles. He'd blushed. Sweet.

So give the receipt to the desk sergeant, nasty old cocksucker, he pulls his glasses down to the end of his nose and looks her up and down, then shakes his head, like, What's the world coming to? Like he wouldn't drop trou in a heartbeat. Where'd you come up with this kind of money, sweetheart? he says. I bet I can guess. Ha ha. Then she has to sit in the chair. And wait. And wait. Then—her heart starts to go like crazy—the red door opens and Rome shuffles through, all cocky, giving her his fuck-look, that's what he calls it. His belt and shoelaces missing, his baggy black jeans halfway down his snake-hips. The desk sergeant gives the belt and shoelaces and pocket change back to him in a brown envelope, holding it out like it smells bad, but Rome takes it by the corner without even looking at him and comes right over to her, her heart going even faster, and, dropping the envelope, grabs the dog-collar with one hand and her ass with the other, pushing her hips right into his so she can feel him, half-hard already, and sticking his tongue down her throat as far as he can. His breath is bad from being in jail, but she doesn't care. The cops all staring, but she doesn't care.

"You miss me, bitch?"

"Oh yeah." She can hardly breathe.

He pushes into her again. "You miss him too?"

"Oh yeah."

"Good. Let's go see how much." And he puts his hard hand down the back of her pants, right on her butt cheek, and guides her toward the front door.

"Stay out of trouble," Stuie perks up, all snotty-friendly.

"Yeah, see you in court, asshole," Rome says, and Stuie's eyes go hard.

The light outside, reflected off piles of dirty snow, is blinding, the air so cold it makes you gulp. He throws his arms wide, flares his nostrils. "Free air, man!" he shouts. "Free!" A fancy lady in a shearling coat stares at the two of them as she goes by; Rome gives her some nasty tongue-flicks. The lady shakes her head and hurries off. He laughs.

"So you really missed me, huh?" he says.

Chia nods.

"I know you did, I just like to hear you say it. You empty out your piggy bank for Romilar?"

She stares at him, not sure what to say, knowing she should lie but somehow unable to.

"Naw, I know, you loaded, right?" He shakes his head in wonderment. "Plenty left, right? Rich girl."

"I borrowed the money."

He snorts and looks at her narrowly. "Say what?"

"Everything I have is in trust," she says, knowing as she says it that he won't understand, it'll only make things worse. "I can't touch it till I'm thirty." Which means never.

"Who loan you money for me? Not your fockin' father, that's for sure."

"Joel."

"Joel? Joel who?"

"Joel at the Sub Shop."

He stops and rolls his eyes. "You mean Gonzo? Hard-On?"

"I—I didn't know where else to get it."

Rome is shaking his head. "Boolshit, boolshit, boolshit. You do this Gonzo?"

She thinks about her thoughts a few minutes ago and feels guilty even though she's done nothing. "Rome, I— No. No."

He has the back of the collar, he's pulling it hard, choking her. *"You do this Gonzo?"*

Now she really can't breathe. At all. She tries to say no, but can't get it out. So she shakes her head, hard, looks at him beseechingly.

He lets go of the collar and she gasps, as if coming up out of the deep water. He's staring at her, his black eyes giant, breathing hard himself. "Lemme get this straight," he says. "Gonzo got a hard-on for you, he gives you a grand, free and clear, you don't have to do *nothin'* for it?"

"Nothing," she whispers. A whisper is all she has.

He turns his head, boring in. "You don't have to *promise* to do nothin'?"

"Nothing."

"Boolshit." He spits. "Fockin' *bool*shit." He raises his open hand, and she squeezes her eyes shut, ready for the blow. He stands there fluttering the hand for a moment, ready to break her cheekbone, to smash her teeth, then drops it, shaking his head. "Fockin' lyin' bitch," he says. "Don't do me no favors." And struts off into the metallic winter sunlight, his laceless sneakers shuffling on the salted sidewalk.

"Rome," she sobs, but he's gone.

# 27

They met, as she had indicated, in the produce aisle of King's in Cedar Grove, mid-morning, when shopping volume would be light. It was a spotless, wide-aisled market, with gourmet everything and cooking classes, and everything, even milk, costing a little more than at Shop-Rite or Pathmark, but you went because it was all so *nice*. It *smelled* nice—something good was always cooking on the demonstration stove—and the nice men behind the meat and deli and fish counters seemed healthier, and happier about themselves in general, than their counterparts elsewhere. They wore clean white lab coats; they smiled reassuringly. They were men who knew what they were doing.

The produce aisle was a work of art, not, as elsewhere, a jumble of disappointments. In King's produce aisle there were twelve kinds of lettuce, every head picture-perfect, and tiny sprinklers went on periodically to make sure they stayed that way. The radicchio was never brown; the arugula looked as if it had just been yanked from the garden an hour before. Mozart played on the Muzak (although today, two days before Christmas, there were tastefully arranged seasonal selections), and the other shoppers always looked as if they'd just gotten good news from their stockbroker. More than once Gail had seen women in full riding regalia, jodhpurs and knee-boots, in the market.

Mario both did and didn't fit in. His houndstooth sports jacket and tassel loafers were right, but there were jarring details, like those semitransparent black silk socks he always wore, the chunky ring

on his stubby pinkie, the yellow-tinted aviator glasses. And Gail
could tell, even in profile, by the set of his plump cheeks and bristly
mustache as he examined the watercress, that he was smiling ironically. At what?

"Oh, hi," she said, trying her best for casualness as she sidled
up next to him.

"Greetings, Agent Double-O Four," Mario said.

She wore a fixed, sociable smile—like a bad ventriloquist, he
thought. "Can't you do a little better than that?" she asked him.

"No I really can't, Gailie, because this is totally bogus," he said,
with surprising good humor. "What am I looking at produce for? I'd
rather be looking at you." He grinned, making sure she understood
exactly how he meant it.

Gail glanced around a little desperately, not moving her head,
and picked up a bunch of parsley. "Could you please play along for
*two minutes*, for Christ's sake?" she hissed.

"So tense, Gailie, so tense. Your neck looks like rock. I could
turn it into melted butter." He reached over and tried to touch her
neck, but she jerked to the side as if his fingers were hot.

"Are you *out of your mind?*" she said. A woman was approaching from the left, mumbling to herself distractedly, rummaging
through the greens as if she were searching for something lost, something of great value. Gail and Mario both stood like statues for a
moment. The woman had long blond hair—dyed, Gail thought, even
as she stood gritting her teeth—and wore big round sunglasses, a
silver fur coat, and black leather pants. She nearly bumped into Gail
before she glanced up over the glasses, which had slid to the bottom
of her pug nose. "Sorry," she said, hoarsely, passing by. Her eyes were
red and swollen. *There's someone*, Gail thought, *as bad-off as me*. The
woman continued down the aisle, still rummaging and mumbling.

"I'm going," Gail told Mario. She started to walk away.

"Gailie, wait," he stage-whispered. "Wait. I'm sorry."

She stopped.

"These carrots look particularly fine," he offered, holding a bunch in front of her by their resplendently green stalks. In fact, they were magnificent carrots.

"I can't do this anymore," she said, in a low voice.

"There's a nice new Korean market in town," Mario said. "I hear they have kimchi."

"Mario, please."

"Sweetheart, you want to stop meeting, there's nothing I can do about it. But you're gonna make me a very sad man. And I don't think you'll be so happy, either."

"I'm not happy now." Her eyes, he could see from the side, were brimming.

"Don't cry, Gailie, OK?" He sounded quite calm, like a cop trying to talk a suicide down from a ledge.

"I'm not going to cry."

"Don't cry."

"I'm *not* going to cry."

"I could make you happy, Gailie."

She stared at the vegetables.

"Think about it, sweetheart. Imagine being happy."

"I can't see you anymore, Mario."

"*Think* about it," he hissed.

"I can't see you anymore." She sounded wooden.

"Not even on a professional basis?"

"I have to go now," she said.

"Gail! Hii!" Lynnie, who had just wheeled her cart around the corner from the baking-supplies aisle, was calling from the foot of produce.

Gail's heart almost stopped. "Oh shit," she said. With a quick, smooth motion, Mario put down the bunch of carrots and picked up another, moving a few crucial inches away from her in the process. "Hii," she called back, as Lynnie approached, her long brown fake-fur shaking and shimmering in counterpoint to her busy walk.

"Hi hi—are you *OK*?" Lynnie said, her tone changing mid-sentence, her dark eyes turning concerned. Then she caught sight of Mario, edging farther down the bin. "Oh—God. I'm sorry. Look, I'll go," she said.

Gail's smile was much brighter than it should have been. "Why?" she said.

Lynnie scanned her friend's face for a second, then seemed to understand everything. "Oh," she said. "I don't know. Hi!" she called to Mario. "Shopping?"

"Oh—hi!" he said, a little lift of surprise in his voice. He nodded and held up a pale green Boston lettuce. "Shopping." He smiled stiffly and moved still farther away, toward the fruit.

"Are you all *right*?" Lynnie asked Gail, in a low voice.

"I'm fine," Gail smiled, actually almost looking fine for a second.

"You sure?"

She nodded, blinking fast.

"You want to go somewhere and talk? Have lunch?" Lynnie offered, brightly.

"I don't think I'd better right now," Gail said, putting her hand on Lynnie's arm. "OK?" The two women looked at each other for a long moment, then Gail dropped the parsley she'd forgotten she was holding into her cart and—leaving the cart, and Lynnie, and Mario behind—hurried down the aisle toward the front of the store.

# 28

The week between Christmas and New Year's always felt, no matter how old Will got, like school vacation, and the office, in the wake of the holiday party—and with many suppliers and customers skiing in Aspen or snorkeling in Grand Cayman—took on a sleepy, dressed-down, halfhearted air, with long, thick silences between phone calls and hushed employee conferences at the coffee machine filling up the hours until early closing, in the blue-gray light of three-thirty or four. This year, for Will, there was all this, and much more: the twin possibilities of infinite loss and seemingly infinite gain hung in the air, like those scales held by the blind lady. The blind lady was Justice. Was there justice in the universe? Often, clearly, not; yet it also seemed— or at least it seemed to Will in his rosier hopings—that occasionally She came through. Would he get what he felt he so clearly deserved, what he had worked so long and hard for, ever since, against all his misgivings, he had gone to work for Jack? Money was what he had gone to work for Jack *for*. So couldn't some real money—especially money perched so near the edge of the table—finally fall his way?

Christmas at the Weisses had been the usual overladen and guilty orgy. The primary guilt had to do with celebrating the holiday at all, a decision Gail and Will, both nonobservant Jews, had reluctantly come to when Danny started to ask questions. The questions were more practical than spiritual: Why, if Christmas was being celebrated all around them, would Gail and Will consider doing anything else? They had no good answer. "Because we're Jews" didn't cut it, because they weren't, quite. So as a sop to the guilt-gods, they also celebrated Hanukkah, as a kind of Christmas tune-up, with just a few presents, and a menorah instead of a tree. The Feast of Lights— it was a pretty name. Plus, the way Will figured it, you could use all the light you could get this time of year.

The secondary guilt, no small deal in itself, had to do with the great blizzard of boxes under the tree and around the living room— most of them for the children, it was true, but toys added up. And then there were the obligatory boxes for each other: a cashmere cardigan and a gold necklace for Gail; a car-cover for the Tundra and a fancy exercise bike, an expensive but backhanded gift, for Will. Christmas was many things, but for him it was mainly a good five grand out the window. And no bonus for him this year, either, not with the sale coming up. Why did all this stuff have to be bought? It was like the bad old arms-race days, he thought: one side escalated, the other had to, too. Nothing short of a major treaty or some epochal turn of events could change things.

And he and Gail were still spending on the promise of the Leviathan deal, spending more than ever, and with fresh abandon, ever since Jack's Friday-night phone call. At first they'd allotted their two million rationally: this much for taxes, this much for paying off debt, this much for a down payment on a new house, that much to furnish it and carry the larger mortgage. This much for mad-money. But then—with the approach of the big new year on the calendar (who knew what would be? maybe archangels would come down and announce the end of civilization as we knew it), and especially as Barney Jessel continued to drag his heels—the money had all blended into a worried, excited blur: it all became mad-money. Will tried to sort out in his head what they were charging up, but he soon lost track.

He'd handed out the employees' year-end bonuses himself, the Friday before Christmas, lingering especially long at Layla's desk, trying to assess the precise degree of sexual promise the gratitude in her eyes contained. It was there; he wasn't inventing it. The eye-play between them had become a teasing game, whose resolution—for there had to be a resolution, didn't there?—he often wondered about. And in anticipation of the sale—even Jack approved—the workers' checks were especially generous this year; so Will could expect that much more gratitude.

There was a feeling you got in your eyes and sinuses at year's end, it had something to do with steam heat, and each day's bright brief light (slowly, thrillingly, starting to lengthen now), and the end of things, and the beginning of things. This was a very big end, and a very big beginning. Will tried to imagine how different he would feel as a man of the 2000s, how it would feel to get up each morning and look at the paper and see that number. Part of him knew that everything would be roughly the same, but a larger part of him didn't believe it. Part of him expected important shifts. Even the light and the shape of space, he thought—irrationally?—must be about to change. And somehow, in the waning days of the year (and of the century, and the millennium; of, it seemed, time itself), his giddy, frightened thoughts all focused on Gary's party.

Poor Fiona, a single, wistful-hopeful, piano-legged Irish girl (her word) of indeterminate, incipiently middle, age, had been enlisted weeks before for the evening. It was a major coup getting a sitter for New Year's Eve, one based, in this case, on the more or less solid promise that Will and Gail would be home by one—at which point Fiona would go out with her friends, "a great rowdy lot," as she called them, and a group that Will, imagining red-faced group-sings in after-hours bars, preferred to think about as little as possible. "But thank God she has *some*one," he liked to say to Gail, who always nodded solemnly.

Gail seemed solemn in general these days, and distant, for a change, and Will—without quite stopping to wonder if his own distraction had anything to do with it—was at a loss about why. Or rather, why *now*? She'd seemed so excited about the money. Then changed so quickly afterward. Women were a mystery to him in general, and Gail in particular. He'd slowly come to accept that their marriage had entered some muffled middle period of diminished peaks and valleys: of spotty, sporadic sex; of constant distraction by the children; of generally separate interests and concerns, fitfully and incompletely shared. Leviathan had seemed to begin to reawaken something in her, or to awaken something fresh, if only house-lust. And yet now, these days, the new sparkle in her eye seemed banked, and directed at some indefinite point over his left shoulder.

They were dressing for the party. Fiona was in the kitchen, chirping merrily in her brogue as she made the children's chicken fingers; Danny was watching a new laser disc of *Independence Day 2* on the new, huge-screen HDTV (it had set Will back almost three thousand; he was obligatorily worried about the money and the even firmer hold the big set exerted on Danny's attention, but he was secretly thrilled with the incredibly sharp picture and the futuristic, flat-black controls). Rachel was flitting between Fiona and her parents' bedroom and bathroom doorways, where she gaped at the entrancing transformation of the two thorny, grouchy people who loomed over her life into a fairy-tale prince and princess.

She gazed at Will as he straightened his clip-on tux tie. He, in turn, gazed at himself in the mirror, flattening the grayer hair on the sides of his head and thinking that—Gail's apparent lack of interest

aside—he didn't look bad at all for forty-three. As proof, he summoned up the approving images of his harem, Patti and Layla. He had
salted away a few electrifying affirmative moments: the time Patti
had touched his knee in the Sub Shop; the time he'd told Layla a silly
joke by the Xerox machine and she'd collapsed, giggling, against his
side, bare midriff and all, giving him such a hard-on that he'd had to
try to multiply 683 by 386 in his head before he could walk back
across to his desk. She wanted him. They wanted him. That his wife
no longer appeared to want him was a problem, but one he could now
and then live with.

He turned his head to check his profile and spotted Rachel.
"Hey, Pickle-puss," he said. "Whatcha doin'?" She grinned and
smoothed her hair with her left fingers, another approving female on
his roster.

"You look so *beautiful*, Daddy," she sighed.

"You're pretty beautiful yourself, kiddo."

She blushed and smoothed her hair again. He really had something working here, he thought. How early it began! "Is Mommy
ready yet?" Rachel asked.

Gail, of course, was still in the bathroom, in her bra and black
panty hose (and what a loathsome, armoring, anaphrodisiac garment
*they* were); it had taken him all of five minutes to suit up, and he might
as well have waited a half-hour. He turned to Rachel. "You know
mommies," he said. "They're never ready." And he wrinkled his nose
merrily—a gesture that, weirdly enough, he now realized, he had lifted
from Patti. *Patti Campesi Mintz*, he thought, his blood speeding up for
a second. He wondered if she'd be wearing something low-cut tonight.


Gail usually drove when they went places—it had been their
habit forever, something that had originally had to do with placat-

ing her, and that he'd continued for fear of ruffling her—but tonight, for general winter purposes, Will drove the Tundra, though the roads and the sky were clear. Still, the last night of the millennium—pregnantly, festively, a Friday—was frigid. The temperature was in the single digits, the stars glittered in a sky as black as outer space itself. Which seemed appropriate: the future was arriving, coming in from out there somewhere.

The future was arriving, and it seemed he and his wife weren't speaking. Much. "Hey," he said, turning to her as they went up the hill. "Hi," she said, without looking at him. The monosyllable, and the lack of eye contact, might as well have been a formal announcement declaring the suspension of diplomatic relations.

"What?" he asked her, meaning, in domestic shorthand, *What is it? Why are you being this way?* He said it with less of his usual mommy-fear than a certain amount of humor: he felt good. He'd worked a half-day, alone, at the office, catching up on paperwork and clearing his desk, so happily efficient that he was only briefly entertained, rather than plagued, by the fantasy of Layla walking in, her close-set eyes gleaming a challenge. After coming home he'd taken a run, to clear out his head, and then, his cheeks blazing from the cold, his thighs still pleasantly throbbing from the final uphill, Will had enjoyed, in his immaculate bathroom—Esperanza had come that morning, her sour face slightly softened by the guilty-generous Christmas bonus he'd given her the week before—the three of man's most basic pleasures that Jack liked to speak of, in his tough Marine way, as shitshowershave. Afterward he'd felt cleansed, purged, as fresh as the New Year's baby himself. His guts and his legs still hummed happily: How could anything, anywhere, be wrong?

"Nothing," Gail said.

"Come on," he said, jollying her.

She turned to him now, her face almost apologetic. "No, really."

The apparent concession was strange, but he accepted it. "You look great," he offered.

She did. She was wearing a long clingy black dress, the diamond earrings he'd bought her for their tenth anniversary, the single strand of pearls that, against her blue-white skin, had once given him an almost pornographic pleasure. His fantasies had moved on. Gail wore a black cashmere coat—dramatic, expensive, but not especially sexy. He'd toyed with the idea of buying her a fur for Christmas, but had had to admit to himself, guiltily, that it would have been erotically confusing. Fur was Patti, soft fur under her naked ass, mingling with her own . . . Oh God. He was hard.

"Thanks," Gail told him.

"I mean it." He tried 37 times 73. Forty times 73 made 2920, minus 219 . . .

"That's sweet," she said, softly, and he suddenly realized: she was *sad*, not mad. It made him feel even guiltier. But sad about what? It would take work to excavate the reason. Was he up to it?

"Is everything OK? I mean, you seem . . . kind of sad."

A silence. What? "A little, I guess."

He hesitated. Did he want to get into this? "What about?"

"I don't know."

Will had the foolish fleeting fantasy that came to him sometimes, that she could read his mind. God, they would've been divorced ten years ago. "Really?" he asked.

"Really," she said.

He smiled, relieved.


A poker-faced maid in a black-and-white uniform dress— Esperanza's cousin, as it happened—took their coats as they came in the double front doors. A jazz duo, grinning raven-tressed guitar-ist and intense ponytailed electric-pianist, were noodling away in the sunken living room. The distant city skyline twinkled through spot-less floor-to-ceiling windows. Will turned to Gail and said, under his breath, "Whoa."

He had never set foot in Gary's house. The place smelled like money. White carpets, stone floors, modern leather furniture that looked as if it had never seen a pet or small child. Over by the dining-room doorway slouched the girl, the pretty one that Joel was so gaga about, holding a silver tray of little brown puffy goodies, her expression beyond hopelessness, as Barry and Sherry Bohrer in-spected the hors d'oeuvres with grab-bag grins. Will looked her up and down: he could see it. He could definitely see it. You had to work around the weird outfit, which somehow managed to be a turn-off and a turn-on at the same time: skintight black-on-white spider-web-pattern pants, ripped tie-dyed T-shirt, giant platform heels in candy-apple red, with sparkles. She wore black lipstick, and her hair, despite the Daisy Mae pigtails, was crew cut on top. But her midriff was bare—poochy little tummy with two rings hanging below the navel—and Will, the boob man, could tell, as she shrugged her skinny shoulders with frantic boredom at Barry and Sherry's refusal to go away, that she wasn't wearing a bra. Small, but nice. Will made a quick mental plan: hors d'oeuvres as soon as possible.

But first you had to greet the host and get a drink. Gary and Ellen were blocking the way to the canapés, standing in the hallway with flutes of champagne, laughing hilariously with Mario the realtor and Donna DiMichele. Mario too was now starting a ponytail, though it was still just a snip of a thing: Gary's salt-and-pepper one, shak-ing as he laughed, hung down between his hunched shoulder blades. ". . . get an *appraisal*," he was gasping, as the champagne in his glass shook. He wiped a tear from the corner of his eye and put the flute to his lips, then had to take it away as the laughter welled up again.

"Am I right?" Mario was saying. He watched carefully, his own laughter a little more contained, as Gary laughed and nodded. The women, in the uncomfortable position of not knowing each other well enough to start a side conversation, were looking at the men and shaking their heads.

"Hey hey—Willy!" Gary squinted with hostish, already slightly potted magnanimity as he threw an arm over Will's shoulder. "And the beautiful Mrs. Willy! Welcome! Happy two thousand!"

"This is Gail," Will said. "Hi, Mario. Donna."

"Good to see you," Mario said, giving Will's hand a firm, business-like shake, then taking Gail's. Only Ellen Berkowitz was at the right angle to take note of Gail's expression as she shook hands with Mario. *Hmm*, she thought. The look in Gail's eyes was of baffled, almost naked vulnerability. Mario, the expert actor, gave her a quick professional smile.

"Glad to meet you, Gail," Gary said. "This is my wife, Ellen."

Ellen and Donna looked a little alike: both were long-legged, big-hipped, dark-haired. Gary's wife, though, was pretty, her dark long-lashed eyes sad but sexy. And, Will noted, she had nice boobs. He stared at her, in the strange position of being interested in her top but not her bottom. Something about this pleased him, though— it gave him an advantage, even if Gary was a better tennis player. Will wondered if the slightly mannish Donna and Mario did it or were just a party-pair. He put an appreciative arm around Gail's slim waist and looked the other two men in the eye: he was going to be rich. It was good, he thought, to be rich and have a wife who looked nice in a black dress. An olive-skinned Latino man, who could have been the brother of the coat-taking woman—in fact he was her common-law husband; he beat her—materialized with a silver tray of champagne flutes. Gail and Will each took one. Gary raised his glass.

"Here's to the new century," he said.

"Millennium," Mario said.

Gary gave him a you-old-jokester look. "Here's to the new whatever-the-fuck," he said. "May it bring us joy, peace—and a shitload of money."

"*Another* shitload of money, for you, Gar," Mario said.

Gary tilted his head modestly. "OK," he said, in a little-boy singsong, and they all laughed and toasted. Will saw, over his raised arm, that Junior and Patti had just come in the front door.

# 29

Larry and Debby Somebody, two excessively pretty people Will had never seen before, arrived late, without many apologies: good looks, it seemed, made up for a great deal. This made twelve at the party—thirteen if you counted the girl, but she mainly sulked around the edges. Now the six couples had retired to the living room, where Gary had turned off the lights so they could dance while looking out at the amazing view, the vast twinkling city spread out over the horizon under an orange-black sky.

Four couples turned on the dance floor while the musicians played something, Will forgot the title, by Carole King. Barry and Sherry were dancing together, as were Larry and Debby; Gail was doing a stiff foxtrot with Mario, and Will, to his amazement, found himself dancing with Patti.

In a way it was too much to take in. First there was her perfume, something he had never smelled before, and driving him crazy—Baise-Moi sur la Planche, by Coty? Then there was her dress, long and black like Gail's, but there the resemblance ended: Patti's was slashed deeply both in front and in back, so that one could either take in the thrillingly unusual sight of the eastern and western (rather than the quite-interesting-enough northern) hemispheres of her breasts, or gaze on a giddily long stretch of tan, toned back. Too much.

Will gazed. He gazed, and sniffed, and held, and felt, all the while trying to dance without stepping on Patti's feet, and striving to make small talk. And now, for some reason, amid the sex-sensory tumult, Will suddenly found himself thinking of Joel, wondering what his friend was doing on the biggest New Year's Eve since the Middle Ages, then remembering back to the lunch in the Sub Shop when Patti had touched Will's knee, smiling, and Joel's dark eyes had looked so strange. Will recalled that the two of them had had something flirty going on at the reunion, but that was just Joel: he'd probably gone back to his room and written a poem about her. Back in high school, when Joel had been thin and handsome and having sex with Cindy Island, Will—who didn't have sex with anyone but himself until sophomore year of college—had felt jealous of him. He was handsome, smart, athletic, funny; girls were nuts about him. Now Will felt sorry for Joel, when he could bear to think about him. Alone in his room on New Year's Eve. Will shuddered at the thought, then immediately put it out of his mind.

He glanced across the room, where Gail was dancing with Mario, standing stiff and straight. What was her problem? Why couldn't she, at least, have the grace to flirt with another man, or pretend to? Lately grace seemed to have deserted her: ill-tempered and distant, she was always knocking things over and bumping into furniture. A few days before, in the kitchen, she had stepped squarely on Will's big toe and barely apologized. Maybe she had a brain tumor. He had an instant fantasy, a millisecond movie: Gail dies, he marries Layla, Patti on the side. Suddenly, unbidden, the children enter in, glum, motherless, meeting Layla. End of movie.

Gail's sadness was a new revelation, one that might have touched him more if he hadn't felt so shut out. He tried to imagine her flirtier, more fun; what *if* she'd flirted with Mario? And what if she really meant it? Now he tried to think, for a second, of the two of them actually getting it on. Teasing himself, half-hard already with the champagne and Patti's perfume and the CinemaScope view of her freckly chest, he had to put on the brakes, in the form of yet another mental multiplication problem, to avoid lapsing into a teenage predicament.

Yet Patti herself was distant, even if she danced obligingly close. As Will carried the conversation—what there was of it—she kept glancing off to the side of the room, past Ellen and Donna, the two big girls now chatting like old sorority sisters, to where Junior and Gary sat, huddling intently and smoking cigars, their faces just visible in the light from the terrace. It reminded Will of one of their tennis conferences, only Junior's brow was corrugated extravagantly, and Gary appeared to be trying to explain something, not quite to Junior's satisfaction.

That was when he saw the bruises.

Patti's chest and shoulders were heavily freckled, but Will's eyes kept coming back to two areas on either side of the base of her neck that seemed, even in the half-light, spotted more darkly. She had powdered herself there, he now saw, with some orangey cover-up, but underneath it, the spots looked purple, almost like finger marks.

His tongue loosened by champagne, he simply spoke up. "Did you hurt yourself?" he asked, rubbing the top of her shoulder lightly with his left index finger.

She winced; Will pulled the finger away, apologizing. "I had a new masseuse," Patti said, quickly. "She was a little . . . overenthusiastic."

"Ah," Will said, excited by the glance into her pampered, mobster-moll life: working off the stresses of shopping. His right hand rested—he had to focus to keep it dry—on her vertebrae-nubbly bare back, just at the point where the incurving spine bowed out (if you were thinking downward, which Will was), toward the coccyx. "Do you ever get a guy?" he asked; blushing, he quickly added, "I mean, a masseur?" Now he made so bold—the music, the darkness, the city lights out there contributing—as to apply a very slight extra pressure on her backbone, by way of teasing emphasis.

But she wasn't having any. "Not usually, no," she said, nervously—thereby eliminating the slightly salacious line of questioning Will had tentatively mapped out. What was more, they had now swung over to the corner of the floor nearest Gary and Junior, where Will could just make out, in the shadows, Gary still apparently trying to explain something to Junior, the orange glow of whose cigar—deepening as he inhaled, then growing paler as he blew out a cloud of blue smoke—pointed straight at Will.


"What is it?" Mario asked, widening his eyes. "What?"

Gail shook her head. "I don't know," she said. Then added, with seeming irrelevance, but as a kind of catchall: "I'm sorry."

"I mean, I feel like I'm at Miss Whoozamacallit's Dancing Academy or something. 'See here, Ms. Weiss, no close dancing,'" he mocked, in a fruity, prissy voice.

She smiled—a little. "I know. I don't know what you see in me."

"Well, I'm beginning to wonder myself."

But this was in a funny voice, too, and he smiled as he said it. That was one of the things she liked so absolutely about him: he never sulked or whined the way Will did; he seemed to understand his power, even when things, temporarily, weren't going his way. No wonder he'd won all those sales awards. She loosened slightly in his arms.

"There. There," Mario said. "See? This is good."

"*I'm afraid,*" Gail whispered, under the music. Her eyes were moist.

"Of what?"

"I'm afraid that if I let go, I'm going to keep falling and falling, and never hit bottom."

"I'll catch you, Gailie."

She pulled her hand from his and quickly dabbed the corners of her eyes, glancing over at Will—whose eyes were still locked on the bimbo. Just his style, Gail thought, putting her hand back in Mario's. "Will you?" she asked.

"In a heartbeat."

She drew him toward her, so that their bellies touched. "*There we go*," Mario said, holding her tight. She could feel he was half-hard. Just then, Will looked over—her heart was racing—and smiled. Her hand in Mario's, Gail waved, and her husband gaily waved back.


The dinner conversation had turned to Barry, who, it seemed, had taken up meditation, or attempted to. ("I just sit there for fifteen minutes thinking about whether the Knicks are playing and stuff like that.") But Will was staring across the long marble table at the girl. She was pretty, he thought; her looks grew on you. She also looked miserable. She had barely touched her food, instead heaping it into satiric little subpiles on her plate as the grinning, candlelit grown-ups loomed chattily all around. After Barry had prated on for a while, she stood abruptly and stalked in her slightly skewed walk out of the dining room and down the transverse hall off the living room (her platform heels tapping on the stone floor), slamming a door at the end. The chatter that followed her departure indicated that she'd been grounded in some major way. Poor kid, Will thought— poor rich kid. And then he thought of Joel for the second time. If only the girl knew how he felt. Then what? Joel, after all, was the one who'd invented something about her; she probably barely knew (or cared) that he was alive. But still Will amused himself briefly with the thought of the two of them together: the perfect couple, in a way, Mr. and Ms. Weird. So what if he was old enough to be her father? Joel was always saying time was a joke, anyway. Will carried it all out in his mind, the two of them moving in together, getting married, having babies. . . . The weirdness would have to fade with bills and babies. Wouldn't it? Maybe they'd have strange babies and live in a little purple house. . . .

A while later Will was in a champagne blur, sitting next to Gail on a huge white sectional couch in Gary's den, along with the whole rest of the party, six couples gazing at a wall-sized television, even bigger than Will's new set, whose screen was filled with a startlingly clear image of a giant lighted ball, at the top of a pole, against a black background. Gary had turned on all the home-theater speakers, and the crowd-noise filled the den as if the crowd were right in there, the bassy outdoor boom of the remote pickup vibrating in the pit of Will's stomach, the treble cries of a hundred thousand revelers getting louder and louder as the hour approached.

Will had taken Gail's hand, and his palm was wet. The moment was so big—too big, like some giant dark object approaching the earth on an inexorable path. He hunched back in the couch, frightened and exhilarated by what was about to happen. Which was what? A ball was going to drop, the calendar was going to change, many zeros would appear. So what? Wasn't it, essentially, just like a car's odometer turning over? You took note of the fact, drove on.

But no, this was more. Will looked around at the men and women dressed in black and white, wondering, for some reason, how far each of them—himself included!—would make it into the fresh century. Each, at best, could tack on a paltry couple of digits to the row of zeros. He thought of the game he and his brothers had played at Hanukkah, ages ago: betting which menorah candle would burn out last. He looked around the room. The women would last longer, of course. One or two might go from cancer or mischance, but most of the men would certainly beat them to it. There were Gary and Junior, on what must have been their third cigars of the night: cigars wouldn't get you far. There was Barry, smiling into the after-dinner cheese plate: his cholesterol must be three hundred. Even Will himself, for all his good habits, all the miles he ran, all the smokes and desserts he avoided (sexual fantasy and whisky on Saturday being his two venial vices), didn't have heredity on his side. Look at poor Jack (Will said a brief, silent prayer here for his father). And both Jack and Louise's fathers had died in middle age, of cancer and a heart attack, respectively.

No, Will's money—handsome Larry aside—was on Mario. The idea surprised him, but something in him felt certain about it. Plump as he was, the realtor had the air of a survivor: he would scrabble over others and emerge rattily triumphant. Will smiled at the thought. Mario did look a little like a rat.

Tuxedoed Mario reclined cozily on the couch, an arm slung expansively around Donna's plump shoulders (she looked strangely sad; or was it just the way the light was falling on her face?), his unshod feet, in semitransparent silk socks, on the glass coffee table. Barry and Sherry leaned forward over the cheeses, still sampling. Larry and Debby nuzzled prettily. Gary and Junior still hunched in intense conference, Gary glancing now and then at the TV screen, Junior not seeming to see it—or his wife, who sat alone, with an entire section of the sectional to herself, staring into space.

The crowd noise pitched up; the countdown began. Will held Gail tighter as the digital display on the bottom of the huge screen raced and jovial, ancient Dick Clark recited the numbers: "Nine, eight, seven . . ." And the couples in the room recited along with him—everyone, Will noticed, except Junior, who sat absently biting his thumbnail as Gary counted, and Patti, whose stare seemed to harden with each elapsing second. On *zero*, Times Square exploded, and the surround-sound speakers shook the den, which also shook from the partygoers' glad cries. From outdoors Will heard the boom of fireworks; through the picture windows he saw an amazing vista, all across the dark spangled plain, of brightly colored rockets rising and bursting. He kissed Gail, who acquiesced, and then, to his embarrassed pleasure, found himself kissing pretty Debby, on his left, and then—simply to his embarrassment—kissing big Donna DiMichele, who blushed. Gary circled the room, giving all the women hostly pecks and the men one-armed hugs; even Junior managed a small smile. The deafening noise from the TV speakers rumbled on and on, till Gary had the presence of mind to simply turn down the volume; still, the boom of fireworks continued outside. Then there was a furious scream from the front hall.

Frowning, shaking his ponytail, Gary went out to look, and everyone in the room followed. Julie was standing by the double doors—in the same outfit as before, Will noticed, with the addition of a short nubbly black jacket and a backpack over one shoulder. She was pointing at Ellen, whose mouth was quivering. Wide-eyed, Julie seemed to take in, but not see, the crowd that had emerged from the den.

"I fucking *hate* you!" she screamed, at Ellen.

Gary went to her side and put his hand on her shoulder. "Julie . . . Jules," he began, but she shook his hand off.

"Let her talk," Ellen said, her lips quivering. "Let her tell me what she thinks of me."

"Ellen, this isn't the time or the place—" Gary began.

"I fucking *hate* you! You're *not* my mother!" Julie screamed.

"That's right. I'm not," Ellen said, quietly.

"Ellen," Gary said. And then, "Jules—"

Julie turned on Gary. "You fucked my mother, so what does that make you?" she said.

"Julie, that's not—"

"You *fucked my mother*, Gary. What—does—that—make—you?"

Gary's mouth worked, but no sound came out. The eyes around him felt like searchlight beams.

"I'll tell you what it makes you, Gar," Julie said. "It makes you my motherfucking father." She was breathing hard. "What it *doesn't* make you," she whispered, "is my motherfucking lover." As Ellen's face collapsed, Julie grabbed the handle of one of the heavy front doors and tried to throw it open, but it caught her shoe on the travel and stopped, vibrating. She stamped her foot in pain, tears starting to her eyes, then flailed at the handle, clawed at it, finally managing to grab it and throw open the door, which hit the wall with a loud bang. Ellen had sat down on the floor. And her stepdaughter stalked out into the frigid night, into the year 2000.

# 30

Ever try to walk down a steep hill in platform heels? She hears the voice in her head, herself to herself, as she clacks down the black street, the top section of Overlook, the long lightless hill just below the crest, under the glittery stars hard as little knives, sharp as the little star-knife Marlon Brando threw in the guy's eye in that movie late at night. She cried when she saw that, sitting alone in the den in front of the wall-sized screen, the picture like real, Gary spent all that money so it'd be real, and it was real, the guy with the star stuck in his eye and blood coming out. How could people do something like that? She's crying now, about that, about everything, but the cold is so cold that her tears cool on her cheeks, the cold is so cold she can barely breathe, the skin of her face neck and belly burning, and she can't stop shivering, she's shivering like a sonofabitch, she's only got the little rat-jacket on, and it doesn't do shit. She's never cold, but this is cold. Ever try to walk down an *icy* steep hill in platform heels? the voice asks, maybe it's just a way to try to keep warm, talking to yourself about yourself. The fireworks keep going *whump* in the sky, and every once in a while a car passes, but nobody even slows down, not even the carful of drunk high-school assholes who open the window and yell something dirty as they go by. Thanks, assholes. *Clack clack*, the heels go, and she has to move slowly, very carefully in the dark, if she doesn't want to land right on her ass. The lights out there are beautiful through the trees, and the fireworks, but she's crying, for Gary and Ellen and Cindy and Rome, and yes, for herself, alone lone lone. She's tried to call him, Rome, like a hundred times, but he won't take her call, he hangs up saying the worst things he can think of, which are pretty bad things. So what has she got left? She could try to go find him, she has a pretty good idea where he is—partying with that fucking scary outlaw D-Life—and who he's probably banging, that useless little hill-whore Alicia, she'd spread it for anything that scared her father, bet her father's good and scared tonight. She could try to go find him if she didn't have any pride, which she doesn't, so what does it matter anyway? She can imagine walking in on him, can see it just as sharply as if it were really happening, D-Life smiling with his fucking gold teeth and trying to hit on her, right in front of Rome, he doesn't give a shit. And Rome with the little whore, spammed out of her mind, her butt stuck in the air like a dog on the street, her eyes nowhere. Rome doing her right there, and not even caring she was walking in—Hey, babe, you wanna join in? Wanna party?—she can hear his cocky voice too in her head, and see everything, as real as on Gary's TV. Hey babe, you wanna join in? Fuck him. Fuck *him*. She's crying hard now, it hurts so bad, love hurts so. Fuck *him*—she would do it. She told him she would be his slave, his dog, his anything, so what does it matter? Join in, be his again. Fuck him.

She finally makes it to the bottom of the hill—not the whole hill, but at least the long steep stretch without lights. Here, on the next downhill, is where the houses begin, a little smaller than the ones up top, but still big, with big cars in the driveways and on the street, lights in a lot of windows, parties still going on. She can see people through the windows, somebody's happy in there probably, and she's still crying with the crazy voices in her head going *fuck him* and telling her to be his dog at the same time. Fuck him, be his dog. She can't stand it. It's a funny section of street, this part of the hill—funny how? She can't think right now, she can't stand anything, but it's funny, the shapes of the houses remind her of something, something strangely good, an island of strangely good in the sea of shit. she can't think. The good goes away. There's another thing she could do: she could make it all stop. She's thought of it a thousand times, thought of all the ways she could do it, wondered if it would change Rome's cocky face for a second, wondered if Gary would be sorry. Or anyone. But one thing: she doesn't want it to hurt. But it hurts so bad now that she believes she could do it, believes it would be some kind of release. But how? The woods are back there, behind the houses, the quarry, she remembers they used to dynamite there. The fireworks are still going *whump*, but less of them now. Probably if she just lay down in the woods by the quarry and went to sleep, probably she'd wake up dead. She laughs a little at that, the idea of waking up dead, but she believes it, she's always believed you go somewhere. Now she's smiling, imagining waking up dead in the woods, and it's summer forever, with no bugs. And you could lie in the sun forever and never get cancer, you'd get a beautiful shade of gold—gold. Gold. It's hit her, all at once, what's funny about this block. She's standing in front of the single house on it with no lights on, staring at this old familiar run-down brick house with the overgrown yard and suddenly remembering the one strangely good thing: Joel.

She clacks up his driveway, super-careful again because whoever shoveled this driveway can't shovel worth shit. Black ice and ridges of white ice in the dark, and the snow so squeaky-cold, it sounds like she's walking on Styrofoam. Under the carport and in the

back, it's all tire-tracky snow: whoever made a half-assed try at clearing the driveway just gave up here. There's one lighted window in
the back of the house, and she thinks, with a sudden flash of actual
happiness, it must be his. Who the fuck else would be home on New
Year's Eve? She can hear him grumping about the useless holiday,
can hear it as if he's in her head: *calendar-worship*. She smiles. He is in
her head. She remembers the walk in the woods to try to see the deer,
remembers the leaves swishing under their feet, remembers his beautiful hands and strange dark eyes. How he loved her but wouldn't
touch her. And now she feels she really loves him back—not like
Rome, but some way. Some strangely good way. She looks up at the
window and thinks of him lying up there, and feels so good, for the
first time in a long time, that all of a sudden she feels like hugging
herself. She reaches down into the snow with her bare hands—it hurts
like hell, even though her hands are almost frozen, anyhow—and tries
to make a snowball to throw, but it's too cold, the snow won't stick
together. So she picks up a little edge of tire-track ice sticking up
from the snow in the back driveway and flings it up at the window.
She's never been able to throw; the ice disintegrates against the
bricks. She finds another piece, throws higher and harder, with all
her might, and it smacks against the glass. She does it again. And
again. Nothing. No one. Is he asleep with the light on? Then she
notices one garage door is open, and looks in and sees a big silver
Cadillac, but the car she's looking for, his beautiful shit-bomb, is
gone.

A long time ago, when boys lived here, the back driveway, a
perfect basketball court, echoed with hoarse happy shouts; these days
only the rusty pole that once supported the backboard still stands,
presiding over a wide empty square of asphalt as dead as the surface
of the moon. Covered with snow, half the square, a triangle, is rutted

by the tires of the Cadillac and the Impala; the other half is fresh powder. She walks out into it now, the dry snow coming up over her high shoes and spilling down into them and melting stingingly against her flesh—she doesn't care—and looks up at the stars. The fireworks have stopped. She's never seen the sky so clear. A white smear that she knows to be the billion stars of the galaxy, seen edgewise, vaults over the top of the sky: an interesting perspective to be stuck with. She stares up at it, craning her neck, until the sky starts to turn dizzily. She wants to lie down to look at it. She lies down. The cold cold snow burns her back and the back of her neck—she doesn't care. She spreads her arms and legs the way you do when you're making a snow angel, so she looks like a star herself, a star looking up at the stars. Here, she thinks, is where she could lie, here is where she could rest and fall asleep and wake up under one of the stars from the galaxy shot down to warm her, a perfect blazing sun. She closes her eyes . . .

. . . only, after a minute, her brain starts to run fast, faster, thinking and thinking, she can't stop. Stop. Thinking she doesn't want to die alone. She doesn't want to be alone. And there's only one way she can think of not to be alone. She stands up, the back of her all glowing with the cold, brushes the snow off the best she can, and click-clacks down the driveway, leaving her angel behind . . .

. . . and goes down the sidewalk to the bottom of the hill, turns right on Wyoming, walks the long block to Verona Ave., and sticks out her thumb. The first car that comes along screeches on its brakes.

Joel is putt-putting down Heatherdell at the wheel of the Good Ship Impala, trolling along at just walking speed, drinking and thinking, thinking and drinking, staring at the Christmas lights. All the houses, each with a world inside, most of them, he supposes, subtle variants of the same world, a world built, essentially, around going out and coming back and watching TV. Even now, toward one in the morning, with a couple of parties still going on on the block and one or two starting to break up, he can see the bright screens flickering (or just the blue flickers on walls, like fires on the walls of caves), on upper floors, on main floors, the world bringing itself to itself. As though the parties hadn't quite been the real thing, perhaps more of an opportunity to discuss television. A funny fact about Joel: he doesn't watch. Hasn't for years. It's not disdain so much as the fact that he can't quite get interested. He remembers *Bonanza*, *Jeopardy*, *The Brady Bunch*, and that's enough for him, the memory of the big barking faces: he doesn't feel the urge to go back and see what new barking faces have been come up with. Irma has a mammoth old Zenith in her bedroom, with a bulgey gray-brown screen and gold grille over the speaker, that she watches night and day; Violet follows her "stories" on the 1968 black-and-white G.E. portable in the kitchen. When he's home, Joel can hear the undertones yattering away, catch the odd bleary image now and then: it's enough.

He comes to the end of the block. There's a house down here that he's come to notice more and more on his trips to the gate (more and more of them alone now, since Will has turned into, or maybe just revealed himself to be, such a pain-in-the-ass—what?— *unbeliever* about the past): a dog-ugly old Tudor, gray on white but dirty, with leaded casement windows (diamond panes downstairs, square up), gold drapes behind them, a badly overgrown yard (so bad that not even the snow cover has been able to disguise it), and, somehow most heartbreaking of all, a corrugated crime door over the garage.

It's clearly the oldest house on the street; once it stood out here in lonely splendor, by itself in the woods, and, no doubt, in good repair. Who lives here? Joel wonders. What do they do behind the drapes, in the garage behind the crime door? He pictures some worn-out old fat guy, sitting in a BarcaLounger with a cigar and a Racing Form, nodding off to *Abbott and Costello*. Do they show *Abbott and Costello* anymore? Probably not. Maybe this guy watches it anyway.

The road through the trees is invisible under powdery snow; he navigates it slowly, by memory. It goes out, curves back on itself once, then heads straight for the gate. Which, he sees with astonishment in the yellow glow of his headlights, is closed.

Shut. How can this be? It's never ever been closed before: it makes his head hurt to think of all this means. The border has been sealed, the last night of the year and the first day of the year have been divided by a full stop, there's no *follow*-through. The present is merely present, all alone, the past has been left to die on the vine, without him. Unless.

He gets out of the car, the engine still running, lights still on, and pushes on the gate. Nothing. Pulls on it. *Nada*. Lifts it, kicks it, same thing. It's frozen, stuck, locked. Someone has locked the gate.

He feels like crying.

Until suddenly it hits him: he could simply step over. What a wacky thought! Step over! Walk through! It might not be the same, but—he blinks gratefully—it might even be better.

He goes back to the car and turns off the engine. The wind swishes through the trees, over the snow, bringing the sound—he can just hear it in the wind—of laughter, of someone, far away in Woodwick, laughing so helplessly, so uncontrollably, that after a moment Joel can't tell if they're laughing or weeping.

★ ★ ★

When he and Will were small (back when Will had brains), they used to play soldiers or explorers in the glen. The glen was in the reservation behind Woodwick's northern edge, down the steep hill where Joel and Patti had made love, far down that way and much farther still, back deep in the past where distances were infinite, bounded only by lunchtime and sunset. There was a brook at the bottom of the glen, with its glorious sweet magic of water running from here to far away, running through the rocks, then pooling deep and clear, then moving on, with the voices you heard in water, and the cool cling in the brook's air on the hottest days.

Joel wants to go to the glen.

He walks and walks through Woodwick, warm in the loden-green duffle coat (now he remembers: a *station coat* was what Saks used to call it in the ad copy) with two just-unboxed sweaters on underneath and two pairs of brand-new Izod socks on inside his Jack Purcell tennis sneakers, which in turn are inside the very black rubber rain boots (with those satisfying black metal clips that have always reminded him of the slotted visor on a knight's helmet) he's had since eighth grade. He's tied the coat's wool hood tight under his chin, the way you were never supposed to do if you wanted to look cool, but who cares anymore? Looking cool, these days, is not high on his list. The world, with the warm hood tight around his ears, has a nice muffled sound to it, especially welcome since the air is so sharply cold that even the street lights look like they could stab you.

He crunches along the snowy margin between sidewalk and curb, pausing briefly across from Cindy's (the house is dark except for one faint light deep inside), where he stifles the urge to throw a snowball at her window: he doesn't want to wake her, she looks so beautiful when she's asleep. Down Glenview, past the little street he and Patti took, Pierce Court, along, along, past all the dark big houses, to the way he and Will used to go, through the Kesslers' yard to the edge of the woods.

Their backyard has a large, expensive-looking wooden jungle gym, which means that either the Kesslers have moved or they've gotten younger and started having children again. (Maybe this batch would turn out better than the other one: mean stupid Kenny, who got elected student council president in Joel's junior year, and just plain stupid Beth Ann, who was always in charge of pep committees and always, like Kenny, had a Miami tan in January.) You're not supposed to cut through their yard, Mrs. Kessler has a thing about the grass, which is precisely why you do it. And then the woods' edge has such an *expectant* look—and you know, once you pass over into the trees, that you've become invisible.

His feet seem to remember, thirty-five years on, the exact rhythm of the woods—where the roots and bushes and trees are, and where there's a kind of path that goes straight over the ridge and then down alongside the hill for a long time, dropping more and more steeply, then switching back the other way and dropping more steeply still. Joel stops, holding on to a young tree for support, breathing hard. He waits as his breath slows down, looking up at the stars, scattered through the branches like Christmas lights. The snow on the forest floor gives off a faint gleam, which, together with the starlight, is just enough to see by. He listens, but now the hood is bothering him, so he unties it and throws it back.

It's as if the world has opened. He can hear the wind, the occasional faint swish of tires on Verona Ave. (the esses, by his calculation, run through the reservation about two hundred yards from where he's standing) and, now, something else: the gurgle of running water.

Is this possible? It has to be close to zero out. He continues down the hill, holding on to branches for balance (when he lets go, they flip up like mares' tails, scattering powdery snow onto his cheek), crunching between the hemlocks and rhododendrons, coming at last to—just where he knew they would be—the big brown rocks that announce the edge of the glen.

It's darker down there, and there, amid the ice and evergreen smells, is the scent he remembers so well, the irony tang of wet rock and running brook. Running? He stops and listens again. Yes. Climbing down between the rocks (barely having to think where to put his feet, they know so well), he reaches the bottom, where the wide limestone shelf he left just the day before yesterday extends out to a little waterfall, which he's thought of, ever since seeing a map of ancient Egypt in the fourth grade, as the First Cataract.

On his hands and knees, he peers over the edge. Between sheets of ice, the water gurgles and rollicks and hisses and purls, merrily, endlessly, mocking all the time he's spent away, carrying on its jolly monologue, speaking in the voices of the living and the dead; even, now, singing:

> *What's your name?*
> *Who's your daddy?*
> *He rich—*
> *Is he rich like me?*

# 31

"Out?" Will said. He was sitting in the office, in the hard, slightly too bright light of the new year, a light sharpened by the fluorescents' buzzing on freshly white walls, painted over the long weekend. He was on the phone with Jack, who sounded hoarse, and therefore even gruffer than usual. A moment before, he'd been staring, for a change, at Layla's butt as she bent over a file drawer: she was wearing tight white pants, and Will had spent a few moments thinking how much confidence a woman had to have in her behind to wear pants like that. Now everything—Layla's butt, the light fixtures, the Far Side calendar on the wall by the water cooler—was turning to stone.

"Out," Jack repeated, testily. Will waited for an elaboration. There was a vast silence on the line.

"Did he explain?"

"He didn't have to, Willy. He found out about me, somehow."

"How?"

"Oh, Barney's a smart fella."

"But who else did you *tell?*" Will felt a strange, small scurry in his stomach: did his father suspect *him?* Had he told anyone besides Gail? Even hinted to anyone? Could Gail have . . . ?

"It doesn't matter," Jack said. "It's out. So Barney's out."

"What'll he do about west of the Hudson?"

"Same thing he's always done. Deal through Empire in Cleveland, lose a couple pennies per gross, and wait to see what happens here."

"Wait to see . . . ?"

Jack had to spell it out for his tenderhearted son. "If I'm dead in six months, then he's got a fire sale. To be blunt."

"But—"

"Willy, you're a smart kid, smarter than me. And you've done a good job playing the hand you were dealt. But you've still got a lot to learn about doing business with people."

Will sat saying nothing, seeing nothing. He knew Jack was right. He was even being kind. Will knew next to nothing about Doing Business with People. It had simply never been his forte. What was it Locke had said? "No man's knowledge can go beyond his experience." At Amherst Will had majored in philosophy—he'd even kept a philosophical notebook once. Where had it gone? (From the basement on Twin Elms Drive into the trash, during Jack and Louise's move to the condo, was the answer; and thence to the Bayonne landfill, where it lay moldering among the disposable diapers and Kentucky Fried Chicken containers.)

He cleared his throat. "Could we . . . uh, negotiate with him?" he asked Jack.

"Barney's out, Willy. He'll be the one to decide when he comes back in."


The smell of fresh paint had always been one of Will's favorites, due to some early-childhood association (which, like most of the rest of his childhood memories, he had purposefully put out of his mind), and it was always heightened by the scent of rising steam heat.

Today, however, in conjunction with the pressure in his head caused by Jack's news—and, perhaps, by the weather, which had turned abruptly warmer, with a fog-producing drizzle—the paint smell felt like a suffocating blanket: he could barely breathe in the office. He had to open the seldom-opened window over his desk, and in the process of forcing it open, broke loose a piece of the rain-rotted window frame. He sat back down and put his head in his hands. More money. The painters had left their bill—two grand and change— neatly in the center of Will's desk after finishing the job; it had been there to greet him when he came in this morning. Now he would have to call a carpenter. One of the perils of owning your office. The main one, of course, being the steadily sinking value of industrial real estate in East Paterson, whose long-awaited corporate renaissance was a bit slow in coming. Will had tried to talk Jack out of buying the building four years before, but, in a strange access of optimism, his father had argued that with the imminent urban turnaround, they'd be sitting pretty when it came time to sell. "It won't hurt to have an asset or two besides my good name," he'd said, gaily.

Now this. Will sat and shook his head, not caring who saw him. *Things fall apart; the center cannot hold*, piped up a voice from freshman English, a century ago. *Mere anarchy* . . . yadda yadda. Was this it? Were things falling apart? He tried to steady himself, to see it all one strand at a time. The sale was falling apart, yes; Jack was sick. Yes. But Jack would get better—his own doctor had said so—and there was still money in the bank. There was still, Will thought, his portfolio.

The Dow had backed off the magical ten-thousand barrier, and then poked back through in heavy but mixed trading just before New Year's. Now everyone was holding their breath, waiting for new employment figures, waiting for the dreaded Millennium Effect, whatever that might be. Some were predicting new heights; some were saying the bubble must finally burst. Meanwhile, though, Will's portfolio—including retirement accounts, college savings, a smattering of stocks, and a potpourri of mutual funds, with heavy emphasis on foreign and domestic indexes—had floated up to well over six hundred thousand. He couldn't quite believe it (he sometimes called the automated brokerage line twice a day to check), but it was true. Six hundred plus! Even without a sale. Not too shabby.

True, he was a little cash-poor. The old rule of thumb was that you were supposed to have two or three months' worth of cash to cover the nut in case things went completely belly-up; Will, whose nut these days was an amazing twelve grand (OK, maybe thirteen), didn't quite have a month's worth. All right, he had a lot less than one: he had about five thousand in the bank, cranking out a steady 3 percent. In addition, he had a twenty-five-thousand-dollar home-equity line, a ten-thousand-dollar credit line on his checking account, and a Visa card with a fifteen-thousand-dollar line (six thousand of that gone, cranking out its own negative 19 percent). And that was it. Forty-nine grand: four months, five in a stretch. That was the safety net. Beyond that were Jack and Louise, then the poorhouse.

Well, not quite. Gail had a little money—in a couple of places, he wasn't sure of all of them. This was her great mystery. She had a small trust fund from her grandfather, and a few stocks: she was always vague about the whole thing. She and Will had a joint checking account, but only his salary fed into it. Her part-time pay from Bache, Halsey—soon to be no more—went into her own account, from which she paid Rachel's nursery-school tuition, the cleaning woman, and Bloomingdale's. Period. The rest, presumably, was gravy, but the one or two times Will had made so bold as to ask about it—and to comment on the inequity of the situation—she'd stonewalled him. Money was power; she wasn't about to yield any of the little she had.

Still, if worst came to worst, she'd kick in. Wouldn't she?

On the debit side, they owed two hundred thousand on the house, about sixty thousand in Gail's law-school loans, the Visa bill, and thirteen hundred a month on the two cars, which were both leased. The American Express bill for Christmas was on its way (Happy New Year!), and it would be at least five thousand—the exact same amount, coincidentally, as he had in the bank.

But more was coming in.

But not enough.

It would have been a good thing if Leviathan hadn't fallen through.

He picked at his tuna sandwich at lunch, sitting at his desk, staring at the wall and wishing things were different. But things weren't different. Things were never different. He tried to call Fidelity; the line was busy. That was odd. Should he be concerned? He decided not to be. Technology was always screwing up.

But then a strange call came from Barry, after lunch: Gary's daughter, Julie—Joel's girl—had been missing the whole weekend, ever since she'd walked out of the party Friday night. The police had been called in. Accordingly, Gary wouldn't be playing tennis Saturday, nor—apparently out of worry-solidarity—would Junior. The game was called off.

No money was one thing; no tennis was something else. The rain, and Will's mood, worsened all afternoon; worse still, he couldn't get his window closed; the broken frame had stuck it for good. Finally he had to ask Layla to tape plastic wrap over it, which made a sorry sight, and deepened his funk still further. He stared out at the rain, and tried to imagine where, in it, was the weird, sad, pretty girl with the odd walk. The more he stared, the more certain Will became that she was dead.

He had once formed a secret theory—ridiculous, he knew; yet it held a certain fascination for him—that he could predict the performance of the Dow, on any given day, by consulting his own mood.

Up meant up; down meant down. It was totally stupid, yet it worked out an amazing amount of the time. He was certainly no stock savant; was he, instead, perhaps, hooked in to some wave or particle body of mass emotion Out There, behaving in bird-flock or fish-school unison?

In any case, he arrived home that night to find, after his colossally bad day, that the Dow industrial index had dropped 250 points, twice triggering the circuit breakers that stopped trading. The employment figures were higher, but not inordinately; analysts were at a loss to provide reasons for the drop. Besides, of course, the Millennium Effect. But that was nonsense. Wasn't it? There was always the chance that bottom-feeding buyers would turn things around, but then, no one was sure if the bottom had been hit yet.

# 32

The gate seems to have been closed for good. He goes every night now, knowing she's gone, and thinking maybe he'll hear her voice in the brook at the bottom of the glen. Stepping over the gate carefully, making sure to do it the same way every time, walking through slushy Woodwick (looking through the windows at the blue lights flickering) in his loden-green car coat, the hood tied until he gets halfway down the hill in the woods. Then untying it and listening to the great ocean of air in the forest, to how it sounds different when the air is wet or dry, thick or thin, cool or cold. To how the woods-sounds mix with the drifting swish of tires from Verona Ave., to how the brook gurgles faintly, then louder (the music rising along with the smells of water and rock and pine) as he descends the steep hill. And then the voices in the water: Morris and Steve and Tommy Dano, and—somewhat to his surprise—Pia Pugliano, a solemn, thin-haired girl who sang and played the accordion in the talent show every year. What's she doing here? *Leukemia leukemia leukemia*, she warbles.

But not *her*.

It worries him—he can hear (and talk to; he talks down there) the dead, but not her, so he wonders what she is, where she is.

He feels as if he'd had a tooth extracted, as if he were probing the gap with his tongue until his tongue hurt from bending it back.

At work he cuts his finger with the sandwich knife—stupid, stupid, he's never done it before, and it's a bad cut, the tendon nicked, he has to go to the emergency room at St. Barnabas for stitches, then come back for a lecture from Larry.

"What is it with you? You're somewheres else—I mean, even more than usual," Larry grumbles, staring at the bandage on Joel's left index finger and shaking his big head.

Joel shrugs. The subject of Julie is, of course, unbroachable with Larry—or virtually anyone else, for that matter.

"You know what you need?" Larry says.

Joel stares at him. He has absolutely no idea what he needs. What does he need? Her, back. And the past to pan out, somehow.

"You need a vacation."

Joel blinks.

"You need a fucking vacation," Larry announces, triumphantly. "When's the last time you even *took* a fucking vacation?"

He doesn't have to think. "I, um . . ." He shakes his head, clears his throat. " . . . never have, actually."

Larry looks stricken. "Never? I never gave you a fucking vacation, over a period of, what—" He looks down, counts on his fat fingers. "—eight years?"

"Eleven," Joel says.

"Eleven years you been here?"

He nods.

"Eleven years?"

He nods again.

"And I never gave you a vacation?"

"You gave, Lar. You gave. I just never took."

Larry shakes his head. "I can't let it carry over, all that time."

"Lar, it's OK. I don't even *want* a vacation."

The sudden vehemence of Larry's response startles him. "Well, you're takin' one," he commands. He looks a little startled himself.

"No human being can work eleven fuckin' years without a fuckin' vacation. Take a week."

Joel raises his hands. "Lar, I—"

Larry wags his sausage-finger. "I won't hear no on this. My dipshit nephew's on break from Fairleigh anyhow; he can come slice lunch meat, it won't kill him to learn something for a change."

"Lar——"

"I won't hear no. Go sit on a beach somewheres—you need money for a plane ride?" He reaches into his pocket, where, Joel knows, he keeps a big wad of bills.

Joel waves his bandaged hand. The finger is throbbing. "Lar, I don't need money," he says. This is quite true. Besides paying for gas, the odd book, and occasional repairs on the Impala, he has no expenses. He's spent close to nothing for well over a decade. He has neither checking account nor credit cards. Week after week, year after year, his paychecks have gone right into a passbook savings account and sat there, compounding interest. He had, last time he looked, something like $189,000 in the account. Maybe it was $198,000. Maybe more. The bank sends him pen-and-pencil sets, greeting cards on holidays.

"You sure?" Larry says, looking a little injured, now that he's in the spirit of largess.

"Larry, where am I gonna *go?*" He has a quick, strange vision, a waking dream: sitting on a beach, under a warm gray sky, the kind of day where the outdoors feels like indoors, in one of those low aluminum chairs, next to Pats. And Julie is a few yards off, her chair turned slightly so only her shoulder and profile—not her eyes—are visible. And still, someone is missing.

Who?

"I don't know where you go, and I don't care," Larry says. "Just go. Now. Here." He takes out the wad, goes *flip flip flip*, the chubby fingers amazingly deft, and takes out three crisp hundreds—Ben Franklin looking vaguely startled, vaguely amused, in his big off-center portrait—and presses them into Joel's limp, unbandaged hand. Joel exchanges glances with Ben. Ben winks. No, that's Larry. "No backs," he says, breathing heavily with happiness. "Get."


Seventeen years ago, when he left Cindy's room, There (going out the way she'd let him in, through the window, then out into the woods where he'd seen the deer), she told him not to come back. "I love you, Joel," she said. "I'll call you when I get better," she said. "I promise."

She didn't call. Not for a year, not for two or three—for a while he looked at the calendar every year on the day. Then he stopped looking, but never stopped thinking, and all he could think was that she hadn't gotten better.

Some people never got better. He had, in his own way, but he knew about people who didn't, he knew what it could be like not to; sometimes he wasn't better, himself.

So she hadn't gotten better. It wasn't the worst thing in the world. He thought of her in the same room, day after day, week after week, year after year, eating the good food, sitting in the nice chairs, reading the fine books, taking walks in the pretty woods. It helped him through the long mornings at work, thinking of her, there. It helps him still.

In his mind, she's never changed.

That night, for the first time, he hears a new voice in the water. The voice is Cindy's, singing not talking, tunelessly, breathily, singing but not talking when he speaks to her. He wants, he needs, to speak to her.

★ ★ ★

"I'm going on vacation," he tells Irma, the next morning, walking into the kitchen with a small plaid-cloth-sided Touristair zipper suitcase he found in the back of his closet. (Inside: a bottle of Jim Beam; a notebook and pencils; some new boxer shorts and Izod socks, still in their plastic bags; his old olive-drab periscope-shaped Boy Scout flashlight.)

The unlit cigarette in his housecoated mother's mouth drops along with her lower lip and dangles there precariously. Violet looks up from the *News*.

"Vacation?" Irma says, as though she were hearing a word in Norwegian.

"Sure."

"Where?"

"The beach," he improvises. He smiles at the sound of it.

"The beach," she repeats.

"Sure."

Violet looks back at her paper. "Wish I was going to the beach," she says.

"What beach?" Irma asks.

"I don't know, Mother. I'll know it when I see it."

"Joel, honey—" Her mouth opens and closes. She's trying, but failing, to express the inexpressible fact that he has slept nowhere but under this roof for . . . many, many years. Irma is afraid.

But her son kisses her cheek, with its smell of tobacco and Pond's cold cream. "It's OK, Mother. I'll be back in a week or so."

She blinks fast, swiftly lighting the cigarette, and introducing a delicious new flint-and-fluid aroma from the gunmetal Ronson she's pulled from the pocket of the housecoat. "That's all you're taking? You have swim suits?"

"Who needs a swim suit?"

Violet snorts.

"What kind of beach is this you're going to?" Irma says.

He walks to the door. "See you in a week."

"I'll make you a sandwich."

"That's OK, Mother." He waves.

"It wouldn't be any trouble—there's chicken in the icebox." She opens the refrigerator, stares at the contents, half-seeing through a film of tears. She remembers making Morris a snack the night before he left for good. He liked her chicken, though it also gave him gas. She removes the dish with its foil-wrapped carcass and holds it out to her son, but, as though a sorceror had waved a wand, he is no longer there.

The *world*ness of the world, the world he hasn't seen in so long, startles and scares him at first: the vast breadth of the blue blue sky, with its little fingernail scratches of jet trails; the width of the highway; and the vehemence of the traffic, the insistence of the cars on always getting their way, on going fast, faster, faster. And then, as he crosses the border and merges onto the New York Thruway (for north is the way he's traveling), the trucks, their huge, spotless grillwork gleaming blindingly, bent on his destruction. For miles and miles he clings to the right lane, traveling a timorous forty-five (for he's also noted, with some nervousness, the minimum-speed signs; he's never heard of a lower limit before), squinting with amazement at the giant sky and the orange-tan-gray-green self-congratulatory highway grass and the brown ecstatic winter trees exploding with holy sunlight (it's January, there's a lot of light around), a quadrillion particles of sheer spectrum color bursting out, it all makes his head so light, he has to sip at the brown-bagged bottle—peering carefully around for troopers—just to cool down.

But then, after an hour or so, after he feels slightly more at peace with the battering sunlight, the hurtling trucks, the implausibly huge landscape of blue farm fields opening out to an incalculable horizon, he ventures into the middle lane (the road has emptied a little, too, which further emboldens him) and tries fifty miles an hour, fifty-five. Sixty. Sixty is bracing. The Impala thrums urgently, its pistons and cams and cylinders challenged, it would seem, to the limit. Giddy with a sudden spirit of daring, he nudges the gas pedal a little more. Sixty-three. Something in the engine begins to squeal. He eases off, back to fifty, back to the right lane, his home.

He jerks back in his seat, suddenly startled by a buzzing in his stomach, a loud noise, as though something not him were in there— but then he realizes it's what's *not* in there: he's hungry. Mid-mornings in the Sub Shop, his stomach will hurt sometimes, but he always identifies the pain with the pain of being there, never hunger, even though food takes it away. He eats just to eat. Now, though, he's *hungry*, it's as if all his nerve endings are exposed, he needs to eat, a lot, *now*. He thinks longingly of Irma's chicken sandwich. Where do you go for a chicken sandwich, though, in the middle of this ocean of highway? It feels like an ocean, he's drifting a little in the right lane, weaving, squinting in the sunlight for food. When he sees the Indian chief.

The big old-fashioned billboard looms up on the right, flaking red paint on a white background, forties-style letters reading BIG CHIEF DINER—FINE DINING & SNACKS—EXIT 38 TANNERSVILLE. He stares at the Indian's stolid silhouette and starts to salivate, imagining both the fine dining and the snacks, both dispensed, his mind's eye and nose somehow tell him, on white linen tablecloths by haughty uniformed waiters, supervised, perhaps, by the Chief himself, impassive in evening clothes. Joel can see and smell and hear everything, even the big-band music ordered up from those semicylindrical tableside jukebox selectors with the stiff pages you turn with metal tabs, and those square plastic push-buttons (some a luscious transparent red, others the same rich ivory plastic as mah-jongg tiles) below.

An exit sign is coming up, coming, coming; he squints: 29. His shoulders sag. He's so hungry, he could get out and nibble grass. How long can it be till 38? Nine miles or ninety? On long car trips when he was a child (all car trips were long when he was a child), billboards would start announcing tourist attractions hundreds of miles early, theoretically to work you up into such a slow-building frenzy that by the time you actually got there, not paying a visit wasn't even an option. SEE AUSABLE CHASM, 300 MI. (what strange quality, he always wondered, was ausability?); HILL OF MYSTERY—GRAVITY REVERSED—450 MI. Can the BIG CHIEF DINER, FINE DINING & SNACKS, be such a case? He imagines finally reaching Exit 38 toward nightfall, weak from hunger, getting off the highway to find himself on the end of a long line of cars. But then, after a mile, a sign informs him that the next exit is 32.

Nor is there any line of cars when, after twenty minutes, he exits at 38. The Big Chief's parking lot isn't even especially full. He gets out of the Impala on rubbery legs, aching knees. His knees and lower back have been hurting lately, often, the tedious heralds of encroaching middle age. His eyes aren't exactly right, either. The two o'clock sun glitters brutally off the car windows and chrome trim. He staggers toward the shelter of the diner.

There's a small foyer—why is there always a foyer?—with a pay phone, a few tourist brochures in a wire stand, and that inevitable diner smell (but how pulse-quickening in this instance!) composed of cigarette smoke, french-fry grease, cheap perfume, the ghosts of old malteds. And a diner—nothing more, nothing less—is precisely what is inside the inner door, the fond fantasy of tablecloths, he now sees, a chimera induced by his hunger.

Which has grown monumental enough to excuse the dirty floors
and counters and the indifferent faces of the waitresses, two old and
one young, behind the counter. Some country song is mewling in the
background. He sits down on one of the drumshaped turning stools,
a giddy memory suddenly emerging, fresh and glistening, of the cen-
trifugal swoosh of blood in his forehead and the sound of his and
Steven's laughter, amid the disapproving clucks of adults, as they
spun and spun on stools like these. *Clatter clatter, spin spin, whirl whirl.*
The joy of turning. He spins, slowly, now, just to give it a try, tucking his knees under to avoid bumping them. It feels good. He tries it
again. And, a little faster, again. One of the old waitresses is paying
attention. Joel sees it, notes her cynical, slightly fearful, sidelong look
toward the kitchen. Does the cook have a blackjack? a baseball bat?
In a sudden rush of thought, Joel can see the cook and his whole family, his house, his gun collection, his angry ancestors . . .

And then, as he spins around again, slowing down, he takes in
the faces of the four or five diners at the tables along the windows
and on the other stools down the counter. A couple of them have
perked up, taking notice of the spinning man. Maybe they'd like to
kill him. Their stolid faces seem to be entertaining the possibility.
It's interesting, Joel thinks: he was less hungry when he was turning
around. Maybe there's a physical explanation; then again, maybe he
just needed to spin.

The staring waitress has placed herself in front of him. "Know
what you want?" she asks, not especially invitingly, as he slowly
comes to rest. She doesn't have a bad face—withered, dumb, but not
bad. Just scared.

Joel smiles—*don't worry, lady*—and shakes his head. "Whew,"
he says. "Whole room's turning."

She lifts her chin, one economic gesture indicating she's heard
him, repeating her question, and telling him she has other things to do.

"Funny," Joel says, glancing around. "Doesn't look that busy to me."

The waitress rolls her eyes. "Lemme know when you're ready." She puts her pad back in her apron and walks away; shaking her head, exhaling through her nose, she joins her friend at the other end of the counter. The young waitress is clearing one of the tables.

"How 'bout chicken?" Joel calls. "You got chicken?"

The waitress pretends not to hear.

He gets off the stool and walks down the counter to where the two women are standing. "You have a roast chicken back there, by any chance?" Joel asks.

The other waitress looks him up and down and makes a face. "Chicken salad, chicken roll," the first waitress says. Reluctantly.

He winces, as though someone had just told him very bad news. As though someone had struck him. "Oh no," Joel moans. "Really?"

They gape at him. Waitress Two is chewing gum very slowly. "'Scuse me," she says, and goes into the kitchen.

"Do you have any idea what's *in* chicken roll?" Joel asks his waitress.

Waitress Two comes out with the cook, a wiry old guy with a brown paper bag on his head and a faded tattoo on his saggy old bicep. Joel stares at the tattoo's greenish outlines for a moment before he can make out what it is: a head of Jesus, staring upward pitifully, into the crown of thorns.

"I help you, chief?" the cook says. He's a tough old bird, leathery skin and bleary blue eyes.

Joel perks up. "Actually, the Chief is exactly who I'd like to talk to," he says.

The cook squints. "Say what?"

"The Chief. The Big Chief? I'd like to talk to him about chicken roll."

The cook leans over the counter, smiling as he assesses Joel's potbelly. "You know what I'd recommend, buddy?" he says, in a low, loving voice. "I'd recommend you take a hike. Right now."

"Being that you have access to large knives, hot oil, stuff like that?"

"Like that, yeah."

"But not to the Chief."

The cook's smile grows broader. "How 'bout I count to three."

"I'd be impressed," Joel says. "But I gotta tell you—I've seen it done."

The cook's smile fades. The muscles in his ropy forearms tense; his big old hands are pressing on the counter. The waitresses seem to be holding their breath. Everybody in the place is watching now.

Joel sighs, turning around with an I-give-up gesture. "I'm leaving," he announces, to the diners. "Hungry. Let the record show that I'm leaving hungry."

"Get the fuck outta here," the cook croaks at his back.

Joel wheels quickly and advances a step, pointing at him, his black eyes hard. "Hey," he says. The cook flinches. Joel's finger is steady. "I've put in some time behind a counter myself," he says. "And I gotta tell you—the Chief would be ashamed of you."

Of There—also known as the Atchison Farr Center for Living —he has sharp memories: a big, cozy, well-kept house, or rather, a big central house, white clapboard with black shutters, connected on both sides to a low, rambling series of architecturally rhyming wings, old-new, set prettily on a wide lawn next to a brown pond at the edge of a pine forest among rolling fields on the outskirts of Farboro, Mass. What Joel most remembers is the smell of the place —a sublime composition of furniture polish, bayberry, and baking bread, with a slight, not unpleasant whiff of antiseptic around the edges—and how it announced itself immediately to the nostrils, seeming to give instant peace and solace for any hurt. The halls were quiet but not oppressively so; the décor was Colonial without being too dark or too cute. The staff hovered in the background, waiting to help or approve. Joel entertained a fantasy of moving there himself, living next door to Cindy, setting up housekeeping by proxy. He knew that it cost thousands a year—tens of thousands, was the rumor—and so was impossible. But it was nice to think about. Cindy read, mostly, and saw her doctor; there were group sessions, but they weren't compulsory, and she didn't like them very much, she said they made her feel shy. So she read, and walked, and ate—a little— and saw her doctor, and rested. Another thing about There was that it had no TV at all. The staff and the residents (they were never called patients) didn't make a big deal about it; they just smiled and said it was too noisy. Joel liked that. It made it all the harder not to be able to move in.

He remembers exactly how to get there: You pull into the center of town, where there's a traffic circle with a Civil War monument and the Farboro Inn across the street, a huge white Victorian house with wide porches looking out over the fields; you jog left out through the fields on an old two-lane blacktop until you start to see a stone fence on your left; then, 1.1 miles later, there's a gate with a discreet plaque, leading to the long, long driveway. He could do it in his sleep, and in fact, he has, many times—and in waking hours too—made the drive in his mind, pulled up the long driveway, walked into the front hall, sighed with the beauty of the ambient perfume, the welcome.

There were rules, but they were like everything else There: they didn't cudgel you with them. Visiting was during certain hours and only in public areas. Visitors were not to enter residents' rooms. And so Joel would sign in and sit in one of the visiting rooms with Cindy, then they'd walk the grounds, hand in hand. They would kiss in the woods, and she would go back to her room alone. And let him in the window.

How could he make love to anyone as beautiful as Cindy Island? It was always a problem. He was once beautiful himself, in a way, but he never quite believed in it, for one thing, and anyway, masculine beauty, for the hetero-practicing male, was a strange, clotted, confusing, and untrustworthy quantity, mostly unusable for the possessor, except as a kind of party trick. Extreme feminine beauty—radiant, no-makeup, traffic-stopping beauty—was also untrustworthy, and intimidating, to boot. Cindy's secret was that she was intimidated by her own beauty, she wore it uneasily, she saw what it did to people and it worried her endlessly.

When they first got together, the way they looked was al-most—almost—beside the point. He had to swallow hard and circle her hurt eyes before he could find a point of entry; she had to look at him and convince herself she wasn't admitting a self-lover. Once she was convinced (though in her innermost, inconsolable soul, she was always afraid), once she let him in, their beauty was a shared joke, a marquee for the high-school envious. (They refused to be photographed for the Most Beautiful page in the yearbook; the honors went to the—vastly inferior—second-place pair, Marci Emberg and Frank Ambrosio, who weren't even a couple.)

But even when they were alone, the joke was edgy. Their love-making was ridiculously tentative at first, pallid at best. (He used to smile grimly at the thought of what people must have imagined.) The blame was equal: he found himself in a state of constant incredulity at her slim, lunar perfection, and the disbelief was infectious. She couldn't come. Later she could, but always in a balked, distant way, as though retreating to the far shore of a dark, frozen lake. When he followed, it was tentatively. They were shy with each other. And since their shyness was part of their sweetness, it was impossible to change.

The last time had been the same, only different. She was on a new medication, to quiet the panic attacks that had become increasingly frequent and severe; it dulled sexual response. He came guiltily, perfunctorily. As they lay together afterward, she half-smiled at some thought so remote that, try as she might—and she tried—she couldn't dig it out for him. In the winter half-light outside her window, not ten yards away, a doe munched on a bush, then, as if at some signal, looked up, directly into Joel's eyes. He and the deer stared at each other for what must have been a solid minute; weirdly lulled, he let his eyelids droop. As he fell asleep, he dreamed the doe was in the room with them.

He reaches the exit as the sun is dimming in the bright hard afternoon sky, and sets off toward the Massachusetts border with the light at his back. The two-lane road, Route 29, rolls through farmland and forest, the declining sun igniting barns and tree trunks with a dull, antique-looking fire, like a gelled spotlight on a moody stage set. The Impala's slate shadow travels in front of him, rising to meet him on each uphill, falling away at every crest. Toward four o'clock he crosses the state line, the tender feeling border-crossing of any sort always gives him magnified, in this case, by the weight of time. He thinks of the New Year's Eve just passed: it is the year 2000. He is driving in the 2000s. Cindy is forty-three. And, of course, not.

Farboro, in the dying light, looks different. Route 29's process into town seems to have been rerouted; some internal alignment in him feels skewed as he drives along an unfamiliar strip of bright boxes in the air: signs. KENTUCKY FRIED CHICKEN, BURGER KING,

CORDERI MOTORS. SNOMOBILE SUPER RIOT. GAMBLERS ANONYMOUS MTG 2 PM WED. How will he find the traffic circle, the Civil War monument? But a minute later he's there, only backward; he's come in the wrong way, somehow, with the inn—still the same—at his right instead of in front of him. So that the left turn will be a right. Except that the stone-fenced fields across the road have, as if in a spell or a dream, become a neighborhood of cookie-cutter-new, brown-shingled houses. From the chimney of one of them, smoke rises sluggishly through the blue air: dogged proof that someone lives where there was nothing before.

He makes the right turn. The houses—nicely landscaped, well designed, but houses instead of fields nevertheless, a busying for the eye instead of a rest—continue for a good half-mile; then, he's relieved to see, the fields pick up where they had left off. He looks at his odometer: a half-mile to go. He also sees that he's nearly out of gas.

The sign on the stone wall is new, a long, corporate-looking bar, half dusty-blue, half steel-toned, the sedate serifed black print reading ATCHISON FARR/WEBCO: A MANAGED-CARE FACILITY/PRIVATE. The sun has dropped behind the trees; a new star glistens low and alone in the cloudless orange-black sky. A sudden panic rises in him, a giant hollowness, an idea the size of the world: he's an idiot. A moron. She couldn't possibly be here. She left years ago. She died. She married someone and had children. Sharp claws clutch his stomach lining. The only thing he's eaten since this morning was a pack of Nab cheese-and-peanut-butter crackers and a can of Nehi orange soda—an all-orange motif, hopeful at the time—at a Texaco station along the thruway. He is full of emptiness, surrounded by emptiness.

But then another idea rises, like a second star: she sang to him in the brook. Dead or crazy, she's around here somewhere. He turns up the driveway.

# 33

The central house, the big white clapboard with black shutters, is no more, has been replaced by a long low mirror-glass box, still connected, as if by some monstrous transplant surgery, to the old wings; with a new bronze abstract sculpture, resembling a butterfly enmeshed in a giant pretzel, in front. The sculpture sits in what must be, in warmer weather, a reflecting pool. The shaggy old front lawn—Joel remembers a croquet set and old-fashioned-looking wooden-slatted chairs—is now wide and empty, as perfectly trimmed as a golf course. The front drive too has been widened, and in a little parking harbor on the left side of the entrance sits a shiny maroon Range Rover with green-on-white Massachusetts M.D. plates. Joel pulls into the next space, noting, after he switches off the engine, a small sign in front of him reading RESERVED FOR DR. SHUMAN.

The furniture-polish/bayberry/bread fragrance is gone, too, replaced in the softly lit, minimally furnished lobby by a faint tang of brass polish mixed with some buzzy electrical smell Joel can't identify, along with the suave, lulling, piped-in sound of a clarinety saxophone, or saxophony clarinet:

> *Things are looking up, they honestly truly are,*
> *improving every minute,*
> *oh, improving, improving, improving,*
> *blink back those tears and see*

the gentle, swelling music seems to say.

288

A woman at the marble desk looks up pleasantly. Joel is wearing the clothes he set out in that morning—his Sub Shop jeans, a new brown Lacoste buttoned to the neck, the car coat, clinking black rubber boots. The front of the shirt is still dotted with orange crumbs from his 11 A.M. cheese-and-peanut-butter crackers; it also must be admitted that Joel exudes a strong, gamy scent all his own, unimpeded by deodorant. Nevertheless, the woman at the desk—a handsome patrician type in a gray sweater, of a certain age, with pearls and tightly pulled-back, gray-blond hair—gazes at him calmly, with, even, what appears to be an air of welcome.

"I'm looking for somebody," Joel says.

She nods as if this were the most natural thing in the world.

"You mind if I sit down?" he says, sitting in a leather-and-steel chair and rubbing his calves. "It's crazy—I've been doing nothing but driving all day, and my legs have totally had it."

"I know the feeling," the woman says, laughing a little. Her smile—the teeth as perfect as the pearls—is ravishing. She has a nice voice too.

He kneads his thighs and focuses all the power of his gaze on her. "You wouldn't happen to have a piece of fruit or something around, would you?" he asks.

Her smile turns to one of genuine regret.

Joel puts his chin on his hand, his elbow on the desk. "I have the feeling you could help me," he says, staring at her.

"I'll do my best."

"There's a girl—a woman—who used to be a p——who used to be here a while ago."

The woman nods.

"Her name is Cindy Island."

The woman looks more serious. She tightens her lips, thinking for a moment. "You've put me in a bit of a spot," she finally says.

Joel's heart trips and stutters.

The woman looks at him with her clear blue eyes. "You see, if she *were* in residence here, I wouldn't be allowed to tell you unless she had OK'd it first. But I do think it's safe for me to say there's no one by that name living here now." She smiles again: it's as though the sun had peeked through the clouds. "Of course I'm afraid you'll have to take it on faith that that's not what I'd tell you if there were." She looks absolutely merry.

"Would you like to go out and have some dinner?" Joel asks.

Her eyes actually look mischievous. "It's very kind of you," she says. "I'm afraid I can't."

"I'm loaded—you could have anything you wanted," Joel says. It's true. He stopped at the bank before leaving town and withdrew $6,543.21 in hundreds and assorted smaller bills: the rubber-banded pile of currency sits in the inner pocket of the car coat like a brick.

"I'm sorry."

He searches her beautiful eyes: they look like the sky over the ocean in August. "You know, it's weird," he says, "but I actually believe you are."

"Charlotte, what is that piece of crud parked in my space?"

Joel turns around. The speaker is a short, definite-looking man in a blue blazer, with tight gray senatorial curls. "Dr. Shuman, I presume?" Joel says.

"Who the hell are you?"

"The driver of the piece of crud."

"Do you have business here?"

"I used to," Joel tells him. He stands and extends his hand to Charlotte, who, with a glance at Shuman, takes it. Joel bows and touches his lips softly to her knuckles, then brushes by the doctor on his way to the front door, emitting a low growl that, he carefully calculates, only the two of them can hear.

★ ★ ★

He stands by the gas pump at the Sunoco station on the Farboro strip, his neck craned back as he stares at the sky. It's a windy evening: the gusts seem to be polishing the glinting stars, which lie jumbled around the black sky as though the constellations had fallen apart. *Lost lost lost*, he thinks. *Gone gone gone.* Although the air is bitingly cold, the wind has a peculiar, flannely softness, almost springlike, and for a second, through the gasoline fumes, he picks up the oddest corner of an important scent, one he thought he'd forgotten forever: the smell of goodness and safety that lingered in the foyer of the red-brick Montclair elementary school he attended until third grade, when Morris and Irma moved to Verona. For a second he can see the back of the SAFETY PATROL poster taped to the wire-glass pane of the brown door, the strange letters ЈОЯТAꟼ YTƎꟻAꙄ above the outline image of a dauntless boy in his white-web Sam Browne belt, arms outspread protectively. And he can smell the smell. He inhales deeply—and it's gone, lost to gas.

Goodness And Safety, he thinks. GAS. Goodness and safety are gone forever. No more goodness and safety. No more protection. The wind blows. The stars glitter.

"Twenty-eight even," the attendant says, and Joel looks back down to see the kid in his brown jumpsuit and red hooded sweatshirt standing next to him, his little eyes all small-town and doubtful. Joel takes out the brick of bills; the kid's eyes get big, he's never seen this much money in one place before. "I need exact after seven P.M.," he says, staring at the bills. "Or a credit card."

Joel shrugs, extends the pile of money. "Here," he says. "You want it?"

"What?"

"Take the whole goddamn thing. I don't need it."

The kid puts up his palms. "Whoa whoa—wait a minute."

"Why not?" Joel asks.

He looks screwy-eyed. "I, uh—"

"Would it make you happy?"

The kid stares at him a long time. "Uh, sure," he says. "I guess so."

Joel keeps holding the bills out. "So why not take it?"

The station's phone rings, a loud burble on an outdoor speaker; the kid jumps. He points at Joel. "Could you wait a sec?" he says, walking backward to the office, as if to make sure this guy doesn't go anywhere. "Just a sec."

Joel follows him to the office; the kid eyes him warily as he picks up the phone. "Snack," Joel explains, peeling a single off the top of the pile and feeding it into the bill acceptor on the machine to buy another pack of peanut-butter crackers. He'll need another dollar to buy a Mountain Dew—he thinks for a second of Larry, and the clock in the Sub Shop—but now he's out of singles, he doesn't even have any quarters; he'll have to wait for the kid.

Who doesn't take his eyes off Joel. "Yeah," he says into the phone. And then repeats it: "Yeah." He listens for a moment, then looks away. "Weird," he half-whispers, as though Joel couldn't hear him. The kid's standing at the station's cluttered brown-gray metal desk, flipping idly through a phone book as he talks. "Just *weird*," he repeats, a moment later, glancing at Joel.

Joel gives him his sunniest smile. The kid winces one back in helpless reflex, then says into the phone: "Call me back in five." In case this guy murders me, in other words. He riffles the phone book's pages one last time, lets it fall shut, and hangs up.

And now Joel's staring at the phone book, thinking the strangest thought. His heart trips and stumbles again. "Could I look at that a minute?" he asks.

The kid blinks. "What?"

"The phone book?"

"Sure."

Joel fumbles through the greasy pages as quickly as he can, his fingers thickened by dread and hope, to the *Is*. **ISLAND TANNING SALON,** in big black letters, is the first thing that jumps out at him. But then, in shy-looking type above it, he sees:

Island C 43 Haymkt

and a number.

He gazes at this for a long time, drumming his fingers on the page while the kid watches him. Joel puts his hand in his pocket for phone change, but he knows what's in there: $6,510, plus a dime, a nickel, and a few pennies.

"Do you have any quarters?" he asks.

The kid shakes his head. "I can't open the register at night," he says.

Joel has the feeling he's lying. "How 'bout in your pocket? Come on. Please. I'll give you ten dollars for a quarter."

His eyes are stubborn, dumb. "You owe twenty-eight even on the gas."

"Right. Right. I forgot. Look—here's a hundred. Just give me a quarter."

The kid's half-smiling.

"Here," Joel says. "You want two hundred? Take three hundred bucks. Consider it a finder's fee."

Now the kid's grinning: this guy's insane, but harmless. When the kid holds out a black palm full of quarters, it looks to Joel like the lost treasure of the Incas.

★ ★ ★

The pay phone's outdoors, on the side of the building. Joel's standing at it, quarter poised at the slot, shivering and shivering. The quarter jumps out of his fingers. It lands in the dirt, next to a big frozen dog turd. Joel picks the coin up and tries to stop shaking, but he can't. He drops the coin again, picks it up again. Finally he manages to put the quarter in the phone and push the buttons.

The line has a country sound, a soft raspy double ring. Two, four, six, eight . . . "Hello?" says a woman's voice, vaguely familiar but somehow wrong.

Joel opens his mouth. Nothing comes out.

"Hello?" the woman says again. This time she sounds annoyed, and Joel can tell it's Cindy. Or, rather, Cindy's voice encased in something, an odd, hard, substance: he imagines a blue-gray stone, dotted with lichen, etched with tiny lines. . . .

"Cindy?" he croaks.

"Who is this?"

"Cindy, it's Joel."

There's a pause. "I don't know any Joel."

"Cin, it's me. Joel Gold."

With a click, the line goes dead.


When he tries back, the line is busy. Same thing a minute later. Same thing—Joel stamps around in the cold, rubbing his hands, hugging himself—five minutes later. He goes back to the office, where the kid, newly rich, is back on the phone with his friend, smiling, feet up on the desk. The smile turns half-wary, half-familiar, when his benefactor appears in the doorway.

"Can you tell me how to get to Haymarket?" Joel asks.

The kid has no idea. "I just moved here last year," he explains. But there's a town map in the desk; Joel unfolds it while the kid reverts to cautious monosyllables on the phone. Haymarket, when he finally finds it, turns out to be a little dead end out past the town dump. He writes down the directions on a gas-station pad.

"Thanks," Joel tells the kid, dropping the map—and another hundred—on the desk. The kid just shakes his head, grinning, as Joel walks out.

It quickly gets dark out on the back roads past the strip, and the streets are a jumble, and his directions seem wrong. He keeps ending up in the same place, facing an old cemetery (the tilted blue-gray headstones dotted with lichen, etched with tiny lines). Then he figures out that there are two Palmer Streets, and that he's been turning onto the wrong one. The correct turn takes him for what feels like miles out into the country, until he sees a town line sign for Dunston and realizes he must have overshot. A U-turn brings him back to a TOWN DUMP sign he missed on the way out, and a tilted street sign that was invisible from the other direction: HAYMARKET.

Number 43 is the last house on the right, a black tarpaper-shingled little place with a dim light behind a brown shade in the windowed front door. The small porch contains a rocking chair but no other clues. Joel gets out and climbs the porch steps. He pushes the doorbell button but hears no ring. Then he opens the storm door, taps on the pane, and a deep-voiced dog comes to life in there, scratching across the floor and then landing *bang* on the other side of the door, clawing and barking enormously, ravenously, terrifyingly.

"Mary, *stop*," he hears a voice call. "Shut *up*."

The dog barks a little more, then whimpers.

"Who is it?" says the voice. She sounds different but the same.

"Cin, it's me. Joel."

He can hear an intake of breath. "Oh shit," Cindy says. The dog growls and whimpers.

"Cindy?"

"You didn't say you were *here*."

He shrugs. "I'm here."

"You've got to leave, Joel."

It's the first time—in seventeen years—she's addressed him, and he feels the old familiar warmth in his vitals, and beneath. He leans against the door frame and sighs. "Why, Cin?"

"Go, Joel. Please."

"Just tell me why."

"Because I don't want to see you, that's why."

"Why?"

"Joel, *please* go."

His knees are giving out, he needs to sit down. So he sits in the rocking chair and rocks for a minute, the cold planks beneath him groaning, as he stares out at the black trees.

The dog growls deep in its chest, in a voice as deep as Larry's. Then Joel hears it snuffle and shuffle its claws eagerly as a lock handle turns and the storm door clicks open.

"You always were a stubborn SOB," Cindy says.

He stands and turns to see—as much as he can see in the porch's shadow—a different person entirely, encasing the remnant of Cindy's voice: a matronly woman with frizzy grayish hair, in an untucked chamois shirt and gray sweatpants, holding on tightly to the collar of a big German shepherd. The dog would plainly like nothing more than to lunge at Joel.

"Mary, for God's sake, *stop*," the woman says, yanking on the collar. The animal sits reluctantly. The woman's staring at Joel. "You look just the same," she says. "You grew a beard."

"Cindy?"

"Yes, it's me, Joel." She sounds annoyed. "I got fat, I got old. What else do you want me to tell you? My brain isn't broken anymore."

"Cindy," he says, his voice cracking. As he steps forward and puts his arms around her, the dog starts to growl and rise, but all at once Cindy, with an angry cry—and a force Joel would have never imagined her capable of—stamps her foot and pushes the animal down.

Where, in this new flesh, is his Cindy? As he squeezes her tightly, weeping, he can smell cigarettes and whisky—but then, at the heart of it, he picks up a faint, familiar lilac sweetness. "Cindy, Cindy," he bawls as he holds her. He sounds ridiculous to himself but doesn't care. She stands rigid at first, but then—shyly, awkwardly—pats him on the back.

"Joel, Joel," she says, shaking her head and patting him. "The past is *past*."

"As you can see, I wasn't expecting company," Cindy says, dryly, as she bends over, breathing hard, to remove a tall pile of books from a worn-out armchair. He keeps searching her new face for her old face; he keeps catching it at unexpected moments and angles. But even her eyes have changed: there's more in them. They know something, not much of it especially good.

She puts the books onto the floor—among other piles of books. Her house is warm, dim, brown, doggy, with books scattered and piled onto every surface, including a couple of disastrously rickety-looking bookshelves. A black wood-burning stove glows in the middle of the large living area. A computer terminal (with a pile of paperbacks on top) flickers bluely in the far corner; beyond it is a cluttered kitchenette. The dog settles into a clear space in front of the couch, its head on its paws but its black eyes watching Joel carefully.

"There," Cindy says, looking with some satisfaction at the cleared chair. "Guest-ready." She motions, ceremoniously, for him to sit. "You want a drink? I forget whether you drink."

"Sure," Joel says. He sits in the chair, sinking below the level of the arms.

She pads over to the kitchen area at the end of the room and returns with what appears to be two shrimp-cocktail glasses. She hands one of them to Joel and picks up a bottle sitting on a pile of books in back of the plaid couch. She displays the bottle to him, bottom first, parodying a helpful wine steward. It's Old Crow.

"I like the name," Cindy says, filling his glass. "I can identify." She fills hers and sits on the one vacant cushion on the couch, resting her ragg-socked feet on the dog's back. The animal grumbles and then, with a last suspicious glance at Joel, closes its eyes.

Cindy raises her glass. "Well," she says. "To surprises. I guess." She sniffs a little laugh, then drinks half the glass away. She takes a pack of Camels out of the pocket of her beige shirt. "Smoke?" she asks.

Joel shakes his head.

She puts a cigarette in the corner of her mouth. "I'm gonna," she says, lighting it. "My house." She smiles as she exhales a cloud of blue smoke, and shakes her head. "Joel, Joel," she says. "You make me very nervous."

He takes a mouthful of the whisky—not as smooth as he's used to—and swallows, sending a nice, eyeball-threatening warmth cascading through his body. "I'm nervous, too, Cin," he says.

She sniffs and shakes her head again. "*Jesus*, Joel."

"Maybe I shouldn't have come," he says. But then, "I had to come."

"Why?"

"Julie's missing."

Cindy's eyes grow hard and distant—strangely, it's the most she's resembled her old self yet. "Missing how?" she asks, staring nowhere, her cheeks sucked in, ready for the blow.

He tells her. The whole story, as he's pieced it together from Larry (Larry reads the newspapers)—the party, the fight, the witness who saw her hitchhiking on Verona Ave.

"So she's dead," Cindy says, simply, at last, still staring.

"Well," Joel says. "We don't know till we know."

Her voice is flat and small; she sounds a million miles away, just like the old Cindy. "Your daughter is dead," she says.


"But I thought Gary . . . ?" Joel says, when his breath comes back.

She looks at him as if she's just noticed he was there. "Gary what?"

"I, I . . . wasn't the reason you were at Farr . . . I mean, wasn't it Gary who—?"

"Who raped me and drove me crazy?" She taps her cigarette ash into her empty glass. "He didn't help," she says. "But he wasn't her father."

"But he thinks—"

"I know what he thinks," she says quickly, leaning back into the plaid cushion. "To a certain extent my livelihood depends on what he thinks."

"I . . ." He opens his mouth but nothing comes out.

"Gary raped me the first time in September," she says, clinically. "And then again in January, at Farr. But I was ready for him; I took something. You and I slept together a week later. She was born in October."

"Uh . . ."

"So Gary sends me a check every month. He sends me a check every month, and I don't come back. That's the deal." She looks at him, more directly than Cindy has ever looked at him before. "That's our deal. What else do you want to know?"

"So I'm . . ." He moves his hands in space, trying to somehow sculpt the reality.

"Her father. Yup. Were, it sounds like." Cindy gazes away again, her eyes damp. She sucks on the cigarette for all it's worth. "So," she says, after a minute. "What's—what was she like?" she asks. "I don't know much."

"She, um." He wipes his eyes. "Walks funny."

"Oh yeah. That was a congenital thing. Hip dysplasia." She sniffs. "They told me it would go away."

"She's beautiful."

"Oh yeah?" She chews on the inside of her mouth for a second. "Well—we were."

"You were," he says, without thinking. This is the old Joel talking. He knows that in the real world, where life is lived as other people live it, people go to excruciating lengths to be diplomatic. For one reason and another, he's never gone to these lengths, especially; yet, now that he looks at Cindy's eyes—her now-eyes—something in him, something new and awakening, realizes that while the first word was the one he meant to emphasize, the second was what she surely heard.

But she blinks it away. "Oh, you were, too, Joel," she says, quickly. "You still don't look bad, though. You're receding a little bit up there—" She points to her temples. "—but it looks, you know, distinguished. And you've put on a little weight. Just like me. "

This sounds flat and hard, a statement of fact, but he knows, somehow, that it's also a question, a plea. He doesn't know what to do; everything is turning upside down. "Remember when I cut your hair?" he says. On one of his last visits, he smuggled in a pair of scissors and, per her instructions, sheared her hair to boy-length. He can see now their two faces in the mirror in her room, the two sets of dark eyes, hers dreamy as she crooned, *Now we're just the same.*

She gives him that direct stare again. "I'm old, aren't I," she says. "Old and ugly."

He stares back at her for a long time. "We don't look alike anymore," Joel says.

"You didn't answer me."

He shakes his head as if he were being startled awake. "I think you're beautiful," he says.


He sleeps on the soft, doggy, plaid couch, under a comforter from her bed full of her lilacy scent, and he falls endlessly, still turning, unable to land or right himself. He hurries through huge, futuristic cities, alone, the pleasant landscapes of the past, with their familiar cast of characters, all destroyed, as if by a bomb. Patti shows up, in a uniform of some sort, leading a limping faceless child by the hand through a crowded railway station in which planes instead of trains arrive and depart. He runs after her, but slams into an iron-like pane of sea-green glass. He shouts and pounds uselessly on the sound-annulling glass; the child starts to turn, but Patti pulls its hand sharply before Joel can see its face, and drags it aboard a plane-train, gone forever. He sits up sharply on the couch, awakened by his own impotent scream. *No.*

The dog, at the foot of her bed in the open doorway opposite, stirs and barks, just once, at his cry. The house is dark, except for the glow from the little window of the woodstove, but now he hears a rustling of sheets and feels, in a sonic alteration, in a hush of the air, her presence in the doorway. "Are you OK?" Cindy says.

"Dream," Joel croaks, his mouth all gummy. "I—" He stops. He wants to tell her how much worse this dream is than anything he's ever dreamed before, but how can he? Where would he start? "Just a nightmare," he says.

She sits at the foot of the couch. "I don't dream much anymore," she says. "Or remember it, anyway. It's a help."

He sighs with simple relief at her company, inhaling her sweetness.

But nothing is simple. "Aren't you the slightest bit curious about me, Joel?" she asks. "Don't you want to know what I do? What I've been doing the last . . . what is it, twenty years?"

"Seventeen."

"Seventeen," Cindy repeats.

"I counted," he explains.

He hears a sniff and a muffled cry. "Damn it, Joel," she says, after a moment.

"I *am* curious," he says, to himself, with some surprise. There's no answer; she sits weeping quietly. He reaches over and puts his arm around her shoulder. "I want to know, Cin. Tell me. Tell me everything."

She takes his hand and rubs his fingers for a long time. "I always loved your hands so," she says.

"Tell me, Cin."

Cindy grips his palm tightly. "Come on," she says. "We'll talk in the morning."

She takes him to her soft bed, where they lie down next to each other and fall asleep like children.

# 34

Through the Tundra's superb, deeply bassy, speakers, Will heard, as he drove to work, that the nude body of a white female approximately sixteen years old had been found by a group of boys in Branch Brook Park, in Newark, near the downtown terminus of Verona Avenue, nine miles from the center of town. The boys had been playing soldiers in the snow when they found the body, its arms and legs hog-tied, the hands cut off, the head and torso burned beyond recognition. The radio report provided all this information: Will had naively thought you weren't allowed to say such things on the air, on a radio station that children might be listening to. Police were withholding any speculation about the crime, pending the checking of dental records. An autopsy, the report concluded, would have to wait until the body thawed.

The caller, a woman, sounded distraught. "Is this Will Weiss?" she said.

Not used to hearing female voices on the phone at the office— Gail almost never called, especially these days—Will thought, immediately, that something had happened to one of the children. The radio report had turned his frame of mind, already edgy about the Dow (which seemed to be skipping down a mountain, from rock to rock, toward the edge of a precipice), jumpy and superstitious:

Layla's pants today were made of some glittery, cruelly clingy material, and she didn't seem to be wearing underwear. It was as though she had upped the ante. If the sight of this (and the sight, and the sight, and the sight) didn't turn him into a pillar of salt, it would surely do harm to Danny and Rachel.

"Yes?" he said, his voice rising.

"This is Donna DiMichele."

The name, so totally out of place in this context, flummoxed him for a moment, and he bluffed. "Hi, Donna."

"You don't remember me, do you."

She sounded so accusing that he was thrown further off base. "Of course I do. From the—"

"Our high-school reunion," she broke in, saving him. "I also saw you at Gary Berkowitz's New Year's party, where that poor girl . . ." Her voice trailed off, informing him that she too listened to the news.

All at once, Will remembered their midnight kiss at the party— a thing in passing for him but not for Donna, as evidenced by her deep blush—and he had the sudden, crazy fantasy that she was calling to suggest they get together. "I know," he said. "Isn't that an awful thing?"

"Terrible," she said, quavering. "I can't stop being shook-up about it."

"I know, I know," he said. There was a silence on the line: What was this all about? Jack would have ordered the woman to cut to the chase. Too polite to be blunt, Will merely lapsed into absurdity. "So, Donna," he said. "Anything else new?" He slapped his forehead.

"I, uh—this is difficult for me, Will."

Oh my God, he thought. Here it came. So he'd been right after all. *Donna, I should stop you right there,* he prepared.

"It's about Mario Dartelli," Donna said.

This stopped *him* for a moment. Though he realized in a second who Donna was talking about, he had never heard Mario's last name before. "What about Mario?" he said, equably. *As if I could care.*

"And your wife."

"My wife?"

Donna's voice broke. "They're having an affair."

His first reaction was disbelief. His first thought was of Mario's semitransparent black silk socks, revealed up to the calf as the realtor rested his feet on Gary's coffee table on New Year's Eve. Gail and those socks . . .? Then, unwilled and quite specifically, his thoughts zoomed to his wife's vagina, to its look and feel and taste, all so very well known to him, and he had an instant equally unwilled vision of Mario's pendulous uncircumcised thing (it must be big; why else?), going in and out and in and out and in and out of his wife's vagina . . .

. . . and Gail enjoying it.

When was the last time she had enjoyed him? He tried to think. . . .

Will felt as if he were going to vomit and have diarrhea at the same time. His insides seemed to be exploding. It was all he could do, as a matter of fact, to keep from throwing down the phone and bolting to the bathroom.

Donna was weeping, gulping air—an unlovely sound—on the other end of the line. "I'mzorryI'mzorryI'mzorry," she gasped.

"Are you sure? What makes you th——"

"I *know*," she burst out, with startling scorn. "I *know*."

"You——"

"I work with the man!" she exclaimed. She blew her nose furiously: directly into the phone, it sounded like. "It's an open secret at Suburban; he's making a mockery of the profession, sneaking around with a customer!"

"A cust——?"

"Not to mention your marriage! And me! Goddammit! And me!" She began to weep, noisily, again.

He sat with the phone half off his ear, staring at nothing, as Donna sobbed and sobbed.


As if finally and demonstrably superconnected to Will's mood, the Dow began its free fall soon after the start of trading, and exactly simultaneous with Donna's call. He first became aware of what was happening soon after he hung up the phone (no easy feat; he'd had to plead illness) and stood, feeling not quite in his body, to go to the men's room. On the way, he passed Nick Georakis' desk; Nick, who did the company's accounts, had a little portable radio that was always on, and always tuned to the all-news station.

Nick was leaning on his desk enclosure, wearing his usual sardonic half-smile as he listened to the station's urgent, galloping chorus-of-violins musical theme. "Did you hear this? It's wild," he told Will.

Will stopped, forgetting his guts for a moment. "At the top of the news, the Dow plummets three hundred more points," the announcer's voice droned, doomily. "Circuit breakers halted trading this morning at—"

Nick shrugged. "Glad I got out," he said.

The news switched to the Hong Kong airport siege: the terrorists were throwing people off the roof. Will went to the bathroom and sat in a stall. He no longer had to vomit, but his insides were in an uproar, groaning, gurgling, clicking. Still, nothing would come out. It was as if he had a cork in him. He leaned forward, pressing his eyelids onto the heels of his hands, squeezing his eyes hard, the way he'd used to do when he was a kid, to see the stars and patterns reeling in the blackness. Maybe, he thought, his mind racing absurdly, this was what you saw after you died, this was all there was. It reminded him, all at once, of a little toy he'd had when he was small, a little metal plunger that turned a plastic wheel decorated with a translucent red-white-and-blue spiral, and made sparks. You stared at the sparks through the translucent disk, through the spiral as it whirled and whirled, hypnotizingly. The plunger *felt good*. It looked nice. That was it. It was as simple as that. It felt good to make the toy go faster and faster, it was nice to gaze at the sparks.

He burst into sobs.

He wept loudly in the tan metal enclosure, unable to stop, not caring whether anyone heard him or not. He sounded to himself like an animal, some animal hurt out in a field somewhere. He didn't care. He sobbed and sobbed, yelping, bellowing, astonishing himself with the noises he could make, then moaning and crooning when his voice got tired. He wept for his lost childhood, for the passage of time, for his father's inevitable death (and his own), and for his wife's treachery—for the sweet love they'd once had, just the two of them, before the children were born. He wept for Vail. Where had Vail gone? Where had anything gone?

After a while he realized he'd stopped making noise. He stood—with difficulty; his thighs had fallen asleep—and pulled up his pants. Emerging from the stall, he saw the face of a crazy stranger in the mirror, a middle-aged stranger with sparse gray hair sticking out in all directions (revealing a shocking, egg white–like expanse of bare temple) and red, Kabuki-like rings under his small swollen eyes.

He blew his nose, fixed his hair with his fingers (carefully covering the offending temples), and washed his face for a long time with cold water. When he looked up into the mirror again, he once more resembled himself, except for the tiny red eyes. He had some eyedrops, but they were back in his desk drawer: he calculated exactly who he'd have to pass on his way back there. Not to mention who might have heard him through the door. But then, what was embarrassment? What had happened to him was beyond embarrassment. He didn't care anymore.

He opened the door. Debby, Nick's assistant, walking by with an armful of file folders, saw him and quickly looked the other way. Nick was sitting again, back in his enclosure, bent over his papers, the little radio still tweeting and murmuring. Will walked over to him. "Any change?" he asked. It sounded like "eddy chaidge."

Nick looked up. He'd worked for the company for a long time, almost since Jack had started it; he'd seen a lot happen. His heavy-lidded eyes appeared unshockable—really, not even remotely sur-prisable. He'd been sitting ten feet from the bathroom door during Will's entire performance, he had heard everything, and now here was his young president looking like hell. Why? He didn't know why; he didn't especially care why. Nick looked up, not even blinking at Will's swollen face, and said: "Down two hundred more. They shut the breakers again."

Will's throat seemed to be swelling shut. "The Big One," he croaked.

Nick shrugged. He'd cashed out of the market near the top, converting his winnings into Treasuries and insured money-market accounts. (He'd also bought fifty thousand dollars' worth of gold.) His kids were through college; he owned his house and Cadillac out-right, plus a time-share in Boca. He could retire now, if he wanted. His secret plan was to leave the company next winter. Nick sat facing a picture of himself, with a dark tan, holding up an enormous sea bass. He could stare at this picture for long minutes at a time. When Will had said, "The Big One," Nick's eyes had gone immediately to the photograph. He had it in him, he knew, to catch one much bigger.

"The Big One," Will repeated, to himself. He staggered away from Nick's desk, catching his toe on the carpet and almost tripping, as if the floor had suddenly turned uphill. He fell back into his chair, picked up the phone, and pushed the speed-dial button for Fidelity's automated line. He'd expected a busy signal, he realized, but not the kind of busy signal he got: it seemed to be beeping at double or triple time, as if something were wrong with the phone lines themselves, as though something were wrong with the world and not just the Dow-Jones industrial average.

He turned to his computer and double-clicked the mouse on the tiny map-shaped icon for USOnline, sending a row of red lights flickering merrily across his modem and triggering a comforting tenor dial tone, followed by seven fast bleeps as the machine summoned, faster than fingers could ever move, the connect line. But this was busy, too, as was the backup number—as were two more numbers Will located in the connection directory. Finally, while the office emptied out for lunch (he barely noticed), after he'd clicked and reclicked the mouse for a half-hour, he heard a silence rather than a busy signal, and thought at first that the line had gone dead. But then came the staticky, quavering whistle of an answering modem, followed by the fast, heart-accelerating procession of connect graphics, and he was on.

He tapped the keyword PORTFOLIO, and the little dark-and-white-quadranted circle that indicated process appeared, and turned. It turned and turned and turned, for what seemed like a year, and then, with a high, plinking, jack-in-the-box chord, a black-bordered message-box appeared on the screen. Due to exceptionally high call volume, the box said, this service was not currently available; he should try calling back in one hour and forty-five minutes.

One hour and forty-five minutes. While his savings, his security, his future, bled away. He sat trying to think, his jaw clenched and his heart racing, and suddenly his right leg began to twitch. He looked at it. His foot was tapping up and down as if it were keeping time to music. Will put his hand on his knee to try to stop it, but the leg kept jumping.

"*Stop*," he pleaded to his leg, but it kept on twitching.

Once, in fifth grade (all at once, for some reason, he was remembering things and not pushing them back), he'd had to take a test on long division, which he had failed to learn. Skinny freckled Miss O'Riley had handed out the test papers, which smelled intoxicatingly of mimeograph fluid, and Will had excused himself and gone to the boys' room. There he had stood, in the middle of the boys' room, amid the smells of wet brown-paper towels and milk farts, with absolutely no idea what to do, until someone came to fetch him. *No way out:* his stomach, he remembered, had felt as though it were weightless, floating in space. That was how his stomach felt now.

Then he thought of a way out.

He'd opened the brokerage account, he now remembered, back in the mists of prehistory, before Danny had been born, by simply walking into the Fidelity office in Newark and writing a check. Surely he could close the account in person. He looked up the office's number and phoned; of course the line was busy. He would go. How much could he lose in the time it would take him to drive to Newark?

He got his shearling coat out of the closet (Gail had bought it for him one Christmas long ago, when she still loved him), threw it on without buttoning it, and went out to the parking lot. It was cold out there—biting cold; mockingly, the January thaw had come and gone, and now the TV weather forecasters were having a field day with their windchills and warnings. "Coldest weather of the century," one quipped. It had been seven on the kitchen thermometer when he'd left the house that morning; now, the Tundra's ambient-air gauge read five. He turned his seat-heater all the way up, power-locked the doors (he was, after all, going to Newark), and clicked on the radio to the all-news station.

The top story was from Wall Street, where a reporter was on the floor of the Stock Exchange, in a panicky soundscape of echoing male shouts and burbling phones. The Dow was down 569 points, and the circuit-breakers were about to be released once more, to give the Bears another go. "Still no word from the experts on whether what we have here is the dreaded, so-called Millennium Effect, or simply a garden-variety January correction," the reporter said, in tones of hearty objectivity. "Back to you, Terese and Harley." Terese and Harley then bantered about the weather—the temperatures were going the way of the Dow, they joked; the low that night was going to be minus ten. . . .

Will had stopped listening. He was on Market Street, in a long stretch of closely spaced traffic lights, every one of them turning red in his face. If he'd been on his way to a dental appointment, he knew, or a funeral, say . . . He couldn't think. He felt as if his veins were closing up. As he wondered where Gail and Mario went to do it, and how they did it, and saw, in his mind's eye, the awful vision of his wife's smile (when had she last smiled for him?), there suddenly appeared, in the glarey-icy midday sun of the present world, yet another stop light, looming up out of nowhere, and bringing with it —very quickly—the rusty sunset–red, Spanish–bumper stickered (*VAYA CON DÍOS; JÉSUS EL REY*) rear end of an old VW Rabbit.

It was a very slight collision, just a kiss, but there was contact. The driver, a stocky, mustached man in a peacoat and a Yankees cap, leaped out and accosted Will while he inspected the bumpers. "Whats-a matter jew!" he yelled. "Jew crazy?"

"It doesn't look like there's any damage," Will said, speaking from a dream.

"How jew know? How jew know?" the man shouted. The few people who stopped on the sidewalk to watch quickly moved on— too cold, too cold.

"Look, I'm sorry," Will said. "But I really don't think your car . . . Look, let me give you my card . . ."

He reached around in the pockets of his coat. There were no cards. "Wait a sec," he said. "There are some in the car."

"Ahhh," the man said, shaking his head. Then he hawked and spat an enormous gob of phlegm onto the driver's side of Will's windshield.

It looked as if someone had broken a small egg on the glass. "OK, mister? OK?" the man said. Then, muttering a stream of Spanish curses, he got back in the Rabbit and drove away.

Will stood and stared at the blob of mucus, which was at once dripping down the glass and freezing. The cars stopped behind him were beginning to honk. He got back into the Tundra and put it into gear, turning on the windshield washer. But the liquid wouldn't dissolve the stuff, and the wiper just skittered over it, spreading a large frown-shaped streak in front of his eyes: he had to crane his neck to either side to get a good view of the street.

There was no parking on the avenue in front of the black-glass tower that housed the Fidelity office; nor was there a single space on any of the three levels of the building's underground lot. He screeched back up the twisty ramps to daylight, turned onto a side street, and put the Tundra in a yellow-striped fire zone with the emergency flashers on. What was a ticket or even a tow? This was a *real* emergency.

The building was across the street from a triangular park, in whose center sat a gray-green metal statue of some bald early-American worthy: the statue was scrawled with graffiti and capped with pigeon shit. An icy wind blew down the avenue. The park's bushes were full of what appeared at first glance to be shiny brown streamers, but which, Will now realized, were the shredded remains of dozens of plastic bags. Where had they all come from? Dirty snow lay around the base of the bushes. He thought of the pretty girl, Gary's daughter, naked and burned—it had to be her. He wondered where her soul was, whether it was flying around out there in the cold somewhere. The wind blew so hard that Will could barely open the heavy glass door. Across the lobby, he saw a crowd standing in front of the Fidelity office.

Two large young men in blue blazers, each with a square steel badge on his breast pocket, stood in front of the doors. They both seemed about sixteen years old. Their cheeks were red, their hair was very short, they had the dim, mouth-breathing look of cheaply hired authority. The young guards were staring down their noses at a small, gray-mustached, high-voiced man who was talking very fast. Will could just pick up the end of what he was saying as he hurried across the lobby.

". . . *clear* violation of SEC regulations," the man said. He had little, clever eyes and a nose like the prow of a canoe. "Clear."

The guard he was addressing shrugged. "We don't make the rules," the other one said, dully.

"You don't make the rules, that's cute. You're only following orders, right?" The man shook his head with disgust and stalked away. Will surveyed the entirely male crowd, which was milling and grumbling indeterminately and, like him, peering through the office's tinted-glass doors, where two scared-looking young men in white shirtsleeves stood behind the blond-wood counter. The young men kept glancing down at their terminals and then out at the crowd.

"Are they gonna open up?" a tall, anxious-looking man with a big Adam's apple asked Will.

"I just got here," Will told him.

"They say not till the close of trading," a fat man said, grimly.

"A lot of good that'll do," said another.

"I'm fucked," the tall man said, staring blankly.

"We're all fucked," the fat man said.

Will stood looking at the doors and the guards for a while, but nothing kept happening. The tall man took out a tiny gray cellular phone, flipped it open, and bleeped a number on the keypad. His mouth opened as he listened. "All the circuits are busy," he said.

"Jesus Christ," a man groaned.

"Man the fallout shelters," someone in the crowd called brightly. "Check the canned goods and ammunition."

"Jesus Christ," the man repeated.

Will turned around and walked back across the lobby. The black floor was dotted with silver speckles: if you stared at them, the speckles looked like stars scattered across space. They reminded him of the time in Ocho Rios when he'd impressed Gail by knowing a few of the stars, and impressed himself by identifying what he believed was the north-ernmost edge of the Southern Crown—a constellation never visible from New Jersey—peeking over the horizon. They had made love that night—

His mind was moving in jerks, twitching the way his leg had twitched before. *Five thousand dollars*, he thought. Five thousand dol-lars was what he had. Four and change by this time of the month, really. If he could get to it. But the bills were coming in, and his next paycheck wasn't for two weeks, at which time the mortgage would fall due. So zero was what he really had, unless you considered the checking plus, the home-equity line, the Visa, all of which—you had to be realistic if all the circuits were busy—might not be accessible. He had about thirty-five dollars in his wallet. How would he buy groceries? Who would he buy groceries for?

He found himself, without quite knowing how he'd gotten there, back at the Tundra, which, miraculously, had neither been towed nor ticketed. The big yellow hazard lights were still flash-ing away. He stared at the chunky yellow lights, so calm and self-assured. He had a car payment coming up, too. He looked at the frozen gob of spit still sitting in the middle of his windshield. The wind had picked up: pieces of broken ice or glass tinkled down the street around his shoes. The world was breaking. His feet were cold. He got out his ice scraper and did his best to remove the spit without looking at it. His stomach felt dicey again; he might need a bathroom quickly. Where was the nearest bathroom? Gas stations aside—and gas stations pretty much had to be aside, except in the direst emergency—back at the office. Twenty to twenty-five minutes away, depending on traffic. He got back in the Tundra, locked the doors, turned the heater on full-blast, and, insofar as it was possible in his present condition, clenched his insides.

He turned on the radio, quickly switching away from the all-news station. He didn't want more news. He wanted easy listening. Long, long ago, he now recalled, in the house on Twin Elms Drive, Jack used to come home from the office and turn on easy listening in the bedroom as he washed up for dinner. How Will had disdained the easy listening, with its soupy, violiny, echoy arrangements of corny songs like "Whispering"! How he yearned for easy listening now! But it was nowhere to be found on the FM band. Where had Percy Faith and Mitch Miller gone? Vanished as he was growing up. He landed on his rock station for a second, with its Music for the Millennium: yet another doomy young voice, chanting over a twanging aboriginal instrument. He didn't want that. On the classical-music station, a bar of Rossini segued smoothly into news of the Dow. He switched again and found some New Age stuff, a saxophonish clarinet sounding tearily hopeful. It seemed just right.

The lights were all green for the trip back. Wasn't that always the way? Will kept wanting to pick up the car phone and call somebody, to talk to someone with the tearily hopeful music in the background, to cry himself—but who might that someone be? Gail? He half-smiled at the grim joke. Joel? Joel would snort at his predicament, would tell Will, as he liked to, sometimes, that he'd buttered his bread, now he had to lie in it. Stock-market stuff and domestic stuff interested Joel not at all. No, Joel would chide him for tying his life up in irrelevancies, then bounce off into some absurd riff about the past, with color commentary. . . .

Will blinked. All at once, he wanted to hear about the past. Suddenly the past seemed like a good place to be.

But the lights kept turning green as he arrived at them, and he wasn't at all confident, in his present state, of being able to dial Joel and drive at the same time.

He would go to the Sub Shop.

He smiled. He would surprise Joel. Will nodded to himself. He would apologize—it didn't matter for what. He would patch things up, and pick up Joel, and they would get a bottle and drive around, and this time, at last, Will would listen and listen and listen. The past seemed like a good place to go.

The sun was starting to set. He was driving west now, straight into it. The sun was descending, over the hills, into steely clouds. The wind was wild, rocking the traffic lights and street signs.

He finally hit a red light. It was a corner not far from the office, Straight and Market. The night shadows were beginning to creep up from the gutters, up mailboxes and lampposts and the sides of buildings; the sunlight was dying up there, and Will wanted it to stay, to stay. . . . An especially violent gust seemed almost to lift the Tundra, rocking it back and forth. A giant cardboard box—a carton from a TV or a washing machine, or something—blew across the intersection. Nobody was on the sidewalk; everybody in his right mind was indoors somewhere.

Will jumped. Someone was tapping on his window.

He looked and saw the kid he'd seen before, here and in Verona, the handsome kid with the big Afro and eggplant-colored skin. Shivering in a ratty jean jacket. No hat, no gloves. The kid was smiling, his close-set, sad-happy eyes almost apologetic, and motioning for Will to open the window.

Will's heart was knocking. He didn't want to open the window.

It was too cold out there. You shouldn't open the window for strangers. But the kid was smiling such a nice smile: as if he weren't a stranger, as though he and Will were old friends, and why wouldn't Will open the window for a friend?

Will did his best to smile back—his face was twitching—and shook his head, fast. *No.*

Then there's a metallic *clink* on his right, and a gush of cold wind, and he looks over and sees the other one, with the shiny strip of metal in one hand and the black thing in the other, getting into the passenger seat. No no no no, Will is saying, his lips all rubbery: to his shame, he's crying again.

Shut the fock up, muthafocka, the other one is saying, pulling up the auto-unlock button. The silky sound of the plungers rising. The Afro kid jumps into the back seat, rubbing his hands. *Whoo,* he says, shaking his head. Why you don't let me in? Iss *cold* out there. He has a high, childish voice.

His chin trembling all over the place, Will looks at the one in the passenger seat. Also a kid. Light brown skin, with a pencil mustache and a big earflap hat. Gold earrings under the earflaps. The black thing nestled cozily in his lap, pointing at Will. You can have the car, Will says, his voice shaking like Mary Tyler Moore. Puh-please take the car.

The light-skinned one shrugs a laugh, mocking him. Puh-puh-please, he says. Fockin' poossy, he says. Listen to him, weepin' and beggin'.

Nice an' warm in *here,* though, the black kid chirps, from the back seat.

You can have my money, my credit cards. Will's taking out his wallet, his hand shaking like crazy.

But the light one stares at it strangely, as if he wants it and doesn't want it.

Drive, muthafocka, he says. Drive to Verona.

# 35

He parks where they tell him to, the turnout in the reservation, just down the hill from the beginning of the esses. "Get out," the light one tells him.

Will closes his eyes. "Thank you," he breathes, and opens his door: they want the car. But the two of them get out, too, and close their doors. Will looks back and forth at them. Light cocks his head, flipping up an earflap, and motions with the gun.

"Walk," he says.

A car passes by, headlights on. The driver must have seen everything, he could've stopped; he didn't even slow down. The wind blows through the evergreens. The stars are beginning to appear; the only light left in the sky is a faint strip of orange over the hills.

"Shee-it," Black complains, shivering, to Light. "Too *cold*, man."

"Here," Light says. He grabs the collar of Will's shearling with one hand, unbuttons it with the other, pulls it off Will's back and tosses it to Black. "From me to you."

Black holds the coat lovingly, stroking the fleece, the soft tan skin. "*Nice*, man," he tells Will. He puts the coat on over the jean jacket.

Light yanks off Will's brown Brooks Brothers gloves and tosses them over too.

"Hey, man, you generous." Black slips on the gloves. "Whoa, shit—is this *bunny* fur?" he asks Will. "Shee-it. Ooh, *man*. Soft as a pussy."

Another car passes. Light looks nervous. "Come on, come on," he tells Will. "Over there." He points with the gun, to a gap in the trees just visible in the twilight. The trail.

Will remembers it from long ago—he remembers everything now. The trail descends steeply and crookedly, around brown pine-needly rocks, to a little waterfall and a spring. He and Joel used to play down there, a thousand years ago—cowboy and soldier and everything else. All at once he remembers his metal soldiers; he remembers a white wastebasket, with a painted cowboy spinning a gaily striped lariat, in his sunny room on Twin Elms. The warm, sunny room. He remembers how the tan carpet felt and smelled when he laid his cheek on it to pretend his soldiers were big. His chest heaves with a shivering sob: he was good, a good boy. He's so cold.

"Move move move," Light commands, prodding his back with the gun. Will trips down the steep trail (it's still covered with crusty snow; not much has melted off in here), grabbing the trees for support, falling from tree to tree.

"Hey, this coat is *nice*," Black says, behind him.

"Glad you enjoyin' it, muthafocka," says Light.

Black giggles. "Hee hee."

They crash down through the frozen bushes till they reach bottom, and there, in the darkness, is the space that has slept in Will's mind for thirty years: his death. The rhododendrons, the wide rock shelves, the gurgling water. A hole of blue-black sky, high overhead, pocked with glittering stars. Black branches swaying in the wind.

"Strip off," Light tells Will.

Will looks at him dully. He's half–bent over from the cold, his arms huddled against his chest.

"Strip the fock off, asshole."

"Don't shoot me please," Will whispers.

"I ain't gonna shoot you, poosy boy," Light says, scornfully. "Don't need to. Come on, take 'em off."

Will unbuttons his shirt with shaking fingers, remembering the smell of Aqua Velva on Jack's rough cheeks. He kicks off his shoes and pulls off his pants and shorts, thinking of the powdery sweetness in the nape of Rachel's neck when she was a baby.

"Socks too."

He bends over to take off his socks. His soles are bare on the icy rock. The muscles in his feet are cramping. He is inconceivably cold.

Light snorts: "Look, you can't even see it."

"Hey man, it's *cold* out, you wouldn't be no bigger."

Another snort. "I'd have more than that." Light takes something out of his coat pocket. It's white. He loops the clothesline around Will's left wrist, pulls tight, and ties the rope to the branch of a hemlock. He walks the remaining length of line over to another tree, loops it around, ties Will's other wrist, then pulls tight—his arms are stretched out wide—and makes a final knot around the second trunk.

Black giggles. "*He* ain't goin' nowhere."

Light gathers up the clothes and shoes. "Yeah—just to make sure."

Will hears a crashing of bushes above, a heavy crunching of snow, sees a flashlight beam flickering around the tree trunks. He closes his eyes, squeezes them tight. He sees a stack of big brown pancakes, a pat of oozing butter, a pool of syrup around the bacon . . .

"Hello, Willy boy," a deep voice says. "That you?"

He opens his eyes and smells spearmint gum. Junior, clacking gum with his big teeth, is holding Will's chin up and shining the flashlight in his face.

"All right," Junior says to Light and Black. "Get the fuck out of here."

They hesitate. Junior shakes his head, then takes a roll of bills out of his pocket and peels off several for each of them. "You can keep the wallet," he says. "Lose the clothes."

Black clicks his tongue. "Aw man, this nice coat?" he whines.

"Keep the fucking coat, I don't give a shit."

"Thanks, Mr. Mintz."

Junior turns to Black. "Listen, fuck."

"Uh-oh," Black says.

"You never met me, you never heard of me. Right?"

They stare at him. "Right," Black says.

"Now get the fuck *out* of here," Junior says.

The two step back, then scramble up the trail, crashing over each other in the dark.

Junior shakes his head. "Fuckin' punks," he says.

After a minute it's quiet, except for the wind and the clacking of Junior's gum. He's turned off the flashlight. "So, Willy boy," he finally says. "Nippy out, eh?"

Will's teeth are chattering uncontrollably.

"You know, I'd kick you in the nuts—if I could find them." He laughs a little. "So . . . did you enjoy yourself?"

"D-don't understand," Will just manages to say. He squeezes his eyes shut again. The strangest thing—he sees everything so clearly: he can read the engraving on the blade of the restaurant knife, see the green trim on the heavy edge of the pancake plate.

"Yeah, I know, it's all a mistake, right? That's how it is with me, too—all a fuckin' mistake."

"Don't . . . under-stand."

"See, that's the funny fuckin' thing, Willy. I can't keep her, anyway. Not where I'm going."

"Don't un——"

"I'm fucked, Willy. Did you ever hear of being fucked so bad that there's nothing you can fucking do?"

The butter is melting, swimming. And there's hot cocoa, with whipped cream. You can eat as much as you want, that man over there with the nice smile says. . . .

Junior sniffs a little laugh. "Yeah, I guess you did." He chucks Will on the cheek. "I guess you did, Willy boy." He clicks the light back on and, pulling up his coat collar against the cold, walks back up the trail.

Will gazes up at the tossing black trees, at the slim arc of stars right overhead, just under Cassiopeia. Andromeda. He remembers everything.


Joel listened to the car radio the whole way home, flabbergasted by the *busy*-ness of the world, the multitude of voices wanting, complaining, confessing, proclaiming, noticing, commenting, wheedling, and selling selling selling. Selling things he had never imagined existed. He formed a vision of the world as a great soft fat globe, its tremendous girth wrapped in pulsing lights, lights pulsing like a neon sign or Christmas-tree display, going BUY BUY BUY. It worried him as a father—albeit as the father of a dead girl—that such things were being sold, that everything was for sale. The world did not seem OK, and he wondered what his place could be in it now, now that the ghosts were dead.

It was true. Steven, Tommy, Morris, even Pia Pugliano—all dead. What a truly strange thing it was to be dead. As he drove south (now crossing the border into Jersey, and coming onto the Garden State Parkway, its orange and blue and red lights floating, all disconnected now, in the wet night air), he tried to wrap his thoughts around it, like the selling lights around the earth, but the idea was too large. He could see the precise contour of Steven's swimmer's shoulder bones under deeply tanned skin, skin that smelled with such desperate sweetness of Coppertone, but he could now be certain he wouldn't encounter the shoulders in the upstairs hall. This certainty contained comfort, satisfaction, and vast sadness.

And Cindy too. He thought of her singing in the brook in the glen, and knew—now that he knew the exact shape, feel, and scent of her body from only twelve hours earlier; knew the grayness of her hair, plumpness of her cheeks, and sharp knowledge in her eyes; knew why she read what she read, and what she did on her computer that brought the checks that, along with Gary's checks, enabled her to buy wood for her stove and food for her dog and Old Crow to drink— that now the water would simply sound like water.

Wouldn't it?

He wondered, still, why he hadn't heard Julie's voice. It gnawed at him, even beyond the absolute emptiness of death. He would have, should have, heard her there.

But then, it had all been a dream anyway. Hadn't it?

He was thinking of buying a new car. He'd told Cindy about his money, and she'd laughed at him. You're incredible, you know that, Joel, she'd said. You want to send me some? He told her, quite earnestly, that he would, but then she laughed again and hugged him, crying, and told him goodbye. Goodbye, Joel, she said. Buy a new car. Buy a computer. E-mail me.

What? he'd said.

So he thought, sadly, cozily, as he drove down the dark empty highway, that he'd buy a new car, something like Will's, all tight and plastic-smelling and good in the snow. It had seemed to make him so happy. Maybe that was what it took—maybe there was some happiness for him too, out there, somewhere.

And what would he do now?

★ ★ ★

The lights were all on in the house, and at first he thought, with his new and sorrowful radio knowledge of the world, that something terrible had happened, that Irma had been murdered by survivalists or techno-terrorists or customer reps, but when he walked in the back door, the house smelled, quite deliciously, of fresh paint.

Irma came into the kitchen, put her hand over her heart, and burst into tears.

"Oh, Joel," she said, as he hugged her, a little stiffly, a bit strange in his body and mind not only from having driven all day, but from everything else in the world too. "Oh Joel," Irma said, "I thought—" She hugged him harder, and cried harder too. "I don't know what I thought."

"What's . . . ?" he gestured around the brightly lit house, seeing now that the kitchen cabinets looked different, that the counters were white and new, that the old clock and radio were gone.

"I've been doing a few things," she said. She was smiling.

"You've been . . . ?"

"Oh, painting, papering, cleaning up a little. Joel, honey, I had the stairs recarpeted. Can you believe it? The upstairs hall too."

He could see, over her shoulder, in the doorway to the stairs, the new gray carpeting, covered with protective brown paper.

"The—" he began, then stopped. He had no idea what to say.

"When you left, it . . . well, it did something to me. Dr. Wasserman says it forced me to come to terms with my Morris's death."

"Dr. . . . ?"

"Dr. Wasserman? Leon? Honey, I've told you about him many, many times."

Joel sat down in a kitchen chair. It was a new chair, blond wood with a cane seat. He shook his head in confusion: he had no memory whatsoever of a Dr. Wasserman.

"Leon said maybe it was time to clean house. So I took a little of my money and did just that."

It was so strange to see Irma smiling.

"Come," she said, beckoning. "I want to show you."

He stood—his knees cracked painfully—and followed her, in a daze. The brown paper on the stair carpet crinkled under their feet. The upstairs hall had been papered in a pale, solid antique blue: no pattern, no visible seams.

"All the lights are on," Joel said.

"To help the paint dry," Irma explained. She put her hand on his arm. "Now, Joel. I want you to prepare yourself."

"Prepare . . . ?"

She opened the door to his room. The walls were antique white, clean and empty, the floor carpeted with the same gray stuff as in the hall. The bed had a sober new blue-plaid cover. Adult-looking. The books, the bulletin board, the shelves full of—everything: all gone.

"My books?"

"I kept a few old things and most of the new, in boxes in the basement," Irma said, and sighed. "But everything old is gone, Joel. In Steven's room too. I made a clean sweep."

"My notebooks?"

She shrugged. "Oh," she suddenly said. "I wanted to show you something." She opened his closet, where the clothes and shoes were neatly rearranged, and took out a shoe box. "With a few little things I couldn't help myself," Irma said. "Look, honey," she said, opening the box and taking out a long plastic object. "I found this behind your old dresser. Isn't it sweet?"

It was a pencil box, circa fifth grade, the sliding top a combination ruler/pencil-sharpener in pale-green transparent plastic. There were still pencils, coins, and ancient bottle caps inside. But it wasn't the contents that interested him. He gazed at the pale green, prism-

edged ruler, and something in the front of his brain, something across
the inside of his forehead, shivered and shifted: he had forgotten. Everything, everything. And, of course, not forgotten at all. For here
it was at last.

There are lights. He shakes his head and tries to open his eyes;
the lashes stick briefly, his tears having frozen. He has lost all feeling everywhere, it seems, except inside his mouth: he can move his
tongue around and taste ice. Is he dead? How can he be dead if he can
taste? He opens his eyes and sees the big white lights and thinks,
dully, for a second, that he's been saved; but then he sees the silver
suits, the long heads covered in silver, the wide iris-less black eyes,
and he knows that something else is happening, he's dead or is
dying. The silver things speak with giant, inside-out voices, saying
nothing he can understand. They prod at him—he can't feel it—and
walk around him with the lights. The wind is blowing up dry snow,
the crystals so beautiful in the white white light . . .

   His eyes close again.

"I have to take a drive," Joel told Irma.

   "A drive?" she said. "You've been driving all day." She put a
hand up, closed her eyes. "Wait," she said. "I'm sorry. I'm sorry,
honey—please forgive me, Leon says it's time to let go."

   Joel blinked and stared at her. "I have to think about things,"
he said.

   "Go. Think. You're a man now."

   Only now. He drove—where else?—up the hill, but not to the
gate this time. Never to the gate anymore. He sighed, hearing his own
breath. There was no reason to go. Instead he drove up Overlook and,

reaching the crest, circled around to Skyview, past Gary's, as though he might suddenly see her walking down the street, as if he could go back and stop her, pick her up and save her. Nothing. No one. A frigid night, the glittery sky electric-blue, the wind smacking the side of the Impala, ice tinkling down the street. A few lights on at Gary's, the party long past. The *past* long past. This was what kept getting to him, that it was all back there, done with. That nobody, nothing, was coming back. Was this actually true? It now seemed that it was, verifiably.

But he hadn't heard her in the water, the old part of himself thought. He'd heard everyone else but her. Maybe she simply hadn't been dead yet, thought the new part of himself, the sensible, credible, overriding part.

But something in him wouldn't let it go: he had to find out. He didn't like this in himself, yet he couldn't help it. He steered the car north, over to Glenview, past Cindy's house—determinedly not looking—and over to the Kesslers', by the edge of the woods.

He turned off the engine, even though it was so cold, and sat as the wind smacked the side of the car. The Kesslers' house was dark except for a single fluorescent on somewhere deep in the interior, patently an antiburglar light: they were probably in Florida. They were always in Florida. Joel sat for a long time, as the inside of the car got cold, and stared at the trees, part of him wanting to get out and go listen for her, the rest of him knowing what he would hear: only water. In the world as he now understood it, Kenny and Beth Ann Kessler, tan and firm-jawed, would command all the voices— the wanting, complaining, confessing, proclaiming, noticing, commenting, wheedling, and selling voices—and soft voices, especially voices in water, were out. The dead were dead. Water was water— except when it was ice. Trees were trees.

Then, staring at the trees, Joel saw lights in the woods. He opened the car door.

# 36

Larry barely looked up when Joel walked in. "Good thing you're back," he rumbled. "That fuckin' nephew of mine was fuckin' worthless."

Six forty-five, Monday morning. The first day of the rest of your life, Joel thought. All at once everybody else's life seemed to be changing—but then, maybe he'd just never noticed before. Take Will, for example: He'd lost two toes. Not to mention his wife. His nose had been saved, however. That was a good thing. It was one thing to lose a wife; it was another thing to have to walk around without a nose.

Or a daughter. For Joel had heard about the body, and it no longer mattered what the water said.

Larry finally looked at him. "Jesus Christ," he said. "What happened to you?"

Joel gingerly touched his pale cheek. He had shaved his beard over the weekend, after he'd heard, had gone down the Steven-less back hall to the old bathroom and worked at his cheeks with scissors and razor until a different person—alarmingly white-faced but strangely un-bad-looking—stared back at him from the mirror. "What do you think?" Joel asked, rubbing his cheek.

"Jesus Christ," Larry repeated, shaking his big head. "You don't look like nobody who would work *here*."

"Well. That's an interesting point you bring up, Lar."

Larry put his hands on his hips. "What? You gonna quit on me?"

"Just kidding, just kidding."

But Larry couldn't stop staring at him and shaking his head. "What the fuck happened to you? You get religion or something?"

Joel was rolling up the sleeves of his shirt, tying his apron. Quickly wiping the tears that had abruptly filled his eyes. "Larry Larry Larry," he said. "Can't someone spiff up a little without a big discussion?"

"No," Larry said.

Acting injured, he would barely talk to Joel for the rest of the morning, which seemed to go much more slowly than normal—if such a thing was possible. When, after filling coffee cups, buttering muffins, and slicing sandwiches for what felt like a full three hours, Joel finally allowed himself to sneak a peek at the Mountain Dew clock, it was nine-eighteen—an hour and twenty minutes earlier than his previous record. His stomach ached actively, so sharply that nibbling on soup Saltines, his usual solution, had no effect. He reached under his apron and rubbed his belly. He thought about what Larry had said. He could quit, but what would he do? Where would he go? He had decided to leave home: he couldn't breathe with all that fresh paint. His room was gone, anyway. And she. The thought of all that was gone caused a piercing pain in his midsection that nearly doubled him over.

"Eh, look who's back."

Joel looked up. It was the yellow-faced guy in the PANTONE CONSTRUCTION T-shirt, chewing on a toothpick and grinning. "Whuss wrong?" he said. "Eat some of your own food?"

"Ha ha," Joel said, weakly.

The guy turned both ways, to an imaginary appreciative audience, then back to Joel. "I'll have the usual," he said.

Joel managed to straighten up. "Refresh my memory," he said. "Liverwurst and onions? Peanut butter and provolone?"

The guy checked his peanut gallery again. "Go ahead, bust my chops," he told Joel. "I love it."

What happened next made no sense. The door opened, with an electronic bell sound Joel had never heard before—had Larry had something installed while he was gone?—and then, out of the side of his eye, he saw someone moving fast.

"Hey Gonzo!"

Joel turned. It was Romilar, in a long black coat and waving something black in front of him, Romilar in a blur, running and vaulting up onto the counter, as the yellow-faced guy fell back, features distorted, palms raised. Romilar squatting on the counter, yanking on Joel's collar and pushing something cold and hard into his cheek. Joel could hear his hard breathing, could feel it hot on the side of his face.

"You're dead, dickhead," Romilar breathed, in his ear. "Give me the focking money."

"I—" Joel said, and there was a white flash, a gulp of air: he had been smacked, hard, on the side of the head.

"Too slow, fockface." Romilar jumped down on Joel's side of the counter and bashed the keys of the register with one hand as he held the gun on Joel's cheek with the other.

The store exploded. Joel sank to his knees, splattered with something warm and sticky, something that smelled like the inside of a package of hamburger. He had been shot. But it was Romilar who lay on the duckboards, one foot weakly kicking, his head in a thick gushing red pool. The walls were ringing and ringing. "Jesus shit," the yellow-faced guy whimpered. "Jesus shit." On his knees on the duckboards, Joel turned and saw Larry, his eyes huge and his lips pressed tightly, his nostrils wide and his big belly heaving under the white apron, the gun in his hands still pointed at Romilar's body.

"*I* fuckin' quit," Larry said.

# 37

The trains went by every half-hour or so, oftener in the mornings and evenings, shaking the whole building and all its old people, who had long ago stopped noticing. In the long afternoons, Will lay on the brown-gold couch in his room, the living room (his crutch lay on the coffee table), noticing the loud rumble but not caring especially, his hands clasped between his knees, staring and staring at the changing daylight on the painting over the TV, an orange and green and black and brown rendition of what appeared to be a Spanish galleon in a storm at sunset. So much turbulence, so little substance—was this, he wondered, his story, too?

After dinner he watched television, rooted to the couch for hours, though sometimes, late at night, he got up and dragged himself to the card table where he'd put the laptop he had stolen from work, and dialed up, from the Internet, images of the most astounding filthiness. Stimulated, repelled, but unable, at first, to look away, he gazed in disbelief as they formed themselves on the little screen. He responded as mechanically as the images seemed to require, but always with the sad underlying memory of actual sex, of Gail. When he grew disgusted with himself, he wandered the Net: his crutch irrelevant here, he was mobile in an exhilarating but also upsetting way; a whole new world had assembled itself, under his nose, without his permission. He thought, for some reason, of the love songs he used to listen to on the car radio—songs that had helped form his world for thirty years, until his world fell apart. The new world had love songs, but they were as thin as the wind: What reminiscence, what metaphor, could vie with all that now-ness?

Sometimes he remembered things—images, names, phrases—and wasn't sure where they came from: TV, the computer, dreams. His mind seemed to be scattering. Now and then, late at night when it all overwhelmed him, he clicked off whatever flickering screen he happened to be watching and called up one of the mail-order catalogues, just to talk to a person. You could ask lots of questions about an item without actually buying anything; it was easy to get into conversations with the operators, most of them women. No doubt some of them were lonely, too.

The days went by. Barney Jessel, as Jack had promised, had bought Weiss Containers at a fire-sale price after the collapse of the Dow, paying just enough to keep the lights on and the doors open, but not enough to subsidize the salary of a cardboard-box prince and heir apparent. Will got a small payout—the bulk of which went toward keeping the lights on and the doors open at his own establishment, which he currently got to look at, from the outside, on weekends, when he swung by to pick up the children.

Did Gail need his money? It was a good question. According to Donna DiMichele, who had told him (and continued to tell him) far more than he ever wanted to know, his soon-to-be-ex-wife had apparently stashed away quite a bit on her own over the last couple of years. Which seemed to make the question of Will's contributions to the household—especially in his severely diminished financial capacity—somewhat murky, except that on this point the courts and the lawyers were firm: the mother, however culpable, kept the house and the kids, the father/breadwinner paid the tab. Owl money. Never mind that he was no longer winning bread, nor that Gail had plenty. She had been officially unemployed for six months, and—cleverly enough—her plenty was hidden.

Jack was on a maintenance regime, fistfuls of super-multivitamins and chemo pills, and seemed in almost unnaturally hearty spirits these days, despite the fact that his portfolio, too, had been hammered as flat as one of those junkyard-compacted cars (which was what had ended up happening to Will's Tundra, but that is another story). He had some cash, a couple of money markets, some gold, inflation-indexed bonds. He and Louise would survive, with only a tiny bit of belt-tightening: one vacation a year instead of two, sharing a car instead of paying two leases. They managed to make it seem cozy— "like during the war," Jack would say, meaning the ancient-history war that seemed to Will to have little to do with life in his parents' precision-landscaped, climate-controlled condo. He went to dinner there once a week, at his parents' insistence, and sat and smiled tightly while Jack gave uplifting lectures about Surviving.

It was early March. As if by sorcery, purple and yellow and pale blue crocuses, with tiny orange tongues, were beginning to pop out of the steely ground; soon would come the real flowering time, and in a strange way (although there were bad hours, at 3 and 4 A.M., when the dream that Danny and Rachel were in the next room woke him with a start, and the realization that they were not pierced him like a spear; he lay on the couch sweating then, with the actual sensation of cold steel stuck in his belly)—in a strange way Will felt as if the simple annual act of regreeting his plantings (Hi, hosta! Hi, hydrangea!) was what he would miss most about his house. He remembered looking out the bathroom window early on a late-February morning and feeling the strong urge to celebrate, with his own seed, the sight of a forsythia whose buds were beginning to set. By way of vegetation, the apartment building had a meager border of pricker bushes in front; Will couldn't imagine celebrating *them*.

Once or twice a day he got up and limped the three long blocks to town, to have a sandwich or a cup of coffee, mostly just to make the walk. He remembered (he remembered a lot these days; in a very real way remembering had turned into his job) this street thirty-five years ago, before the apartments had been built, before everything, when there had been old brown Victorians backing onto the train tracks instead of low yellow-brick housing blocks like the one he now inhabited (and the trains had been the old World War I–vintage dark olive Erie-Lackawanna cars with wicker seats, rather than the brushed-steel space capsules of Jersey Transit); he remembered a camp-out sleepover in dead Bobby Augenblick's backyard (the house was still there, across the street, repainted a cheap flashy off-white), a night whose simple yet racy highlight had been a 1 A.M. walk into a Verona center eerily, almost erotically, somnolent.

It had been a quaint quiet town then (the malls were just starting to be built; anticipation was high), with small shops run, as though in a movie about the nineteenth century, by actual shopkeepers, with eyes that knew you. He often walked, whole in his mind, into the old stores now (as his one good foot and one bad jerkily propelled him to the town of the present), savoring their lost odors and colors and textures: the sublime powdery sweetness of DeSoto's, the bakery, always so much better than anything they actually produced; the thrilling important Scouty bouquet of web belts and mess kits and crisp green uniform shirts in Beman's Boystown; the swooningly lovely fountain-pennish tang of both the town's stationery stores, Grose's and Holman's. The overstimulating sensory magnificence of the two toy shops, Vincent's and Leo's, the former just slightly more downscale but dignified by the exalted Depression-era manners of its kindly eponymous owner; the latter as flashy as suntanned, goateed Leo, and predictably overpriced, but all the more heart-stopping for its big-ticket toys, its whiff of rich-kid decadence.

Will sighed. The past had overtaken him. He couldn't seem to let it go, or vice versa. In his mind he browsed the shelves of the old library (the building still stood, now used for storage), with its brown-glass-floored stacks, its perfume of bindings and mucilage; he wandered into the big downstairs waiting room of the town's (now brutally Sheetrocked and arc-lit) turn-of-the-century railroad station, which was filled with a yellow morning 1920s haze of sunlight and cigar smoke. He had next to nothing to do with the present town, with its Blockbuster and automatic tellers and Sports Bar and lounging self-important miscreants. With its lingering air, like a pervasive smell, of dull panic about the dead girl. His one concession to the present was his regular patronage of the corner store that had once, in the Eisenhower through Johnson administrations, housed the Library Lounge (a poky establishment that somehow managed to survive by now and then selling the odd book and greeting card); that then (after brief, unproductive interludes as a florist and a real-estate office) did business for a quarter-century as the Sub Shop; and that today, under the new management of Will's apartment-mate, was known as Gold's.

He has made some changes. He's always hated change, and here he is making changes. The first is coffee. People seem to love it— Joel has never quite understood why, but people are wild about coffee, and so he put in an expensive espresso machine and a whole new refrigerator case for the two dozen varieties of beans he now keeps in stock. A plump, pretty girl comes at lunch and makes fancy sand-

wiches, things with sun-dried tomatoes and cheeses Joel's never heard
of. And the coffee and the sandwiches have brought in a whole new
kind of customer, and so, although he's just beginning to understand
what newspapers are good for—it was in glancing through a *Star-Ledger* that he learned of the disappearance of electrical contractor
Norman Mintz, wanted for questioning in the kickback trial of union
officials—Joel also keeps a rack of papers for the new customers to
read. Clean-shaven, wearing neatly pressed khakis and brown tassel
loafers, and a blue dress shirt with a little polo player over the
breast—Irma bought him a box of them as a parting gift—he stands
and stares in amazement at his fellow-citizens, leafing through the
*Times* and sipping Kenya Roast. (Among them, at least once a day,
Will, staring into space over his drooping stock section and cooling
cup.) Here, in the rustling of newsprint and the aroma of coffee, is
the world he stepped aside from for twenty years. Is it worth coming back to?

Joel smiles. He has a secret, a real thing: Julie is alive.

# 38

He knows there was a time, not long ago, when he might have imagined this, when her phone call might have been either a real phone call or anything at all—a dream, a whim—but things aren't that way now, he's surrounded by facts, with their curious clear chunkiness, their crisp outlines and solid shapes. He hasn't had time to feel oppressed by it, the world feels newly minted.

And new since her call. It came one morning at three, while Will was thrashing in his sleep in the next room, crying out. Joel got to the kitchen phone on the sixth ring, and her voice went through him like a drill. He had so many questions, all at once. What had happened? Where was she? Who was she with? She wouldn't say much. She was headed west. She was happy. Don't tell anyone, she pleaded. She would phone again soon.

He didn't mention Romilar. He didn't mention—well, the main thing. Still, why would she call *him*? Why him? Why did she ever call him? We know things we don't know we know—that much he knows. He so wanted to tell her, yet couldn't get the words in, or out. He'll be ready the next time she calls. He wants to tell her everything.


But it all still leaves him with his own life. Which is what, precisely? He asks himself the question often as he walks to and from work. Happiness is actually possible now—he's drinking less; he's lost weight; he's thinking of taking some night courses at NYU (the city!)—but there are times, in the evenings, when he looks up from his book (Will lying in the next room watching television, its idiot squawks and cajoling music not even tempting Joel) and wonders why.

One bright morning, after a night of steady rain (the old furniture-scraping rumble of thunder heralding, like the sound of an orchestra tuning up, the start of spring), he stops in his tracks on the way down the sidewalk and gazes at the telephone wires across the street, dripping in the early sun, each wire sparkling with a prism of the keenest possible colors, colors he couldn't even begin to name. Maybe, he thinks, this is his answer.


"Hey!"

It's the first hot day of June, June of the year 2000, and he's running across Verona Ave. on the flashing DONT WALK with an envelope full of cash, trying to make it to the bank before it closes, but the familiar voice halts him as the traffic starts, and he wheels around.

"Pats," he says to himself. He dodges the moving fenders, walks over to the strange white economy car double-parked in front of the flower shop (flower smells are drifting, dizzyingly, out the open door), and bends down to the window. "My God," Joel says. "Pats."

They kiss, and something about her mouth is different: warmer, softer. She holds the kiss for a long time, and when he stands back up to look at her, light-headed, she's beaming and very beautiful.

"You're tan," he says.

"I'm pregnant."

He leans on the car's windowsill, suddenly short of breath. "Ah," Joel says, trying to smile.

"Feel," she says, taking his hand.

"Pats."

"Come on." She pulls his hand down inside the car and presses his palm over her round warm belly. A shifting shiver in there startles him; he tries to pull his hand back, but she holds it there: she's strong.

"It moved," he says, amazed.

"He's a lusty young fellow," Patti says, grinning. "Very impulsive."

"Congratulations," Joel says.

Her eyes search his for a while, as if daring him to guess. "Congratulate yourself," she says.

# 39

It's happening again: The columns of the *Wall Street Journal* are in motion, jumping and rushing and circling and blinking, their normally dependable phalanxes of type moving too fast to comprehend. Will blinks and looks up to steady himself, his gaze slowly rising over his cup—he switched to decaf when the problem started, but it doesn't seem to help—and turns for solace to the familiar, cozily walnut-trimmed confines of the coffee shop, where all is as it should be: Paul Desmond playing on the sound system, an academic-looking couple at the next table chuckling pleasantly over something, the Intense Young Person in the corner, with his beret and double espresso and Artaud.

And, in the far corner, the brown-skinned man in the brownish green suit.

This is interesting. Will stands slowly and carefully, making sure his legs are steady. There's Joel behind his new wood-and-glass counter, talking with the sandwich girl: they both look happy. Will stares at his friend. It's true—his features are animated, his eyes alive, his cheeks smooth and pink. How strange, Will thinks. Searching for his own happiness, his mind turns, in its old tic, to his portfolio, only to realize how little remains.

The man in the green suit looks happy, too. Standing at the newspaper rack, Will keeps glancing over at the broad smile on the side of his face. It's a familiar face—Will thinks he remembers it from somewhere far away. But what's he smiling about? He's all alone; he has no book or newspaper. There's only one way to find out. Will turns toward the man's table . . . and then, underneath, sees the feet, bare and white-nailed and beautiful.

Now he knows who it is.

"Tommy?" Will says.